The Book of Ghaan

Part One

By Colin Darney

Copyright and Disclaimer

The Book of Ghaan, Part One

Disclaimer

This is a work of fiction. Names, characters, places, and incidents are either the product of the author's imagination or are used fictitiously. Any resemblance to actual persons, living or dead, business establishments, events, or locales is entirely coincidental.

Colin Darney

Foreword

Hello!

Thank you for choosing to read part one of The Book of Ghaan. I'm putting the foreword here, instead of with the body of text, because I want this book to come across a certain way to the reader. And my reason for that is style.

I purposely made an effort as I wrote this book to have it come across like a 'lost tome' to the reader. The titles and certain words are in Latin to give it that 'old feel', and if some of the things you read come across as 'flowery', that is the reason for it.

You will quickly notice that the story is told from the point of view of a narrator, who bounces back and forth in his remembrances through time. He is an old monk, near the end of his life, and is remembering the events of his youth. And if every now and then you hear the wizened voice of a grandfather while you read this, I have succeeded in what I set out to do.

The story begins on the next page with the Indicium, and that appellation starts the book. Everything from the Indicium to the Apostille you should consider part of the story, with the Foreword and Afterword encapsulating the ancient tome that old monk wrote.

I hope you enjoy what you find.

Thank you again for reading,

Colin

Indicium

I hereby attest
and affirm
that all the
words herein
are true.

May the
Pantheon
have mercy
on my soul …

Abbot Makun
Derring,
1547 a.f.

Intercessionem

Never in the sixty-two years that I have been blessed and afforded by the Pantheon would I have ever assumed to recount and make testimony to the terrible deeds precipitated by our order's encounter with one Rahdimus Ghaan. It could be said that the man was a victim of circumstance, afforded by the ancients with a malicious malady transmitted by blood in accordance with nature, though most would not. Yet regardless of how that poor soul was afflicted with the provenance of our Pantheon's damnation, his arrival heralded diabolical events and tumultuous change upon our order that we could not prevent or deflect. A change that has altered the thinking of all who encountered him, that I have either been blessed or cursed through the course of events to bear witness to. And my role during those times, limited though it was, must be communicated accurately for those who follow after me to take charge of the office of abbot, and lead the Monachi Spirae, whom they will eventually oversee.

To whomever shall in the future read this humble tome, I charge you with the following goal: Read this vehicle of truth, then embody its provenance so that you may guide our blessed order into the unknowing future through our many gods' grace. For the truths I held bright and clear when I bore witness to the events I shall communicate herein, were later shaded to grey by the discovery of uncomfortable evidence that fills me with both heartache and unease. And that disquiet has followed me these many long years, through the events I bore witness to, as well as the conflicts between those events and the knowledge that all men of my time hold in their hearts to be true.

I charge you, my successor, to hold onto your judgements, and to contemplate upon the ramifications of the knowledge I shall impart herein, before you author up your eventual decision to determine my grace or damnation in your eyes. I have thought long upon the events I shall communicate, and weighed the decisions I made to guide our order upon the scales of spiritual purity as best I can understand them. In the eyes of the Pantheon, it is my hope that I will be received into their bosom having been found to have chosen wisdom over frivolity, and humble grace in the place of diabolical pride. And it is my sincerest hope that I will be gathered unto the Pantheon upon my eventual death, to bask humbly in their glory while I rest from the many labors of this long life that I have been forced to endure.

But, if in the wisdom granted to those who follow after me, my decisions are found wanting, I charge my successor with this: a humble warning. The insidious nature of mages and magic cannot be determined by blood alone, as we now understand their provenance to be. And our thousand-year charge to eliminate its spread through castigation, purification, and the breeding of those most holy, is, in itself, inherently faulty. For magic and mages are for some unknown reason able to rise up in the most unexpected of places, completely at odds with the tight strictures our blessed order strives to enforce. And I must conclude, possibly somewhat heretically, that mages and magic are natural to our glorious world, as well as our blessed though humble existence, in spite of being the authors of our Pantheon's ignominious fall.

For despite all of the safeguards and barriers that we who reside within the Towers of Knowledge have put into place, upon both ourselves and on others since that horrid day of our many gods' fall, I have been faced with quite the uncomfortable conundrum. In spite of our ecstatic vision to eliminate mages and magic in hopes of restoring our beloved Pantheon, stomping them out wherever they have been found, purging entire bloodlines to eradicate their sinful spread, making agonizing decisions that pierce the hearts of all pious men to rectify their heretical existence, I have made the most worrying discovery.

Of all the evils of magic and mages we have encountered, I am forced to admit this uncomfortable truth: Despite everything the Monachi Spirae have done over these many centuries, mages and magic can be found no matter where a mortal soul may look. And in spite of my many pious prayers, and endlessly hopeful yet desperate entreaties that I have inflicted upon our beloved Pantheon during my many moments of weakness, and yes, even during my repetitive attempts to repent my sins through the mortification of my own flesh, I have discovered this about those heretical mages, a most curious yet damning surprise.

That despite everything we have done, I, myself, am one.

May the Pantheon have mercy on my soul.

Abbot Makun Derring
Authored in my own hand,
Day 192, 1547 a.f.

Capitula 1

My tale begins, as many stories are wont to do, a number of years before the time of its writing. The year was 1508, After the Fall, and I was twenty-three years of age at the time. Our order had survived where many others living during that time had perished, and our existence was one of relative peace. Relative in the fact that one may have peace if one hides well enough, for though monsters still roamed, we had achieved stability through perseverance, and had actually started to grow and expand our humble community. And that growth is where I have chosen for this story to begin ...

"… and it appears your studies have been going well, Brother Derring. The brother recorder has been pleased."

"Thank you, Abbot Dreise."

"Have you completed your charge, young Derring?"

"I have, Abbot. This past month has seen the completion of my copy of Ammondon's Greater Works, and both my reproduction of the texts and the knowledge afforded therein has been most enlightening."

I bowed my head towards the abbot in unstated thanks for the opportunity to copy such an exclusive work. It was unusual for it to have been given to a newer monk like me, and I knew the order to do so had most likely been given by the abbot himself.

"Such was my hope." The abbot smiled before continuing, pulling both the original and my copy onto the surface of his desk. "I must say that I am most pleased by your work, as well. And on the recommendation of the brother recorder, you are to be removed as one of our lay brothers, and relocated to the providence of the brother recorders to further protect and catalogue the knowledge we protect herein," he said, indicating our abbey as he waved his hand around the room

"Thank you, Lord Abbot."

"You are most welcome, Brother Derring. In acknowledgement of your success, it is my decision to grant you the day to conduct yourself as you see fit. You are to consider yourself free of your normal duties until you report to the brother recorder at sunrise tomorrow. Until then, I believe you have a close friend who has been anxiously awaiting the results of our meeting."

I bowed my head, hiding a grin, as I too could hear my childhood friend pacing in the hallway outside. The abbot continued to fondly smile upon me, smoothing the black and silver filigreed stole of his office before sliding both hands into the opposite sleeves of his deep purple robe.

"Go, young Derring, and know that the eyes of the Pantheon are upon you."

"Thank you, Abbot Dreise."

The stocky abbot lifted his hand as I bowed my head once more. I kissed his ring of office before I departed the room with a wide smile. Then immediately after shutting the door, I was bowled over by my curious though nervous friend.

"Makun, what did he want?"

"Who?" I teased.

My skinny friend, Chaltic Harn, had been sure I was in trouble when word of a private summons had come while we broke our fast earlier that morning. He was currently almost wringing his hands, clenching and unclenching them both inside the voluminous sleeves of his dusky red robes. The red robes being the same as the ones I wore, as well as what all the brothers of our order commonly covered themselves with.

"The abbot, you imbecile!" Chaltic fumed, knowing full well I was teasing him. "What did you do now? It couldn't have been the ink."

"Me? I didn't do anything. I am completely innocent."

I turned away to make my way down the gray and white speckled stone hall, hiding another grin. Chaltic gaped, then followed quickly after as both our steps echoed off the plain stone walls of the Spire. We were in the upper stories of the monastery, the only section kept livable after the Fall, yet it still felt empty even with all our brother monks living there.

"The abbot doesn't summon people for nothing, you idiot! I'm sure your endless pranks finally caught his notice and got you in trouble."

"No, he does not. And I do not prank."

The silence between us stretched, Chaltic gaping once more.

"Surely you jest? Just yesterday? With the pail of water?"

"How was I supposed to know one of the brother healers was

standing below that window?"

Chaltic rolled his eyes. "Because Brother Vorise is there every day tending his flowers while he watches that girl in the village you are both pining over."

"I do not 'pine'."

Chaltic snorted. "Oh, yes, you do. But that's beside the point. What did the abbot want?"

"Well … it seems I am being removed from my position with the lay brothers."

Chaltic gasped. "You're what!" He grabbed my elbow, spinning me around. "You're being turned out? Removed from the Spire?"

"No …" I grinned.

"Damn you, Makun! Why are you taking this so calmly? The only reason to turn you out of the lay brothers is if you are being excommunicated!"

I couldn't help it and laughed, causing Chaltic to growl with frustration.

"Why are you laughing!" he demanded.

"Because I'm being promoted to brother recorder instead."

I chuckled again watching Chaltic's jaw drop, then managed to walk a few more paces before my childhood friend caught up.

"But you are only twenty-three!"

"Yet I am still a brother, like all who are graced to reside in the tower under the Pantheon."

"Dammit, Makun! You know as well as I do that no one is considered to become a brother recorder before they've achieved their third decade of life." Then he went on to quote: *"A brother must mature in both flesh and spirit before being allowed to progress in the eyes of the Pantheon."*

And when his quotation ended, I allowed my grin to grow even more. He caught sight of it, frowning mightily, before I simply met his eyes and said "Yup" in the most uncultured way possible.

"Aaargh! You are impossible. Tell me you're moving into the repository. Where will you be stationed? Are you going to be assigned your own desk? In the Hall of Knowledge?"

I decided to give in, seeing my friends frustration reaching its peak. "I don't know yet. The abbot has given me the day off. I report to the brother recorder at sunrise tomorrow."

"They won't even let you have breakfast before you meet?"

I laughed, continuing my journey outside. "I'm sure he will, but I'll have to wait and see."

I was holding onto my excitement, valiantly keeping myself from shouting for joy, but it was a hard thing. Two years as a lowly aspirant, then three as one of the novices helping the friars in the village below. Then my indoctrination into the monastery, becoming one of the lay brothers until my gift with speech and translation was found. Then four more long years as a lay brother, performing whatever task was assigned to me by the grace of the abbot, until just a few months ago, when I was assigned to copy one of our most famous works.

Nine years total since I was selected from amongst the other entrants in the village below. An orphan, a stranger who no one quite knew who exactly my parents were, or had been. Only knowing that my parents had been found lying among the other villagers who had died during one of the innumerable monster attacks many years before. An orphan who had been granted mercy and acceptance by the abbot, despite having an unknown family line, and in his forbearance allowed to live and grow into maturity within the community we all toiled to preserve under the eyes of the Pantheon.

And now I was to become one of the trusted brother recorders? Charged with the care and preservation of the many works our Tower of Knowledge guarded in the halls below? The tower in which we all reside?

Oh, the feeling I held knowing that was glorious.

I almost whooped, stepping out of the speckled stone hall into the edificium which ultimately led to the world outside. The edificium was one of the few decorated chambers within the tower, with depictions of almost every god lining the walls. There was Ni Hols and Jaq'lenne, Amos the builder, S'rah the guide to the spirits, and Dy'an the god of the sun. And there were more, many more, along with the gods' images, unfortunately some of whose names had been lost during the Fall. But the edificium held them there in memoriam, making sure all who passed through the confluence of these hallways would see our gods as they passed.

That, and any who entered the spire was faced immediately by the symbol of our order, embossed on a circle that was centered inside an eight-pointed star. It forced one and all to remember the glory of what had once been, and how vital the Monachi Spirae, now simply known as the monks of the Spire, charge was to protect our knowledge against any and all.

Chaltic and I chatted as we passed through the edificium's outer gates, past its two immensely thick impenetrable doors, and into the sunlight outside. It was recorded in the histories that the doorway of the edificium, which was the sole portal allowing entry into our Tower of Knowledge, had remained closed for almost a century after the Fall … but surely that was an exaggeration. Records of those times were scarce at best, even though the recorders of those days worked diligently to ensure the survival of their brother monks after the initial incursion. But the choice those poor past souls made to ensure their survival, instead of keeping good records, was an understandable decision. And I was excited that, now as a brother recorder myself, I may have the opportunity to explore and read the stories of that time, hopefully sometime in the near future.

"So, where are we going? And what are we doing outside? I would have figured you would be bothering the other brother recorders by now," Chaltic said as we walked through the courtyard.

"I figured I'd take a walk down to the village. Maybe take an afternoon stroll in the sun."

"And possibly see that pretty girl of yours? What's her name again? Jan? Jan Isterlin?" my friend teased.

He knew damn well I'd been trying to attract her attention for years, right after she'd blossomed into maturity with her coming of age. She'd seemed receptive, too, and as long as our blood was determined to be a good match by the brother healer, our union might possibly be approved.

I just had to work up the courage to ask her for it to be forthcoming.

"Hello?" Chaltic rapped his knuckles on the side of my head. "Oh, exalted brother recorder … Hello in there. Get that stupid smile off your face before the brother protector sees it."

"Knock it off Chaltic. Like Brother Sedimont gives a solitary damn if I smile."

"*A monk of the spire should always remain silent, holding their emotions and knowledge in check, before such things can be used against them,*" Chaltic quoted.

I could almost hear the strict Brother Sedimont saying those words in my head. "That has to do with people we don't know, dummy. Not people down in the village."

"Right, right …"

"See, you can be taught."

"Has nothing to do with anybody down there. Especially not that girl whose ass and tits you've been drooling over for years now."

Chaltic skipped away as I swung at him, laughing while I chased him through the courtyard, then under the outer wall. The outer wall had been built during the time of the reformation, begun almost a thousand years after the Fall by the records we had. It was an impressive edifice, guided by our friends, the dwarves, when they unexpectedly came knocking one day on the edificium's gates, built into the side of the mountain.

The dwarves of Nächtaltom were the only contact we had in the outside world. Surviving the mage storms by hiding deep inside the earth, as we had, they bravely emerged to discover what was left of the world. Triumphant on discovering our forefathers after many years and innumerable hardships, they traded with us to this day, providing us food and ore in exchange for potions and knowledge.

The outer wall had been their first gift, though the design was the actual gift more than the wall itself. Built over the process of twenty years, it was an impressive stone edifice that blended itself almost seamlessly into the walls of the Spire, the mountain that hid our home. It offered a place of refuge and a means of escape to the villagers outside, somewhere they could run to for safety during the many mage storms and monster attacks.

The limited records of the time while it was built were heart rending, and the losses the brothers had taken had almost brought our community's survival to an end, but thankfully the wall had eventually been completed. And that wall, which was almost as thick as the height of two men, protected the gates of the edificium from the random destruction that occurred, and the many monster attacks outside.

Passing through the outer gate, then underneath the inner and outer portcullis over the bridge beyond, we emerged to a high vista. The view afforded to those who lived high up on the Spire was stunning, and stretched far off into the distance. Records from before the Fall stated that the land before us was once a plain, mostly flat, that had been tilled and farmed for grain. But the wild beauty that the forested hills we now saw afforded us was in complete contrast to those ancient tales.

Rolling wooded hills stretched beneath us as far as the eye could see. Dangerous and deadly woodlands that were filled with monsters, which was the name the uneducated villagers had first coined to call the alter-beasts of our time. Rumor had it that every monster we had ever encountered had once been a natural thing, horribly mutated by the mages and magic during their war with the gods. Then those poor beasts had been further perverted by the mage storms which had raged frequently in our skies ever since. But, honestly, no one rightly knew.

However, one thing was for certain. Only a few foolhardy souls had ever wanted to find out what was out there. And those brave explorers who descended from atop our mountain into the deadly woodlands below, almost none of them ever came out.

"Gods, I love this view," I said, simply standing there to take it all in.

"You always were a dreamer." Chaltic shook his head as he stopped at my side.

"And there was never an artistic bone in your body."

"Nope. Too much work to be done," he agreed affably enough.

I shaded my eyes, looking far off to the horizon in the east. "Do you think the city is still out there?"

"Són?"

I nodded my head. "Or any survivors?"

"It's been fifteen hundred years, Makun. If there was anybody left, they'd have been here by now."

"They said you once could see the Pillar Gates of Són from here."

Chaltic snorted. "Wishful thinking and tall tales, that's all that is."

"Gods, I wish it was true …" I fell silent, continuing to scan the skyline as I was known to do.

I caught sight of a mage storm forming on the horizon a bit to the north, its black and red clouds flashing with deadly intent of what I knew would be a purple and green lightning, striking down from above. The sounds would be deafening, loud enough to cause one's blood to flow from the ears for anyone who was caught outside in it. Then the winds it created would rip the trees from the ground, roots and all, and fling them high up into the air along with anything else

10

it caught in its path. Then whatever it had negligently cast asunder would fall back, crashing into the scarred earth below, to shatter on the ground upon impact, if it hadn't already been destroyed by the dreaded lightning that continued to fall. The many scars of their passage littered my view.

Thank the Pantheon we are so high up that most of them pass by beneath us.

Chaltic warily eyed the distant storm as well. "You can spend your time looking off into the distance if you want to."

"Don't you ever wonder what's out there? What happened to the people before?"

Chaltic looked outward, contemplating what I had asked by the look of him, then gazed down into the village below. "Sometimes," he admitted. "But most of the time I keep my eyes on what is right there before me," he said with a grin.

"Yeah? What's that?"

"Pretty girls … like that Jan Isterlin girl down below." He nodded his head towards a bunch of women gathered around the tiny waterfall that trickled out of the mountainous wall of the Spire. They clustered around the pool by its base, gathering the water the fall provided for the villagers' use, the only fresh water they had. "I think I'll go say 'Hi' to her."

"Chaltic!"

My friend laughed, skipping ahead as I chased him down the winding path to the village below.

The village outside our walls was a new thing. Well, new in the sense of events, that is. Founded only a little over a hundred years ago, the villagers had finally outgrown the courtyard the dwarves had helped us enclose and needed somewhere else to go. Since no one was allowed to enter past the edificium into the Tower of Knowledge unless they were monks, by longstanding tradition, as well as the strict order of the abbot of that time, those found wanting were denied the safety of the tower. And with nowhere else to go, they decided to settle and build their homes on the small plateau outside, found below our outer wall.

It had taken two generations of hard work, and the death of many a soul, but the mountainous terrain of the Spire had finally begun to yield fruit. The laborious task of tilling the mountain soil to support the crops the dwarves had traded seeds for us to grow, afforded just enough yield to get by. And further enhancing the fields by using the knowledge that we guarded ourselves, it allowed the villagers to improve their lot, giving them the drive to cautiously descend our mountain to acquire timber to construct permanent homes. It wasn't a gloriously productive operation by any stretch of the imagination, but it was much more than our forefathers had known during their times many years before.

And it was certainly an improvement over our staple crop of mushrooms. The hideous things the dwarves loved so much could be grown in droves down in the catacombs of the tower and were the main part of our diet, stretching into times immemorial. They were edible, to be sure, but that was about all that could be said for them. And there were only so many ways you could prepare a mushroom until even the most steadfast soul was heartily sick of them.

But, at least now we had various plants and grain to supplement them. They were stunted things compared to some of the illuminations I had seen of the farms before the Fall, depicted as gloriously waving fields as far as the eye could see inside the books we guarded inside The Hall of Knowledge, but they were plants and grains nonetheless. And Chaltic and I laughingly ran past one of our fields as we made our way down the switch-backed trail and into the village itself.

We were greeted by a couple of odd looks, as well as a few smiles, but the villagers knew us well. As lay brothers, we'd assisted the friars for years now while they toiled down here in the village. The friars managed the teams of novices and aspirants, who worked alongside the villagers to ensure the daily chores that guaranteed our survival were done.

I'd always felt bad for the villagers; people who had been skipped over, deemed unworthy for some reason or other to become a monk of the Spire. It'd always been a mystery to me as to what criteria the monks were chosen by, something determined by the council of seven, but a person's time spent as a novice or aspirant was when they were evaluated.

But whatever the reason, the people who lived here had a good heart, and their numbers had quickly grown as they were free of the strictures my other brothers and I lived by. Maybe as a brother recorder I would find out some day, but the villagers outnumbered the monks now four or five to one. They were uneducated and simple to be sure, taught as best as we were able, but to the last, they were the foundation of our surviving society now, no matter how little knowledge they held.

"Slow down, you blasted monks!" a gravelly voice shouted.

We turned to look, seeing Untark Mar glaring at us while he leaned on his spear. He was a hulk of a man, absolutely bulging with muscle, and the self-titled protector of the village … just ask him. More of a bully, really, than anything else, he'd originally been an aspirant before he was thrown out for almost beating another man to death. The brother protectors kept an eye on him because he had been so bitter ever since that day, and he and a clutch of other rough men hung about together. They practiced with their spears while ogling the women, truly all they ever seemed to do.

"Yes, Master Mar," Chaltic laboriously replied. Mar had beaten him in a practice bout once, and Chaltic had never forgotten or forgiven it.

"Yes, Master Mar," I echoed, bugging my eyes out at Chaltic.

It was always good to be polite, even though technically the monks outranked the villagers. It wouldn't be very politic to remind Untark Mar of that, and starting problems with the town ruffian the day I was promoted to brother recorder wasn't something I was going to do.

Chaltic rolled his eyes, though nodded his head to acknowledge my gentle chastisement.

One of the friars hailed us, waving the two of us over his way. He was teaching a class of some kind, surrounded by a circle of aspirants and young villagers. Beyond managing the novices and aspirants, the friars were the outreach of our order, spending most of their time in the village with the masses. Technically under the office of the brother teacher, the friars worked independently of the monks to spread the word of the Pantheon to the villagers, and look out for promising children who might one day become monks themselves.

They also looked out for possible mages, alerting the brother protector for that, but I didn't know much about them. A mage hadn't been discovered among the populace in almost a hundred years, and I only knew that because the last culling and burning of a mage was required history to read during a monk's education. Regardless, the brother protectors practiced daily with their weapons in the courtyard above, preparing for the day they were needed to destroy another mage. And the brother protector's skill at arms exceeded that of the brute Untark Mar by leaps and bounds.

We helped out the friar by answering a few simple questions about life in the monastery for the class before we moved on. Eventually arriving at the pool at the base of the fall, I caught sight of the lovely young woman I pined over. Jan Isterlin was a few years younger than me, but not by much. Brilliant yellow hair, along with a set of devastatingly deep blue eyes, she was a vision that haunted me during my waking hours whenever I thought of her, which I admit was quite frequently. And she seemed to return my interest, quirking a smile my way before a flush rose to her cheeks. She ducked away, seemingly shy, then her mother called out for her. Then she glanced my way once more before she walked past, joined by a gaggle of giggling women.

"Ah, curses! Struck out again," Chaltic teased as he watched the alluring backsides of all the women walking away.

I smacked him on the back of the head, ignoring his complaint of "Ow!" while I watched my Jan go. And I was rewarded for that when she glanced my way to catch sight of me watching her, which started a bunch of giggling amongst the women once again.

I sighed.

"You're never going to get her if you keep letting her walk away," Chaltic said sagely.

"We'll talk eventually."

"Eventually, huh?"

I caught Jan glancing my way again. "Yeah. I'm almost sure of it."

Chaltic fell silent as we watched the women wander off. "Think her blood will be a match for yours?" he asked as he took a sip from the pool.

"I don't know."

"Has the brother healer said anything?"

"I haven't asked yet."

"Gods, Makun. You're pining over her as bad as this, and you don't even know if the genealogies will allow it?"

"Nobody knows who my parents are, Chaltic, remember? All he can do is say yes or no."

"Bet you hate those strictures now, huh?"

I shrugged, hoping beyond hope the brother healer would say

yes, but dreading he would say no. It was the main reason that had forced me to remain silent, beyond simple shyness, that is. The strictures had kept our community free of any inherited mutations since the Fall, but I was forced to admit that because of my parentage, I was an unknown. And the terrible tales the histories told? There were reasons for those strictures. It was very possible I would be ruled to remain alone.

Who was I to challenge what was? Or forever shall be?

"It is what it is." I sighed. "Come on, Chaltic. Let's go wander around," I said as the last of those alluring backsides disappeared behind one of the houses. Well, one backside in particular, at least. I sighed again watching it go.

"What do you want to do?"

"I don't know. Spar?"

"You're that bored?"

"We could always go explore."

"Outside the wall?" Chaltic glanced towards the villages' palisade. "Are you crazy?"

"No." I grinned.

Chaltic grunted. "Fine. Spar it is. Anyway, let's wander back up to the courtyard. That way Untark can't see how bad we do."

Laughing at his exaggerated shiver, I led the way.

Capitula 2

Alas, that first meeting with the brother recorder was not to be the next day. For it was as if once fate noticed that I was being promoted to my new position, it lit the spark that fired up the flames of events to come. Then the first troubling happenstance came, and it came swiftly, without omen or warning. The first mage storm to threaten our survival in many a long year, and dare I say, generations ...

It was that first terrible crash of thunder which alerted us to the storm.

Coming around the northern edge of our mountain, the first whisps of those reddish black clouds began to swirl. Pushing along with them was the normal rains, the indomitable deluge that always accompanied any of those storms, but it was the roar of thunder which scared us. For that thunder was a portent and symbol of the ancient war, the war that had destroyed the world.

CRASH – BOOM!

The bell in the village began ringing as the winds picked up. Brother protectors began running through the halls towards the gate of the edificium. Then spilling out into the courtyard where Chaltic and I were still practicing, my brethren charged towards the outer gates of the wall.

Chaltic and I were caught up in the flow, running towards the outer gates along with the brother protectors as another crash of thunder pealed. The sky grew steadily darker as I cast a wary glance towards that swirling cloudbank of impending doom, and I saw the red there tinting everything inside as something flared anew. I knew what we were doing was madness, but we had to get everyone who could to take shelter inside.

BOOM! the thunder rumbled again as we exited the tunnel, then looked out over that normally pleasant view as the first patterings of rain began to fall. And I looked down into the village, seeing the people there waver in what they should do: evacuate to the tower or remain in their homes. There were large problems with either, no matter which way they would choose.

"You! Lay Brother!" one of the brother protectors shouted my way. "Help close the gates!"

"But the people!" I whipped my hand down towards the villagers scurrying our way. I saw Jan down there with the other women, all of them rushing our way in panic. "It is our duty to save those we can!"

A whistling wind began as he responded. "It's a mage storm!"

"And those people will die if they're caught in it!"

I knew the brother protector's sole duty was the defense and preservation of the tower, so his conflict was clear. But it was one of our duties as lay brothers to ensure the welfare of the people, and I was honor bound to do so.

By the Pantheon, I will not let anyone die if I can prevent it!
CRASH – BOOM!

The wind picked up even more. "Fine! But the gates close the moment any lightning comes near! We must protect the tower!"

"Just keep the gate open!" Chaltic yelled as I nodded, in total agreement with what I was doing.

Both of us sprinted down the switchbacked trail towards the village, roughly shoving those who were already ascending the trail to hurry up even faster. The scattered patterings of rain had increased into a growing deluge, lit a strange red from within by some crazed glow in the clouds. Then flashing and flaring with an intensely green light, another CRASH – BOOM sounded from the clouds above that told us to make haste.

Jan was sobbing with the other women when I arrived by her side, all of them scampering up the trail my way. "Makun!"

"Jan! Get up the trail!"

"My mother! She's down in the house!"

"I'll find her!" Another CRASH – BOOM sounded. I stared up into the swirling evil of that mage storm which threatened to destroy us all. "Go! Get to the tower! I don't know how long the gates will stay open!"

She latched onto me but I pushed her away, shoving her bodily up the trail towards the tower. My duty was to all of these people as a lay brother, no matter how much I wanted to stay by her side. And I was going to do it, no matter how much in that instance I didn't want to, nor despite the fact that I wanted to soil my robes.

Another flash of virulent green flared from above, followed by a deafening CRASH – BOOM! I couldn't believe the storm had snuck up on us so quickly as I ran to catch up to Chaltic, who was already shoving novices and aspirants up towards the tower from below.

The rain was coming in sheets now, the robes of my order completely soaked through. People were scampering my way, screaming and yelling as they pushed their way up the switchbacked trail towards the tower, all underneath another CRASH – BOOM!

I began shoving and pushing people along with my brothers, sending whoever we could up that perilous trail. The wind howled, the rain flew, the crashing and booming sounded, but I did my duty as a monk of my order, sending all that I could towards the safety of the tower. It grew evilly dark, but still I and my brothers did not falter, performing our duty to the Pantheon to save who we could.

They were still our people, even though they weren't actually our brothers. And it was this thought, that had been carried by my brethren through time, that saw our community through.

CRASH – BOOM!

Then the inevitable happened. A bolt of that deadly lightning landed nearby, spreading its evil through.

Brilliant green light flared so brightly, it completely blocked out my sight, when that bolt of diabolical magic landed somewhere close by in the village. A thunderclap sounded almost immediately thereafter, luckily blocked by some of the villagers' houses. I knew without the houses blocking some of that terrible din I would be insensate right now, bleeding from my ears as I'd read so many others had done before me, but the noise was tremendous. Slamming into my chest like the Pantheon's own fury, I struggled to breathe as I fought for my senses, all the while staggering wildly to the side.

"Come on!" Chaltic shouted, waving towards a group of villagers who'd been stunned the same as me. They'd been almost completely thrown off their feet. "Get up, you! Run! Run for the tower!"

"You bloody monks can go to your tower!" Untark shouted, sprinting into view. He bent with a group of his men to help the other villagers up onto their feet. "We don't need your bloody tower!"

"What are you saying, man?" Chaltic shouted.

"Your tower leaves everyone behind!"

I was stunned by the vitriol in the man's words, but there simply wasn't time for it now. Everyone needed to escape.

"The tower offers you safety!" I shouted.

"They already closed the gates!" he sneered, shoving the villagers back towards their houses. "You know that as well as I do! You think they'd keep them open for the likes of us?"

CRASH – BOOM!

"Your houses don't offer you any protection!"

"They offer more than you monks do!" Untark retorted.

I couldn't believe what he was saying. I knew he hated that he hadn't been chosen to be a monk, but I had no idea the hurt went so deep. I simply gaped at him, staring stupidly as he hurried the villagers away.

CRASH – BOOM!

"Makun! Come on!" a soaked Chaltic shouted, pulling at my saturated sleeve. The streets were deserted, mud flowing in growing rivulets while the rain only grew. Chaltic shoved me towards the stampede of villagers still on the trail, running for their lives to escape to the tower.

BOOM!

I tripped and fell, mud splattering everywhere as we struggled up that slick switchbacked trail in the villager's wake. Then another brilliant bolt of green lightning descended from above, it's perverse magics producing another tremendous explosion while my panic only grew. The lot of us stopped thinking as we struggled to escape, the outer gates still above us, thankfully still hanging wide open. But as the sky darkened even further and that terrible wind grew, all I could think about was the fury that raged and boiled all around us, and the terror of the mages that still wildly grew.

CRASH – BOOM! sounded from almost on top of me, but thankfully not accompanied by a bolt of that deadly lightning. Nonetheless, I slipped again, and so did most of my brothers. So did almost everyone else for that matter, as we struggled to escape the rampaging storm. But desperately climbing the trail towards the outer gates, I watched as the first people made their way through, and my hope started to grow.

Another brilliant bolt of green lightning shot out, crackling across the sky like the evil it was before it lashed out at some structure below. The explosion blew everyone off their feet again, a weird tingling coursing its way through my body as the ringing in my ears grew. I shook my head to clear it as I pushed myself up to my elbows and knees, struggling against the strange sensations prickling and tracing along every part of my body, but I only knew I needed to flee.

CRASH – BOOM!

"Go!" I croaked to my brothers, my voice strangely hoarse. And putting actions to words I struggled to my feet, Chaltic grabbing onto me once more and pulling me along with the others towards shelter. Our only shelter: the gate which had been left open, that led to the courtyard, and into our tower beyond.

We eventually did make the gate. A terrifying ordeal punctuated by crashes of thunder, the howling of wind, the stinging impacts of that horribly cold rain, and the endless slipping and sliding because of that devilishly slick mud, but arrive we did. Stumbling my last steps through the mud that seemed determined to stop us, I held onto the stone walls of the tunnel as another deafening CRASH flew. Then ducking inside I gathered up speed on the dry ground of the tunnel, bursting out into the courtyard beyond along with my brothers to make our last dash to safety.

But the courtyard was full.

Panicked villagers and terrified brothers were packed against the gate of our tower, the gate to the edificium which was now closed. A friar was shouting for attention, trying to gather the rest of the novices and aspirants to achieve some form of control, but the people weren't listening. And on seeing that, Chaltic and I both glanced at each other knowing as lay brothers that it was our duty to help that lone friar …

… No matter how much I wanted to join them in panic and scream.

CRASH – BOOM!

✳✳✳

Thus began the longest night of my existence, that terrible night in the storm. Pushing people against the inner walls of the courtyard, we managed to get the people out of the howling wind as much as we could. But the constant crashing and booming of thunder from the skies above made the stinging rain seem as if the spells of the mages from that ancient war had come to tear us asunder again.

And it only picked up as that terrible night wore on.

Joining my brethren, I did what I could, helping those that were with us to take shelter. And as night slowly fell and that terrible storm continued to rage, I learned something new. That the red of those demonic clouds glowed and swirled in some chaotic pattern. Some crazed kind of order found in that sinister light, that pulsed and breathed while it flickered hatefully above. Then flaring into a jagged webwork that crackled its way across the sky, it pulsed, before the next brilliant green bolt of lightning flew.

Soaked entirely through to the bone, I am sure my pallor only increased upon seeing that. That, and the strange tingling that pulsed and tickled its way all over my body as those lightning bolts flew.

I had never prayed so fervently as I did that night. Desperate in my need to have salvation and mercy delivered unto me by the many gods of our Pantheon, I abased myself. And as I fervently prayed, so did my brothers, joining us in a litany of devotion some of the villagers had never seen before as the sky wildly raged. I came to lead my section, Chaltic another, the friar led his, but all of our voices were lifted in ecstatic praise beseeching the Pantheon to save us.

And our salvation came true.

Sometime in the beginnings of morning the last toll of thunder sounded. The swirling black clouds slowed and then scattered; the howling wind no longer blew. Then the pelting rain lessened, easing back into its scattered patterings, and then into a gentle mist before that ended, too.

I helped Jan to her feet, her and a few friends having joined my group sometime during the night, and we joined the rest who were rising. No one said a thing, all of us stunned by what we had endured. We moved as a group, checking and seeing that everyone with us was alright, and we found that we were.

Then scared and miserable, we moved to see what else we might find. The first of us entered the tunnel through the outer wall, to look out upon the village, and on whatever was left below.

A cry came up from one of the novices, then another, and then a third. Jan gripped my hand in an iron grip, but I was too stunned to notice. Following the rest of the group, we made our way back through the tunnel until we stood on top of the trail leading down into the village. And there I saw what the evil storm had handed to us, and what remained of our once peaceful community.

There were vacant spaces in what I saw down below. Ragged

craters here and there where houses once stood. I saw bodies strewn amongst the muck, some were whole, some were in pieces, but those still, forlorn people were everywhere that I looked. A moan of desolation grew from somewhere beside me as all of us looked down, but I really didn't care who made that sound. No, I was still dealing with the devastation, the damage the war of the mages had brought with it, in whatever form it flew.

***

Then began our recovery from that devastating storm, almost a week and a half worth of work before it was all through. The only thing good that could be said about what happened is that the village's stockade wasn't damaged, but that was about it. And despite the vitriol Untark Mar had spewed, he did do some good, leading his group of armed villagers to protect the rest of the people until the gates of the Spire were opened.

And it was a full day before those gates were opened, the entirety of the brother protectors guarding the entrance as it swung by. By then Chaltic and I, along with the friar and the other lay brothers had organized the village along with the elder, gathering and securing the bodies in case any predators came by. One of Untark's men insisted he saw some creature scuttling its way up the wall of the stockade, but no tracks or marks were ever found, and he had been up for over a day's worth of hours. So, he was sent to bed, to rest and recover, everyone attributing his sightings and insistence to hallucinations from being overwrought and exhausted.

He never did change his story, though.

The entire council of seven came out with the brother protectors to survey the damage, not so much as a scratch on any of them, having rode out the storm in the tower. Chaltic and I, along with the friars and other lay brothers, assisted their tour and were congratulated for our efforts. Many exclamations and prayers to the Pantheon were given, but the lay brother, Brother Randilon, quickly had us return to our duties, going back to assisting village.

In all, over a hundred people died that terrible night, either directly through being killed by the lightning and explosions, or indirectly through the concussions the impacts had caused. Two score houses were destroyed outright, with the remainder losing their roofs and their porches, some with pieces of timber amazingly driven straight through their walls. And the mud that the deluge had produced hampered our relief efforts, the calf-deep morass sticking and clinging to everyone who thought they could pass through.

Jan had found her mother, their family home miraculously surviving without significant damage, but others were not so lucky. And I lost sight of her after the second day, Jan's family taking in other survivors to house and shelter, along with a mother and young boy. But I was too busy being one of the lay brothers, the backbone of my order, to worry and pine over her too much. For we were working as a community to recover, to return to order the evil the leftovers of that ancient war had caused for us.

We found there was a new scar on the land when everything was over, some testament to the damage the storm had caused. It was a strange linear track that descended the mountain. Starting somewhere above us on the north side of the Spire, the brother protectors said it ran for almost as far as the eye could see when you stood in its track. They trembled after witnessing the results of the ancient mage's fury, lifting their voices in prayer to the Pantheon to find comfort.

But their prayers did not comfort me.

No, what I mostly saw was that wherever that track travelled, the earth had been stripped away to expose almost bare rock. Every living thing had been annihilated along that evil course, trees and plants cast wildly asunder. Boulders had been flung far; impact craters surrounding wherever they now lie. Bare trunks were completely denuded of foliage, stuck into the ground here and there like a scattering of skeletal spikes. And even stranger things, like that eerily distorted branch that was found imbedded into the side of a rock, a branch that hauntingly glowed green.

We burnt that branch, that evil reminder from an even viler time. Then we led the village in a search for any other mage-born alterations of the Pantheon's grace. Thankfully, we found none. And even though that story from Untark's man was hurriedly repeated as a reason to continue to search even more, the abbot declared the village was safe.

Then, leading our order and all of the villagers in prayer, the abbot lifted his voice in public praise to the Pantheon. Giving thanks for seeing us through, he blessed one and all in reverent words of wisdom and exaltation. Then beseeching continued guidance from our lost gods, he led us in a solemn remembrance for the unlucky ones who had perished. Though despite their deaths, they had gone on to bask in the Pantheon's good grace.

I went to bed that evening, exhausted but safe inside the cell I shared in the tower. My thoughts drifted to what I had witnessed, the terror I had seen, the evil magics I had been exposed to. And I prayed to the Pantheon that night, prayed as I never had before, thanking them for the grace they'd shared in their unknowable wisdom to keep me and those with me alive. To allow us all to survive, to learn and grow from what we had endured, to earn wisdom from what we had seen, so that we could continue the sacred mission of our order:

To bring about the Pantheon's inevitable return.

And I went to sleep on thinking that. That, and wondering if I could live up to the honor the Pantheon had shown me … despite the evil of those ancient magics I'd endured.

Capitula 3

It was after that somewhat sleepless night, my long overdue meeting eventually occurred.

"Brother Derring, good morning to you."

"Good morning, Brother Ansilin." I inclined my head. "This humble one thanks the brother recorder for receiving me at such an early hour."

Brother Ansilin chuckled, the ancient frame of the head of the brother recorders quaking amidst his laughter. "So formal, young Derring? You remember your training well. Yet one must remain humble in the eyes of the Pantheon," he teased.

"Yet one must also show respect for one's superiors, lest arrogance precedeth one's fall from grace."

Brother Ansilin broke into amused laughter as one of our order's general tenants was parroted back to him. His open amusement was one of the things that I'd always loved about this brother monk, and it stood him in good stead amongst the dry and dusty tomes he managed.

It was a welcome relief from the past few days of recovery, that laughter.

"I see the teachings of Brother Margonest have been planted well and born fruit."

"The brother teacher has certainly given seed to the forest of my mind, Brother Ansilin. And after these many years of that field he planted being tended to by Brother Randilon, a verdant valley has formed, ready to take upon its duties to provide for our order."

Brother Ansilin smirked, then curiously began looking around at his feet. As the silence stretched without him making any response, I had to ask. "Did you lose something, brother?"

"No …"

"Then what are you looking for?"

"The pool of excrement I have wandered into, that spews forth its filth from your mouth so readily at this ungodly hour of morning."

I chuckled on seeing the amused twinkle in his eye. Then the brother recorder turned away, leading as we entered the scriptorium of The Hall of Knowledge. The voluminous scriptorium was essentially the heart of our order, where aging books – some all the way back from the time of the Fall – were copied and recopied to preserve the knowledge we were meant to guard. Rows of desks lined the hall, as well as the transient shelving to hold the books that were brought up from the library deep below.

Both the scriptorium and the library below made up The Hall of Knowledge, though the scriptorium was all anyone else except specially designated brothers ever saw. I looked around the room with keen interest, my mind taking a fancied flight imagining all the treasured knowledge those who worked here saw on a daily basis. And on every desk, I saw a volume some brother of our order was currently working on, though the hall remained bare of my other brethren at this early hour.

Brother Ansilin tottered with his cane down one of the long aisles, approaching a desk along the left wall which was bare of any work. "… and this one will be yours, young Derring."

"Thank you."

"Sit, please, and familiarize yourself while I continue on."

I did so, lifting the top of the desk to take stock of the equipment inside.

"As you know, most of the brethren I have been chosen to lead spend their days copying works from the library. Each has a separate duty, be it the copying of words, illuminating our beloved manuscripts, or binding our labors to protect them for future generations. It is normal for people chosen to become a brother recorder to begin with book binding, before working their way up through increasingly more detailed work, to have their journey culminate as one of our blessed illuminators."

"I have heard it to be so."

"Good. Then would you find it problematic to begin your journey there?"

I fought not to frown, remembering the book I had reproduced through my own efforts that led me to sit at this desk. Hiding my disappointment, I took a cleansing breath before replying. "No, Brother Ansilin. The labors of a brother recorder are yours to guide."

"Excellent. However, you must do better in the future to hide your disappointment from me, young Derring."

"My apologies, Brother Ansilin."

He waved the apology away. "It is of no matter, because this is not where you will begin your journey under the eyes of the Pantheon."

I looked at him with surprise.

"No, young Derring, your journey will follow another path."

"Brother?"

The brother recorder smirked. "Did you seriously believe that someone the abbot oversaw himself, that I then personally requested, would begin their path as any other brother of our order?"

"Brother Recorder?"

"Ah, it is good the young can still be surprised." He smacked me lightly on the shoulder with his cane. "Smile, young Derring, for you will begin your journey here as a recorder of history. And while not doing that, you will learn a few forgotten tongues we still have the translations for. There still remains untranslated works within the library, and you will begin your duties by bringing that knowledge into the light."

"Thank you, Brother." I bowed my head, understanding the high honor I'd just received. Only a chosen few were given access to untranslated works. And usually those who had, had worked diligently in the hall of knowledge over many years to earn the privilege to access those works.

"You have earned it. I am not the only member of the council of seven who have had their eye on you. Your diligent work since becoming an aspirant of our order has not gone unnoticed. I have just had the pleasure of beating my other brethren to you." The old man smirked.

"Still, Brother, I am honored."

"And I say again, you have earned it." He squeezed my shoulder. "Your copy of Ammondon's Greater Works was a flawless reproduction. Though the fact that you also diligently reproduced an ink stain amongst one of the illuminations did cause some hilarity with the other recorders. It was flawless work."

I cringed, not having known I'd done that.

But Brother Ansilin chuckled, obviously picking up on my embarrassment, then changed the subject. "Here, you will be needing this," he said, gently tossing a silver disk my way.

Eying the metal medallion, I examined the filigreed lettering that surrounded the central flame depicted in its center, which was the symbol of our order. The metal shown in the soft light of the hall, slightly different from the bronze badge I kept on a thong around my neck, which left it hanging close to my heart. I realized its lettering was a silvery blue, oddly glistening as I moved it back and forth in my palm.

"While here, within the scriptorium, you will not need this. However, when retrieving one of our other works, this will allow you to pass the doorway and access the library below." He pointed his cane towards a closed door at the far end of the hall.

"Thank you, Brother." I bowed my head again, understanding that by being given access to the library, I had been granted another honor. "I will not abuse this trust."

Brother Ansilin snorted. "Of that, I have no doubt. Neither does anyone in the council, so allow your fears to rest on that matter. Just keep it safe. You have proven yourself many times over these past few years, Brother Derring."

He squeezed my shoulder as I bowed my head again. It filled my heart almost to the point of bursting, hearing his open acknowledgement of my successes and labors to reach this point. And I admit that my chest tightly clenched as I found myself suddenly wracked with emotion by the elder man's open and heartfelt praise.

"Come," Brother Ansilin said after I had regained my composure. "It is time to break our fast. And while you escort this old man to the refectory, I will join my other brethren in offering my congratulations before we celebrate your new appointment. But before I do, remember that there is much left in life for you to experience, Brother Derring, and your position here is just the first of your steps upon it."

✳✳✳

"Access to the library!" Chaltic exclaimed.

"Yes." I grinned, spooning the morning meal into my smiling lips.

"Whose cock did you slobber over?"

Someone further down the table snorted, almost spitting the mushroom gruel through their nose. Chaltic glanced their way, then turned his accusing eyes back on me. Another brother at our table began pounding on the poor fellows back.

"No one's, you ass. I'm to record the histories, then translate some of the remaining works."

"By the Pantheon, you lucky bastard." Chaltic grinned. "Only you would go from working with animals to being a trusted brother recorder in one day. Bastard."

I grinned, simply spooning up another bite of my gruel. After leaving me to join my normal table, the brother recorder had joined the other members of the council of seven. The council sat apart and above the rest of us at a table by themselves, where they could oversee the entire refectory. All the monks inside the Tower of Knowledge were here to take their meals together, and every one of us sat on long benches at our tables in the enormous hall.

Quiet chatter filled the room as we broke our fast together, interspersed with laughter and exclamations here and there. We were a happy community, despite Brother Sedimont frowning towards any open expression of hilarity, while hidden away in our mountain hall. Things were tough, but, by the grace of the Pantheon, we endured. And the evidence of our successes surrounded me, by the number of brethren amongst whom I now ate.

We numbered almost two hundred souls now, each generation increasing that number by one or two more despite our many deaths. It was a paltry number compared to the villagers outside, maybe a quarter of their total population, but our lives were much safer now. And the villagers respected that, respecting that those we accepted into our order to live inside our sacred halls would use our knowledge to protect everyone outside.

It wasn't always that way.

And reading between the lines in our histories, I saw evidence of many times where our previous brethren had made the choice of sacrifice. And in the process, they chose to meet the Pantheon themselves, in order to protect the knowledge we held and guarded for the greater good.

Our losses, over the years, had been great.

"Do you know what you'll be working on first?" Chaltic asked.

"Not yet. Brother Ansilin said the other historians would meet with me to instruct me on my duties."

"The ones who follow the abbot around?"

"Do you know of any other historians?"

"No. Ass. But they're nothing but glorified secretaries."

"And yet every single one of them has access to the library." I'll admit I said that last bit quite dreamily, thinking about the hidden wonders I now had access to and would soon find out about.

"Look at you. You'd think you'd just spent the night experiencing the carnal delights of Jan."

"You cockwobble. Like you aren't the least bit jealous not having access of your own."

"Well, yeah. But you don't have to go all orgasmic about it at the table."

The man who'd snorted before, snorted again, but at least it didn't go up his nose this time. I glared at my friend while he grinned unrepentantly back. We both knew he was jealous, any of our order would be, but he also knew that I'd earned it. The Pantheon knew how many late nights I'd put into my studies over the years.

"Brother Derring?" another brother asked.

"Yes?"

"Good morning. The brother recorder sent me. I am one of the historians," the red headed man said. "Once you have broken your fast, join us at our table over there." He pointed. "We want to welcome you unofficially before we join the chanters for morning prayer."

"I will, thank you."

The man nodded before walking away, and, of course, my friend couldn't hold onto his peace. "Already being invited to a higher table. Pretty soon it just won't do for you to be associated with the rest of us." He grinned.

"Oh, get over yourself, Chaltic. Besides, now that I've been promoted to a new position, I might need someone to run errands for me. I wonder who that might be?"

"You wouldn't."

"Oh, I don't know. I think I may suddenly find myself too busy to do the laundry, clean my room, empty my chamber pot ..." I grinned back.

"I swear to the Pantheon if you even try ..."

"Try what, lay brother?"

"Ass."

"That's brother recorder ass, to you." I grinned.

The rest of the table laughed as we continued to poke fun at each other, not an ounce of anything beyond gentle teasing included in our banter.

After finishing my meal, I joined the other brother recorders at their table, being openly invited to break my fast with them every day if I chose. I was pleasantly surprised, having wondered if my sudden elevation may have been taken the wrong way. But my fears were unfounded, the group openly welcoming me and already being friendly as one made a jest about the ink stain on the illumination at my expense.

It was the start of a beautiful day, and I stayed and chatted with them until the bell that summoned us to our morning prayer began to toll. At least, I didn't have to rebuild the village.

✳✳✳

"... the gods shall guide us and keep us, accepting us into their bosom at the end of our days," the chanters intoned.

"The Pantheon shall save," we all sang in reply.

"Protect us. Guide us. Keep us. Raise yourselves and come forth to shelter us against all harm."

"The Pantheon shall save."

"For we are all that are left to stand against the encroaching darkness. To keep safe all knowledge, so that our successors shall inherit the fruits of our many labors. To reside in our hidden place of safety, and teach those who wish to listen to the glory of your heavenly bodies. To stay ever faithful, so that upon your return you will find those who still believe."

"The Pantheon shall save."

"We say this in the many gods' names. Upon this glorious day, beginning the five hundred and thirty-eight thousandth, three hundred and fifty sixth day, after the Fall. We still remain, those who choose to believe, your faithful servants. We humbly pray."

"The Pantheon shall save."

I bowed my head towards that lone candle upon the alter as the harmony of our chant dwindled off into its quiet echoes. And my brethren bowed along with me, all of us joining in, in honoring the gods who had come before. The daily ceremony underway held deeper meaning for me this morning, as I thought upon my changing position, and the honors that had been bestowed upon me.

Our order had chosen that lone candle to represent the many gods as a group, at some unknown time in the past, long before my birth. Sitting upon the mottled stone alter that encompassed our faith, its loneliness belied everything that that symbol stood for. And behind its solitary flame, seeming to frame that burning candle within its blank center, was a carved standing circle entombed upon the speckled stone wall. Surrounded by the carved runes in our many gods' lost tongue, the candle reminded me and my pious brethren of all that had come before.

Most of which was now lost.

That innumerable monks of our order had offered up their lives to protect over the ensuing years.

It was a heady thing to think about that morning.

I gripped my medallion tighter, then without much thought pressed it to my forehead before planting a tender kiss upon it. It was a display of deep religious conviction, and something not wholly embraced by the totality of our order. In truth, I didn't usually embrace such open displays, but on this day, I chose to show my fealty to the entire pantheon of gods for all my brethren to bear witness to.

The brother chanter, Brother Barkon, moved to the dais inside the Hall of the Pantheon, where we all were, and took up his place behind its gilded lectern. We took our seats upon the benches as he looked out over the hall, seeming to meet every one of our eyes. He had held his position as the head of those who recited the graces for twenty years, and his knowledge of the gods before the Fall was unmatched. Yet for all his wisdom, he fought daily against the insidious passage of time, and the loss of knowledge that inevitably followed the turning of years.

He bowed to the abbot, our chosen leader sitting in his bedecked and adorned chair one step below that of that lonely candle, whose flame danced slowly back and forth in the air above the alter. The abbot was again dressed in his formal purple robes, his black and silver filigreed stole dangling loosely across his shoulders. In contrast, the rest of us wore the dusky red robes we worked in daily, though for the morning chant we openly displayed the medallions every one of us bore.

It was a heady experience to see every member of our order

present within the hall, and only those accorded with special dispensation, or some other important duty, were ever excused from our daily prayers.

"Today, I chant to remember from The Book of the Fall," the brother chanter intoned. "Chapter eighty-nine, page four hundred and forty-two, verses three through thirty-three. I begin my chant …

"And in the final hour, the deceiver rose from the protection his insidious lies provided, to stand and take his place before the alter. He spread his arms to begin the beautification, and all who were present looked on with great interest. The heads of the various orders, the important folk, and yes, even the gods themselves, were present to bear witness. And yet, the person who had been chosen to perform that sacred duty was not to come.

"For on this day, a diabolical scheme would overtake the masses. The favored ones had taken it upon themselves to cast down the gods from their rightful places, and their plotting and betrayal was now ripe to bear fruit. Embracing the grace that had unknowingly been bestowed upon that vile deceiver, the foul mage raised his arms up in supplication. But this act of pious worship was unknowingly a lie, and the ecstatic vision that should have been displayed for the glory of our many gods, was used instead to author in one of the basest of treacheries.

"For taking upon himself the grace that was due in honor of the gods, the deceiver cast what he had gained down upon those present, bringing vile devastation upon the holy temple. And in its demonic reds and diabolical greens, it destroyed our church. And then began that which followed: The War of the Fall."

The brother chanter looked out over the gilded hall, filled with every one of my brethren, and the silence within was profound. As this passage, known simply as the Canticle of the Deceiver, was rarely spoken except on the holiest of days … and this was not one of those days. Nor was the Canticle ever chanted in open worship, usually only to be read in private, during deep and personal prayer during the turning of the year.

The brother chanter did not break the uncomfortable silence he'd made, a few brothers bowing their heads and rocking back and forth as powerful emotions overtook them. I raised and kissed my medallion once more, looking away to the many idols along the walls that depicted the individual gods, and then to the many empty pillars that contained not a single image. As those empty places were for the gods whose idolatry had been lost during that terrible time, some of whose places we only knew that a god should be there, not even remembering something as simple as their name.

All because of that lone deceiver, a mage.

"We say this in remembrance of their grace," the brother chanter intoned, breaking that horrible, terrible silence.

"The Pantheon shall save."

"The Pantheon shall save," the brother chanter repeated. Then knowingly nodding his head while he looked around the room, he paused before intoning, *"The mages must die."*

Then every one of us affirmed, *"All mages must die."*

Capitula 4

Many months passed by as I learned my new role within the Tower of Knowledge, hidden within the mountain we all knew as the Spire. Chaltic informed me about the rebuilding of the village, how houses were demolished and used to rebuild others. How superstitions spread as families were uprooted and housed in temporarily rebuilt homes. One bright point was the mother and boy Jan's family had taken in spent their time helping others, but despite that, Chaltic said the entire place was a mess.

I, however, was educated upon my new position, which revolved around bringing books up from the library – which I was now allowed access to – so that their care and preservation could take place through the efforts of my fellow brother recorders. I was also afforded special access to rare tomes, which I began to translate, learning many things about life beyond our humble walls, about the many lost towers, and the civilizations that were once present during those ancient times.

And after reaching some equilibrium in accordance with my duties, I was slotted into the rotating schedule that all of the historians shared. To sit and bear witness to the happenings around the abbot, and record those occurrences for posterity's sake, so that future generations can hold in their hands the evidence of the events that occurred ...

"I think we are done for the day, Brother Derring," the abbot said, pushing a stack of papers away from him across the desk.

"Yes, Abbot. Are you going to retire?" I asked, hoping he would say yes.

The abbot grinned, glancing out the window before returning to me. "Somewhere you wish to go, Brother?"

I valiantly fought against squirming, it being an open secret now that I spent most of my free time in the village with a particular lass I just might possibly be pursuing. My time was my own if the abbot chose to retire, but if not, it was my duty to be his escort until such a time he chose to finish for the day. This early in the afternoon, I could visit Jan both before and after the evening meal. A rarity for me in my new position, and one I was looking forward to with hope.

"To the village, Abbot Dreise. However, my desire to visit will only occur if my duties before the Pantheon are fulfilled."

"Your duties to the Pantheon will only be 'fulfilled' at the time of your death, young Derring." The abbot smirked.

"I meant for the day. My duties for today," I hedged.

The abbot chuckled. "Then you are in luck, because I have no more need for someone to follow me around and watch my diligent performance of paperwork." The abbot studied me for a moment. "Is there something you wish to request of the brother healer perchance? Based on your repeated visits to the village, young Derring?"

I felt my face heat, surprised by his delicately wrought question. I was not ill, so the only reason to consult with the brother healer was because of the genealogies. No union was approved without knowing the histories of the persons involved, as ignoring family histories led to fearsome mutations, along with the possible spread of mage blood. Every union was recorded by the brother recorder, births, deaths, and any mutations or dangers involved.

No one with any recorded abnormalities in their history was allowed to become a monk. Every union with a monk was closely researched so that our pure blood was not diluted. The inbreeding I learned that happened after the Fall would never be allowed to resurface, and the danger of some bloodlines mixing with certain others was feared, because it could possibly produce a mage. This was something our order had taken upon itself to ensure would never arise again, and the horrible, blood-filled decades and centuries until we learned that lesson was something I'd discovered the history of since becoming a brother recorder.

The knowledge haunts me to this day.

"No, Abbot Dreise."

"Then is there something you possibly wish to request of me?"

To make a request of the brother healer was an open acknowledgement that you had interest in pursuing to couple. To ask it of the abbot himself, it was as if you were openly declaring before the Pantheon your desire to court. Jan and I had not reached that point yet.

"I … I have no requests to make at this time." I only hoped one day to be worthy enough to make that request.

"Hmmm. As you will." The abbot smiled, turning to look out the window once more. I followed his gaze, glancing past the massively thick shutter that was pulled open to one side. "Do not put your duty before all other considerations, Brother Derring. The Pantheon understands our mortal afflictions. And besides, without the carnal pursuits our mortal coil demands of us, how would our order endure to survive?"

I gaped at the abbot, before, I was sure, turning a brilliant red. For the abbot to so openly discuss something taking precedence before our duty to the Pantheon was unheard of, but he had slowly opened up to me, and given hints of his inner thinking during my time at his side. But still, his comments were a surprise.

"I can see my words have embarrassed you. Forgive me, Brother. Your day is your own, you may journey to the village if you should so choose."

I bowed my head, still fighting my hot cheeks. "Thank you, Abbot. Should I–"

Running feet could suddenly be heard approaching the abbot's door as I dwindled off, then cries for the abbot began sounding through it.

"Abbot! Abbot Dreise!" a brother shouted before the door burst open. The brother was covered in sweat, obviously having run a long distance.

"What is it?"

"Demons, Abbot! Demons are invading the village!"

"Demons?" The abbot strode towards the window. "The alarm hasn't been sounded."

"The brother protector sent me, Abbot." The brother gasped, still catching his breath. "He requests your presence in the village."

The alarm bell began sounding at that moment, its tolling telling one and all of a possible attack that was imminent. The abbot continued to look out in silence, before turning back to the room. "Brother, return to your duties and prepare for attack. Brother Derring, I no longer believe your afternoon is free."

I gaped, then quickly accompanied the abbot down the speckled stone hall, through the edificium and out its thick gates, which was currently being partially closed. Hurrying into the courtyard, we were joined by a squad of brother protectors, the militant arm of our blessed order. Each one was outfitted with a leather chest plate beneath their robes, wielding a long hammer half as tall as a man, with a spike affixed to its back end. They formed protectively around me and the abbot, informing us they were there to escort us safely through the outer gate, then down to the village where the brother protector awaited our presence.

So, we followed them. Through the outer wall, and then down the switch-backed trail to enter into the village where a gathering of people were seen in the distance. Untark Mar was present, along with his gaggle of rough men, every last one of which was armed with whatever they had, and armored in padded cloth, which was the best they could do. The man looked worried, but barely glanced our way as wailing villagers streamed through the buildings and up towards the courtyard to hide as we passed.

The villagers' panic was blatant. Doors were slamming as mothers herded their daughters into their homes. Fathers were yelling for their sons to pick up whatever arms were available to them. A scythe appeared here, an axe seen there, even one man with a short sickle turned out to defend his home. All manner of equipment was on display as talk of demons and devilry sounded from one and all. And all turned to the abbot for help and guidance upon seeing him.

But we did not stop.

Cries and yells for absolution by the common people followed us as we hurried through the village, which pointed towards Chaltic's reported increase in superstition. A few wailed for the abbot, lifting their voices to be saved by the Pantheon, but still we did not stop. Their prayers followed us, lifting my heart upon hearing them, while at the same time filling me with dread for whatever had stirred them up so much. And I caught myself watching behind me as despite myself, disturbing thoughts of devilry and mages infiltrated my mind.

The abbot and I advanced to the opposite edge of the village, which was closest to the end of our plateau, and the territory we controlled. We passed the wooden stockade as we strode through one of its open gates and into the open plain beyond on the mountain's side. Then walking over a rise in the terrain, we looked down to see a huge gathering of men, armed to the teeth, with an odd collection of figures off to the side. Each one of those figures was the size of an older child, with huge eyes and demonically pointed ears, carrying bows fit for their stature, along with multiple quivers of arrows.

"By the Pantheon! They are sprites!" I exclaimed as I identified one of the creatures.

The abbot nodded but kept going, yet his pace noticeably increased.

A large group of our brother protectors stood between the party of men and sprites and our village, preventing any further advance. Even from some distance away the air surrounding that confrontation could at best be explained as tense, and I wondered if it would come to blows. All of the monks had some proficiency with fighting – we practiced it regularly; there were still many monsters after all – but admittedly, any noticeable skill with armed combat was not something I had been blessed with by the Pantheon.

And that made me nervous.

"What happens here?" the abbot demanded.

"Abbot Dreise," Brother Sedimont replied. Brother Sedimont was the brother protector, head of the militant arm of our blessed order. He was armed the same as the rest, with his shoulder-high spiked hammer, standing amongst his other men to prevent the unknown party's advance. "These … people … are seeking shelter. They say they've been attacked. Their leader is poisoned, and the sprites of the wood brought them to us for solace. They are heavily armed and I advise caution. We have no idea who they really are."

The party of men made sounds of protest after Brother Sedimont's statement, but it was the sprites who advanced next to speak. Making a strange gesture by crossing one hand over his eyes, then in front of his face, the lead sprite strode forward to within speaking distance. Then eying the abbot for a moment in silence, he spoke.

"The forest greets the mountain home," the sprite said in an almost unintelligible accent.

The abbot copied his gesture, replying in kind. "The Spire greets the sprites."

"Your people. Sick, tired, long journey," the sprite spoke again.

His halting speech was difficult to understand, like it was coming from the mouth of some wild animal. I was stunned the creature could communicate with us at all.

"These are not my people," the abbot disagreed.

"Your people," the sprite insisted, meeting his eyes squarely.

The abbot looked towards the party of about fifty men, who were milling only a short distance away. They were haggard, carrying a man who was obviously holding onto his last vestiges of consciousness. They looked mean, or maybe wary – at the time, I didn't have the experience to tell – but what I saw of the group made me glad for the brother protectors.

"I have never seen these people before in my life," the abbot replied.

Then a musical conversation was taken up amongst the group of wild sprites, obviously in response to what the abbot said. I was stunned again, hearing what was obviously their speech, even though it was as if the noises I'd heard from the forest below were what was being reproduced now. The sprites eventually seemed to come to a consensus as that first speaker turned his head back towards us.

"The forest says people are yours," the sprite intoned.

"The forest?" the abbot asked.

Then the sprite eyed him for a moment longer, before reaching into a pouch at his side. Taking something from it, he tossed it underhand to the abbot.

"Your people," the sprite declared, as the abbot fumbled to catch the thrown object.

Then holding the copper or bronze object he had caught up to the light, he raised the square, palm-sized object up to study it. It was a curiously decorated square, though obviously heavily adorned. I immediately thought nothing of it, beyond being curious about the script I saw there, and looked back towards that sprite while wondering why the creature thought the object was something that would be significant to us.

But the abbot? The abbot suddenly froze.

Abbot Dreise's head whipped up in shock, then he eyed the wary party of men, completely ignoring the sprites in the process. "For knowledge forfends," he said loudly to the other group.

They looked back and forth amongst themselves, quietly discussing something before one of the men haltingly replied, "What?"

"For knowledge forfends." There was something hopeful, and yet incredulous in the abbot's eyes.

"What you say?"

"Dammit …" the abbot dwindled off. "For knowledge forfends … forfends … dammit, that's the wrong word. What's the original phrasing?" the abbot mumbled.

"Are you reciting the first canticle?" I asked.

"Yes. The passage … what was its original translation?"

"Third verse?" I asked, only recognizing it because I'd recently translated the original phrasing written in another language.

The abbot nodded.

"It's not simply one word. In old Harlatan, it goes: 'For the sharing of knowledge wards against all evil–"

I was cut off as the semiconscious man completed what I was saying in a broken tongue. "For in the light of truth, ignorance and deceit cannot flourish." His strangely lilting voice added a curious cadence to the original words of the passage.

"By the Pantheon," the abbot breathed. "Sedimont! Escort these men – No, these brothers! – to the outer courtyard. Send a runner to prepare for their needs."

"Brother Abbot?"

"By the Pantheon, man. Hurry!"

"Who are these people, Abbot?"

"They are our brothers," the abbot answered. "Brothers from another tower … Another tower of knowledge …"

Then we gazed at these new men with widening eyes. Our shock simply froze us in time, and not a single one of us noticed the sprites, who were quietly slinking away.

✳✳✳

Thus ensued a flurry of activity as the newcomers were escorted, admittedly somewhat begrudgingly by the brother protectors, through the village and up into the courtyard. There, though, the brother protector put his foot down. Brother Sedimont adamantly refused to allow the newcomers beyond the edificium's outer gates, to which the abbot ultimately agreed. But into the courtyard the newcomers were led, a sorry group of travel worn figures, all of whom basically collapsed in place once their journey to it was complete.

Brother healers and others came out from our halls to give solace to them, distributing food and blankets, clean water and collapsable cots, all of which was part of our emergency supplies. They were a sorry group, blankly staring around as if they couldn't quite believe what was happening to them as my brethren treated their ills. And while all of this was going on, Brother Sedimont argued vehemently against allowing any of them into our halls, only grudgingly determining that the most wounded would be allowed inside to be treated within the Hall of Healing.

The abbot strangely agreed, not questioning or arguing with the brother protector's desires or wishes as events went on, though he pushed for them to have everything they could. A handful of the sickliest newcomers were immediately laid onto cots, then carried inside by lay brothers while accompanied by brother healers. But when that semiconscious man who had spoken was loaded onto a cot to be taken inside, the entire group of newcomers immediately became alarmed. And almost, dare I say, enraged?

"Where he go?" one of the newcomers haltingly demanded.

"To the healers," a brother healer explained.

"He no go! No take!"

More of their group stood up, hands travelling towards weapons as the brother protectors approached, taking up combat stances themselves. The tension escalated quickly, Brother Sedimont shouting orders to subdue anyone who took up arms.

"No take Ghaan! No take!"

"He'll die," one of the brother healers patiently explained to him. Calmly continuing to speak in the face of the newcomer's fury was one of the bravest things I ever saw. "He appears poisoned. We can't treat him out here."

The man in question seemed to arouse, speaking in a slurring foreign tongue to the angry man who was objecting. The man protested whatever was said, but the first man didn't respond, slipping back into semiconsciousness, then his head lolled to the side. The angry man seemed ready to explode on seeing that, but settled himself to speak angrily with those who were attempting to carry this man.

"Ghaan go, me go!" he declared, and his intention was obvious. The semiconscious man, obviously this Ghaan the man was talking about, apparently wasn't going to go anywhere without this man going along.

Brother Sedimont was about to respond back but was stopped by the hand of the abbot. "If we take Ghaan, you go along?" the abbot asked.

The man narrowed his eyes, obviously thinking it through, but responded after only a short time. Nodding his head 'yes', he replied more calmly, "Ghaan go, me go."

"I agree," the abbot declared, overriding any of Brother Sedimont's concerns. "If you have issue with it, place a guard on them," the abbot told the brother protector. "Take them to the Hall of Healing. Ensure all who can, survive."

The last I saw of Ghaan that afternoon was the lay brothers carrying his unconscious form into our halls past the gates of the edificium. Those thick, thick gates. The gates that had protected us since the time of the Fall. That had never been breached once they were closed.

And had never, in all our order's long years, failed to protect us from harm.

Sometimes I wonder at how naive we've been, and thank the Pantheon for how we've endured ...

Capitula 5

Thus ensued one of the most frantic times I had ever experienced. Used to the calm and placid ways of the tower, I was utterly unprepared for the hurried orders of the abbot, nor the shouted commands of the brother protector for the newcomers to hold. They seemed somehow at odds over what we had encountered: One man frantically stirring the pot of ingredients these new men added to our community's feast, while the other simply wanted them to simmer in place, staying exactly where they were.

Our brother protectors were hurriedly called up as a whole by Brother Sedimont, armed and armored in our tower's limited supplies to stand guard upon the edificium's gates as if an incursion was already underway. They questioned every soul who even thought to pass that indomitable entry, the lay brothers being delayed in bringing our lost brethren merciful supplies as the brother protectors took stock of what entered and left our hallowed halls in detail. But eventually the brother healer himself simply stood inside the gate, glaring at every brother protector who even deigned to consider interfering with his mission to provide and give succor.

While all of this was going on, I was relegated to a role I was untrained for: the interviewing of those who had come. Sitting at one of the travelling desks we sometimes used to teach classes in the village below, I spoke haltingly in my barely understandable Harlatan to whomever of these new men took the time to respond. I got a lot of confused glances and incredulous looks from the newcomers, until I made the discovery that they were not from Harlatan at all, that lost nation being one of the newcomer's neighbors from before the time of the Fall.

I learned the people before me were actually Lehntarnese. Not a helpful discovery in the moment, but my new awareness allowed me the chance to report my findings to Brother Ansilin, who promised a book of translations from that lost state that he hoped would be helpful. Regardless, it was close enough to another ancient tongue I'd been translating, but had never spoken, so an attempt at speech could be made. But between my broken attempts at speaking their language, which had been considered long-lost to us, and the generous sallies the newcomers made in our tongue, communication eventually took place.

These people, armed and armored as if expecting a return of our god's ancient war, had been travelling for over a year to reach this place. Our limited ability to communicate left many questions unanswered, but that they were the only remaining survivors of their entire people was made clear. They were overjoyed to find another inhabited tower, specifically labeling our home by its ancient title as one of the 'Turres Servorum', or a Tower of Knowledge, but were at the same time disappointed by what they had found. The root cause of their disappointment remained unclear, and the older warrior I spoke to guarded his reasons well when I asked, but finding us here seemed to relieve some underlying tension that man held, that apparently he had been carrying for a long time.

With his scarred and scored armor only loosened, though never fully removed, he haltingly spoke to his group's needs. Water and food we readily supplied, and though they were obviously cultured, their ravenous hunger overtook simple things like proper dignity and decorum. Pouring our clean and purified water into his hand, the warrior looked at it in amazement before he drank greedily, obviously entranced by such a simple thing as clean drink. Then messily stuffing his face with such an everyday thing as our offering of unleavened bread – the only thing we had immediately on hand – he chewed while speaking with his cheeks bulging out, almost comically seeming to be afraid that if the food wasn't eaten, it would immediately disappear.

Leaning guardedly against his pack when he had finished a first loaf, the warrior, whose name I eventually learned was Vortiid Beln, spoke in his distinctly fluid and warbling tongue to the other travelers in his party. I apparently had become somewhat of a friend, or at least nonthreatening, as their ease around me was quite evident while I continually tried to communicate, and was markedly different than the reception the rest of my brethren received who had arrived to help. I even got an unguarded smile and nod once Vortiid's belly became full, before the man called out to some of the others in his group. Whatever he said in that liquid tongue was lost to me, but I received a few more nods from the rest of the hardened group as they slowly lessened their guard and took their ease.

Then, as the last of our temporary cots was brought out and occupied, I glanced aside to see Chaltic leading a group of brothers in erecting one of our large tents, setting it up against the wall of the mountain and out of the wind. The Lehntarnese watched them while it was erected, some gradually falling asleep and snoring after their bellies became full, while others strove to remain alert.

There seemed to be a distinct divide within their party that slowly came out, between those who slept and those who watched. And with almost unspoken direction, one part of the group fell asleep, while the rest either stood or sat on guard and continued to watch. It seemed like it was a long-practiced thing, this divide I discovered. And as I studied them, three distinct divisions, along with their leaders, became readily apparent.

Of the sleepers, the man who seemed to settle them down was a brawny figure. His armor was a mix of ring and scale – something we had no access to, and I only knew about because of the library – with a stained red tunic underneath. Hugging a curved sword, he lay in repose, almost as if he was posing for his likeness to be preserved through art. But fall asleep he still did, with his weapon in hand, the same as roughly a third of the overall party who had fallen asleep with him. Then among and in the center of that grouping, I noticed some women.

Amongst the rest, those standing walked and observed what was going on in pairs or trios. Seemingly led by a skinny man, that one checked in with every one of his people quite frequently. A quiet word here, a jest there, he seemed completely at ease. But his and his men's eyes watched every motion and thing, nothing coming to within a few armlengths of their overall group before those men halted themselves to silently observe, then moved to intercept every one of my brothers if anyone came close. They didn't interfere with the delivery of food or drink, but anything else they called into question to that older warrior Vortiid, who sometimes haltingly posed a question to me before answering. The standing men were ever on edge. Never relaxing, no matter how much we suggested they do so. Their leader just silently observed. His brown clothing blending into the mountain, despite the chain he wore.

The third group was led by a portly man, who seemed like he was more of a type to enjoy any comforts we could possibly provide than to accompany such cautious men. This man's bulging belly was encased by a metal breastplate, the only armor he wore overtop his green clothing. And while his group sat or lounged as they observed, he took stock of the group's equipment. Surprisingly deferred to by the more muscular and masculine men around him, he almost looked like he was trying to keep count of the group's supplies. Tallying and memorizing the rations they had, he led a few to redistribute their belongings more equally amongst the group.

And while all that was going on, Vortiid did his best to quiz me in his broken and barely understandable attempts at our tongue. Obviously in charge of these people, he told me they were all that remained while he kept watch over everyone around him, as he nibbled on some more food and drink. Then after I dismissed the brother protector who came to stand by my side when Vortiid fell silent, we haltingly spoke back and forth, gradually becoming more adept with our words, and getting our points across. There were some eyebrows raised in response to the brother protectors' presence, but beyond a few comments in their foreign tongue, nothing was obviously said in regards to Brother Sedimont's stern orders regarding his men.

I was eventually able to take stock and determine they numbered sixty-two, a tremendous party to be found wandering the wilds alone. Almost being a small army, their numbers were most likely the only reason they had survived their journey, and Vortiid seemed to allude they had originally numbered many, many more than what we saw here. He alluded they had encountered the sprites some days ago – the creatures able to convince them to follow them here after being unable to supply them with something … something important – but whatever that thing was, was unable to be communicated because of our barriers of speech. But it seemed they had lost their supply of whatever it was they required, and the man they named Ghaan was somehow either reliant or dependent upon it.

Vortiid tried to communicate to me whatever it was, insistently, and dare I say, almost tenaciously so, but I simply did not understand him. It sounded to me like a plant, maybe an herb, or possibly some mineral of the earth. But even calling the head of the brother recorders, our aged Brother Ansilin, over to listen, we were ultimately unable to make sense of each other, and Vortiid let the subject drop.

It was a few hours later, after the healers had taken some of the Lehntarnese inside to the Hall of Healing to treat, when a few of their men returned and hailed those outside in what appeared to be a relieved expression. It was difficult to tell, the men's expressions constantly on guard and kept strangely reserved, but I watched as Vortiid seemed to allow every ounce of stress he held onto to flow immediately out of him upon hearing it. And then the first unguarded expression of satisfaction and trust crossed his face.

Then he became solemn once more.

"You speak truth?" Vortiid asked, though in reality it was more of a quiet demand.

"Yes?"

"Ghaan no dead?"

"No." I looked at him oddly while I shook my head. "We will do everything we can to help him."

"Help Ghaan." Vortiid nodded his head. "This good."

"We are going to help the rest of you, too."

"Help Ghaan. Important. We wait."

I gave him another odd look. "We can help all of you, you know."

"Help Ghaan." He thought for a moment. "First," Vortiid insisted. "Ghaan …" he dwindled off, obviously searching for the word he wanted. Then giving up, he continued "Ghaan important."

I nodded, wishing our communication barrier wasn't there, but pleased by the simple fact we could communicate at all. I was about to question him as to why they were so concerned about that particular man when raised voices suddenly echoed out through the gate. The walkers amongst the Lehntarnese took notice, stopping their patrols as almost every one of their number turned towards the edificium. Yet I still noticed a significant part of their number turned to face the other way, as those who had been sitting reached for their weapons, while some of the sleepers arose.

The abbot and the brother protector eventually walked out through the gate, deeply involved in a heated conversation of strong and conflicting opinions. I had seen more angst on display between the two of them today than I had seen in my entire life, and the open conflict between them was surprising.

Following behind Brother Sedimont and the abbot was one of the Lehntarnese, someone who had escorted their men into the tower. He hurriedly moved aside to speak to the portly man in charge of the sitters.

"… don't care for their ease, it is a security risk to the library."

Brother Sedimont was barely holding onto his temper, his strong words pelting out towards the abbot.

"They are our brothers, Sedimont! What risk could our brothers pose to our way of life? Even if they come from another tower!"

"The risk of anyone who is armed to the teeth! They look more like brigands than our brothers of old, and I question your thoughts and assumptions on this matter, Abbot Dreise!"

"Look at them, man! Look!" The abbot waved his hand towards their group which was resting off to the side. "They barely made their way here. We have their seriously injured members already inside. These people can barely move! And you already have those lying on cots down in the Hall of Healing under guard as if they were mages themselves. No, Brother Sedimont, we must offer them succor, and offer them quickly. The best we can is what they deserve."

"Succor, yes. Quarters inside the monastery? Absolutely not! If I must call for the council of seven to emergently meet on this matter, I will. No matter the importance of their discovery or coming, we must be mindful of what we protect. You know this, Abbot!"

"And what better place to provide for them and offer them succor but within our very own halls? Where every facility we have is readily available! Not out here in the weather under a tent. I say again, they are our brothers, man!"

"The barn near the southern palisade. Or the house vacant next door. There are other dwellings in even less repair than these we can quarter them in since the mage storm. These places can provide shelter for these men until the veracity of their story and their demeanor can be verified."

"You would have them crowded into empty and dilapidated structures within the village? They are barely livable! You are hard, Brother Protector Sedimont. Unfairly and unfortunately hard. These are our brethren, I tell you!"

"And if they are, I will pray for absolution for my deeds before the Pantheon this day. But until then, opening up the lower levels of the tower for those we don't know a single thing about is too great a risk."

"Risk, you say!"

"The council of seven would agree, Abbot Dreise. And in times of strife, the protection of our community falls unto me. Should we meet with them to discuss opening the tower to armed men we know nothing about?" Brother Sedimont challenged.

The abbot froze before the glaring man, then visibly calmed himself, running his hands over his formal robes to smooth them while he thought. Everyone knew the tower was much larger than the section we used, the unopened sections travelling deep into the mountain below. They were held in a sealed state as a place for the villagers to evacuate to, indeed as a place for all of us to escape to, in case of a monster incursion or a coming mage storm, as they were used only a few weeks before. To place the Lehntarnese there simply made sense, as our monastery definitely had space. But Brother Sedimont's point of not knowing these men at all made his suspicions make a dangerous sort of sense, too.

Glancing towards Vortiid, I noticed the man's shrewd eyes taking in their heated words while the two approached. I wondered how much he understood, and it was the first time I questioned if he truly had as much difficulty with our tongue as it seemed. I looked around towards the rest of the group as I thought about that, and took in that more than one of those faces seemed to understand much more than I had previously assumed.

"Brother Derring," the abbot called out. "Tell us what you have learned."

Brother Sedimont seemed incensed he was not addressed or answered, but held his peace as I answered the leader of our order's call. I slowly glanced from the brother protector to the abbot before answering, deciding it would be unwise to bring up his angrily flushed cheeks. And I looked quickly away from his answering glare when he noticed.

"Their party is from the lost land of Lehntarn, Abbot Dreise. Communication is difficult, but I have learned they have been journeying for roughly a year. They seem to be the last survivors of their people, but admittedly we've had some difficulty in expressing everything we want to." I waved my hand to indicate Vortiid. "Regardless, they lost some important thing I have yet to determine, then the sprites brought them here after they met them looking for it."

"And in regards to their tower?" the abbot asked excitedly.

"We have not discussed it. I apologize, Abbot, but I was mostly keeping our conversation to their immediate needs ... to assist the brother healers and the lay brothers."

"And their needs are?"

"Beyond the immediate, we are only discovering that." I bowed my head. "Again, I apologize, Abbot Dreise. We are still in the early stages of discussing food and drink, clothing and shelter, basic necessities so that they may sleep in peace while our brothers' man the outer gate. I haven't even begun to discuss any further needs of theirs, or any of their wants."

Vortiid stood up from where he was, deliberately setting his sword and brace of daggers aside. He offered the abbot his hands before speaking. "Thanks food. Rest." He nodded. "Coming good."

The abbot moved to take one of his hands, but Vortiid reached past his hand to clasp forearms solidly with Abbot Dreise. But Brother Sedimont only had eyes for the weapons that were left on his pack, and I followed his gaze to take in their used but well-cared-for countenance.

"I am glad," the abbot replied.

"Need place. People," Vortiid continued, glancing toward the tent we provided that his people were under. "Go tower?"

"No," Brother Sedimont quickly responded, producing a frown from the abbot. "A place will be made for you in the village below."

The abbot looked like he wanted to argue, but Vortiid answered him before the abbot could speak. "Place good. Other people good. Rest, go?"

"Yes, you may take your rest until that other place is made ready for you," the abbot answered, taking control of the conversation. "Is there anything else you need? Anything more we can do for you?"

Vortiid looked towards me before speaking. "Need food, water, voice speak. Have food. Have water. Boy speak." He nodded towards me. "Take boy speak?"

"You wish to take Brother Makun to translate for you?"

"Makun? Makun speak, yes." Vortiid obviously took that as some kind of blanket agreement. "We see Ghaan? We see …" then he said some word none of us understood.

"Yes, you and your people can go see your man, Ghaan," the abbot answered.

"With an escort," Brother Sedimont quickly added, followed almost immediately by the abbot's quick frown.

"This good. Is good." Vortiid nodded, extending his arm again.

He clasped forearms with the abbot, then insisted on doing the same with Brother Sedimont, though he visibly applied more strength to the brother protector than he had before. "Rest. Sleep. Village …" He dwindled off, then pointed to the sun making a path like it was travelling across the sky. He kept making a motion to indicate it was rising.

"Yes, you can stay the night here. Tomorrow we should have your quarters prepared."

"Is good."

"And it gives us time to inform the villagers," Brother Sedimont said. His tone conveyed that the coming conversation would not be easy, nor an entirely acceptable one.

Capitula 6

It was another day before the superstitious villagers allowed the party from Lehntarn to occupy those abandoned buildings. A day made even worse by another mage storm that had come close, thundering in haunting echoes while it raged its vile destruction outside, within full view of our settlement below. And while staring in fear towards that apocalyptic storm, wondering whether it was going to come near like the one before had, the villagers' desires in regards to these unknown strangers was made clear.

Furious conversation between the abbot and Cor Tam, the village elder, broke out as soon as the suggestion was made. The elder was the village's leader as much as the abbot was ours, and though the kind old man was normally receptive to anything the monks put out, hosting strangers from somewhere far away was apparently asking too much. With rumors that the almost never-before-seen sprites were sneaking around to steal babies by the superstitious villagers, that and the suddenly resurfaced rumor about 'the creature' that was purportedly seen during the mage storm, the diminutive creatures' association with either the elves or the hated mages of old was considered a certainty. And since the party from Lehntarn had arrived in their presence, the newcomers were considered damned as a result.

Because of this I was again relegated to a duty that was not normally my own. Sitting to the side of the abbot, I communicated my tale of what I had found out about the strangers who had come here. Being almost put to question by any and all, I struggled to communicate what I had learned to the scared villagers. Harsh questions, and even harder accusations, befell the abbot as he insisted that the Lehntarnese could not be housed inside the tower. And amidst shouts and yells of magecraft and demon worship, Abbot Dreise struggled for calm.

How he remained so collected in the face of all that, I simply do not know. But even though he was noticeably flushed, he maintained a calm and even tone in the face of their anger. Putting their fears to rest, he answered every last one of their questions, building upon what I had told them to calm their fears. But with an unshakable will, Elder Tam refused to be budged from his stance of intransigence, eventually forcing the abbot to call one of the Lehntarnese over to publicly be questioned by him.

Escorted by the brother protectors, it was that grizzled warrior Vortiid who came over to be questioned by the villagers. Nodding to me as he approached, his face took on a flat though wary look as he faced the crowd. And though it was obvious the villagers feared him, the hands on the various tools the villagers had taken up as weapons to defend themselves with were firm.

I noticed Vortiid's hand stray towards his belt, brushing past the place where he kept his sword, but he must have left it behind as his belt was bare. Frowning without looking away from the villagers, he strode to my side, staring into their angry and fearful faces in apparent challenge to whatever they saw. Then still without looking away from any of them, he spoke as that distant thunder rumbled.

"You call. I come."

The abbot looked his way, eventually giving up on Vortiid looking back at him while the silence stretched uncomfortably long. "Thank you, ummm…"

"Vortiid Beln," I prompted the abbot.

"Vortiid." The abbot nodded his thanks my way. "These people have some concerns and wish to ask you a few questions."

Cor Tam snorted at the abbot's politeness. "Questions, me arse. You one o' them demons, stranger?"

"Demon?" Vortiid replied, slowly sounding out the obviously strange word.

"Them pointy eared bastards who left all 'o us to die?" Cor Tam hooked his thumb towards us. "Them monks be teachin' us plenty about them demons. They done walled themselves up after they helped them damned mages kill off the gods. You one of them?"

"We've never said–" I began, but the abbot cut me off.

"That is not one of our teachings, Cor Tam. The elves secluded themselves in their homeland, wherever that is. But they did not help the mages cast down the gods that we know of. It has only been passed down that they did not assist or defend."

"Assist, defend, seclude … fancy words fer' fancy actions. Means nothin' to me. If they didn't fight, they didn't help. And if they didn't help, they might as well been helpin' them mages."

A series of noisy agreements came from the crowd, the villagers obviously not caring at all for the distinction we'd made. But Cor

Tam wasn't done yet.

"An' I don't care one bit what you or those dirty diggin' fools who come to trade have to say. You an' the dwarves are the same, usin' fancy words to confuse where simple speech would be best." The elder worked his mouth, and then spit on the ground at his feet. "Demons one an' all, I say. An' I'll not be havin' any of 'em in my village."

"No demon," Vortiid's voice cut in, drawing attention back to himself once more. He clenched his fist, then struck himself in the chest twice in a deliberately paced repetition. "No demon. Guard. Tower." He pointed up towards our walls. "Fight long, fight hard, come here. Want rest. Want peace."

He paused to look around at the surrounding villagers, his halting speech somehow having silenced them all. Then he looked back to the elder, meeting Cor Tam's eyes for a long moment before he quietly spoke again. "Want peace. Swear. No fight. No demon. No …" He struggled for a word, then shook his head. "Peace. Swear."

"An' what'll you be doing with your 'peace'?" Cor Tam challenged.

"Do? Peace? … Live."

"Just live, huh?"

"Live." Vortiid nodded. "Eat. Sleep." He looked around towards the crowd of villagers. "Live," he finished simply.

"A more appropriate answer couldn't be found," the abbot said following Vortiid's pronouncement.

"An' what'll they be doing while they 'live'?" Cor Tam was obviously not ready to let his resistance go.

"Well first, brother Makun here will be cataloging their journey. He seems to have formed a rapport with their group, and with the help of the library will be forging improvements in our ability to communicate with them."

That was news to me.

"And then he will be working with those from Lehntarn to add their story to our own. To research any new ideas they bring, which might improve our lives and our situation here."

"Sounds like a bunch of goat droppings to me," Cor Tam replied.

"Who knows, Cor Tam, what new knowledge they bring? Tales of things we've forgotten, things that were never recorded, things that seem commonplace to them that never even occurred to us.

Their coming here could be a gift from the Pantheon, and spark a new age for us upon the Spire."

"Aye. And fifty armed and armored warriors could also bring about our doom." Elder Tam frowned. "Taken to our breast like a swaddling babe, only to have their innocent clothing hide an alterbeast, soon to tear out our throats." He spat again. "I don't like it, Abbot. I don't like havin' them here. I don't like your oh-so-smooth speech. And I don't like havin' strangers we don't know a thing about behind our gates."

"Do you like having the wisdom of the library to aid you and your village, Elder Cor Tam?" the abbot challenged, obviously having had enough. "To have us help you and your villagers as we all recover from the depravity of the Fall?"

"You know damn well we do." The elder's nostrils quickly flared.

"Then this is what the monks of the Spire require of you," the abbot pronounced. His curt rejoinder was glaringly at odds with how he normally was. "The Pantheon has graced us with these people's coming, and the village that we help to protect will set aside a place for their rest. Unless this is too much of a burden for you, Elder Cor Tam?"

The abbot's tone had become deeper the longer he'd spoken, until in the end it was almost a basso growl. But before elder Tam could reply, Vortiid's voice broke in once more. "Want peace. No fight. Will work. Protect place." Vortiid opened his arms to encompass the entire village.

"And there you have it, Elder Tam. Out of the mouth of a stranger … that the Pantheon sent in their wisdom to grace your village to help protect it from harm. The same stranger who offered to work alongside those who would refuse his people a chance for safety, without making a single request in return. Is your heart so jaded, Elder Cor Tam? So callous to the needs of these common men that you would turn away those seeking shelter with nowhere else to go? Are you so cold?"

"No."

"Then here they will stay." The abbot bestowed upon the elder a smile that contained not a single ounce of warmth in it. "I thank you for this chance to discuss things with you, Cor Tam. I will continue to see your needs are met while our guests from Lehntarn reside here."

"Wonderful."

"Will that be all?"

"Aye." Cor Tam scowled.

"Then I will leave Brother Derring here with our guests. With that settled, I'm certain you now have enough time to show them the buildings you so humbly will make ready for them to occupy."

Cor Tam didn't reply to that, just watching the abbot with his beady eyes before the leader of our order rose and walked away. But he must have forgotten I was there, for I saw him glare, and then snarl in silence, at my departing abbot's back.

"I've always hated you ever since we were children, Dreise," he mumbled. "You always did lord it over people whenever you could, you righteous bastard."

Vortiid looked to Cor Tam, then turned to watch the abbot still walking away. The villagers started mumbling, dispersing back to their homes, most likely to inform their loved ones that the strangers were now going to live with them.

And the looks Vortiid got, were unfriendly.

The abbot and his escorting brother protectors had almost ascended the switchbacked trail to the walls before Cor Tam spoke again. "You ain't changed one bit."

Then the old man spat.

***

I'm not quite certain what made me keep Cor Tam's comments to myself, but I did so. Something about the statements he made, made me uncomfortable, and challenged one of the basic foundations of everything I knew. That someone would apparently hate the abbot was an entirely new thing to me. And that someone would say so, and do so openly, was something I found deeply troubling ... all the way to my core.

Again, Vortiid seemed to understand what had been said, much more than his ability to speak let on. Cor Tam eventually let go of his glare, leading both of us to the far southern end of the village where the abandoned house and barn stood. It wasn't much, but they were sturdy enough structures, and the most livable we could provide at the moment.

The house was a large square with a loft that spanned the entire length of its structure, originally housing two entire families, both of which had died of a sickness last autumn. There was also a smaller building off to the side used for storage, which had originally been an elder son's cottage. It too was serviceable, currently filled with junk because of the villager's superstition regarding that long-gone sickness, but it was possible to house six to ten people depending on how tightly the people were packed inside.

Then the barn was last. A large structure, it currently housed the plows and harnesses the villagers used in the fields. It had once housed a herd of mountain tarn, a hardy animal that lived among the peaks, that we used for food. Squat to the ground and surprisingly quick moving, the naked animal had not a single ounce of fur covering it. But it did have a thick wall of fat that kept it warm and safe from the elements where it lived.

Its meat was stringy but filling, and the creatures could survive on the most limited of things. They had been introduced to us by the dwarves, brought all the way from their home in payment for important information we shared. And we had accepted their offering readily, the mountain tarn able to provide us with a musky milk, as well as us being able to use their skin for leather.

Able to climb and hang off the sheerest of surfaces with their many toed paws, they survived on the alpine scrub, warding off predators with their impressively curling horns. They were almost impossible to catch in the wild, and had been a large boon to our community before the time of my birth. But our herd had been lost when I was a babe. Another alterbeast having gotten behind the palisade one night, slaughtering the herd as well as some of the villagers before the brother protectors could take it down.

That episode had been what had led to the formation of our villagers' levy, and what that bully Untark Mar always referred to whenever anyone challenged why he didn't work in the fields like the others. Our abbot had worked diligently to replace our herd, as had the abbot before him, ever since their loss. It was hoped that one day we might succeed, but we had been unable to capture any replacements, though many died seeking a way.

It was hoped the dwarves might bring more with them when they returned next. But until that time, the barn that had once housed that herd of creatures stood vacant … and the things kept inside that empty barn could be readily moved aside to house our Lehntarnese guests.

Why we couldn't just put these people in the empty places inside the tower was still a mystery to me, but after seeing the abbot's most recent interaction with the village elder, I wasn't about to ask the abbot to explain. So Vortiid, the elder, and I toured the two structures as we haltingly communicated to Vortiid that this is where the people from Lehntarn would stay.

"Stay here?" Vortiid asked.

"Yes. These buildings are for you to occupy and use. Blankets, food, and other supplies we will bring down for you," I replied.

"Stay here?" he asked again.

"Yes."

"Not tower?"

"No. Not in the tower. You will be staying here."

Vortiid mumbled something in his own tongue, half underneath his breath, then he eyed me shrewdly without saying anything more. He seemed to be thinking about something quite determinedly, assessing some need or thing he allowed to remain unspoken while he watched me. Then he walked off, entering and then reentering the buildings he had already seen before he spoke again.

"You stay? Here? Speak?"

"No. My quarters are in the tower. I still have my duties there."

"You stay. Speak to people. Speak to Ab-bot." He waved his hand towards the elder, before he pointed towards the gate to the tower, high on the mountain over our heads.

"I'm sure I'll be down daily. I will still speak for you," I assured him. "And I will Translate for you when I can."

"No. We stay. You stay. Speak good, people. Ab-bot."

Vortiid seemed quite insistent on this point, so I said the first thing that came to mind. "I can certainly ask. The abbot already said I'd be here daily. I'm certain that arrangements can be made."

Vortiid nodded firmly. "Good. We stay. You stay. Come, go. Visit sick people all day."

"You want to see your injured?"

"Yes. Come, go, all day."

"We're certainly not going to keep you away from your people, Vortiid." I did my best to put his concerns to ease. "No one in the tower will keep you away from your people."

A sudden snort came from behind me. I turned to see Cor Tam's face quirked in a strange half-smile.

"What?" I asked.

"Nothing, lad. Nothing at all."

"You stay. We stay. Come, go. Speak. Live," Vortiid interjected.

"I hear ya', stranger. I hear ya'." Then Elder Cor Tam went on to show something else about the barn he'd apparently forgotten about to Vortiid.

I followed along, haltingly interjecting in various languages whenever a moment of confusion set in, but my mind was on other things. On why Cor Tam would snort in derision when I said Vortiid would be allowed to see his people. And then why Vortiid seemed so insistent on having me by their side.

I was only a little over twenty years old when that first encounter took place, and it is understandable looking back now why the interactions didn't fill me with dread. And in my naivete, my only concern at the time was how I was going to convince the abbot and the brother recorder to allow me to stay to help out. Not on the hows and whys of what had been said. Nor upon the impacts such little statements and gestures would have in the future.

Capitula 7

Thus ensued a few days of settling in for the party from Lehntarn. It was a trying time, filled with superstition and the getting over of fears by the villagers. But the Lehntarnese worked stoically to, not so much as to fit in, but to reside peacefully in the site provided.

Where their differences were blatant, there were some challenges. For the Lehntarnese were not apologetic for the way they were at all. And though they seemed to find the superstitions of the villagers curious, they were accepting of them, and made efforts to be as non-threatening as possible. Keeping mostly to themselves and in groups when moving about in our larger community, it was an apparently deliberate tactic not to stir up too much trouble, and their decision and affect there helped.

But within their own territory, for that is what they considered the buildings we had provided for them to be, they were completely unapologetic. Manning their grounds in shifts, they were ever vigilant of the site they protected, a third of their people always being under arms. And though they did not do anything else beyond patrol around the structures they settled in, it alarmed the villagers to have an unknown armed camp inside their walls.

The villagers also did not like the Lehntarn's multiple-times-a-day travel to change their guard upon their sick members, but the villagers remained silent and only watched from afar. Except for the mother and boy Jan's family housed, that is. Jan told me about how the boy had lost his father and had not a thing to do, so I put him to work running errands for me. And apparently some of the stories he told about what the quiet-though-strange people did in private made their way through the village, and eased some of the villagers' fears.

However, his telling did nothing to ease the fears about the Lehntarnese's strange insistence on patrolling outside the villagers' stockade. Multiple times a day they went, doing nothing overtly threatening – beyond the fact that they were armed – but the villagers didn't like it at all. Neither did the brother protectors, but these new people paid not a soul a single mind, simply going about their business with a nod and a smile whenever they were asked.

My role in all of this was what the abbot had previously described, and what the Lehntarnese had haggled for. Yet I quickly found myself strangely at odds with both the brother protector and abbot, championing for the people of Lehntarn to be granted more than they were initially offered. And, working as a poorly trained translator between the many disparate groups.

Working with the aspirants and novices, I organized them without asking permission to help carry necessary supplies down the hill to the survivors' new quarters, not thinking at all about directing them assist. But after that was already in progress, and then coordinating with Cor Tam, Untark Mar, and even some of the brother protectors themselves, to have the Lehntarnese come and go from the hill without problems, my decisions were called into question. And my taking it upon myself to see to these new people's comfort and needs, along with enabling their movements, were of an obvious issue.

Though the Lehntarnese did come to my aid by expressing their thanks in my superior's presence while my questioning occurred, the brother protector's displeasure was clear. His angst was disagreed with by the abbot, which began a tense discussion between the two, and I soon found myself standing as if I was a child stuck between his squabbling parents. Yet when I sought to explain myself and my actions, this brought about the disapproval of the abbot, who seemed to think I should be seen and not heard.

The abbot felt that he should have been the one to offer any of our supplies after the Lehntarnese had requested them, and the decision to do so wasn't my place. Nor should I have assumed to coordinate with Cor Tam per the abbot, or Untark Mar by the brother protector, or with the other brother protectors, which was agreed on by both. But that I was simply trying to do my best was a grudgingly concurred upon truth by my two leaders, despite their continued uncomfortable discussion and disagreement over the Lehntarnese, that continued between them both.

It was an impressively uncomfortable time.

Yet despite my many missteps, my role with these new people was agreed to remain relatively unchanged. It was decided that I would continue to sleep in my own quarters within the Spire, but from the moment I broke my fast until I returned to sleep, I was to spend every waking hour with the people from Lehntarn ... and learn everything I could. It was a fascinating experience for me, exposed to a living culture the monks of my order could only read about in barely legible books. But it was also a time of high stress for me, as the demands I was under were many and varied. For Abbot Dreise was most keen on learning the tale of the Lehntarn's lost Tower of Knowledge, and anything regarding its secrets the people from Lehntarn were willing to share.

"… And you came from your tower?" I asked Vortiid, sitting outside in the yard before the barn. I was behind a travelling desk once again, a brother protector lounging nearby having long ago accepted the Lehntarnese meant me no harm. But the brother protector, Brother Sedimont, had insisted upon a brother protector being present, so here we were.

"Yes. Lived in tower. Left tower. Came here."

"But why did you come? Why come here? If you had your own tower, its walls would have protected you."

This was a sticking point, something about the subject not quite coming across sufficiently in words while we spoke. I knew it was a matter of translation and Vortiid's limited use of our tongue, but it was almost like he had decided to deliberately avoid speaking about his reasons. He had been named a brother by the abbot, so this simply could not be so, but his limited vocabulary was quite obvious and the entire episode was frustrating me to no ends.

"Yes. Tower protect. Live tower." He made a motion with his hand that alluded to a large amount of time passing. "Tower not protect. Not …" he searched for a word, "safe. Leave."

I sighed, annoyed that this point had come around once again. Rubbing my head, I resisted the urge to snap at him in frustration for the repetitiveness of our conversation. The abbot had kept me awake much later than I would have chosen to be the night before, insistent I discover more about these people and the tower they came from. He had even come down this morning to the village, pleasantly chastising me in front of the Lehntarnese to use greater efforts and apply myself more to understand their comings to the Spire.

I tried again. "I understand that, Vortiid. Your tower used to be safe, where you lived. Then it wasn't safe, and you came here. But what I want to know is why? Why was your tower not safe? What happened to your people? What forced you to come out of your halls?"

The older warrior smirked, telling me he damn well knew he was stringing me along with the look. The impertinence of his grin shocked me. That he would so irreverently acknowledge he wasn't telling me what I wanted to know, it simply drove me to distraction.

I scowled, then sighed again. "And how did you even get here in the first place. The library describes many hundreds of thousands of leagues between here and Lehntarn. Across an ocean, if such a body of water actually exists, and is not just some kind of child's tale. Did you walk? What is the word … Sail? Have ships?

But instead of answering, Vortiid continued to watch me with that damnable smirk, almost daring me to ask the same thing again. Gods, I hated that look. If I didn't find the answer, the abbot was sure to be irked.

"Dammit, Vortiid! Would you just tell me!"

Vortiid laughed. "Many questions, Makun."

"Brother Makun," I insisted, letting my frustrations finally come to the fore.

"No brother me." Vortiid laughed.

"I don't care! And how far did you come? Our maps of that area were destroyed. By the Pantheon, Vortiid, you have to tell me something. This 'tower safe then not safe, we leave' is getting old."

Vortiid observed me for a moment in silence, then nodded his head. He called over to one of his patrolling countrymen, beginning a conversation with him in their liquid tongue which caused that other man to raise his eyebrows and inspect me. Eventually, the conversation caused the other man to grin and then laugh. Then Vortiid turned back to me, that insolent grin returning again to be plastered across his face. "We get map. Show."

"Map? What map?"

"Lehntarn map."

"You have a map of Lehntarn?" My voice rose in surprise, causing heads to turn. "I could have read the map and avoided asking all these questions hours ago!"

Vortiid chuckled, which annoyed me even more. "Monks no trust. Abbot no trust." He pointed to the brother protector lounging off to the side. "Warriors no trust." Then he pointed towards a few villagers who were trying and failing to appear uninterested in what we were saying, and the Lehntarnese they were poorly spying upon. "Villagers no trust."

"I get that. You're new to the area and in a strange land."

"Makun ask questions. Try help. Try speak. Do help. Do speak." He watched me for a time, then slapped me on the shoulder a lot rougher than I was used to. "Stay here, many day. Angry, still talk. Try trust Makun."

"You mean you don't trust the monks, the abbot, or the villagers, but you're trying to trust me because I've stayed here for a couple of days like you asked?"

Vortiid nodded his head. "Makun speak, yes. Try Makun trust. Show map."

Vortiid's words set me aback, his stated rationale once again confirming to me that he was not a stupid man. He seemed humored by me, but also respected me, somehow understanding the unenviable position I was in trying to learn about a people I could barely communicate with. My frustrations with him slowly dissipated as I sat back to study the man, watching Vortiid in silence as the humor I saw in his eyes continued to shine forth.

I wish I could have peered into his head to read his masterfully hidden thoughts, but there was nothing for me to do but continue to ask. And I knew my endless questions would remain ever unanswered, no matter how much I pressed the man, so I resigned myself to wait. And on seeing my eventual though frustrated acceptance, Vortiid nodded his approval.

Eventually that portly man, the one leader, arrived at our side. His breastplate was notably absent, and he was hugging an oiled-canvas pack to his chest. Vortiid introduced the man to me as Gritilli Van, his name the only thing we were able to convey because of the limited words we shared. Gritilli nodded his head to me, friendly though seeming reserved, as he started to open the pack. We hadn't spoken before, but I knew he was in charge of one of the Lehntarn's three shifts. And his men seemed to respect him, not a single one of the more manly and in-shape members of his group raising a single eye towards his corpulent mass.

Very carefully unwrapping another waterproofed parcel inside the pack, Gritilli set a thick tome down upon my desk. Then gently opening its cover, he paged through it until he found the section he was looking for. Turning the book so I could see, an extraordinarily illuminated drawing depicted a circle in the tome's center, in blues, greens, and browns. Then connected to that central circle touched half-formed-circles on either side, these half-circles also curiously colored in the same hues as before.

Filling the page were characters in a language I'd never seen before, but before I could ask a single question Gritilli spoke up. "Lehntarn," he said, pointing to a section in the lower right part of the central sphere. Then pointing to the right most half-circle, he indicated where a series of miniscule humps formed a line. "Monks," he said, then passed his finger between the two. "We go," he finished, obviously done saying whatever he could.

There was a swath of green to the north of where he said the monks were, a region of bare brown below, and a huge expanse of blue between where he had originally pointed to, and where we now were.

Waiting as I looked between him and the picture he indicated, it slowly dawned on me he was showing me where his country was located. Then it hit me that this simply drawn picture was a map of the entire world. The world as they knew it. Something none of us knew.

"This is a map of the world?" I reverently breathed.

Every map of the world the monastery had was damaged, some burned or soiled beyond repair. Brother Barkon and the other chanters told of how our Tower was invaded during the Fall, but records of that time were spotty at best. To have an intact map that showed our entire world in such simple terms was a gift of the Pantheon, and needed to be preserved for all time. Brother Ansilin would be ecstatic, the abbot even more so.

"Map," Vortiid agreed. "No map Makun tower?"

I didn't even glance his way. "No, we have no maps. That section of the library was destroyed during the Fall. It's how most of our forebearers died. The tower was battled over until we beat off the invaders. It's why we sealed off the library – shut ourselves off – to protect the knowledge we had left."

"Tower … invaded?"

"Invaded … ummm. Monsters invaded the tower according to the chanters. They killed most of our people until they were beaten off or destroyed." I pointed towards his sword, the thing never out of reach even though he rarely kept it on his belt anymore. "Our forefathers fought them off. Made war on the monsters? The ones the mages brought."

"Tower fight. Made war. Lost map?"

I nodded, figuring this was the best we could reach based on our understanding of each other at the time. "To see a map like this … Vortiid, this is amazing." I leaned closer towards that priceless tome lying there so simply upon my desk, peering intently at the picture before me with miniscule lettering here and there all over the map. "By the Pantheon, I have to tell Brother Ansilin about this! The abbot will be thrilled."

Gritilli slammed the book shut, narrowly missing my nose. "No," he declared. "No, Makun." His emphatic response left me no doubt that seeing this wonder was for me, and me alone.

"But why not?" I asked as that amazing tome was hurriedly wrapped up in its protective cloth and stuffed back into that unassuming pack.

Gritilli began speaking aloud in that fluid tongue, the defensiveness of his speech coming through in his tone, even though I didn't understand a single one of his words. Vortiid replied, their conversation going back and forth as I hurriedly grabbed for a piece of blank parchment. Smearing the ink in my haste, I sketched my remembrance of that priceless map in a sloppily applied drawing, doing my best to accurately depict everything I had seen before my memory was lost.

I had roughly drawn the basic outline of our globe and labelled Lehntarn and the Spire before I noticed a tense quiet. Looking up, I saw both Vortiid and Gritilli frowning at me. Gritilli looked angrily put out, his chubby face flushed with what he now saw. But Vortiid seemed to understand and sympathize with my haste, though he was obviously unhappy as well.

"Don't you understand? To have a map of the world? The things we could learn just by simply knowing where things are? It has to be preserved before it is lost to time once more," I insisted.

Waving a hand in the direction of Gritilli's pack, I tried to convey that tome's priceless importance. Unfortunately, it was also the hand that was holding my quill, and my motion sent drops of ink flying towards the two of them. And, of course, a droplet of ink landed squarely on the pack I had insisted we protect.

On seeing that, I cringed.

Vortiid smirked on seeing me cringe, saying something to Gritilli in his own tongue. The portly man lost some of his flush, but he hugged that pack back to his chest once more. Then flicking the ink off with one hand, which miraculously didn't even leave a stain, he gave me a curious look before turning away and reentering the house from which he had come.

I watched him leave, my eyes unable to stop longingly staring after the pack until it had completely left my sight. Then I sighed, turning back to my hastily drawn recollection of the map, damning myself for not asking if I could copy it sooner. Then I damned myself for opening my mouth at all, wondering if they would ever let me see that amazing book ever again. Or any other of their books, for that matter, which caused me to frown. Then I sighed once more, casting sand across what I had drawn in defeat, hoping the brother recorder and the abbot would accept what little of the world I had managed to record.

"Makun."

I looked up at Vortiid, who had a very serious look on his face.

"Makun, map no help. Me help. People help. Makun help. Map no help. Book no help."

"But the knowledge …"

"Know-ledge?"

I pointed at my head. "Knowledge. Things you know. Remember."

"Know-ledge help," he agreed. "Makun, me, people, help more." Then Vortiid nodded his head as if what he had said was somehow profound.

I nodded as well, accepting what he had said in defeat. "You are, of course, correct. Without each other, where would we be?"

"Yes."

"I still wish I could see that book."

"No book. Makun, Vortiid, speak."

I sighed, dusting the sand off that incredibly important sketch I'd just made on the sheet and put it aside. Then pushing back from my desk, I moved my scattered papers and the ink away from me, settling in for whatever Vortiid had to say. "Fine. Speak."

I admit I was frustrated.

"Good. Makun, Vortiid, speak. No write, speak. Makun write, no speak. Help Makun. Speak Lehntarn. Speak walk far. Speak people. Make abbot no angry speak Makun. Make pro-tec-tor no angry help Lehntarn. Have Makun here, stay here, speak Vortiid more. Help more."

No, Vortiid was not dumb, not dumb at all. And with the pronouncements he made, I no longer had any doubt in my mind he understood everything that was said much more than he let on. To be able to pick up that I was under pressure from the abbot to learn what I could, despite the advanced words the abbot had used, left no doubt. And that the brother protector was suspicious of them, with what little Brother Sedimont had said, it only confirmed it. The nod Vortiid gave me on seeing my shrewd look solidified my suspicions.

"Why help me?"

At first, I didn't think he was going to respond. But before I could look away once more, he did. "Makun no angry."

"Of course I'm not angry. I'm trying to learn."

Vortiid nodded. "Makun want learn. Abbot no learn. Sed-i-mont no learn. Monks no learn. Makun want learn."

"What do you mean we don't want to learn? Everybody is thrilled by your arrival and what it could mean. If it wasn't for Brother Sedimont's concerns, you'd be inside the Spire right now."

"Yes. Makun want learn. Abbot want …" he trailed off, searching for a word but eventually gave up. "Abbot want thing speak. Sed-i-mont want no fight monk tower. Abbot, Sed-i-mont, no want learn. Want thing. Makun want learn."

"Well, of course they want specific things. They're both in charge and have specific duties."

"No. No du-ties. Want things. No learn."

I didn't understand what he was trying to say, and damned the limitations of language we were under. Vortiid was apparently frustrated too, running his fingers over the stubble that graced his shorn head. Mumbling to himself, he eventually looked up and met my eyes again.

"Makun stay. Makun, Vortiid, speak. Makun no go."

"Fine, I won't go. What do you want to talk about?" I asked, reaching again for my papers and quill.

"No write. Speak. Vortiid no speak Makun write."

I looked at him oddly, pausing my reach across the desk for my things. Slowly easing away from my papers, I settled further back onto the camp stool. Then watching Vortiid in silence for a while, I wondered what he wanted to talk about that he didn't want me to make a record of. It admittedly had me curious, and something told me that Vortiid's offer made here and now was him taking a big leap of faith.

"I agree."

"Vortiid, Makun, speak? No write?"

I shut my book, then placed the scattered papers underneath. "No, I won't make any records," I said as I capped the ink.

He wet his lips with his tongue, glancing over towards my escort, the brother protector that was still lounging off to the side. My brother was nodding as he slept, and admittedly, I hadn't even noticed when he fell asleep.

"No speak abbot?" Vortiid asked.

I frowned. "What could you possibly say that you would want me to keep from Abbot Dreise?"

"No speak abbot?" Vortiid repeated.

"No, I will not make any promise to that. If something you say could bring harm to the Spire, I will inform my superiors … as I am not only required, but am wont to do. The safety of the group comes before all."

Vortiid frowned, turning that over inside his head before he replied. "Vortiid no speak all."

"Fine. But if you are hiding something that could bring harm to the Spire, to anyone, even the villagers, I will hold you to blame."

Vortiid frowned even more, but then nodded his head. "Yes. Lehntarn no fight Spire people. Vortiid no speak all."

"Fine. Then what are we going to speak about?"

Vortiid called out, the leaders of the three sections of their party quickly responding to his summons. The four of them spoke for a while in their tongue, Gritilli frowning my way a few times, yet without any heat in his look at whatever was being said. But the others barely glanced in my direction, ignoring me entirely as was their way, though there were quite a few looks towards my set aside papers and my tightly capped ink.

Then an uncomfortable silence fell, and I suddenly found myself under three sets of flat and judgmental eyes, with Vortiid off to the side. First one and then the next responded, the skinny man obviously disagreeing with whatever was said by the group. But the other two agreed with what Vortiid apparently proposed, the skinny man shaking his head 'no' while saying "Ghaan" over and over again. But his refusal was seemingly overruled by Vortiid, and he settled himself with a frown as he and the rest sat back to study me alongside their leader.

"Makun," Vortiid called for my attention. "Gritilli Van, Pormult Dor, yes." He indicated Gritilli and then the brawny man in sequence. "Xer Jeman, no." He indicated the skinny man, and I was glad for the introductions because their names had been curiously avoided until now. "Makun no write? No speak abbot? Speak abbot, Sed-i-mont, fight only?" Vortiid questioned.

"Yes. Like I said, I will not promise to tell the abbot if something you say can harm our people. But if you want to tell me something in confidence," I glanced towards the sleeping brother protector, "I can agree to that."

Xer Jeman grunted after I finished, but the rest remained silent. Another quiet conversation between the four of them took place, but an agreement was finally reached. I sensed grudging acceptance at best. Then the four turned back to me.

"Makun. Vortiid speak Makun long walk. Vortiid speak Makun Ghaan. Vortiid speak Ghaan Lehntarn people. Ghaan save people," he emphatically said that last bit. Then in his broken speech, Vortiid went on to describe their haunting journey …

… And how they had come here.

Capitula 8

Sitting with their backs to the wall of that home we had given to them, Vortiid went on to tell the tale of how they had arrived. A lot of it was difficult to understand, involving a copious amount of hand waving and back and forth questioning to get their point across, but understanding was eventually achieved. And as our conversation went on in the afternoon sun, even a few of the villagers wandered closer to hear the newcomer's incredible tale.

"Fight. Many, many, fight, Makun," Vortiid said. "Fight …" then he frowned, searching for a word. He looked up, then chopped his hand repeatedly while moving it left to right, all the while glancing at the sun, before then looking at me expectantly.

"Time?" I guessed, then thought about his gestures. "For a long time?"

Vortiid nodded. "Fight many time, Makun. Me fight, they fight." He indicated the men beside him before he pointed to a man walking by with his boy. "Old fight. Young fight." Then he frowned, obviously searching for how to say the next part he wanted to.

Pormult pointed at the man and his boy. "Father?" he asked.

"Yes," I replied. "That is a boy and his father."

Thus ensued a quick conversation in their tongue before Vortiid spoke up once again. "Many father fight. Father father fight. Father father father fight," he insisted. "Many time father fight."

"You're talking about history. You're talking about generations of fighting."

"Gen-er-a-tions?" Vortiid shrugged. "Father father father fight."

"We'll come back to it," I said, realizing we didn't have the linguistic background to cover the term.

"Back?"

I shook my head. "Father fight?" I prompted.

Xer Jeman grunted, scowling at Vortiid. Then he spoke up saying, "Father fight."

Pormult agreed. "Father fight. Father father fight. Father father fath–"

Gritilli mumbled "Father father father father fight."

It was all quite comical. Then Vortiid cut them all off, waving a hand to encompass the four of them. "… father fight, Makun." He said something to the others in his own tongue, then they all fell silent while looking at me.

"All your fathers fought?"

"Yes." Vortiid nodded emphatically, then waved his hand to encompass everyone from Lehntarn in sight. "Father fight."

"Everyone here, their fathers fought?"

"Yes."

Then Vortiid frowned before he looked up. Pointing at the sun, he moved his hand as if to drag it across the sky. He looked at me to make sure I was paying attention, then dragged his finger across the sky the same way, over and over again. Sometimes he would mime a shiver, other times he would pant like he was hot.

That was easy enough to catch on. "You're trying to say years? Seasons? Time?"

"Time, yes." Vortiid nodded in thanks. "Many time fight."

"How many time … dammit, now you have me doing it. How long have you been fighting?" I corrected myself.

"Long?"

"Ummm." I pointed to the sky, then moved my hand slowly in imitation of his, shivering at one point then panting at the next before saying aloud "One." I repeated myself four more times, counting each year I was trying to communicate before he caught on.

Vortiid nodded. "Many long time, Makun. Many long time father fight."

"Dammit, I need to know how long," I mumbled to myself. Looking around, I grabbed up two handfuls of pebbles from the ground. Then placing one on the ground, I pointed to it and said "One," waiting until I was sure I had all of their attention. Then I placed two pebbles and said "Two," before repeating the procedure, adding a pebble each time until I reached ten.

Then looking to Vortiid expectantly, I asked "How long have you fought? One year?" I dragged my finger across the sky. "Two years?" I dragged my finger twice across the sky the same way. "How long Vortiid?"

Xer Jeman eyed me shrewdly, saying something in his own tongue without looking away. Vortiid answered him calmly, but something about Xer's tone left me uncomfortable as the two of them continued to speak. Then Xer himself spoke up, "Monk fight?"

"Do we fight?"

"Yes."

"Yes, we fought. We haven't fought in a long time. There are monster incursions, but the ones we can't overcome we retreat into the tower." I pointed back up to the gate.

"Monk father father fight?"

"Our forefathers fought." I looked at him in confusion. "I mean, everyone fought when the gods were lost during the Fall, and we still fight when need be. But we, along with every other survivor of the apocalypse, are doing what we can to rebuild society. Every soul lost is another person that cannot help bring about the return of the Pantheon. So no, we do not fight, not unless we have to."

"Monk no fight," Xer said somewhat dismissively, looking again towards Vortiid.

Another conversation ensued before Vortiid looked at me again. "Makun fight?"

"No, I have yet to be in battle. I have trained for it, all the monks have, but only the brother protectors regularly fight or train for it." I indicated my sleeping escort.

Xer snorted, then Pormult did as well, but Vortiid continued to speak. "Makun, Lehntarn fight many time."

"I understand that."

"No. Fight many time," he insisted. He dragged his finger across the sky. "One day, fight." He pointed towards the single stone before he dragged his finger across the sky again. "Two day, fight. Three day, fight. Ten day, fight. Many ten day fight, Makun."

He pointed towards a boy playing in the dirt by one of the villager's houses, not that far away. "Boy?" he asked, and when I nodded in confirmation he continued. "Vortiid boy, fight. Vortiid father, fight. Vortiid fight. Pormult fight. Xer fight. Gritilli fight." He waved a hand to encompass their entire area once again. "Lehntarn fight many time."

"All of you fought? How many years, Vortiid." I dragged my finger across the sky. "How long have you all been fighting?"

Vortiid looked to Gritilli, and the portly man talked to him for a time. Then looking at me, Gritilli pointed to the cluster of ten pebbles and asked "Ten?". And when I nodded in confirmation, Gritilli picked up a single stone and deliberately said "Ten." Then he picked up the rest of the pebbles, as well as every pebble within reach. Then he started to put them down, one beside the other, keeping ahold of my eyes as he named every single one of them he set down "Ten."

He kept ahold of my eyes until he ran out of stones, then glanced down towards the little pile he made. Then he looked back up at me, holding his hand about waist high over the pile, and said "Many ten time fight, Makun."

There was a lot of space between his hand and that pile.

"You've been fighting the entire time?" I asked incredulously. "For that much time to have passed, you have to have been fighting since the Fall." I couldn't bring myself to believe what he was saying.

They talked amongst themselves before Vortiid confirmed, "Yes, Makun." Then he held his hand up, thrusting it out towards a bush nearby while making a whooshing sound as he did so. Then he brought his hands back together, before he whipped them apart as fast as he could, mimicking the bush being blown asunder. "Since many fight time, Lehntarn fight."

"My gods. Are you saying you've been fighting nonstop since the war of the gods?" The sheer idea of anyone experiencing such a thing left me astounded.

"Yes. Lehntarn fight, ten, ten, ten, father time, Makun."

"By the Pantheon …"

The four of them nodded, a dour look passing between them all. Then Pormult, that brawny man who never seemed to take off his ring and scale armor, uttered a short phrase. Then all of them drew the back of their thumbs down their left cheek, before chanting a series of words.

It was a strangely ritualistic display; however, I was completely astonished.

"Well, no wonder you came," I mumbled, just beginning to go over the ramifications of such a thing in my head. "You've been fighting for fifteen hundred years. Just considering that fact is utterly astounding."

Gritilli gave me a curious look. "Time?" he asked. Then prompted, "Fifff–" drawing out and emphasizing the 'F' in the word. He gestured for me to repeat what I'd said.

I took up one of the rocks and held it up to him. "Ten." Then I picked up ten rocks and said, "Ten ten." And after setting them all down together in their own little pile next to that lone stone, I named the ten stones I'd named 'ten' in my pile as "Hundred."

Seeing his understanding, I searched the pile for stones that were larger than the rest. Miming something tiny with my fingers, I picked up a lone stone and said again "Ten." Then miming something larger before picking up a bigger stone, I said "Hundred." Then placing ten large stones down beside the pile I had named hundred, I said "Hundred, Hundred." Then placing my hand over the pile of larger stones, I looked him in the eye and said "Thousand." Then I pried up a cobblestone from the ground and said again "Thousand" as I named it.

All four watched as I then proceeded to count out five large stones and then set the cobblestone down beside them. I looked up to make sure I had all of their attention before I declared "Fight time Lehntarn. One thousand …" I nudged the cobblestone, then I picked up each of the larger pebbles one at a time counting aloud "One, two, three, four, five hundred years. One thousand five hundred years Lehntarn fight. Yes?"

There was no way this could be true, it just wasn't possible, but as a brother recorder it was my duty to make certain I was clear. And to be able to finally report hard facts and findings to my superiors drove me ever forward. I waited patiently as a conversation ensued between Vortiid and the other leaders, taking a sip of my tepid water from the cup on my desk that had baked in the midday sun.

The ensuing conversation went round and round, with Gritilli picking up a tiny stone, then a larger stone, then the cobblestone, and ensured his understanding that they represented ten, hundred, and thousand. The four of them moved the stones around for a bit, discussing their placement with great care before Pormult got up, went into the barn, and returned with a handful of seeds that had been left over from one of our past harvests. Then handing the seeds to Gritilli, they talked a while longer before the corpulent man turned back to me.

"No. No fight one thousand five hundred, Makun," Gritilli declared.

"I thought so," I answered him, and began wondering where the breakdown in the explanation had occurred.

"Makun," Gritilli interrupted my thoughts, waiting until he had my undivided attention. He held up a seed and named it "One" while he shook the hand holding it emphatically in the air. Then he pointed to the smaller stones naming them "Ten", the larger stones he named "Hundred", then the cobblestone he stated "Thousand."

"Yes …" I replied curiously, wondering where all of this was going.

"Makun, Lehntarn fight …" Then he proceeded to put down eight seeds, five large rocks, and then a single large cobblestone before he looked back up towards me. Pointing at each of them in turn, he said "Eight, Five hundred, One thousand, years Lehntarn fight, Makun."

Gobsmacked, I corrected him without thinking "One thousand, five hundred and eight years," but I was barely paying attention. I totally ignored him when he nodded, repeating what I had said without me really hearing it at all. But then he fell silent as I incredulously met his eyes.

That was the date, this year's date, one thousand, five hundred and eight years after the Fall, something I had heard only this morning, as I had every morning this year during the opening chant before we started our day. That these people were claiming their country – their entire society – had been fighting the entire time, it stunned me to the core.

For fifteen hundred years they'd been fighting? Without a single stop? Without end? For the Pantheon's sake … It just boggled the mind. Vortiid had even mimed magic, meaning he knew what it was, or had encountered it, or at least his people had known what mages were after the Fall.

My mind blurred and then blanked as wild thoughts raced one by one across my head. Then my rampant considerations crashed to a sudden halt, as one thought, a thought that came to be of singular importance before all the rest, rose to the fore. "By the Pantheon, Vortiid. What in the gods' name did you fight?"

"What fight?"

"For fifteen hundred years … No, for fifteen hundred and eight years." I nodded to Gritilli. "What in the Pantheon's name did you fight?"

The men looked between themselves, but it was Xer Jeman who captured my attention. Holding my eyes, he mimed cutting his throat while saying something in his own tongue. "What Makun speak?" Then he mimed cutting his throat again.

"Slitting someone's throat?"

A conversation ensued before he tried again. He repeated "Slitting throat?" Then he closed his eyes, before he slumped to the ground while making gurgling noises.

"Dying? Dead?" I guessed.

"Dead," Xer Jeman agreed emphatically, then looked to his countrymen before returning his eyes on me. "Lehntarn fight dead, Makun." Then he pointed to the pile of stones Gritilli had laid out. "Lehntarn fight dead. Many father father fight dead." Then he pointed to me. "Monks no fight dead."

"My gods." I couldn't even begin to imagine what he was saying. "No. We didn't fight the dead. Monsters of many kinds … Ummm, Monk father father fight many monster." I waited until Xer nodded in understanding. "No monster attacks have come in almost twenty years."

"No monster twenty year?" Vortiid questioned.

"No."

He pointed in the direction of the forest. "Many monster, Makun. Trees," he declared.

"Yes. There are many monsters in the forest. Most don't come up here. We hide when they do." I pointed up to the outer gate, which ultimately led the way back into our hidden tower. "Most of the monsters don't even know we're here. We do everything we can to keep it that way, but we fight the monsters if and when they come."

Vortiid nodded in understanding. "Monsters not dead, Makun. Dead fight every day. Every one day," he insisted. "Dead no stop. No stop, Makun. Father, father fight. One thousand, five hundred, eight time," he finished, pointing to the piles of seeds and stones as he named them.

Then his horrible declaration led to a lull in the conversation, punctuated by another rumble of thunder from the mage storm that raged alongside our mountain.

Far, far below …

Capitula 9

"Lehntarn fight dead, many time, all time. Fight protect tower. Fight protect people. Many fight. Big fight, little fight." Vortiid held his hands out miming what was said. "Lehntarn always fight. Protect tower. Tower protect people. People fight dead," he explained.

"Lehntarn big," Vortiid declared, making a huge pile of stones. "Many time fight, Lehntarn little." He took a stone, one stone at a time from the pile, making his finger travel across the sky before he took each one. "Many time, many little." He continued taking stone by stone until only one stone was left.

"You're talking about years."

"Years, yes. Lehntarn fight many years."

He hoisted that single pebble and named it "Tower." Then he moved his finger across the sky, saying, "Tower fight many year. Fight–"

Xer Jeman interrupted, growling something that stopped whatever Vortiid was going to say. Nodding his head, Vortiid continued. "Fight dead many time. Many die. Father die. Boy die." Then he pointed a finger to a passing woman, questioning me with his eyes.

"Woman. Mother?"

"Mother. Yes. Many mother die. All die. Father, mother, boy, dead. Lehntarn fight father, mother, boy."

"Huh?"

Vortiid looked to Xer Jeman, then Xer made that gurgling sound again. "Dead?" he questioned.

"Yes?"

Then he mimed dying again, and then shook upon the ground after he had allowed himself slump over. Xer then made an eerily whistling sound from his partially opened mouth, almost a whining-like growl, like he was some kind of fighting cat, before he clumsily rose to his feet and started stumbling about the yard.

Vortiid pointed to Xer. "Lehntarn fight dead. Dead kill father, mother, boy. Father, mother, boy, dead. Dead fight Lehntarn." Then Xer returned to his seat.

"They fight you again after the dead killed them? They come back to life after they die?"

I must admit, my voice had become quite high.

"Yes," Vortiid confirmed, despite me not wanting his confirmation one bit. "Dead kill. Father, mother, boy, come life back? Father, mother, boy, dead," he declared.

"That's horrible," I breathed.

"Horr-ib-?" Pormult questioned.

"Horrible. Bad," I explained.

Pormult grunted. "Bad …" The brawny man snorted. "Dead bad?" He snorted again. "Monk no know."

"No, I have absolutely no idea how bad. How did you survive?"

"Fight," Gritilli simply answered. He mimed writing then said, "Me fight." He mimed holding something to his chest, then imitated the cry of an infant. "Mother fight." Then Gritilli held his hand up about the height of his waist. "Boy fight. All fight, Makun."

"All fight," Vortiid agreed. He picked up a cobblestone before he met my eye. "Many thousand dead."

"Thousands?"

Vortiid nodded. "All fight. All kill father, mother, boy …" Then he pointed to the boy who was playing nearby once again, and mimed a set of breasts on his chest. "No boy. Makun speak no boy?" Then he mimed breasts once again.

"Girl? Daughter?"

"Yes, daughter. Many thousand dead all fight. Kill father, mother, boy, daughter. Hide tower. Protect tower." He mimed eating food. "No food. Many thousand dead. No …" Then he clapped his hand on the earth.

"Ground."

"Yes. No ground. Many thousand dead. All kill. Lehntarn fight. Lehntarn little. Lehntarn tower. No ground. No food. Many die. Die? More dead."

"You were fighting a losing battle. Every person the dead killed came back to life to fight you," I shivered, "until you were cornered in your tower."

"Cornered?"

"No way out. No escape."

"Yes. No escape. No food. Ghaan–"

"Vortiid!" Xer objected.

Thus ensued a heated conversation between Vortiid and the man, with both Gritilli and Pormult looking on while they both remained silent. Eventually Xer chopped his hand down emphatically, before he looked towards the other two. Then Pormult and Gritilli looked at each other and nodded, apparently agreeing with whatever Xer had said.

Vortiid nodded, apparently accepting the will of the group before he spoke again. "Dead many. People little. No food. Lehntarn escape. Ghaan Tower. Ghaan lead. Ghaan save Lehntarn escape. Many die escape." All four of them stroked their cheeks again in that ritualistic gesture. "Lehntarn escape. Come here."

"By the gods. So, this is why you are all that is left? Out of your entire people?" I asked. My horror at what he had just told me filled me with fear.

Vortiid looked towards the others before returning to me. "Yes, Makun." He waved his hand to encompass where his people were in the village. "All Lehntarn people." He cast his hand out from where we now were. "No Lehntarn people," he finished quite solemnly.

I shook my head, stunned by how profound those statements were. "To think, all that is left of an entire civilization is here …" I shook my head. "This is amazing. I'm so glad you have come."

"Glad?"

"Glad, glad …" I mumbled. Then I smiled and said "Happy", then frowned and said "Sad." Then I smiled again, saying "Happy. Glad."

"Ah. Yes. Happy come."

"And you came through the forest?" I asked, remembering the map I had been shown. They had come half way around the world. How in the Pantheon's name had they made their way here?

"Forest? Trees?" Vortiid asked, pointing down towards the trees far below.

"Yes."

"No come trees, Makun."

"Well, how did you get here then?"

"Long walk."

"You walked across the ocean?"

"Ocean?"

"Big water? Ocean? You walked across that?"

"No. No long walk ocean." Then he looked to the other three, asking a question of them with his eyes. Xer nodded, saying something before Vortiid began to speak once again. "Come elves."

"Elves!" I exclaimed.

Vortiid shot me a curious look, then glanced again towards the others before continuing. "Yes, Makun. Elves."

"No one's seen an elf since before the time of the Fall!"

Vortiid shrugged, then turned away as the other three began a conversation between themselves. I sat back in my stool, listening though not really caring at the moment what was being said around me. An entire civilization stuck in a loop, in a battle without hope, fighting their own dead. Loved ones who came back to life to kill those who were still living, thus being forced to fight them. Being slowly driven back into their tower, year after year, then having to escape from there because there was no food. Then doing whatever it was they did, to appear in the land of the elves … their story was simply amazing.

My mind whirled at the implications of what I had heard, and all of the questions it left me.

"Makun?" a sweet voice asked.

I turned to see Jan, the beautiful girl I had longed after for so much time. She speared me with those two devastatingly blue eyes, which brought me to speechlessness whenever she looked at me the way she was. She was smiling at me as she walked my way, a basket cocked on her hip filled with the day's laundry.

"Hello, Jan." I waved, bringing the Lehntarn's conversation to a halt. They watched as she walked over, a rosy hue coming to her cheeks as she advanced underneath their impenetrable gaze. But she weathered their looks anyway, glancing their way a few times before deliberately fixing her eyes on me.

The dichotomy between seeing her and the story I'd just learned threw me.

"I thought I heard you were down here." She smiled sweetly. Flicking her eyes towards the four other men, she asked "What are you up to?"

"Learning their story." I waved in the group's direction. "They've come from far away. A complete other country, if you can believe that. They're just starting to tell me a bit about their journey."

Vortiid cleared his throat, then chucked his chin towards my Jan. "Makun. Who people?"

Jan looked at him oddly, unused to his halting speech, but I understood his question. "Vortiid Beln, this is Jan Isterlin. Jan, this is Vortiid Beln, Pormult Dor, Xer Jeman, and Gritilli Van," I named each one of the Lehntarnese leaders in turn. "They appear to be the leaders of their people, and I'm learning their story from them."

"How do you do?" Jan asked, bobbing a quick and obviously uncomfortable curtsy.

The men watched her in silence, then Vortiid turned to me. He got an odd look on his face considering something, then said something to the other men, got a reply, and then smirked. "Makun. Father, boy." Then he dropped his arm between his legs, letting his arm flop like a gigantic cock. "Mother, daughter." He mimed again breasts upon his chest. "Word father, boy; mother, daughter?"

Jan blushed beet red, much to the amusement of the men, but I answered readily, hoping that my cheeks weren't as red as they felt. "Do you mean man and woman?" He cocked his head at me, so I mimed my arm between my legs and said "Man", before I mimed a pair of breasts and said "Woman."

"I don't think this is a conversation for me," Jan started, but Vortiid quickly cut her off.

"Yes. Man, woman. Makun man. Jan woman. Jan Makun woman?" Vortiid asked.

If Jan could have gotten any redder, I didn't know how. "No. Jan is not my woman." I had hoped one day to prove to the council I was worthy to be coupled with her, but that was the last thing on my mind right now.

"Good woman." Vortiid eyed her up and down, then turned to me and grinned. "Makun need good woman. Make Makun man."

"Ahem. Yes," I choked out. I made a point of not noticing that Jan was now red from the shoulders up.

"Is this what you are talking about down here?" Jan challenged, her eyebrows rising despite her brilliant blush.

"No!" I waved my hands defensively, but the men from Lehntarn just laughed as I struggled.

Vortiid laughed along as well, saying "Good woman" as Jan continued to glare at me. "Jan Isterlin," he called for her attention. "Makun good man. Makun want learn. Help people." He waved his hand around to include every Lehntarnese in sight. "Good."

"I already know that," she half snapped.

Pormult snorted, laughing at me with his eyes, while Vortiid laughed aloud once again before he continued. "Jan Isterlin speak yes, Makun ask. Life time little. Jan, Makun, boy, daughter."

I knew I was blushing furiously now, and I was thankful Jan didn't completely understand what Vortiid was trying to say. "I haven't asked yet, Vortiid," I struggled out.

But Jan whipped her head around towards me.

"No?" Vortiid asked.

"No. I haven't told the abbot about that, either. Though I'm certain he has already guessed."

"Excuse me?" Jan asked.

I helplessly looked between Jan and the four Lehntarnese. All of them were laughing uproariously at my uncomfortable situation, while Jan just watched me like a hawk from the side.

"Is there something you want to tell me, Brother Derring? Or perhaps ask?" Jan challenged.

"Ummm. Gods. By the Pantheon, I wanted to do this another way," I mumbled. "Jan? Miss Isterlin?" I cringed when I asked that because her expression didn't change. "Would you care to go for a walk with me this evening … or maybe later this week?"

I refuse to admit I squeaked out that last part.

"A walk?" she flatly stated more than she asked.

"Yes?"

The men of Lehntarn both snorted and chuckled as she continued to stare down at me, her blush seeping out of her shoulders and neck until only her cheeks were still colored. Then she quirked a corner of her mouth into a grin, and answered "Maybe," which she teasingly drew out. Then spinning in place, she cocked the basket of laundry daringly back onto her hip while she slowly strutted away.

The other men guffawed, but she didn't look back even once. I know, I watched her walk away, until she eventually disappeared.

"Happy." Vortiid laughed. "Woman happy. Good woman. Makun ask good woman Jan. Happy," he said before he laughed again.

"I think you mean funny," I grumped. "Not happy."

"Funny, happy, glad … Monk many word happy."

I glanced the way Jan had gone causing the men to laugh once again. I took a deep breath and then sighed, wondering if I was going to be made to pay for how that episode had gone on, then forced the entire thing out of my mind.

"You were telling me your story," I prompted, hoping to change the subject.

There were a few "Jan good woman" and "Makun ask good woman" before the story started back up again.

Vortiid started it off after a brief discussion. "Lehntarn come elves. Elves no want Lehntarn. Elves feed, speak, protect. Heal. Ghaan talk elves."

I caught the sharp look Xer shot towards Vortiid, but the older man kept going.

"Elves speak Lehntarn no stay. Lehntarn …" he looked around before reaching out for the stones. He spoke with Gritilli for a while before he went on. "Lehntarn two, ten, two hundred elves."

"There were two hundred and twelve of you left when you got to the elves?"

"Twelve?"

I motioned ten and two together, naming it "twelve."

"Yes. Two hundred twelve Lehntarn. Stay one year elves."

"You lived with the elves for a year?"

He looked at me oddly.

"You stayed one year with the elves?"

"With." He nodded his head at the word. "Yes. Stay one year with elves. Elves speak, Lehntarn knowledge." He tapped his head.

"You learned? Took knowledge?" I mimed the process of taking.

"Yes. Elves speak, Lehntarn took knowledge. Learn?" He tried out the new word, seeing me nod my head. "Stay one year. Elves speak Lehntarn go. Lehntarn go. Elves … food." He mimed passing me something.

"They gave you food?"

"Yes. Gave. Gave many food. Speak Lehntarn go. Speak many man. Mountains." Vortiid pointed to the Spire behind me. "Many mountains. Lehntarn long walk mountains, go find man. Many die long walk." He eyed me for a moment. "Orcs," he explained.

"Orcs!" Elves and now orcs? Fighting the dead? Coming from the other side of the world? I could barely believe it. This story was becoming more fantastical the longer it went on.

"Yes. Many orcs. Many fight long walk mountains. No fight, Lehntarn see ocean. Big water, find man. Many man little people." He pointed to the village behind me. "Monk people many, man people little."

"You mean there weren't many of them. They were few."

"Yes. Few. Few man speak Lehntarn no stay. Few man fear. Speak many man long walk find many people. Lehntarn go long walk big water. Ocean. Find many man. Long, long walk."

Vortiid pointed his hand towards the sky, drawing his finger across it once more. "One, two, year Lehntarn long walk. More die. Find many man. Fight, protect, many man no fight. Speak. Long speak, no fight. Lehntarn walk many man. Find big many man. Big, big, big. Find king. Speak many man king place. Tatdavarr."

"You discovered the lost city of Tatdavarr?" I exclaimed.

That fabled city had been reported lost during the Fall, the chanters had said so. In our oldest chants, from our most ancient of tomes, that gilded city was claimed to have been able to feed the entire world.

"Lost? No lost, Makun. Big, big place. Gate. King. Many man. Many speak." Then Vortiid frowned. "King want stay. King want thing. Want, want, want. No give, no protect, no learn, king want. Speak Lehntarn fight, king protect. Stay king big house, many food, many women, many speak. Lehntarn speak, Ghaan speak, king no speak. Want thing. Lehntarn no stay. King angry. No fight, angry speak, Lehntarn protect."

I was utterly enthralled by what he was saying as Vortiid continued. "Ghaan speak, king speak, speak tower. Tower many long walk Tatdavarr. King angry. No Gate. No food. No speak. Lehntarn go. Walk, walk, walk. Many long walk. People die. Find mountain, more orc. Big orc. Little orc."

One of the men grunted at this, and it sounded like this was some kind of sore point, but I didn't look up to see who it was. "Little orcs?"

Vortiid looked at me questioningly then stood. He held up his hand about head-height and said "Big orc." Then holding his hand a little above waist height, he said "Little orc."

"Their children?"

"Children?"

"The orc's boy, daughter," I explained.

"No. Little orc."

"But they're not children?"

Vortiid looked confused, turning the word over in his head before shrugging and sitting back down. "Many little orc," he said once more. Vortiid nodded to his countryman, shrugged, then continued his tale. "Lehntarn fight big orc, little orc. People die. Leave mountain. Find tower. Not tower." He pointed insistently up towards the gate. "There tower. Mountain not tower. Little king tower. Big water. Not ocean," he insisted, then shook his head.

"Ghaan many speak little king not tower. Lehntarn stay. King speak happy fight orc, little orc, mountain. King speak Lehntarn stay. Fight. Lehntarn no stay, find tower. Mountain tower no tower. Little king angry, want stay. Fight Lehntarn night, people die. Make war on mountain tower. King people die. King people speak no war. King die. People speak new king. New king speak Lehntarn go. Ghaan many speak. King many speak. People many speak. Lehntarn go." As a group, they turned solemn. "Lehntarn go. Lehntarn find tower. Long walk."

He pointed to the sky once more. "Not year. Many day. Day, day, day, day, Lehntarn walk. Find tree. Many, many tree. Find monster. Many, many monster. Fight, fight, fight. Ghaan speak long walk tower. Lehntarn speak go mountain tower, speak new little king. Ghaan speak little walk tower. Lehntarn walk tower."

Then he turned more somber. "Find monster. Monster fight, people sick. Sick, sick, sick. Monster fight many Lehntarn, Ghaan save. Ghaan fight monster, Ghaan sick. Sick bad, bad. People speak Ghaan die." He seemed to remember the episode poorly.

Then Vortiid sighed, but his voice picked up almost in wonder. "Lehntarn find little tree people." Then he shrugged. "Little tree people find Lehntarn? Lehntarn no speak little tree people speak." He grinned, then said "tree people" once more like he couldn't quite believe it. "Tree people sprite?" he asked.

"The people who brought you here?" I held my hand at about a sprite's height, then mimed two long pointed ears and large eyes.

Vortiid nodded.

"Yes. We call them sprites."

"Tree people sprites," he chuckled. "Tree people; sprites. Yes. Find sprites. Sprites find people." He shrugged once more. "Little walk sprites. Find monks. Walk here." He patted his hand on the ground once more.

"Makun learn. Makun knowledge. Makun speak?" Vortiid asked.

I just stared at him in amazement. "Speak? I don't have any idea what to say. Vortiid …" Then I glanced to the others. "All of you, your journey was amazing."

Vortiid nodded. "Many Lehntarn people die. Want people live." He waved his hand behind him. "Monks protect? Safe?"

"By the Pantheon! Yes, you deserve to be safe."

Vortiid nodded, something about him seeming to relax upon hearing my words.

"But why don't you want me to tell any of this to the abbot? Nothing you told me seems like it should be a secret." I furrowed my brow towards them all.

A discussion began between the men, not a heated one, but one filled with concern. It was obvious that Xer Jeman didn't want a lot of what was said shared, mistrustful by the tone of his voice. While it was just as obvious that Vortiid thought I should be informed even more. It came down to the other two, Pormult and Gritilli only speaking a word here and there while the conversation went on. Then eventually whatever they were talking about came to an end, Xer nodding to Vortiid before the older warrior turned back to me.

"Makun speak abbot? Speak abbot Vortiid speak? Speak long walk?"

I nodded my head. "Yes, I'll tell him your story."

"Good. Speak abbot Ghaan save people. Ghaan sick. Monk people save Ghaan. Lehntarn people happy monk save Ghaan."

"Of course, we'll save him. We're doing everything we can."

"Look heal, yes."

"But why didn't you want me to tell any of this to the abbot?"

Vortiid eyed me for a moment, then he glanced towards his compatriots before he said anything more. "Makun, no abbot speak this."

"Okay?"

Vortiid nodded. "Makun, Vortiid no speak all."

And I was left wondering what it was that Vortiid hadn't said.

It should have kept me up that night, but it didn't. How naïve I was then ...

Capitula 10

"The dead brought back to life?" the abbot questioned. His disbelief was palpable.

I glanced towards Vortiid, worried the proud warrior might take offense at his tone, but his blank stare held no allusion to his feelings. Turning back towards the abbot and the other members of the council, I simply answered his question. "Yes, Abbot Dreise."

The boy that had been helping me and the people of Lehntarn scuttled in, glancing at the council before refilling mine and Vortiid's drink with a clatter. The Lehntarnese had plied the boy with food to come over and run errands for them by himself after our conversation the day before, the villagers reporting that they seemed enthralled by the young. They played with the boy until his mother came looking for him, Vortiid never interacting, but watching on with a thawing reserve. But Gritilli was thoroughly enamored by the youngster, seemingly finding joy in simply seeing the boy smile. Everyone from Lehntarn investigated the boy's laughter after he'd gotten over his fear of them, and even the mother smiled after ensuring the newcomers meant her boy no harm.

"Boy, enough," Brother Sedimont snapped.

The boy from the village froze, staring in fear at the council sitting high above on their dais. Vortiid reached out with his hand, patting the boy on his shoulder before letting his hand drop.

"The boy is just refilling their drinks, Brother," Brother Margonest said. The brother teacher smiled kindly down to the boy. "His actions are not interrupting the council."

"They do not need someone refilling their drinks. Our brother and our … guest … are not infirm."

"No, they are not," Brother Camdal agreed.

The brother healer's aged voice was a comforting thing as he spoke up from his place amongst the council. His calm and wisdom had seen our community through many crises, though the man had never held any aspirations to take charge. He simply supported from behind with his calm wisdom, letting the decision makers drive policy while he concentrated on healing.

"But the boy brings no harm, Sedimont," Brother Camdal continued. "The desire to serve others is a grace in the eyes of the

Pantheon."

Brother Sedimont frowned, but nodded his head. The aged Brother Healer was one of only a scant few in our order who ever referred to the other members of the council of seven by name, and it only reinforced how apart he was from the politics of his position. The brother protector, Brother Sedimont, had always aspired to one day lead the other brother protectors and was keen in regards to his title, as every brother inside knew. He was never overly arrogant about it, he just insisted upon its use.

"This is beside the point, brothers," Brother Randilon said. The lay brother glanced down the table towards the other members of the council. "It is not in my purview to lead us in discussing matters of security. But if such a threat is reported, no matter how far-fetched, shouldn't we at least give credence to its existence, and plan?"

"But the dead come to life?" the abbot once again questioned. "Such a thing defies reason."

Vortiid frowned.

"And even speaking about it is an insult to the Pantheon!" Brother Barkon sputtered.

The brother chanter had scoffed when I first reported that part of the Lehntarn's tale, muttering about fairy tales and mage-born fantasies. His refusal to believe what I reported to the council surprised me, and he had begun quoting chapter and verse out of The Book of the Fall before the abbot had silenced him.

"You, Brother, are a disgrace to your position to bring such a foul tale into our presence," Brother Barkon said as he speared me with his eyes.

"He does as is required of his position," Brother Ansilin chided the man, coming to my defense. "Was not Brother Derring asked to discover their history? To bring directly to the abbot anything worthy of note? I seem to remember that conversation, Brother."

"You believe such a tale?" Brother Barkon scoffed.

"It is not my place to pass judgement," the brother recorder replied. "The duty of all brother recorders is to simply preserve what is, and what also has been … *So that those who come can pass judgement on those who have come before, under the eyes of the Pantheon's good grace, to bring about the return of their rightful place*," Brother Ansilin quoted from The Book of the Fall, much to the brother chanter's chagrin. "As it ever has, such deliberations are made in peace and wisdom, not through fear and alarm-driven dispute. Do you see yourself as the sole arbiter of our order? The only one able to make such a determination, Brother Barkon?"

"He sees no such thing, Brother Ansilin," the abbot chided in return. "His alarm is reasonable, no matter how fantastical their story seems."

The boy, whose name was Eldso, had remained frozen while the council spoke, and I took their short pause to get his attention. "Boy, the Hall of Healing, you know it?"

He nodded his head yes.

"Run along now. Go there and let the one waiting with their man Ghaan know we may be longer than expected."

The boy nodded and ran off, glancing to Vortiid as he did so. Vortiid had explained he was the one to relieve the man who now sat with Ghaan, and I expected with the way this council meeting was going that we would still be here for some time. Vortiid nodded my way in apparent thanks for letting the boy go, but not once did his countenance change from remaining blank in the face of the council.

"At least the boy is now gone," Brother Sedimont said. "There will be no tales or rumors spread, filled with inaccuracies, by one of those ignorant villagers. All we need is a panic."

"Yet we must still discuss the tale's impact," the abbot stated. "Vortiid? The dead come back to life? Yes?"

Vortiid glanced at me once more with that blank face of his before he replied to the abbot. "Yes." His look told me all I needed to know about why he had not wanted this tale to be told. I felt a bit guilty, but he had said I could let my superiors know.

"It seems fantastical," the abbot trailed off. "Are the dead on their way here?" His question seemed to alarm the rest of the council, all of them eyeing Vortiid and I both.

"No. No dead." Then he said a word in his tongue I didn't understand.

"I'm sorry?"

"No dead." Vortiid paused for a moment, before pointing to the ground at his feet.

"There are no dead here?" I asked.

"Yes, no dead here."

"Many invaders have died on these slopes," Brother Sedimont challenged.

Vortiid just slowly turned his head, his flat and blank eyes coming to rest upon the brother protector without a word. Vortiid didn't utter a single sound, just stared at the man until he turned back to the abbot. By his expression, Brother Sedimont was not pleased.

The abbot glanced towards Sedimont before speaking. "And you reportedly lived with the elves. Travelling the lands for over a year, meeting many peoples, including places we once thought lost?"

Vortiid simply stared at the abbot.

The abbot stared back, before in frustration he spoke. "Is this not true, man?"

"Abbot know. Why ask?"

"Impertinence!" Brother Barkon declared.

The abbot placed his hand upon the man, returning the brother chanter to quiet. "I simply wish to affirm that what Brother Derring has reported is true?"

"Abbot know," Vortiid repeated and then settled back, obviously not going to say another word.

Brother Randilon grunted, but it was Brother Ansilin who spoke next. "Maybe you can assure us of the tale's validity, Brother Derring?"

"Brother Ansilin?"

"Is what we have been told true?"

"As is my duty under the Pantheon, Brother Ansilin, all I have reported is true. As you have instructed I must in my position, I convey only the words spoken, not my thoughts or reflections upon them."

"And they told you all these things?" He waved his hand towards Vortiid.

"Yes, Brother Ansilin."

"The dead come to life? Living with the elves? Lost cities and peoples? Battling orcs, men, monsters, and what not? We have at least seen the sprites with our own eyes," he confirmed as he looked around the table before he turned back to me. "They reported that all of this is true?"

"Yes, Brother Ansilin."

Then a silence fell, a few of the councilors pushing away from the table to sit back in thought. A few speared me with their eyes, the brother chanter foremost, but it was the abbot who spoke next.

"And there was nothing else?"

I suddenly felt as if I was under the eyes of a great predator, a meal waiting to be snatched up before being snacked upon. Vortiid had admitted to me he had not told me all, using his own words, and the man slowly turned his blank face towards me while I stared back at the abbot.

I have no idea what made me say what I did next. To this day, I do not know if what I did then was right.

"No, Abbot. There is nothing else I can factually report."

Brother Ansilin nodded his head, raising an eyebrow towards the other councilors in affirmation of what I had just reported, but I suddenly felt like a fraud. I glanced to Vortiid, seeing the slightest of nods before he looked away.

What am I doing?

"The elves are known mages," the brother chanter suddenly put in.

The abbot turned towards him, something in his eye betraying a strong emotion before he turned away again, but he did not speak.

"And the city of Tatdavarr was thought lost," Brother Margonest returned. "What is your point?"

"How do we know they do not bring the trappings of the enemy with them?" Brother Barkon speared Vortiid once again with his eyes.

"The trappings of the enemy?" Brother Camdal calmly asked. "A people who come to us in need? With many of their own injured, sickly, and poisoned? I humbly submit I think you forget your own teachings, Barkon. Does not the Pantheon wish us to give succor and healing to all those in need?"

"Yes, but we must still be vigilant and wary in case the wicked must be purged, Brother Healer," Brother Sedimont rejoined. "Such is the duty of my order."

"Your order, Brother Sedimont? I thought we were all monks under the eyes of the Pantheon?" Brother Ansilin questioned the man.

"Enough," the abbot broke in. "The Lehntarnese arrived with barely the clothing on their backs. I was there. I saw. And so did you."

"I do not dispute the facts, Abbot Dreise. But who knows what evils they may have upon their persons. Things they do not see as such, but which every pious man must fear." Brother Barkon looked towards Brother Sedimont before he turned back to the abbot. "They should be put to question," he declared.

Vortiid frowned mightily.

"I do not believe so, Brother Barkon," the abbot replied. "There is no mage here to invite the strictures. These people come to us in need, and are from another tower. They will be given succor, and their needs shall be met."

"But Abbot—"

"I said, their needs shall be met." The abbot looked down the table. "If you wish to question them, follow young Makun to the village and do so. He seems to have developed a rapport with them." The abbot waved his hand airily towards me. "But survivors of another tower will not be put to question. Not while I am Abbot, anyway. Have I made myself clear?"

There were some unhappy faces and less happy sounds from those at the table, but the rest of the council made some indication of acknowledgement before the abbot turned back to me.

"Young Makun?"

"Yes, Abbot?"

"I charge you to turn your attention to chronicling their journey. It is of the utmost importance, and I believe Brother Ansilin will agree."

The brother recorder nodded.

"As such, consider yourself entirely removed from your other duties, Brother Derring. More so than before, concentrate solely upon preserving a record of their journey from this time forth."

"Yes, Abbot Dreise."

"I believe The Hall of Knowledge can do without Brother Derring, Brother Ansilin?"

"Yes, Abbot. I am most secure in Brother Derring being pulled away for such a duty. He is ideally suited for this task," the brother recorder agreed.

"Then that is my will." The abbot nodded to everyone around the table. "You will begin with their arrival to the elves. Put pen to paper regarding their fantastical tale, so that all who come in the future may read and reflect upon what the Lehntarnese saw."

"Yes, Abbot."

"And because the validity of their story has raised some concerns, you will report directly to me for the duration," the abbot concluded. "I expect you to summarize what you have learned every evening, Brother Derring, at the evening meal."

Brother Sedimont raised his eyebrows at this, but I simply nodded my head.

"Is he to eat at the high table then? Declare everything he learns openly before the rest of our brothers? In open conversation, Abbot?" the brother protector protested.

"No. Good point. Hmmm. That will not be best, no." He looked around the table. "It is best done in private, no? After the evening meal then, Makun. You will report to my office and we will discuss what you have learned."

I nodded my head.

"And that other matter?" Brother Ansilin prompted.

"Is best discussed amongst ourselves," the brother chanter quickly said, cutting off any other reply.

A scattering of "Agreed" made its way around the table, then the abbot turned back to us. "Brother Derring, Vortiid, thank you for coming. You are excused."

"Yes, Abbot Dreise," I replied, bowing my head before I got to my feet.

But Vortiid simply looked around at the council, his blank face not giving anything away. Then he rose, scanned their eyes once more before turning his back, and simply walked away. I heard a snort from the brother chanter but did not turn my head to look. And I followed after Vortiid into the speckled-stone hallway, and away from the council, finding myself hurrying to catch up to Vortiid's conspicuously long stride.

I looked questioningly his way but he did not slow down, not until we approached the Hall of Healing.

"Makun," Vortiid said quietly.

"Yes?"

"No speak abbot Vortiid no say all."

"No. I no speak. … Dammit. Now you have me doing it again." I glared at him as I griped, then took a calming breath. "No, I didn't say anything."

Vortiid grunted and then asked, "Why?"

"You asked." I shrugged, not really thinking anything more about it beyond acknowledging my discomfort.

Vortiid looked my way and then stopped, glancing towards the door to the Hall of Healing before he turned deliberately my way. "Vortiid thank," was all he said.

Then he gripped my arm, raising it until we held each other's forearms in our left hands. Then he very deliberately nodded his head towards me, stroking his left cheek with his right thumb as he did so. Then he stroked mine in the same manner.

"Vortiid remember."

Then he let go, entering the Hall of Healing without another word, to relieve the one who was watching Ghaan.

Capitula 11

Two days passed, and my life narrowed down to concern itself only with the Lehntarnese.

Following the abbot's directives, I recorded all I could about their comings to this land, along with their initial meeting with the elves. I learned much – and I remember my hand cramping being forced to write so much and so quickly – but it was a frustrating time as well, as I knew that Vortiid and his countrymen were holding out on me. Because no matter what questions I asked, or how I worded things, there was a sudden problem in understanding whenever certain subjects came up.

I learned all I would ever want to know regarding how the elves lived, and how the people of Lehntarn were quartered. Their language we touched on a little, as well as interesting tidbits of elvish culture not contained in the books we had. But of the elven mages and magic the abbot asked about so much, I was unable to transcribe a single word. Despite the badgering the abbot hinted that he was receiving from the other members of the council, on this subject, the Lehntarnese would not budge.

Yet despite my frustrations it was also a time of joy, as Jan made sure to stop by and keep me company quite frequently, letting her interest show. I endured quite a bit of ribbing from the Lehntarnese over this, Vortiid especially finding my tongue-tied rejoinders to Jan's sometimes open flirtations hilarious, but I took it in good stead. And Jan seemed to enjoy how the men tortured me, joining forces with Xer Jarmen of all people, to ensure some commentary was made to embarrass me whenever she dropped by.

Jan and the men of Lehntarn had moved to take the boy even further under their wing as well. The name Eldso ended up being frequently heard, and though I had only had him run infrequent errands for me before, he quickly became a fixture inside the Lehntarnese camp. The people of Lehntarn seemed to be working up towards almost adopting him, and the boy happily ran errands for their group while finding pleasure in doing whatever they asked. And Jan seemed to take a particular liking to the boy as well, disturbingly so, mothering him periodically, and then looking up at me with an unusual smile I couldn't quite place.

Admittedly, her looks worried me, and my friend Chaltic took a great liking to teasing me about it whenever he caught sight of her face. But despite the growing signs of Jan's interest, I concentrated on my duty to pursue the abbot's orders in recording the Lehntarn's escape. And they didn't seem to mind Jan's presence while we spoke, simply nodding her way whenever she sat down beside me when her chores were done.

Obviously, I kept my concentration on my questions and writing despite her alluring presence. Definitely not upon the way her blouse sat, or how close she was. Yet the men of Lehntarn still smiled and noticed, though they seemed to take pity on me and chose not to tease me so much when she was right there. Though they still did so quite frequently, no matter what I wished.

"They really lived with the elves?" Jan asked, propping her arms on my desk to lean over my writing.

I valiantly did my best not to look down her blouse while she leaned. "Yes. For a little over a year. We worked out the number."

Vortiid, the bastard, grinned merrily. Then he chucked his chin towards Jan. "Makun woman ask. Speak Makun," he prompted.

"She is not my woman," I protested, fighting against blushing furiously at his continued teasing and pressure.

But Jan had a teasing grin upon her face as well, the twinkle in her eye telling me she was enjoying the situation wholeheartedly. "I agree, tell me more about their story, Makun."

I turned my head to meet her eyes, and by the Pantheon I swear she leaned even further. I was turning furiously red by now, desperately trying not to look to the way her blouse openly hung. I think I cleared my throat, utterly unable to form words while Jan and the other men chuckled.

"Scoot over," she said, bumping me with her hip so she could share the camp stool I was sitting on.

Now I was certainly unable to form a coherent thought, feeling her radiant warmth coming through my robes from beside. And after pining for her for so long, I cursed myself an idiot for being completely unable to say a single word. But Jan simply bestowed upon me a quirky smile, brushing a lock of her hair behind one ear before turning away towards my writing.

"This is their story?" she asked, lifting the corner of one page to flip back and forth through my work.

"Yes. What little of it we've covered." I could smell her, a floral scent that seemed to pervade the air around me like a cloud that exuded the heavens' grace.

"And this here?" She pointed to a sketch I had made a few pages back, something Vortiid and I had worked out in the dirt before I committed it to ink.

"I think it's one of their cities, from what he's describing. They appeared close to this place when they came to our land. The elves called it Siri'ni Kii'ay'va, Vortiid tells me. It is a grand place, the likes of which no one has ever seen since the times before the Fall. If he isn't pulling my leg with what he's telling me, that is."

"Is this its name here?" Jan pointed off to the side of my sketch, towards one of the longest words on the page.

"No, here. By this little village here." I threw her a curious look, watching as she leaned closer to the page while she ran her finger slowly along the letters. I could see her silently mouthing the word as her finger moved. It was something we taught children to do to help them learn. "You can't read?"

"No. Not well." She flicked me a quick glance. "Not many of us can."

"Us?"

"The people in the village." She seemed uncomfortable admitting that to me.

"It's relatively easy." I didn't understand. I'd been reading and writing every day since I was little up in the tower.

"I doubt that." She frowned. "Only the monks have the learning."

"Noooo. Brother Margonest and the other brother teachers instruct everyone," I corrected.

"Only on what they need to, Makun." She pushed another lock of her hair behind one ear. "How many of us need to know how to read?"

I frowned. "Well, that's not right. Everyone needs to know how to read."

"To do the laundry?"

"Well, no." I frowned more. "Here. Look here." I took out a blank piece of parchment, quickly writing down the alphabet. "You know the alphabet, correct?"

"I'm not stupid," Jan protested, frowning my way.

"I'm not saying you are. Look here. This is your name." I spelled out her first and last name, sounding out each letter as I wrote them, one at a time. Then I wrote out my own name, doing the same with each letter as they appeared on the page. "These are our two names."

Jan frowned at me. Then looked down towards my writing before looking back to my eyes. "Why are you showing me this?"

"Well, everyone should know how to read and write."

"Everyone, huh?"

I looked at her in confusion. "Yes?"

"Makun, the only people who need to know how to read and write are people like you."

"People like me?"

"Monks. You monks and your tower."

I was confused. "We all live here together."

"Some more than others." She turned back towards my writing.

"I don't understand. We all do what we can under the Pantheon."

Jan sighed. "Yes. Yes, Makun, we do." Then she deliberately changed the subject. "This is my name?"

I was still giving her a curious look, but she ignored it, staring at me until I responded. "Yes. Do you want to try?"

She nodded and clumsily took up the quill, allowing me to guide her in taking up ink without sloppily making marks across the page. The tension of the previous moment slowly eased as I guided her into making her letters, slowly teaching her to write her name. We spoke while I did so. Jan admitting that most villagers only learned their letters as children, readily forgetting them when they weren't chosen to become a monk of the tower.

This astounded me as I had assumed that the villagers read and wrote as much as I did, which was every day, as a matter of fact. And facing the fact that there wasn't even a single book in the village, that we monks did not bring with us, was a jarring one. Chosen at such an early age to be an aspirant, I'd never really lived a life outside of the tower, and had always been quartered inside. And our conversation that afternoon taught me many things about everyday life, that disagreed with what I had assumed.

We had moved on from our moment, having totally forgotten the reason for me being there as I taught her more things. And I was even more attracted to her as the time went by while she sat there beside me, her hip pressed firmly against my own, as she very endearingly poked the tip of her tongue out between her lips when she concentrated. I looked away from the page as I studied her, enthralled at the way the sun played across her hair while she haltingly wrote.

"I think I got it," she said after finishing what she had been doing.

"What have we got here?" I glanced down at the page, then spotted an error. "No." I chuckled. "That's not your name. You've combined yours and mine."

"Hmmm?"

"You wrote Jan Derring," I pointed out. "Derring is my last name."

"I know." Then she suddenly quirked a smile my way.

Vortiid, who I had forgotten was sitting right there, and had been for hours, let out a mighty laugh as I turned brilliant red.

Jan looked quite pleased with herself, then acquired that sheet of parchment. "I believe I will be keeping this, Brother Makun Derring. Thank you very much for your teaching."

I struggled to speak as that paper was folded up, then neatly tucked into her blouse while Vortiid laughingly told his countrymen what was going on in his own tongue. Jan seemed to take great delight in my embarrassment as she continued to hold my eyes.

I knew then and there she would be receptive to my asking, and I wondered what the abbot would say when we met next. I was sure the question's reception would be positive, the abbot had already hinted so, I just had to get up enough courage to ask.

I grinned, happily knowing I could pursue my affections, but anything I had been about to say was suddenly cut off.

"Vortiid!" One of the Lehntarnese men sprinted into the courtyard. "Vortiid!" the man repeated. Then on seeing him, he went on to hurriedly speak in their tongue.

Vortiid listened to whatever was said and then cursed. There was no doubt about that, even though I didn't understand a thing that was said. He then leapt to his feet, calling for his countrymen as the third of them that were on duty ran out on guard towards the yard. They took up station around the compound, hands everywhere upon weapons as I looked, and there was a flurry of activity, because almost as one, the men of Lehntarn were suddenly armed and armored before me. Then Vortiid turned to me, suddenly glaring at me, and seeming utterly furious.

"Makun go Ghaan! Vortiid go Ghaan. Go Ghaan now!"

"Um, sure," I babbled as Vortiid grabbed me, setting me on my feet as he caught an armored shirt someone had thrown his way in one of his hands.

"What's going on?" Jan exclaimed.

"I don't know."

"Makun woman go! Makun go Ghaan now!" Vortiid replied, strapping on his sword and his many knives, then he immediately dragged me off through the village.

The man who had come to warn Vortiid sprinted off ahead, and I watched as he ran without slowing up the steep switch-backed trail and in through the outer gates. Then a party of Lehntarnese men joined me and Vortiid, eight of them in all, every one of them armed and armored with flat faces and piercing eyes, seemingly ready to face whatever fate might encounter them. They hurried me up the hill, the pace of the group increasing after the eight joined the two of us, and admittedly I struggled to keep up.

The brother protector who was my escort that day hurried along behind, awoken from his nap by the commotion and obviously as confused as I was. But the Lehntarnese didn't slow down to answer his many objections even once. Not even seeming to pay a single bit of attention to him as they advanced upon the outer gate.

The inner courtyard was in a flurry, a commotion ensuing as the Lehntarnese man who had sprinted ahead of us could be heard loudly protesting to someone in his own tongue. Then we advanced as a group to where he stood, our party's simple mass bodily blocking Brother Sedimont from exiting the edificium's gate and proceeding into the courtyard. The brother protector was scowling mightily, then I understood what was going on as one brother protector after another arrived to join their leader in blocking the Lehntarnese men from advancing any further into the Spire.

"Brother Sedimont!" I called, becoming nervous after seeing Lehntarnese hands drifting slowly towards weapons. "Brother Sedimont! What is happening?"

"These people are hiding a mage!"

Gasps came from all around. "A mage?" I protested. "There hasn't been a mage found near the tower in generations!"

"There is one now!" Brother Sedimont declared.

"Ghaan now!" Vortiid demanded, advancing until his party stood threateningly beside their lone countryman. They loomed over Brother Sedimont.

"Get out of my way!" Sedimont thundered.

"Ghaan! Now!"

"You can see your damned man after the brother protectors have done their duty!" Brother Sedimont returned, sneering the Lehntarnese way. "No one shall treat with a mage! It is the will of the gods!"

Shouts of "Make way! Make way!" were heard coming from inside the edificium. Then advancing, surrounded by another group of my stern-faced brethren, the brother protectors escorted out the suspected mage in chains.

"You can thank us later," Brother Sedimont testily explained, there being nothing in his voice that was friendly at all. "This mage was doing something to your almighty Ghaan! You are lucky we kept an escort on him, otherwise your man would be damned. Just like this one! So much for your objections now." Brother Sedimont sneered.

Then I got my first look at a hated mage. The first one discovered in generations. And at first, I thought the mage was abnormally short. Then I realized he only stood a little taller than my waist. Then the mage turned towards me, tears streaming down his face as he cried out my name.

"Makun! Makun! Save me!"

And all the while, that mage, the boy, Eldso … his eyes glowed blue.

✳✳✳

I will never forget the boy, nor the looks he gave us as he was quickly put to test …

Dragged in chains to the village square, the boy was kept under close watch while Brother Sedimont and the brother protectors guarded him. Decrying his apostacy, the legitimacy of which could not be denied, Eldso's fate was quickly determined. And despite the wailings of his mother, and the protestations for mercy those few who had the temerity to speak out made, his fate was quickly sealed.

The destiny of all mages had long been determined; their sentence passed down through generation after generation ever since our beloved gods' fall. A fate designed to ensure that nothing they were or did could ever escape. Knowledge that had been passed down to every single last one of us, the survivors, since the time of the apocalypse they caused. There was only one thing for a mage, despite his age:

Death and cleansing … by fire.

The pyre was quickly built while Eldso wailed in his chains. And I was stunned, utterly moved to speechlessness, as me and my brothers looked on. The entire council of seven turned out, wearing their official robes and adorned by stern faces. Even the kind and forgiving Brother Camdal looked pitilessly down upon the boy, never once lifting up his voice to challenge his fate. And as the boy's mother was dragged back by the arms of our brother protectors, Eldso was led to the pyre in chains and secured to the stake affixed in its center.

Then proclaiming his fate in a loud voice, Abbot Dreise looked out across the assembled masses, not a single villager or monk of the tower anywhere else but here to view the damnation of a mage. The boy continuously wailed, his voice hoarse, his eyes glowing blue as if some kind of water or demonic liquid seemed to seep from his skin in an attempt to escape his punishment before the gods.

Then his mother screamed as the torch was brought out.

Passing it to the brother protector himself, my brethren stepped away as the council of seven moved up to the fore. Then the abbot cried out once again, "Is there any reason this mage should avoid his fate?" His harsh voice seemed to echo throughout the village, crushing underneath its weight any thought that one might have to plead for the boy's mercy.

"My boy!" his mother wailed. "My Eldso! No!"

I felt a hand creep into mine, Jan staring desperately for me while the tears poured from her eyes. The silence that fell over everyone besides Eldso's mother was astounding.

"Then let its punishment be so," Abbot Dreise declared. He nodded to the brother chanter.

"As it was written in The Book of the Fall, so shall it be," Brother Barkon intoned.

The brother chanter's voice came forth, heard easily by one and all. Beginning the chant, The Chant of Death, the chant every one of us had been taught, he began in a minor chord. And every single person there listened as we proclaimed our duty, one out of the history books that we had never expected to use.

"*A mage has been found,*" Brother Barkon's voice rang out.

"A mage is found," we brothers replied.

"*A mage's fate has been sealed.*"

"A mage's fate is sealed."

He continued the chant, his lonely voice sounding its sorrow for our lost gods, and their unknown fate, as we echoed a haunting reply.

To protect us all,
Their deaths must come.
To prevent another apocalypse
Under the eyes of the Pantheon's grace.
We still remember,
We who dwell,
Here, in this lost place.
To protect what we knew before,
What is now,
And whatever may come to be.
We put this mage to fire,
To purge its soul,
To make this body clean.
To pay for the treacheries of the Fall,
And for our forefather's many mistakes.
So that the gods may come again,
And grace those who still remain
We pray with all our hearts.
So mote it be.
We, who still remain.

And as my robe progressed from damp to soaked while Jan cried heavily upon my shoulder, Brother Sedimont sternly advanced with his torch. Putting the flame to the pyre, the kindling took to light. Then the wood caught and crackled, its snapping and popping strangely loud as the brother chanters lifted their voices in ecstatic praise to the Pantheon.

Their song was a hauntingly strange counterpoint to the near-silent weeping of Jan, and clashed entirely with the wailing of the boy's mother.

And Eldso? Eldso fixed his shining blue eyes on me. Tears poured forth from his eyes as he loudly cried out for me to save him. His young voice wailing "Makun" and then "Vortiid", then he rattled off the names of the other men from Lehntarn he knew. Then he cried "Jan" in a high, terror-filled voice that shattered the square, Jan shuddering against my chest as she sobbed when he did so.

But she did not reply. For she knew, as well as I did, that an unclean mage could only bring damnation upon us all.

And as the fire flared up even more, and the boy's flesh caught to light, his wailing voice screeched out for his mother. Copious blue fluids poured forth from his skin, hissing and steaming as they fought against the purifying flames of the fire.

But over time, the flames won out.

"Mama!" he cried, his skin crisping as his clothes caught fire. Then as if in proof of his insidious shame, his entire form went up with a loud *whoosh*. A pillar of bright yellow flame rose up, with only his two glowing blue eyes hauntingly peering forth.

His mother broke free, throwing herself towards her boy before the brother protectors caught her once again. And with a final terrified cry of "Mama!" Eldso fell quiet, the glaring blue of his eyes amidst that pillar of flame suddenly going out. Then that horrible silence fell again, only broken by the crackling and popping that could be heard amidst the chanters singing their praise to the Pantheon.

I will never forget the smell of his burning flesh, nor how it came like roasted meat to my nose. Nor will I forget how long I stood there, staying to bear witness until there was nothing left of the boy except ash. How Jan stayed with me, along with most of the others, staring in shock at how quickly it was discovered and ended, that damnable mage.

A mage that I knew. That I had interacted with. Laughed and played with. That Jan, who still wept into my chest, had held and smiled to as if the boy was her own.

Eldso,
I will never forget you.

May the Pantheon have mercy on your soul.

And as night fell while I sat upon the ground before that lonely pyre, cradling an exhausted, sleeping Jan to my chest, I looked upon the glowing chains that had once confined his body. Chains that looked strange and demonic in the diminishing light. Chains that seemed to encompass all that we had done that day, to the shame of our souls.

It made me feel numb, watching that and them there. And those ancient restraints rested uncaringly upon the ashes of Eldso's remains, ash that was indistinguishable from what was left of the wood. Ash that, looking upon it, looked the same no matter what it once was. The ash we would all eventually become, lying upon the coals of our damnation. Driven uncaringly on by our faith.

The entire episode made me think.

But I was not alone in my viewing. For bearing witness alongside us all were the Lehntarnese. Standing amongst themselves, they had not once made a noise, not since ensuring Ghaan's safety. Stoic and silent, every face blank and yet grim, they looked on. Then when the flames were finished, and all that remained of Eldso and the pyre were glowing embers shining dully beneath the chains, Vortiid cried out.

That lone word he cried seemed to convey some extreme anguish, some hurt that none of us could ever share. And upon hearing his cry, every last one of his countrymen bowed their heads. Then they solemnly thumbed their cheeks with one hand, before they quietly returned to their new home. The home we had given them. Their stated last chance to find safety and peace from where they had come.

Every last one of them was armed and armored as they made their way to their new home. And every last one of them seemed to look upon the monks, the village, and everything else around them with new eyes, and in deep thought. And not a single one of them seemed to find peace with what they saw.

That stood out to me, their leaving. That, and the way Vortiid met my eyes from the other side of the square. Looking over the haunting remains of the Pyre, almost looking directly through the links of one of those glowing chains as he did so, he watched me.

He stopped as his gaze held onto mine. His blank, stoic eyes peering into my own. They told me something, something frightening and new.

That for the first time, he truly saw me.

We paused as Eldso's mother was escorted back to the tower by the brother protectors in chains. The mother of a mage, soon to be put to question herself.

He watched them.

Then we met eyes again after that group had passed. Something told me what Vortiid saw did not comfort him. He did not see it as just. It did not leave him feeling relieved.

And staring through the links of that red hot chain … that had only recently bound that boy-mage … I discovered a new feeling, some new emotion.

That I was suddenly filled with shame.

Capitula 12

The following day was somber.

"Makun," Chaltic whispered. "Are you okay?"

"Hmmm? Yes. Fine."

Chaltic glanced at me, but whatever he was going to say was interrupted as the chanters paused in their hosanna, and time came for us to sit down in our pews.

It was the morning after Eldso's burning … *His ending* … and we raised our voices in acclamation to the elimination of another evil, hated mage. The problem for me was, for the first time in my life, I found myself unsure. And unsure of what exactly? … I was unsure of that also. Unsure, here, in the center of my faith.

What a feeling.

"The Pantheon shall save."

I repeated the affirmation along with my brothers, staring up at the alter without really seeing it. Then as a whole we bowed our heads to that lone candle – the one that represented all of the gods who'd walked among us before they had been so heinously betrayed … by a mage – then the brother chanter stepped up to the gilded podium on the dais.

"Today I chant from The Book of the Fall, chapter forty-two, verse twelve," Brother Barkon said. He looked out over the congregation, allowing a silence to fall. Then stepping away from the podium, an unusual circumstance in itself, he moved directly in front of the alter to face every one of us before he spoke.

"And the gods said: We love you all."

He paused, nodding as if he heard someone stating a point he had agreed with. Then he looked towards that lone candle, then towards the abbot, before he once again looked out over us all.

"The Pantheon shall save."

"The Pantheon shall save."

Brother Barkon stepped down from the dais, walking the central aisle as he moved among us and met our eyes, one by one. He took his time, taking our measure while we waited for his eulogy, leaning upon the podium as was his wont. But instead of returning to the dais, which was his norm, he spoke from among us, and I was barely able to see him as he continued to move.

"Love. They love us all. The writers of our sacred text certainly taught us so. Line after verse singing their praises. They love us all," he dwindled off, turning about to continue to meet everyone's eyes.

"But who do they love? Everyone? Do they love the murderer? The adulterer? The rapist?" he questioned, seemingly genuinely interested in our response. "Do they love everyone equally? The bad? The good? The father who beats his child? His wife? The mother who curses a man's line?"

He continued to look around, then he asked: "Do they love the mage?"

Brother Barkon paused, then he pointed back towards that lone candle. "There they are, watching us as we give praise. Their memory, at least. What we remember of them. After the mages killed them …" He shook his head, paused, then repeated, *"We love you all."*

He turned his back on us, looking back up towards the alter and that lone candle there. Then he ascended the steps, walked up to the stand's side, and plucked the candle out of its holder. A few of the monks gasped, but he looked over his shoulder to observe us, completely nonchalant about what he had done.

"It is only a candle, after all," he explained. "Brother Randilon leads the people who make them." He waved to indicate the lay brother. "You all know our brothers who winnow down the fat of those animals we harvested for the candles' production. How it stinks while they make them. Taking a creature's raw substance, then discarding the impurities they find that are mixed in, until we are left with something clean that can produce light."

He twisted the candle around in his fist, peering at it this way and that, as if a candle was something he had never before seen. "We even make them out of the substance of monsters. Those altered beasts who haunt us still, from that evil time before. … The time before the Fall."

Then his head snapped up towards us. "Does it make this evil? The candle, here? Do we reject their offerings? Do we refuse to take advantage of the products they provide us after we kill them?"

He shook his head. "No. No we do not. We battle them, seek them out when we can if they return to their lairs, for they have become truly evil. But then we take advantage of and utilize what is offered to us. But do the gods love them as well? They made those beasts, you know. Or at least allowed their creation, wherever they are. Whatever those creatures originally were, we no longer know, but they did bring those vile creatures into being. The gods must have loved them once. So should we curse them for what they've become?"

He slowly looked out over the congregation. "No. The book says their change was brought about by war. But should we welcome them into our arms without just certification? Without judgement for what they can do? What they are? Without any due caution? Or assurances? … Should we love them?"

He placed the candle back into its holder. "The answer to that is no, as well."

He lowered his head towards that lone candle, before doing the same to the alter, then towards the illegible lettering around the circle carved into the stone wall behind it as well. Then he turned back to us, studying the assembled congregation for a moment before he spoke once again.

"We kill them, wherever and whenever they find us, because they will slay us if we do not. We must fight for what we have, to keep what is ours, so that we can survive. To make safe our home – our lair, if you will – from any invasion by the enemy that seeks to take from us what is ours." He waved his hand to encompass the hall.

"For like the monster, an altered beast – or *alter-beast*, as the villagers name them – we also fight to survive. And as the pinnacle of our gods' creation, we must base our decisions upon what we hold to be righteous and true. That despite our many challenges and the world's uncertainty, and the trials and tribulations we face, we *will* someday make our world safe … which will bring about the return of the gods. But to do that, there are hard choices we must make. Choices that may haunt us, that we make for the survival of us all."

He nodded his head towards the abbot, before he returned to looking out over us. "*We love you all*, they said. *We love you all*. They did not say that their love holds everything inviolate. That everything in creation should be treated without harm. That we should hold everyone and everything beyond reproach. It simply says: *We love you all*. But it does not say 'who' is that 'you'. Who *exactly* that unknowable group is, that the gods love.

"So, who is it they love?"

He paused to glance over us once more.

"I do not know," he finally admitted.

But then Brother Barkon shook his head. "I can tell my brethren this much, though: The Book of the Fall did not come to us through the words of a monster. Nor did it come to us from the wilds, some unknown group, or from some place out of legend that is very far away. That book came to us from our forefathers, the ones who had survived the war, and the remembrances it holds sum up our knowledge of that evil time. So that those of us who came after its writing could make our judgements quickly, using established wisdom. Not having to waste time repeating the past's due diligence, to do what is right in the name of the gods."

He walked over towards the gilded podium on one side of the alter, then lifted up The Book of the Fall to show us before he slammed the book back down. The boom echoed its way throughout the Hall of the Pantheon, the reverberations returning time and time again while Brother Barkon looked out over us all.

"Brother Ansilin? How many times has the story of our order's survival been recopied?"

"Dozens, Brother Barkon."

"And does that diminish its worth?"

"No, Brother."

"No," Brother Barkon continued, "as the brother recorder says. Despite the many years that have passed since our many gods' fall, it does not diminish this book's worth. Nor does it diminish its words, the knowledge it passes on, or the love our gods have." He looked out over us once more, then paused. Slowly caressing the book with one hand as he studied it, a pregnant silence fell before he looked back up at us once again. "Nor does following the wisdom it holds diminish the worth we all have."

He waved a hand in the direction of the edificium. "Through those impenetrable gates of our blessed and hallowed tower, we witnessed and partook of a foul episode that was forced upon us. The discovery and burning of a mage. A boy." Brother Barkon seemed to look directly into my eyes. "One that some of us knew and had grown quite close to."

Then he glanced away.

"An innocent, some would say. Without guilt or reason for the punishment prescribed in our holiest of texts, that all mages must face. That the boy had no bearing at all on what had occurred during the Fall, or the struggles of our order's past. That the boy should have been guided by us, taught by us, taken into our bosom, because the gods professed by their own words that: *they love us all.*"

The brother chanter began to pace across the dais, waving his hand once more towards Brother Randilon who was sitting with the rest of the council. "But like the chandlers I mentioned, we must also winnow the dross from the fat that initially makes up all that we and our community are. Because do we take the *alter-beast* to our bosom? Allow a monster to eat from our table? To suckle and grow fat from our breast?" His countenance became like a caged beast while he paced.

"No. No, we do not. We kill the predator so that the predator does not kill us. And as such, we live on, able to ensure the safety of all those we love. So that the gods may grace us with their presence once more, when our work is finally done."

Then Brother Barkon stopped directly in front of the alter, and placed his hands into the opposite sleeves of his robe. "But some may ask: If they are gods, where did they go? Why have they not answered our prayers? Why haven't they come? We give them honor and praise. We kill the mage. They are our gods. They hear our prayers, notice our many sacrifices … Do they not?"

There were even more gasps from the congregation this time. His words were as close to heretical as one could get, without being blatant. Most of us were stunned by what we had just heard.

Then he nodded his head once more. "They are our gods. And they *are* gods, most assuredly. And they do hear them. But what prevents them? What stops them from coming? What spoils their return? And, damn it all, to what dark place did they go?"

He waved his hand towards the book once more. "The Book of the Fall, chapter ninety-one, verse one hundred ninety-nine: *And the gods said: We shall return.*"

He allowed the silence to stretch once more.

"Powerful words, those words are. They make a promise, but they do not say when. They love us, they will come again, but they do not tell us exactly when. We fight, we protect, we strive, we survive … we chant to remember, give honor to their name … but what should we do until then? Sit on our hands? Accept whatever may come? Simply live our lives however we wish?

"No, brothers. It is our job – no, our duty – to prepare for their return. Because the book gives us a clue, and I once again bring your attention to the words it says.

"The Book of the Fall, chapter eighty-nine, verses thirty-two and thirty-three …

"*For taking upon himself the grace that was due in honor of the gods, the deceiver cast what he had gained down upon those present, bringing vile devastation upon the holy temple, and beginning that which followed: The War of the Fall.*"

Brother Barkon raised his hands above his head, tilting his head back as if in ecstasy as he continued his sermon. "We must prepare, brothers. We must pray, we must praise, we must take these holy words to heart. For it is our duty to ready the world for our gods' return. And we must make decisions that are sometimes not to our personal liking. Such as to seek out and kill the altered beasts that haunt us, and seek to inhabit the safety of our lair. To protect that which is ours. To spread the words and teachings of the gods, so that those we encounter can remember who they were, and prepare themselves for the glory of their return. For like the chandler, we must winnow the fat from the dross we find, so that we can make something grand of ourselves and bring forth the light to our eyes."

He paused to lower his hands, and then met some of our gazes. "And the mages are one such example of the dross we must cleanse," his voice rang out, carrying easily to one and all. "For they are the most dangerous. They betrayed our gods' trust. Taking it upon themselves to lift themselves up, the mages began to see themselves as our gods' equal. Then they stole the grace they were due, and tried to do away with the gods to hide their depravity. The arrogance of their deeds, along with the shockwaves of that horrible betrayal, foretold of the coming apocalypse. And that vile episode began the war that ended everything we once knew. The war we now name: The War of the Fall. The one our forefathers fought and survived their way through."

He seemed to meet my eyes once again. "The safety of one and all cannot be ensured while a monster inhabits our lair. The candle cannot give off its glorious light while it must burn its way through the dross left within it. And the world the gods have gifted to us cannot recover while a mage remains alive after The War of the Fall."

There was an uncomfortable silence that followed. "We cannot trust them, brothers. Their treachery is written … and the gods surely listen and watch what we do."

He stabbed his hand towards that lone candle. "Because one day, the gods will come again. In all their glory, in all their wisdom, the gods we sing our high hosannahs to, they will most certainly come. And on that day, they will give us their thanks, and reward us for what we have done here. For our trials, and our many tribulations. For the years and years of harsh survival the members of our order have been forced to endure. For all of that, they will welcome us into their bosoms, and return us, the pious, to grace. And then they will live with us like they had done once before, because of our unwavering faith over these many long years and generations.

"For every one of those hard decisions we made, and yes, even the killing of a boy-mage, the gods will thank us. Because there is one thing that all of us must remember, and we must remember this one thing before all others, as we clear the dross from the fat to bring about our spiritual purity."

He paused again to meet all of our eyes.

"We must remember what the gods have decreed, as it is written. A message passed down from those who came before, to those who still remain. To those that heed their words, and do not sink knowingly or unknowingly into betrayal. To everyone that still remembers, who chooses to remain pious, and seeks to be pure …"

He waved his hand back towards that lone candle.

"We love you all. Those are the words that they said to us. To those of us who live by the hard decisions. To those who remain pure. To those of us who fight for the gods return. For their grace … *We love you all."*

Then the brother chanter bowed his head in solemn reflection, before lifting and planting his lips upon the medallion of our order. That symbol we all wore. The one hanging upon all of our chests.

His words were soft, but they carried easily in the hall's silence. They carried to one and all. "The Pantheon shall save," he said to us.

And then just as solemnly the congregation replied, *"The Pantheon shall save."*

Our words echoed and mingled together around the hall, striking and combining against each other in a heady experience. Ricocheting off of the walls and the many busts of our lost gods until the silence eventually returned, it affected us all.

I watched as many heads became lowered among my brethren. How fingers were clenched upon many medallions, and how glistening tears were shed in their eyes. How Brother Barkon's words had affected us, how they had washed over us all. And I found myself drawn out of my previous state, my somber mood somewhat lifted by what I had heard.

Unfortunately, I then began thinking.

And while my brethren seemed to be uplifted by what Brother Barkon had said, I experienced a different vision. One that saw Eldso in flames, chained upon that lonely pyre, while his mother was still screaming against it all.

I glanced down upon the symbol of my order, its silvery sheen gleaming there upon my chest, and I wondered to myself. Then a terrible and heretical thought came into existence that insidiously spread its way across my mind. One that I kept to myself, only allowing the shadow of it to escape my heart as I listened in silence to my brothers who were currently lifting their voices in ecstatic prayer.

I remembered that innocent seeming boy, whose smile had brought warmth to my heart over the short period of time I had known him. Who had done nothing wrong, not as far as I knew, beyond being born a mage. Who Jan had laughed with and held in her arms and lap, and with whom even the Lehntarnese had played.

Who had called for me to save him, then called out for Vortiid, and both of us had done nothing. Then he had cried out for his mother, the only one who had run to him, but even she had been held back… by my brethren, the brother protectors. And after he had been reduced to ash, the look Vortiid gave me … That, and the dampness of Jan's tears upon my chest.

I was uncomfortable with what had been done.

What I had done …

And what I had not done.

Uttering those thoughts surely would have brought me before the abbot for question.

And I pondered that in silence, listening to the high hosannahs of my brothers as they prayed.

And I found I had to ask myself …

What if I was the monster?

… And I had no answer.
And that horrible thought followed me for the rest of the day.

Capitula 13

"Ghaan go," Vortiid insisted, staring at the brother healer.

I had been hurried to the Hall of Healing, being told there was some disturbance the Lehntarnese were the center of. Vortiid was facing off against two of the brother protectors, who stood between him and one of our chirurgeons. Vortiid was completely red in the face, him and the other men of Lehntarn that were with him appearing absolutely unwilling to take no for an answer.

"Vortiid? What is going on?" I asked, angling to insert myself as a wall in between the two parties, and whatever was currently taking place. I relaxed a bit as both Vortiid and the brother protectors turned their way towards me, ending their tense face off. Unfortunately, this meant that I was now underneath both of their frustrated gazes. But as the Pantheon willed it, I was there and determined to make peace.

"This … man … wants to remove one of my barely stable patients from under my care!" the chirurgeon complained, obviously against this mode of action.

"Ghaan awake. Ghaan come, go village. Now."

"He can barely walk!"

"Carry!"

"You'll kill him! I refuse to let you take anyone, only for them to die!"

"Ghaan Lehntarn, no monk! Ghaan go!"

"It matters not, you ignorant barbarian! Brother protectors!" the chirurgeon commanded. The brother protectors took up their hammers, obviously preparing to use force.

"There will be no bloodshed in The Hall!" a new voice thundered, Brother Camdal hobbling to the fore. The aged brother healer walked unsteadily their way, hurrying, his sheer presence bringing everyone's angst and animosity down. "Explain to me why you would take up arms inside the Hall of Healing! Now!"

"This man wants to remove my patient!" The chirurgeon glared.

"Is this patient their countryman?"

"Yes," the chirurgeon replied, obviously wondering by his tone why that fact would possibly matter to the brother healer in the least.

"Is the patient going to immediately die?"

"No," the chirurgeon hedged. "He awoke some time ago, asking for water. He's taken that and fallen back to sleep, though he seems weak. We've made him comfortable."

Brother Camdal nodded, turning to Vortiid. "Makun here tells us you can understand us more than you speak. Do you understand his condition?" He waved his hand towards Ghaan, lying there under his blankets through the door.

"Yes." Vortiid was obviously fighting his aggression, him and those with him barely keeping their hands off their weapons.

"And you realize we cannot continue to heal him to the level we have, if you keep him down in the village?"

Vortiid glared, but it was Ghaan himself who answered. Well, he didn't actually answer the brother healer, he spoke to Vortiid in their own tongue. After a bit of back and forth, which ended with everyone from Lehntarn stroking their cheeks with their thumbs, Ghaan tiredly turned to the healers.

"I will return to my countrymen," he stated weakly, never once opening his eyes.

His coherent sentence amazed me, with only the accent making it strange to be heard.

"You require rest and more healing. I cannot possibly make the tonics you require down in that village, or the condition it's in," the chirurgeon replied. "Your recovery depends on my direct intervention!"

Vortiid and his men bristled, but Ghaan spoke up once more. His voice was very weak. "I will return to my countrymen."

Brother Camdal glanced between Ghaan and the chirurgeon, before looking at me. "Stubborn, aren't they?"

"They are, Brother Healer, but they take the safety of their own to be paramount. If you prevent this, you will start a conflict," I cautioned. "Their care of this man is assured."

"Then their man can go." And after silencing the protesting chirurgeon with a stern look, he continued, "We will need to provide them with instructions."

"I am ready to record, Brother Camdal." I reached for my case, the document bag hanging from my belt was something I kept with me at all times, anymore.

"That is not necessary, young Makun. Our brother chirurgeon will provide you with instructions, along with everything that is needed." The brother in question frowned, but held his silence after another look. "Can you even get up?" Brother Camdal asked Ghaan.

"No."

"Then you will need to be carried. You two," he addressed the brother protectors. "Fetch a stretcher and return with it." Then he turned to Vortiid and the other Lehntarnese. "I assume you will be carrying him?"

"Yes. Carry Ghaan village. Go. Now."

Ghaan said something to him in their tongue which caused Vortiid to frown, but he stood stalwart against any objections. He conversed back and forth with Ghaan as the brother protectors left to return with a stretcher, the brother healer's word being law within the Hall of Healing. I heard my name mentioned inside that conversation in their liquid tongue many times, then Ghaan turned his head to me, weakly assessing me for a moment before he spoke up.

"I have you to thank for speaking for my countrymen?"

"I spoke to them, not for them. I don't know if doing so deserves any thanks, but you are welcome if it does."

"Understanding and discourse between strange peoples is important," he continued weakly. "Ever since ... what do you call it?" He looked to Vortiid. "Ah yes, 'The Fall'."

"You are much better educated than your countrymen," Brother Camdal commented.

"Not better educated, better spoken," Ghaan replied. "There are many more knowledgeable than me," he wheezed out before a cough.

As the man was taken over by a series of weak coughing, the brother protectors returned with the stretcher. Lifting Ghaan up through utilizing the blankets found underneath him, he was quickly moved to the stretcher which was raised and carried by the rest of his people. Vortiid nodded his head towards me, a guarded nod of thanks if I'd ever seen one, but it was the most he'd given me since the night of Eldso's burning. But as they began walking away with their man, the chirurgeon began voicing his frustrations once again, and protesting the brother healer's decision.

Surprisingly, it was Ghaan who stopped them.

However, he did not address the chirurgeon. Reaching out to me with a single, weak hand, he stopped his countrymen's procession. Then simply stating "Come to me when you have their instructions."

Then he patted my arm with that single, limp hand.

Then he gave a weak command to his countrymen, rolling onto his side as I watched them carry him away to the village. I ignored the chirurgeon's continuous complaints.

***

"… I cannot answer that question, Abbot. I have not conversed with the man."

"But why would they insist on taking him?" he pressed me.

"I do not know." Though I was sure it had to do with the boy's burning. "They are very protective of their countrymen, and Ghaan in particular. I've reported this to you already and often."

"Yes, yes, but they've never insisted on taking any of their other people until they could walk on their own. Surely this is unusual."

"I agree, Abbot. It most certainly is. But their man Ghaan is held in high esteem by them all. Surely the other brothers would treat you differently than say myself, or my friend Chaltic, if the situation was reversed?"

"Of course. Though you do sell yourself short, Makun. But according to Brother Camdal, their man is half dead. Surely, they know we can provide better care for him here than down in the village."

I shrugged, not knowing what else to say. The brother healer had been quite insistent that Ghaan be allowed to leave, and the only reason I was here was because of the chirurgeon's ongoing complaints. I'm certain it would have never come to the abbot's immediate attention otherwise, and I still had to get the instructions for Ghaan's care down to the village.

"What is their motivation for taking him down there so suddenly?"

"Abbot?"

"Come now, surely you know."

I didn't immediately answer. "Abbot? What's happened to the boy's mother?"

He seemed thrown off by my question. "What's happened? She's being put to question by the brother protectors. Brother Sedimont is leading her purification according to stricture." Then he looked at me oddly. "What does the mage's mother have to do with this?"

"A look they gave me."

"Bah." The abbot waved my words away. "The burning of anyone is horrible, yes, but surely they cannot be upset over the destruction of a mage. Lead them in prayer if it still bothers them. Come, now. You've spent days with these people. What drives them? What keeps these people going?"

I was stunned. I didn't know what else to say. His dismissal threw me. "Peace mostly, Abbot Dreise. We've discussed my reports."

"Yes, yes, I know that. But what motivates them? What truly resonates with these people?"

I thought about it for a moment, still thinking about Eldso's mother being dragged off in chains. She was being put to question, tortured, here, in the tower. Right now, as a matter of fact.

I couldn't come up with anything right then and there beyond one thing. "Honesty, Abbot. If there was one thing I think they respect more than any other, it is honesty. Or maybe honor, they certainly revolve a lot of their actions around that."

"Honesty? Honor? Gods, where did these people come from?" Abbot Dreise muttered to himself. Then the abbot completely changed the subject. "Have you been down to the library yet?"

I was pulled from wondering where Eldso's mother was.

"Abbot? No. I've been with the people of Lehntarn learning what I can, and recording their story … as you instructed. Has there been some concern raised regarding the performance of my duties?"

The abbot waved my concerns away, not answering. "Come. Ansilin and I have found something."

Then the abbot rose, guiding me through the speckled stone walls of the tower and into the scriptorium. I hadn't been there in days, my fellow brother recorders looking up from their copying as the two of us walked by. But the abbot continued to the front of the room not noticing, nodding to the other historians as he came to the lone door. Fishing his golden amulet out from underneath his robe, he studied it for a moment as if he had been taken unawares by a sudden thought upon seeing it.

Then shaking whatever it was off, he placed his medallion's filigreed face into the mirror-like impression that had been carved into the door's surface. A subtle 'click' was heard, then a series of grinding and clanking sounds reverberated before a suddenly strange thud, then the door shifted itself open. The air equalized with the scriptorium in a sharp breath that gusted out into my face, then the abbot pushed the speckled door open, its surprisingly thick width moving easily upon a set of invisible hinges. Then the abbot continued quickly through, motioning for me to follow him as we descended and entered into the depths of the library.

I'd always imagined the library as a dark and ominous place, but I had been surprised by the light ever since I'd entered it for the first time many weeks ago. Descending a gently sloped set of stairs to enter into an open room, we found ourselves in a well-lit chamber branching off in many directions. With the same odd lettering that was found behind the alter marking each of those passages, each hall led to a particular place.

My knowledge of the library had grown when I became a brother recorder, and I knew that each of those branches led towards a particular subject, being delineated in a particular way. But even though that was the case, floor after room was found inside the library in an endless array of chambers. And a dizzying amount of knowledge had been protected here by the monks of our order, collected and stored ever since the time of the Fall.

I expected to turn in the direction of the healing arts, but the abbot turned in a most peculiar way, which was away from the main hallways we used which led to the various room's subjects. Instead, the abbot led me towards the center of the Spire, towards the vertical opening that bisected and travelled from head to heel through our mountain's heart.

Our footsteps echoed in the surprisingly well-lit hallways as we passed room after room filled with books. It always amazed me how the halls seemed to possess their own inner light, especially in the deeper places found inside the tower, and we knew from The Book of the Fall that it was only by the grace of the Pantheon that this was so. And their grace was kept ever upon us through our daily prayers, the ones we made in the Hall of the Pantheon, and the light they shared with us was a sign of their favor.

The brother recorders witnessed this daily, honored to be exposed to the Pantheon's good grace. But the abbot was set in his course and remained silent, not even glancing to either side at the sign of our god's favor. No. He strode quickly, almost purposely through, obviously lost to his own thoughts. Then shortly before the double doorway that exited the library, which travelled deeper into the mountain, he turned aside towards an unusually closed door.

Unlocking the door by inserting his medallion, I found myself in a small room where someone had obviously been studying. The desk I saw was littered with scrawled parchment and sat in one corner, while a couch and a chair rested along another two walls. A soft carpet was underfoot as well, well preserved though faded, and it was something that was as close to priceless as any of our books ever since the time of the Fall.

And by the look of it, this one might have been from the time of the Fall itself, or at least a copy of something made during that time. It's fine pattern and threads were something we could no longer produce on our own, and the intricacy of it astounded me. It felt like a shame to be walking on it but the abbot never stopped even once, striding busily over the grand thing to the desk to rearrange the mountain of books I saw there upon it.

"Here we are," he happily said, turning one of the manuscripts towards me. The tome was ancient, I could tell that by just glancing at it, but the abbot seemed unconcerned. "This is a book of Lehntarnese origin. At least, that is what Brother Ansilin has assured me."

"Is this his study?" I asked, honestly never having thought about where the brother recorder spent most of his day.

"Yes, we each have our own workplaces inside the tower," he said absentmindedly. "But that is not the point. Brother Ansilin and I have discussed that if you could gain our newcomers' assistance in translating this … book, it would give us more insights into their language which may help us determine our future goals. We have no idea what this book says. Ansilin can only identify maybe every tenth word."

"Their goal is to settle, Abbot …"

"Yes, yes, but I need to know what drives these people." He shook his head distractedly. "You have been an asset, young Makun, but do not stop now. Here, take this work and join their group down below. I realize there has been some recent friction since the mage's burning, but we cannot let such a minor thing interfere with building up our rapport with these people."

I think I blinked at him, my mind blanking at the abbot calling Eldso's burning a 'minor thing', but I know I ultimately nodded in response. Then taking up the heavy tome over my shoulder by its specially designed strap, I carried it into the hall as the abbot resecured the brother recorder's office. And then leaving the library, we made our way back through its hallowed halls into the scriptorium, where we locked the vault door behind us.

Removing his golden medallion, the abbot turned towards me. "Excellent. Now gather your things and return to the village. They should be very interested in the tome you bring."

"I'm taking this book outside of the tower?" I blinked a few times in astonishment, struggling to comprehend.

The abbot laughed. "Well, you're certainly not going to be able to show them the book from up here. And I think the brother protectors might turn them away, simply because of their presence, if they suddenly show up. No. Today, you shall go to them alone. Now off with you, young Makun. And I expect to hear good things from you later today, after you work with them on the translation."

I didn't quite sputter, but it was hard to hold onto my dignity. The abbot however didn't notice, simply clapping me on the shoulder as he turned and walked away. But even the other historians followed him with their eyes as he left the room, intensely disbelieving.

"You're removing that tome from the library? The abbot wants you to take one of our most ancient texts to the village?" one of the other historians hissed at me in disbelief.

"Apparently, yes."

"But … you can't," another one sputtered in surprise.

"What do you want me to do? Refuse?" I looked at him helplessly.

The rest of them simply looked back at me in stunned silence, all of us knowing the number of books that ever left the library was a limited thing. Very limited. And the books that were certainly weren't any of our older tomes.

Yet this one was ancient.

And the few that ever did pass through the guarded doors of the scriptorium?

Those, their numbers were few.

I still shake my head thinking about that book, and what the abbot hoped to accomplish. If I had only known …

Capitula 14

Despite my many misgivings, I went with that ancient text down to the village below. I felt decidedly naughty of all things walking with that book out through the gates of the edificium. But either nobody knew what to do about it when they saw me, or nobody cared. For I wasn't stopped even once as I carried that ancient tome out through the courtyard, through the outer gates, down the switch-backed trail, and then into the village below.

Jan met me as I strode between the buildings, walking alongside in silence while glancing at me from time to time. "I didn't know they let you take books out of the Spire."

"They don't. Normally, that is."

"Then why did you bring that one?"

"To translate. It's in their language."

"You don't look so sure."

She'd always been very observant. "I'm not," I admitted.

"And without any escorts?" Jan looked around. "Where's your protector?"

"The abbot feels they would be a limiting influence on our visitors."

She pinched her lips, turning away from me in silence. Then glanced my way before she replied, saying "I don't like what has happened."

"Hmmm?"

"Eldso."

"The mage," I corrected automatically.

She frowned even more. "He was a little boy, Makun." She looked kind of hurt.

I sighed, then admitted somberly, "Yes. He was."

She seemed to detect my mood, and appeared to take comfort in what I had admitted when she reached out to interlace her fingers with mine. And we walked that way in comfortable silence until we made it into the compound where the survivors from Lehntarn were found. Just her sheer presence gave me peace, and I hoped one day to convince the council to allow us to couple. The comfort she gave just being there by my side was simply that great.

The first thing I noticed was their compound was under guard, much higher and more alert than it had been before. People I had met who usually granted me a small smile of acknowledgement barely glanced my way or stared at me in silence, returning to being intimidating like how they'd originally been when they'd arrived. Walking up to one of the men, I saw Pormult off to the side and turned his way. The brawny man saw me, taking in me and my book with Jan at my side, and then frowned. But my familiarity with the man told me I could approach and not be refused.

"Pormult? How are you?"

He glanced back and forth between the two of us but only grunted in reply.

"Is Vortiid here?"

A few of their men wandered out of the buildings, two coming out of the barn armed and armored and expecting a fight by their look. Pormult only looked at me, not even glancing their way as the two armed men moved to stand at his back. Then the three of them eyed me, while even more men came out of the buildings to watch.

I glanced back and forth at the surrounding men, raising my hands to show that I came in peace. "I mean no harm. I couldn't even hurt you if I wanted to. We can come back if this isn't a good time." I found myself very aware of Jan as she pressed herself up against my side.

"Makun come." Pormult said loudly into the air, as if announcing my presence to a ghost. Then he looked past and beyond me, as if he was expecting someone else to arrive from the direction I'd come.

I glanced back and forth in the direction he looked. "There's nobody else coming, Pormult. It's just me. Jan can leave if it's a problem," I concluded, wanting to get her away. The tension in the yard was beyond anything I had expected to find here. I needed to keep her safe.

"I can speak for myself," she admonished me, but she didn't turn away from watching the Lehntarnese. She did squeeze my fingers tightly with her hand, though.

"No men?" Pormult asked.

"Men?"

He mimed what I eventually understood to be one of the brother protector's hammers.

"No. I'm on my own today. There are no brother protectors following me."

Pormult grunted once more.

"Again, I can leave if it's a problem," I said after a moment.

Someone spoke in their liquid tongue from inside the house, with Pormult responding quite quickly. Then Vortiid exited the door, staring at me with a pair of emotionless eyes. "Why Makun come?"

I nervously glanced at Jan before answering the man. "To continue our talks? We still have much to learn. I brought a book you might be interested in."

Vortiid didn't even glance the book's way. "Why?"

I searched my brain to find an answer that would satisfy him. Then I remembered something he'd said once. "To learn."

"No learn. Monks burn."

"We don't burn learning."

"Burn boy," Vortiid accused.

"The mage." It still hurt to think of Eldso like that.

"Boy."

"He was a mage."

"Boy!" Vortiid insisted.

I sighed, looking at my feet before admitting that to him as well. "Yes, he was."

"Monks burn boy."

"Yes. We did." I looked up at him helplessly, wondering what else I could say. There was nothing, and something in my eyes must have shown it.

Vortiid nodded. His eyes were still flat but a voice from inside interrupted him, and I saw some annoyance cross his face as he tilted his head to answer. He kept staring at me, his blank face I realized was only a façade for his fury, but he never once looked away. He only kept searching my eyes. Yet his conversation with whoever it was inside was filled with a series of strong emotions that didn't once cross his face.

The dichotomy of it was surreal.

Eventually the voice inside concluded and Vortiid stepped aside, waving for me to enter. I hadn't been inside the house since they'd made it their own, and I found it wasn't much different than when it was empty. The only glaring thing that stood out to me now were the weapons and armor everywhere I looked, all within arm's reach of someone inside or by a strategically located position.

"They tell me you've been talking with them since we arrived," a feeble voice said.

I looked over, seeing Ghaan sitting in a chair under a pile of blankets, with his feet propped up on a stool. There was a cluster of his countrymen standing around him, all staring back at me with blank, emotionless eyes. If the purpose was to intimidate me, it was working.

Jan must have seen it too. She squeezed my fingers, almost hugging my arm.

"Yes. It is good to see you up."

"Is it?"

"Yes?" I looked at him in confusion. "You were poisoned."

"I was," Ghaan agreed. "It takes it out of one, doesn't it?"

"I wouldn't know. I've never been poisoned."

"Never left your tower?"

"No. Not that, either."

"Have any of you?"

"What?"

"Left your tower? The village? The surrounding countryside?"

"No. Well some, but not far."

"I see."

He spoke to the surrounding men, a long speech in their tongue that went on for many minutes. He seemed to be promoting some point, something that wasn't going over very well if I was any judge of their expressions. But I had to admit I really didn't understand them as a people, and began to wonder if I'd assumed some things that I shouldn't have, or wished I hadn't.

Ghaan eventually finished up, then returned to looking at me. His expression wasn't as standoffish as the rest of the Lehntarnese, but was still guarded, so I decided to speak up. "I'm hoping we can keep talking. Me and your people."

"Why?"

I waved to Vortiid. "To learn."

"What about?"

"For instance, you speak our tongue – what we know from history was labeled as 'the common tongue' – much better than any of your men. How did that come to be?"

"I have a talent," he replied. "And you do not speak 'common' Makun Derring. Our people do. Your Imperial is quite difficult to understand."

"Imperial?"

Ghaan waved my question away. "I came to learn it as we journeyed here."

I frowned, disappointed by his blatant change of subject, but we were at least talking, and Jan's fingers had started to relax on my hand. "You must be very well educated to speak many tongues."

"Perhaps."

"I believe that you are. And there are many things we could learn."

Ghaan nodded, waving his hand towards the book. "The tome you bring?"

"A book of Lehntarn, or from Lehntarn. We're not entirely sure."

"Then why bring it?"

"To help us to communicate. If we can translate the words, it will help us accomplish that goal." Ghaan didn't look impressed, so I kept going. "We don't have anything translated in your speech. The closest we have is from Harlan, but that country admittedly uses a different tongue."

"The tongue of our enemies."

"Just so," I acknowledged the point. "Which leans towards a certain partiality in translation."

He studied me. "You seem very interested in this."

I decided to go with the truth. "It is my only duty right now. I've been reassigned to communicate with your people."

"They are not my people beyond being my countrymen."

"They seem to think so."

"You think?"

"Definitely." I waved my hand towards all of the lurking armed men standing protectively around the room. "Simply by their actions."

Ghaan fell silent, not answering as he studied me more. He glanced at Jan a couple of times, saying something to one of his men before returning his eyes to me. A chair was brought out for her, the man bringing it motioning for her to sit repeatedly, and not satisfied until she did. Then the man returned to his place, Ghaan still studying me as I stood quietly by Jan's side.

My silence seemed to impress him. "Let me see this book," he eventually asked.

I gave the ancient tome to him, Ghaan simply plopping it down upon his lap on top of the blankets. I winced at how he treated that priceless text but held silent, knowing that him accepting it at all was important to how this meeting would go. But Ghaan ignored me, turning the pages one by one before grabbing a bunch of them in one hand by the corners and allowing them to slip rapidly through his fingers. He stopped at one page, reading a random passage before continuing on, seemingly amused by what he had found. But he slowly started rubbing his head, Vortiid looking on with concern before the warrior frowned.

"I can return if you are not well," I offered, seeing Vortiid tense. I wondered what the abbot would say if I left the book with them.

"No. I have rested enough."

"Then can you help me translate this book?"

"Most certainly." He seemed humored by my request. "The question is if I should."

"I'm sorry?"

"Will you burn us if you learn things by doing so? Things with which you would disagree?"

"Why would we burn you for translating a book?"

"You burned an innocent boy alive from what my countrymen tell me."

"A mage."

"Yes, I know. Yet he was still an innocent."

"No mage is innocent."

"Are you so sure?"

"It is what the teachings tell us."

"The teachings?"

"The Book of the Fall."

The man fell silent, studying me with his eyes. Vortiid said something to him, but Ghaan didn't respond. He simply kept studying me with those eyes.

"I would like to see this book," Ghaan eventually said, pushing the ancient tome I'd brought aside.

I was a bit dumbfounded, not expecting that reply at all. "Ummm, certainly. I can have a copy brought to you."

"I will help you translate that."

I frowned. "Not the tome?"

"Maybe that, too." Ghaan offered, glancing aside at the ancient work. "After we review your text, however."

"The Book of the Fall," I said, making sure I understood.

"Just so."

Ghaan started rubbing his head again, then grunted as he came across a particularly uncomfortable place. The next question that formed upon his lips was interrupted as Vortiid called out to him in their tongue. Ghaan frowned but remained silent, rubbing his head as the silence stretched, and then nodded. Then a woman came out of another room, pouring Ghaan some steaming liquid for him to drink.

I looked at her, having totally forgotten that the Lehntarnese had any women of their own with them. They must have kept them cloistered and hidden inside their camp since the time of their arrival, because I hadn't seen one since. That realization must have shown on my face.

"Yes, we have women," Ghaan said, back to studying me.

"I'd forgotten. I haven't seen any of them since you arrived."

"They are to be protected and sheltered, as it should be. They bring life to the Way."

"The Way?"

"Yes," Ghaan answered, without pausing even once to explain. "It is why she sits and you stand."

I had no idea how to take this statement and remained silent, never before encountering any of their cultural concerns between men and women in my conversations with Vortiid. I glanced uncomfortably Vortiid's way, wondering how many times I may have previously stumbled.

He remained stone faced, however, but it was Jan who answered. She quietly stated, "Thank you for the chair."

"You are most welcome, mother," Ghaan answered.

Jan turned pink. "I have not birthed any children of my own."

"You will in time. So says the Way."

She glanced at me, confused and not a bit understanding, but I couldn't offer any help. I didn't understand what he meant either.

"Thank you?"

"You are welcome, mother. It is the way."

Ghaan nodded, saying something to the other men who nodded in Jan's direction as well. Then Ghaan returned to rubbing that seemingly particularly painful spot. Vortiid called out, and then the first woman returned. She took over Ghaan's massaging of his head, another woman bringing out a steaming cup of something for Jan to drink while smiling her way.

The woman answered my inquiry, simply saying "Tea" to when I asked, as Jan hesitantly sipped at the drink. Then Jan seemed surprised and pleased with its taste, taking a deeper drink.

"It is the custom of my people to offer food and drink during peaceful conversations," Ghaan mentioned.

I nodded in understanding.

"It shows you are not having any thoughts about conflict, as you cannot eat or drink with any weapons in your hands."

I nodded again when he paused.

"I would like to see this book, Makun Derring."

"Brother Derring, or simply Makun."

"Derring then."

I was totally non-plussed. "May I address you as Ghaan?"

"Yes, I have no title."

I wasn't quite sure I believed that, but Ghaan kept talking.

"Something you might think about while you are leaving to go get that book," Ghaan began. "We have been at war for a millennium. We hold women and children to be special. They embody what we are, what we have, and whatever good things may be." He paused to study me. "They embody the hope for us all to go on."

I nodded my understanding. "Thank you for sharing. I will remember."

"Good. Now go." He leaned back, relaxing into the fingers of the massaging woman. "Return with your book so that we might go over and study it. We have questions for your woman."

I looked down at Jan. "Do you want to stay? You don't have to if you don't want to. This is my duty, not yours."

"On my honor she will be safe," Ghaan interrupted, never once opening his eyes.

I frowned, but it was Jan who answered him once again. "I can leave whenever I want?"

"Yes, mother. None here would stop you if you wish to go."

"Then I would like to stay. The tea is good. Can I have another cup?"

Ghaan said something and the second woman assumedly left to go get her more tea.

"Go get your book, Makun." Jan smiled. "I'll wait for you here."

I frowned but nodded my head, accepting that Jan had assumed the role of a bridge over the tenseness in my relationship with the Lehntarnese.

It really wasn't what I had wanted, and it wasn't ideal, but I accepted it for what it was. And as I made my goodbyes, Jan smiled at me and my acceptance as the woman arrived with another cup of tea. Then leaving through the door, I exited the yard and made my way back through the village to the tower to retrieve a Book of the Fall.

And then it hit me.

Ghaan had never once offered me tea. Or anything else for that matter.

And neither had Vortiid.

Capitula 15

When I returned with a copy of The Book of the Fall, it began a multi-day journey of translation and discovery about our differing origins. I had assumed that our two towers were similar, but I was quickly disabused of that notion by Ghaan. And in between his headaches, he explained that the tower he came from had an entirely different purpose. Instead of storing and holding onto their knowledge like ours did, his tower performed only one thing.

And that purpose was to teach.

Though they did have books there, there was no voluminous library of texts that spanned every subject like ours. No, what their tower had was useful everyday things. A clean supply of water, a rooftop system of fields, a storage area under the ground capable of housing thousands upon thousands of souls, which is what it eventually did. The tower of Lehntarn seemed to be the center of their entire nation before the Fall, he described, and where they had turned to with all of their needs.

And Ghaan himself was one of their prelates, a difficult term for me to quantify with my system of beliefs. It held no religious significance Ghaan insisted, but the reaction of their people seemed to disagree. Maybe he was telling the truth, maybe he was not, but whatever significance his title held, his people were behind him, solidly.

Ghaan himself was a gregarious man, my initial interaction with him not at all the man's norm or true self. He was kind, easy going, and made himself readily available to all of his men. He refused that they were 'his men' of course, but even I could identify that lie for what it was. The people of Lehntarn almost waited on him hand and foot, not coddling him, no, but readily meeting every one of his needs without a single complaint being uttered. And it was quite shocking to me to see someone as objectionable as Xer Jarmen getting up without complaint to get Ghaan more of his tea whenever he asked.

The women of their group seemed to be around more, now that Ghaan was up and around, and he spoke to them often. I couldn't quite say or determine if he was involved with any of them, but their care for him was as obvious as their pampering was also. And they seemed especially upset about his headaches, shooing me and Jan away whenever one of them came on.

But the days passed as we discussed and poured over my order's holy text, Ghaan gradually translating its words into his own tongue as our conversations went on. The abbot wasn't especially pleased by this, asking why the tome we had brought wasn't being translated like he had asked. But I could not answer his questions, Ghaan simply stating he wanted to understand the teachings of The Book of the Fall in an attempt to find common ground with us, and understand its meaning.

Regardless, I came to identify that there was a lot of innuendo to the Lehntarnese language through Ghaan. Little things, that would have been completely overlooked if you weren't fluent in their tongue. And as I became more familiar, it seemed like a lot of misunderstandings between our two groups could have been boiled down to their countrymen looking for meanings in what was said to them that simply wasn't there.

We were enjoying our most recent laugh over a slip up while relaxing and taking a break – me finally realizing that when the book said that when the gods travelled to their private place, it didn't mean they left to move their bowels. The inanity of that inference by the Lehntarnese threw me, but Ghaan seemed to find how flustered I was hilarious. Though if Brother Barkon was here right now, he'd be throwing a fit. To imagine the gods even moving their bowels, well, that was as close to being violently heretical from what I knew of the brother chanter's mind as anything could be.

"Brother Derring?" someone called from outside.

I rose from my seat, setting the water I'd brought along aside as I moved to the door. Opening it I saw Chaltic, who brightened upon seeing me. "Chaltic, what are you doing down here?"

"Coming to find you. The abbot has sent for you."

"Did he say why?"

"Yes. The dwarves are arriving. He wants you to bring the people from Lehntarn to meet them and help translate."

"The dwarves?" I was astounded. The last trade caravan they'd sent us was years ago, and it was a fortuitous occurrence it was happening now. I also couldn't wait to see a dwarf.

The dwarves of Nächtaltom we considered an ally, helping us through the times of the Fall. The goods they provided to us were gifts from the gods, while the knowledge we shared taught them things that allowed their people to become more self-sufficient. They had also brought us many things in the time of the ancient past, giving them to us to store and care for along with the rest of our tomes. The pure fact that they did so we knew was an incredible sign of their trust, and the monks of the Spire cherished the relationship between our two peoples greatly.

"Did your friend say dwarves, Makun Derring?" Ghaan asked from inside.

"Yes. They are allies of ours. Friends. Their last trade mission came to us when I was a child."

"So long?"

"They must travel unassisted through the high mountains to get here. It is a dangerous journey, and they say they always lose someone whenever they come. It's always for an important reason when they arrive."

"Then you must not keep them, or your abbot. I will have someone go with you."

"You're not coming?" I glanced back, noticing one of the women bringing Ghaan more of his tea.

"No, Derring. My headaches are especially strong today. I am not fit to travel."

"As you will," I agreed. "I hope you feel better."

He was telling the truth, as whenever he had one of his headaches, he was all but inconsolable. They were debilitating, and always seemed to precede some sort of episode or 'spell', as the villagers put it. I shook my head at their superstitions, remembering Ghaan's last bad headache that had left him mumbling and drooling before he was carried off to bed.

It always seemed darker around their camp during one of his spells. I truly did hope he felt better.

I wouldn't want to travel around with one of those either, I thought as Ghaan and I agreed to meet whoever he sent once they arrived in the village square.

Leaving their yard, Chaltic and I made my way through the houses and smiled as Jan joined me. The people from Lehntarn had become quite taken with her, and I was pretty certain whatever they asked her when I left them alone had been the reason for their thawing attitudes towards me. But whatever they'd asked her she remained tight-lipped about, blushing bright red when I had originally asked her what the Lehntarnese had wanted to know.

"Hello, Chaltic," Jan smiled his way before turning towards me. "Did you hear about the dwarves coming?"

"It's the reason we're here."

"It's amazing!"

"The abbot sent me to get him," my friend agreed, grinning at me when Jan closed the distance to give me a hug.

The bastard was increasingly bothering me to ask Brother Camdal to look into her lineage. I appreciated his teasing, but I wish he'd just knock it off. I had too much going on right now to devote my time to what Jan would need, or maybe desire. She deserved the best, my best, not the leavings some monk had left over when he was tired and thinking of bed. And I wanted to make sure everything was right for her, doing everything I could to ensure she and I would stay together to live a happy life.

But, admittedly, thoughts about taking that step scared me. And not a single one of my fears stopped the grins.

"Well, I'm glad you two came," she hooked her arm into mine causing Chaltic to grin even wider. "I've only heard stories about the dwarves. To see any of them in my lifetime will be a treat. My mother said the last time they came there was a feast." There came a bit of yelling from up ahead. "Well, as long as Untark can calm down," she said, identifying the yelling voice.

"What has Untark stirred up?" Chaltic asked.

I could have bluntly cared less; the brutish man having caused Chaltic nothing but problems my entire life, and then me through association with him. *At least he doesn't act up around the people of Lehntarn*, I thought, remembering how intimidated by them he seemed to be. But for the rest of us, he hadn't changed one bit.

"Elder Mastin died overnight," Jan said.

"Who's he?"

"One of the old men in the village. His son found him dead in bed this morning."

"Was it unexpected?"

"No. Well, yes. But it wasn't as if no one had expected it eventually. He was sickly, and had terrible allergies his entire life."

"Oh, you mean the man with the cough," I said, remembering one of the villagers who always seemed to be being taken care of by one of the healers in the Hall of Healing.

"Yes," Jan nodded. "It looked like something bit him from what his son was saying. His family is in mourning, but isn't up in arms about it. It could have been a bee for all they knew. But you know Untark, always making a scene about everything."

Chaltic snorted.

"I sure do," I agreed, glancing the voices' way as we passed another one of the houses.

A cluster of people were carrying a blanket-wrapped body out of a house further down the side path, Untark and a few of his men helping though arguing with the ones who were carrying it. Untark seemed pretty upset.

"What's his main issue?" I asked, seeing one of Untark's men who seemed like he was upset enough to start stomping his feet. Then I watched as the village elder, Elder Cor Tam, shook his head at the man before saying something, then began walking away towards the square.

"That it needs to be investigated," Jan replied. "You know the strictures. Any unusual death must be reported to the Hall of Healing so that an investigation can take place. Just in case there's some new infection or a disease that's developing into a plague that could kill us all if it spreads.

"That, and Untark's man is going on about that creature again." Jan rolled her eyes. "The man was *old*, Makun, and his family is against investigating anything else. They just want to grieve. They're going to bury him later today."

"You really should report it," I replied.

"We already did. And your brother healer has already come and gone earlier this morning. Untark and his man just don't want to let it go."

Chaltic shrugged, giving one last glance before we passed in between the next row of buildings and lost sight of the group. "Then there's nothing left to do. If the Hall of Healing has already cleared his death, it's done and over with."

"I know," Jan answered. "Like I said, he just doesn't want to let it go."

Sometimes it bothered me how used to death we all were, Jan already turning the conversation to something else. We had to be, inured to death I mean. I knew that. It's not like the area we lived in was safe. And death, disease, and injury were a part of everyday life. But Jan's easy turning from the death of someone she knew, to inane conversation about another villager, bothered me for some reason.

Then I remembered how she had wept over Eldso, and took comfort in my arms while she cried. I studied her as Chaltic and her talked, seeing her glance towards that blanket-wrapped body from time to time. Then I saw her frown before looking away, and I reassured myself on knowing her heart was pure.

Just too used to death, as everyone of us were.

We reached the village square, moving to its center where some of my fellow brothers were. The abbot had not yet arrived, maybe choosing to have the rest of us escort the dwarves to the tower, but quite a few of the others had. There were brothers from all of our delineations, clustered together and talking in anticipation of welcoming the dwarves. And as we moved to talk with a few of the people we knew, the people that Ghaan had sent started to arrive.

Surprised by his choice, it was Xer Jeman who had come. The objectionable, skinny man would not have been my first choice of who to send to meet a new people, but admittedly I didn't know him well. He had three others with him, the four of them chatting softly together, each and every one outfitted for war. They seemed to have put some effort into making their armor more presentable, and it looked like they had gained a bit of oil or wax from somewhere, using the substance to make their things gleam.

But what was most surprising was that they escorted one of their women. She was a slight thing, wearing the simple unfitted dress that the rest of their women wore. But over top of her everyday costume she wore a wide decorative belt, that almost spanned the entire space from her waist to an area low on her hips. It was adorned with woven colorful threads and banding that striped it here and there, which definitely caught the eye. And in and amongst her plaited hair she wore strands of decorative beads, hanging from a braided red cord that had been twisted throughout her hair quite delicately.

She looked exotic and mysterious, all at the same time. And Jan must have caught me studying her, elbowing me in the ribs when she caught me watching. "Something interesting you over there?"

"No!" I objected.

Chaltic just snorted behind me.

"I thought so." She moued, then planted a quick kiss on my cheek. "Keep your eyes over here … preferably on me."

"Yes, Jan."

Chaltic simply laughed even harder.

She was smiling at me while I blushed – what about I wasn't quite sure – but my embarrassment became quite happy when I saw the northern gate of the village's stockade open up in the distance. The main road through the village, more a wide path than anything else even though we called it a road, ran north-south with a gate on each end, and I could easily see all the way to the stockade. I motioned to get Jan and Chaltic's attention, then Xer Jeman noticed and his party walked over to join us, looking that way as well.

"Makun Derring, dwarves come?" Xer asked.

"I think so," I answered, glancing his way.

Then I noticed the woman behind him was jingling every time she moved, with tiny metal beads on even more strands that were hanging from the belt behind her. She nodded in my direction before turning back to look the gate's way.

"Xer Jeman speak dwarves?"

"If there is a moment," I agreed. "No one is going to stop you. Anytime the dwarves come is a celebration."

Xer nodded, speaking to his countrymen as they all turned their interested eyes in the gate's direction. The woman asked something in a soft voice, then Xer replied in the gentlest manner I had ever heard from the man. I was trying to listen in, having struggled to learn the basics of the spoken Lehntarnese language over the last while, but Jan caught my attention. "You can talk later. Look there, the dwarves!"

And then I did see them, being escorted into the village through the stockade's main gate. Leading the dwarves was a stout fellow, his beard reaching down just past his knees as he rode a marintan in.

The creature was one of the strangest I had ever seen, but I recognized it from what I had read. With its front legs almost twice as long as its back ones, a marintan's torso was oddly sloped backwards, giving the thing a curious gate. Combined with a narrow, elongated head, and a tongue that was almost as long as my arm, the marintans lived on the high cliffs and ledges amongst the mountains. An extremely hearty breed, they lived off the scrub and dense plant life they found in the mountains, keeping themselves safe from predators and monsters through a simple strategy of staying as far away from them as they could.

To most they were not worth the effort to tame them, it simply being too difficult to find them in the first place. But the dwarves had not only found them, they tamed them, and they used them to pull their laden wagons, having long ago discovered the marintans' strength.

The dwarf leading the procession came to a halt alongside many of his people once he reached the village's center, but the rest of their caravan was still coming in through the gate. Then he looked around before dismounting that odd creature, having been hailed by Brother Margonest and some of the other brother teachers as well. The brother teachers stood as a group to the side of the surprisingly frowning Elder Cor Tam, as well as Untark Mar's armed people, smiling in greeting towards the party of dwarves.

"Hail Nachtaltom," I heard the brother teacher say through the noise of the crowd.

"Hail ta' tha' Spire," the dwarf in charge replied. "It's been a long time."

"It has indeed, friend. The years have treated you well," Brother Margonest continued.

"Do I know ya'?" the dwarf replied, his voice coming stronger as Xer Jeman and I moved to get closer. His people, along with Jan and Chaltic, went with us, our group causing quite a stir as we pushed our way through the surrounding villagers.

"You must not recognize me, friend. I am Brother Margonest. I met with you when your people came to us last."

"Margonest? Ya' were a young man when I last been here."

"That was almost twenty years ago friend."

"Maker, ya' human's age fast." The dwarf shook his head.

"That we do, Peltic. But at least we can see farther." The brother teacher grinned. "You always were short."

Peltic guffawed, walking up to shake the man's hand. "It be good ta' see ya', old man."

"And it is good to see you." Brother Margonest looked over him towards the caravan beyond. "Still wanting our potions and teachings?"

"Aye. We be needin' some, an' some other things as well," Peltic agreed. Then he caught sight of my party approaching. "An' who do we have here?"

"This is young Brother Makun. One of our recorders, recently elevated to his position."

"An' these people?" Peltic asked, looking towards the people from Lehntarn.

"Survivors from far away," Brother Margonest began before he was interrupted.

And what happened next surprised me, as I am pretty sure it surprised the dwarves and everyone else as well.

Making a very deliberate bow, Xer Jeman moved with the others to stand in front of the dwarf. Then in a clear voice, he repeated a phrase in their tongue. The gravelly words that the dwarves spoke came fluidly from his mouth, then he moved so that two of his countrymen stood to either side of their woman. Then the woman advanced, jingling all the while, before kneeling and kissing each of Peltic's stunned cheeks.

Then the men from Lehntarn knelt also, each banging a fist to their chests before running a thumb down their cheeks. Staring into Peltic's wide eyes, they bowed once more before Xer Jeman clearly said to him and his countrymen so that we all could understand, "Cathaganlire lost, dead."

Then Xer Jeman slowly bowed his head until it rested on the ground before them.

The effect on the dwarves was profound.

Capitula 16

My recollection of that incident is admittedly hazy with the years that have passed by, but one thing I do remember quite clearly was my shock at the Lehntarnese speaking to the dwarves in their own tongue. And something that has haunted me over the years is my remembrance that the dwarves responded quite haltingly, as if they had difficulty responding in kind to what was said. Was there some kind of lingual drift? An issue with what was said that Xer Jeman could not somehow convey? Some other issue that happened before me?

I and my brethren were doomed to never know, for as soon as the party from Lehntarn mentioned Cathaganlire the dwarves stopped everything they were doing. And one of the elders that had accompanied them had fought against his jaw hanging open, if I was any judge of their people. But with a quick though limited back and forth in the dwarvish tongue taking place in the village square, the woman, whose name I found out later was Hestialee, removed the thick belt she wore and presented it to the dwarves.

And that presentation honored them, greatly.

The party from Lehntarn lowered their heads, the woman holding out the thick belt and its beads with both arms as if she was making an offering to the gods.

Peltic reached a shaking hand out to touch it, gently stroking the belt before backing away, making no move to take it. His countrymen joined him, seeing the belt still being held there, and the moment for them was obviously profound. They spoke between themselves in their own tongue before addressing Xer Jeman, but whatever was said exceeded his ability to understand and reply.

"Peltic?" the brother teacher prompted, everyone in the square confused and curious about what was going on.

Peltic just blinked at him, obviously mentally coming out of some other place. He openly forced himself to respond. "They bear the token of Cathaganlire," Peltic explained in a strangled voice as he lowered himself to one knee. Then he ignored Brother Margonest entirely, as he concentrated fully upon what was before him, and spoke again to the Lehntarnese.

Whatever that back and forth in dwarven concluded, it was not a happy tale. A few of the dwarves began wailing, while all of them tightened the hands on the weapons they bore, but every last one of them stood rooted in place as Xer Jeman conveyed whatever story he told. The gate to the stockade closed with a soft boom behind them as the story went on, sounding like an explosion in comparison to the deathly quiet of the dwarves, but not a single one of them turned back to look at it as they held themselves riveted by his tale.

Then, with her arms blatantly shaking from still holding out that offered belt, the woman began lowering the gift because of the strain. But springing forward, Peltic reached out and clasped onto her wrists, holding up the strangely honored belt and its beads, yet still not making a single move to take it. Then remaining there somewhat intimately with the woman, Peltic looked to Xer Jeman to continue his tale.

But his tale was over, the Lehntarnese man having finished conveying whatever information he had to say. A few halting questions went back and forth in dwarven, but the meat of his story was obviously concluded.

Then Xer Jeman and his party did something even further. Kneeling as they were, they planted their fists on the ground before them, then bowed their bodies to look down at the earth. He said something in the dwarvish tongue again, some short phrase or acclamation, but whatever he uttered, its effect on the dwarves was once again profound.

The dwarves as a whole slammed their fists to their chests. Their stoic faces were harsh and drawn, all fifty or so of them having left their belongings behind to hear Xer Jeman's tale. Then barking a quiet command while still kneeling and intimately holding onto the woman's hands, Peltic commanded some honor or salutation from the rest of the dwarves. Three more times the dwarves pounded their fists to their chests, never breaking their verbal silence, while tears poured from some of their faces. Then lifting his voice to cry out to the heavens, Peltic intoned some desperate plea.

"Fäschandi Cathaganlire ayie De'Mal!"

The silence that followed was only broken by the soft shuffling of feet, my fellow monks and the villagers having no idea of what was going on. But that quiet moment did not stretch on for long, Peltic shortly thereafter taking the offered belt into his own hands.

Then leaning forward, he gently kissed the woman upon both of her cheeks, before he planted a single fist in the ground as well. Then he bowed to the Lehntarnese, almost abasing himself in the process, just a few degrees less than the Lehntarnese had been, as if he had been granted something profound.

The dwarves came to their feet, then as a group came forward to assist Xer Jeman and his people to rise also. The dwarves made certain to touch them, every single one of them offering a pat or a grasp of some kind. Then the dwarves wandered off to do whatever they'd been doing before, not a single one glancing back to where they had been, leaving Peltic behind.

But despite their apparent nonchalance, I noticed there wasn't a dry eye amidst the group. And I wondered what it meant, that belt and that scene, knowing that Vortiid had already told me that he had not said all.

Xer Jeman nodded to Peltic and then spoke to his countrymen in their own tongue. Then the group of Lehntarnese nodded to each of us, making a point to differentiate me from the monks, before they nodded as well to the villagers. Then as a whole, they turned and walked away.

Brother Margonest was as openly as confused as I was, and gave voice to our thoughts. "Peltic? What in the Pantheon's name just occurred?"

The dwarf in question watched the retreating backs of the Lehntarnese in silence, until they were completely out of view. Then he turned to Brother Margonest, looking at him as if seeing him for the first time, before he spoke. "Warriors honoring a pledge," was all he explained.

"Warriors?"

"Aye," and it seemed that was all Peltic was going to say. The dwarf took in a great breath before letting it out, glancing at the belt in his hands. Then offering it slowly and with great care to a weathered dwarf standing silently beside him, he turned back as that dwarf took it away. "We have trade to convey."

"Are you going to explain that?"

"No."

The brother teacher was entirely nonplussed by his curt response, but after a pause must have decided it was best to move on. "Okay. Well, your people's usual quarters will be made ready." Brother

Margonest waved to Cor Tam, the village's elder then stepping to the fore.

"As ye can see, we already have a bunch of new visitors," Cor Tam stated. "But, I guess we can make space for ye well enough." I was surprised he didn't sound pleased.

"We can take our place by the fighters." Peltic looked off in the direction Xer Jeman had gone.

Cor Tam exchanged glances with Brother Margonest. "Aye? We don't be having room that way," he cautioned. "We're knowing you don't like staying in our houses. The only thing besides that over there is some empty space and buildings we haven't repaired."

"My people will take it."

"Peltic, we cannot have time honored allies staying here without a roof over your heads," Brother Margonest gently admonished him.

"We been campin' fer three weeks ta' get here. Campin' behind your walls will be easy enough." Peltic waved his hand towards the stockade.

"At least allow us to provide our pavilions for you."

"Aye, we can accept that. They be bigger, anyway."

"Then it is settled. Come, I'm sure the abbot is waiting to greet you."

Peltic nodded easily enough, walking off with the brother teacher to ascend the switch-backed trail that led to the outer gate. But I noticed he glanced frequently toward the way that Xer Jeman had gone, and the dwarf's countrymen did also, almost hurrying away to set up their camp.

The open space Cor Tam had spoken about was only a short distance away from where the Lehntarnese were. I was certain a meeting between those two groups was soon in the offing.

***

"It is becoming annoying that I'm always the one coming to get you," Chaltic griped.

"Then send someone else."

"When the abbot tracks down Brother Randilon, then the lay brother tracks me down – in person, I might add – all to give me orders to find you, you do whatever they wish," Chaltic complained.

I glanced over at Chaltic, both of us hurrying through the halls of the tower, its white and gray speckled stonework passing us quickly by. Why in the many gods' names I was being summoned to the ongoing trade talks, I had absolutely no idea. But it was like Chaltic had said. When they called you listened, so off we went.

I brushed at my most formal robe, then laughed at myself as 'my most formal robe' was the only other one that I had. Then I glanced towards Chaltic, seeing him doing the same.

Being told to find me down in the village, bathe, and then appear within the span of two candles was understandably annoying, and I appreciated what he'd done. I'm certain he had other things going on as well, other duties he was responsible for which had to be set aside to come and find me. And he was just as confused as I was about what was going on, as he had been told to stay by my side once we appeared.

"Don't wipe the polish off," Chaltic admonished, seeing me fiddling with my medallion.

"You polished it?"

"And mine as well." Chaltic nodded. "I was told to bring you, both of us done up as if for the years turning. So, yours and mine got polished."

I glanced his way, turning the last corner that led to the Hall of Teaching, and nodded my thanks. It explained what he had been doing while I was bathing. We didn't have much polish because of how difficult it was to produce, and as such its use was strictly regulated. As far as I knew, only the council of seven frequently used it. So, the pure fact that it had been released for our use only added to the mystery of our summons as we approached the Hall of Teaching.

The brother teachers had been responsible for conducting our trade talks since the dwarves had found us, all those generations ago. Talks with the dwarves were always conducted in their hall, and it was generally an open and easy space. Once a week the older village children would enter the hall, being instructed in more advanced topics than what the younger children learned in the village below. It was a kind of weaning, this more advanced learning, the older boys being watched and assessed to see if they had the intelligence it took to enter our ranks. And I remembered my time spent there with warmth, before a small packet of sadness passed as I remembered the brother teacher who had taught me, now many years long dead.

The doors to the Hall of Teaching normally stood wide open, giving the vast space a welcoming presence that the rest of our tower somehow lacked. However, as we rounded that last corner, we found both of the doors closed, with a grouping of brother protectors there at their side. Chaltic and I slowed, bringing our breathing under control, and by the time we reached the two closed doors we were ready to face whatever reason we'd been summoned for.

"They're waiting on you," one of the brother protectors told us, opening one of the doors for us to pass.

I looked a question towards him but he shrugged in reply while we strode in. Then turning to glance further into the room, we passed the many desks and pillows that were scattered about the floor as we advanced upon the central table. The huge table I recognized, normally being shoved up against the wall and stacked with textbooks along with a selection of snacks and food brought from the refectory. But today it had been set up with an assortment of large chairs, and had been moved towards the room's center, with a place set aside for everyone who sat at the table.

"Ah, good. Thank you for coming so quickly," the abbot said as he glanced our way.

The council of seven was all present. Along with the Abbot, the Brothers Chanter, Recorder, Healer, Protector, Teacher, and the Lay Brother, they all sat in their places. Then in a grouping of their own sat Ghaan, the woman who had met with the dwarves before, along with Xer Jeman, Gritilli Van, and two more of their people. And finally, with them, or maybe immediately beside them, sat a gathering of dwarves. Peltic, the only one whose name I knew, sitting alongside five of his own people.

The abbot waved towards two empty places, me instantly understanding and motioning to Chaltic for the two of us to take our seats.

"They're here now. Perhaps we can continue?" The abbot looked to the dwarves.

"Aye," Peltic said. "Where's yer book?" he asked, looking squarely at me.

"My book?" I replied, still not having a single clue as to what was going on or why we were here.

"Brother Derring," the brother recorder called for my attention. "Their man Ghaan wants this event recorded. There was some objection to the other historian recording for them."

"Objection?" I asked, not understanding how that could be.

"Yes." Brother Barkon frowned as he said that, Brother Sedimont frowned as well. "Apparently the objection was that the more experienced brother who was recording wasn't you."

I glanced among the other members of the council of seven, and felt like I was a prey animal who had been suddenly caught. I had no idea what to say to the leaders of our order in that moment, but the aged Brother Camdal eventually broke the tension I felt.

"Which is neither here nor there, is it not? He is still a historian, correct?"

"Yes. And is performing his duties admirably under a large amount of stress," Brother Ansilin defended me.

"Then there should be no issue," Brother Camdal concluded, then looked towards Chaltic. "We needed someone to run errands for us anyway."

"It is still highly unusual," Brother Barkon stated, his eyes going to the abbot. "His inexperience at his post is a concern."

"Unusual as it may be, Brother Derring remains a historian and one of our recorders. You made no complaint to his elevation." Then Abbot Dreise waved a hand towards Ghaan and the dwarves. "If his services are requested, and there is no reason for us to deny them, then in the Pantheon's name, I say, let it be."

Brothers Barkon and Sedimont both frowned, seemingly only a bit put out over my inclusion, and held themselves silent. However, interacting with them for most of my life, I clearly picked up on their profound disapproval.

I took that moment to voice a most necessary question. "Am I to assume the role of secretary for this meeting?"

"Yes," the abbot answered.

"I see."

"Also, it is unusual," the abbot waved towards a desk that had been set off to the side, "but the dwarves and our survivors from Lehntarn wanted you to sit at their side while you did so."

This caused brothers Sedimont and Barkon to frown even further.

I had absolutely no idea what to say, eventually stating "I did not bring my things, Abbot. I am unprepared."

"Chaltic can get them," Brother Randilon offered.

"And now I'm your slave," Chaltic whispered the joking

complaint in my ear.

"Go get his papers and tools for him, Brother Chaltic. We'll wait for you here. There's enough left over from the last historian for Brother Derring to do his work until you return."

"Yes, Lay Brother," Chaltic answered as he left the room.

Xer Jeman said something to Ghaan in their own tongue, then Ghaan spoke up. "Are we now ready?"

"As long as you are," Brother Barkon replied. His annoyance was obvious to me, but Ghaan made no comment. I was sure that he knew, regardless.

Brother Ansilin waved me to the historian's desk to gather the paper and ink. I got them and quickly returned, sitting at a space made for me by the dwarves and the Lehntarnese before turning to a new page and begin performing my duties.

Conversation around the table resumed, dry and dull talk about what the dwarves had brought with them and what they hoped to achieve. For the most part they had brought ore and a herd of mountain tarn, and looked to exchange it for specific potions and learning they needed, but there were a lot of other things they had brought with them as well.

It was the most unusual trade conversation I had ever read about, with very little dickering or bartering taking place. It was mostly a conversation about what could be parted with without undue burdens being placed on either side of the event, and it seemed like the values of the various things being exchanged had long been determined. And it surprised me to find out that closer to eighty dwarves had arrived, and every single last one of them had carried some tradable item in their packs.

First, we talked about food revolving around a new strain of mushrooms, and what could be learned consulting the library regarding the mineral makeup of the mountains the dwarves came from. Then there was a desire to reference any and all dwarven works, which sparked a refusal to have those works removed from the library, but their ability to be accessed could be granted for an acceptable quantity of iron.

The mountain tarn they brought were offered, which led to a dickering over the quantity of potions we could brew that the dwarves had lost the making of since the Fall. And this led to a discussion of what the Lehntarnese could offer when their ears perked up over the potions, and what talents and abilities they may bring to the table, along with the knowledge they held.

The banality of the discussion descended into dryer and dryer points which barely required me to lift my pen, and it had me wondering the longer it went on …

Why was I here?

Capitula 17

I eventually learned as the talks progressed that another reason Brothers Barkon and Sedimont seemed so upset was that the dwarves had insisted on the people of Lehntarn's inclusion, throwing off the trade talks beginnings until their people arrived. Neither the brother chanter nor the brother protector understood the dwarves' insistence, both being creatures of conservative habit and not understanding why things had to change, but the dwarves had apparently been adamant. So, despite what my order's leaders had wanted, the talks had been delayed.

Then, when the trade talks had finally started back up again there seemed to be some disagreement with the historian who was recording. Apparently, it was simply an issue that Ghaan and the people from Lehntarn didn't know him and hadn't worked with him before. That, and supposedly there had been some misunderstanding in translation that couldn't be resolved.

Brother Barkon alluded to this many times as the talks went on. That, and there had been a prior conversation that had taken place in dwarvish that none of the council could understand. Brother Sedimont had apparently taken issue with this as well, the Dwarves and the Lehntarnese men speaking about things between them where he couldn't understand, and supposedly it had gotten a little bit heated before it had been resolved.

It was Ghaan who had spoken up for me, asking for me to come to the meeting and be present to record. The dwarves agreed to this after another conversation between their two groups in dwarven, and deferred to the people of Lehntarn.

Brother Sedimont had not been pleased.

The 'why' to their insistence in my inclusion was apparently just simply that the people of Lehntarn knew me, but that was enough for the dwarves. They bluntly said that if the people of Lehntarn wanted someone special to make a recording of the trade talks, the people of Lehntarn would have it. And as everyone in the Spire knew, the dwarves would wait until the end of time for something to happen after they had made up their minds.

The two senior brothers still shot looks at me as the day went on, but I kept my head down and concentrated on my writings while doing my best to avoid their irritation.

Brother Barkon glowered. The brother chanter always one to defer to tradition which would have the most experienced historian in our order recording, which I was most definitely not. And Brother Sedimont continuously frowned at me. I knew, based on my years of interaction with the man, that he was mad at my elevation above a more experienced historian, who in his head was therefore my superior.

It was an uncomfortable experience until they ultimately decided to ignore me.

My friend Chaltic they basically turned into a servant, having him go and fetch various things between refilling everyone's drinks. And the rest of the council of seven decided to ignore us both, the only sign of our presence being the scratching of my pen upon paper, and Chaltic constantly coming and going for random things. It was surprisingly exhausting, and I was glad of the breaks Brother Camdal called out for, roughly once every hour.

"The fighters' speak well of ye," Peltic said to me at one of those pauses.

"Thank you?"

"Yer welcome. Any friend o' theirs be a friend o' ours. Nächtaltom will remember."

"Thank you again." I glanced in the people of Lehntarn's direction. "I am just doing my duty."

"As ya' say."

"Peltic," the abbot called. "I have a question off topic."

"Aye?"

Something about the way the dwarf responded seemed guarded to me, and I glanced at the dwarf before turning my attention upon the abbot.

"Why do they call you 'grey rocks'?"

"Oh, that. The grey rocks be tha' name o' a cliff where we live. Fought a battle there, I did."

"Some importance I take it?"

"Aye. A bit. Be tha' first of me name."

"Huh. I would be honored to hear the tale."

But it was then that Ghaan interrupted. He greeted Peltic in dwarven before returning to the common tongue, totally ignoring the abbot. I still didn't know why he named our tongue Imperial, and he had refused to explain why so far. "A question for you, Peltic."

"Aye?"

It was almost comical how quickly Peltic responded, and the abbot seemed totally nonplussed for a moment while he watched them begin to speak.

"We are looking for a plant or an herb in this area, and wondered if you might know of it."

"Aye? I can take a look, but I'm no apothecary," Peltic admitted.

"We have some in our camp. The supply is limited, and we haven't seen any in our travels since we acquired it originally."

"Aye? Where's that?"

"We received our original supply before we left from the Vale."

Ghaan's casual utterance about the home of the elves silenced the conversations of everyone around. The lands of the elves and the elven people was something that no one knew anything about, and the people of Lehntarn had been remarkably tight lipped about it. They shared general things about the elves, sure, but when it came to discussing specifics, they suddenly closed down.

It had been quite frustrating for me, and for him to so casually bring it up in open conversation was surprising.

"Tha' Vale." Peltic stroked his beard while his voice trailed off. "If it come from tha' Vale, it be possible tha' yer supply is all that'll ever be," he warned.

"We were told we could find more in the world."

"Told, were you?"

"We lived with them for a time."

Peltic glanced around at everyone listening, and then frowned. He asked Ghaan something in dwarvish …

… But Ghaan responded to him in common. "They call it *kiftala ton mar*. We were told that many would consider it a weed."

Peltic frowned some more at that, then continued to stroke his beard. It was amazing to me to hear what I assumed was fluently spoken elvish, uttered so casually from Ghaan's mouth, but no one else seemed to be amazed. Now more than ever, I wanted to sit the man down and talk to him long into the night until he answered every last one of my questions.

"That sounded decidedly elvish," the brother teacher commented while Peltic thought. He walked over, Brother Margonest almost dragging Brother Ansilin along with him in the process.

"It was." Ghaan nodded. "It is the name of the plant we are looking for, as spoken in their tongue."

Gritilli Van said something to Ghaan, and by his tone, Gritilli was not entirely pleased. But Ghaan responded easily enough to his corpulent countryman, whatever being said in their tongue between them silencing Van's stated objection.

"Ye still have some?" Peltic asked.

"Yes," Ghaan responded. "A small amount is still left from our travels."

"I can be looking …" Then Peltic said something to one of his countrymen in their gravelly tongue, turning back after the dwarf responded. "Aye, I thought so. Maess died on tha' way here. Our herbalist," Peltic explained. "But Ferdid there trained with him. We can have him take a look when we're free."

"I would appreciate that."

"Ye have but to ask," Peltic nodded.

It was very curious to me how the dwarves so easily agreed, and almost seemed to defer to the Lehntarnese. They'd never acted this way with us. I know; I read it. I'd tried to ask about it during a previous break, but got nothing from them to give me any insights into their interactions. It was as if it was some private family matter we were seeing, and I was a distant family member looking on from afar who was destined to never know.

"We are very curious about your stay with the elves," the abbot interjected.

"I am sure that you are." Ghaan nodded. His statement easily conveyed that there would be nothing else forthcoming.

The abbot tried again. "If the herbalist from Nächtaltom has gone on his journey to rest in the arms of the Pantheon–"

"The Maker," Peltic interrupted.

"As you say," the abbot readily agreed. We all recognized the name the dwarves gave to their god.

"If the herbalist has gone on to rest with the Maker," the abbot resumed, nodding in the dwarves' direction, "we can offer our knowledge from the library. There are many books on plants in the area that we could offer for you to peruse."

I was somewhat stunned by the abbot's offer. The books and the knowledge our library held was a closely guarded treasure. That he would just offer it so casually threw me.

Ghaan paused in reflection upon hearing this, asking first his own people and then the dwarves something in their respective tongues. He began rubbing his forehead, nodding to the various replies he received, but then seemed to descend deep in thought. Gritilli Van seemed especially frustrated by the way he was speaking to Ghaan, but Ghaan silenced him with a short inquiry. Whatever Ghaan asked left the portly man without a single reply.

"This seems very generous." Ghaan looked up to watch the abbot, rubbing his forehead while apparently considering how best to reply. "We are discussing trade between nations here." He waved towards the table. "What will your offer cost my people? The people from Lehntarn?"

The abbot smiled gently his way. "Cost? We should not discuss cost. There is no cost between brothers. Besides, this is a place of learning. Your knowledge of distant lands and the foreign peoples that you have encountered and lived with is a treasure which would cost you nothing to share. We would be happy to assist in your search for this plant while you shared this."

The look Peltic threw him told me he suspected the abbot was up to something, and I most certainly agreed. It was the first time I had ever thought poorly of the abbot, as I knew, along with everyone else within hearing range, that our tower jealously guarded every bit of our learning. One of the key points of the trade talks between us and the dwarves was our knowledge that we protected and held. To say or intimate that the sharing of our tower's knowledge cost someone nothing was simply inane, and utterly untrue.

Peltic obviously agreed, saying something curt to Ghaan in the dwarven tongue, but Ghaan didn't so much as respond to him in the least. He simply eyed the abbot while he continued to rub his head.

"We would certainly treasure anything you might offer to share," Brother Ansilin prompted him, the brother recorder was always one who simply treasured knowledge for what it was. He was always ready to share anything he knew, as well. He had almost become a brother teacher himself, I learned, years before he had assumed the position he now held.

"Access to books on plants in the library? And help in identifying the plant we seek? In return for sharing our tales of the elves?" Ghaan asked.

"Something more than general, I would think," the abbot

countered.

Ghaan frowned. "This is acceptable."

Gritilli looked like he wanted to chew nails, but remained silent.

But it was the dwarves who spoke up. "We have some knowledge of the elves, as well," Peltic offered. "If it can lessen the burden on the fighters, we will see what we can add to whatever they say."

Ghaan nodded, and again I was stunned. The dwarves offered nothing for free. Ever. Not once since we'd known them.

"We were not aware that you had any contact with the elves," the abbot prompted. There was a slight narrowing of his eyes along with a subtle frown as well.

"No. Ya weren't," Peltic simply stated.

And that seemed to be the end to the conversation. The awkward moment was interrupted by Chaltic returning to refill everyone's glasses.

✳✳✳

The brother teacher was deep into the discussion of minutiae regarding exactly how many potions and of what type we were going to trade for every head of mountain tarn we received when we were interrupted.

It was the next day, and our talks had progressed beyond the party's general openings. The council of seven for the most part looked bored, but they remained present despite what their duties usually demanded of them, delegating their responsibilities to other brothers in the tower.

The door to the Hall of Teaching was abruptly opened by one of the brother protectors, and in walked one of our healers. "Excuse me," the brother said before turning to Brother Camdal. "Another villager has passed overnight. The strictures have been met with his passing. Your inclusion is quite clear."

The brother healer frowned. "This is two in three days." He turned towards the abbot as if he was about to speak before he returned to his healer. "The cause?"

"He appeared to pass in his sleep."

"Any marks like the last?"

"Insect bites, nothing more. The villagers are upset. There's talk about the creature," the healer rolled his eyes, "and then some suspicion it could be the fault of the dwarves."

Peltic turned red in the face. "Fer' what?" he demanded.

"The villagers are superstitious," the abbot explained, waving the dwarf down. "They suspect anything new and are quick with their suspicions. They are already tense because of the survivors' arrival." He waved a hand to indicate Ghaan and his people.

"Ya' can tell 'em we didna' bring nothin'!" Peltic insisted. "An' damn ye fer' any suggestin' it."

"Let us not be hasty," Brother Camdal soothed, trying to calm the dwarf's fiery temper.

"It be an offense ta' our honor!"

"And we understand your position," Brother Margonest agreed. "But as the abbot said, the villagers as a whole are superstitious, and they simply don't understand. They are quick to make ignorant judgements."

"Ignorant. Ha! On tha', we agree," Peltic grumped.

"What else can you tell us?" Brother Camdal asked the brother healer, interrupting whatever Peltic had decided to say next. Everyone in the tower knew the dwarves were quick to anger when it came to their honor.

"Nothing, brother. He was older but not elderly, and his death comes as somewhat of a surprise."

"Insect bites, you say?" Brother Sedimont inquired. "Were any unusual insects seen in the area around?"

"No, Brother Protector."

Brother Sedimont turned a raised eyebrow towards the abbot. "Two deaths in three days?"

"One of which was not in the least unexpected."

"One death then," Brother Sedimont readily dismissed the other man's death, almost casually. "It could be some new creature," Sedimont hedged, "another altered beast. We should probably take a look to be sure."

"Agreed," the abbot replied. "Brother Camdal? Can you have some of your healers accompany the protectors?"

"Certainly, Abbot."

"There is also some talk down in the village about being cursed," the healer said. "I did what I could to put an end to it, the friars and lay brothers are also, but that warrior of theirs was talking about it being something to do with the 'demons'. I believe he meant the sprites."

"Ya' seen sprites?" Peltic asked, seeming surprised. He cast a quick glance towards Ghaan.

"They brought the people from Lehntarn to us," the abbot explained, his distracted response immediately began a conversation in dwarven between Gritilli Van and one of the dwarves.

"I find it difficult to believe that the sprites would have anything to do with this," the brother recorder said. "Everything we know about them says that they never leave their forests. It would be highly unusual."

"Everything we know about them comes from storybooks," Brother Sedimont replied. His dismissiveness towards what Brother Ansilin had said was readily apparent.

"Be that as it may, those storybooks are quite consistent," the brother teacher explained. "We would be foolish to dismiss what they say."

"But it could be possible," the brother chanter said next. "The sprites never defended the Pantheon either." He put a lot of weight on that final statement, like what he had just said was in some way of singular importance.

And I blinked at what he had just said, taken aback that it was important enough for him to mention it in the first place. Even if they were somehow at fault for what had happened to the gods, we did not have the manpower to challenge the sprites. Their forests surrounded us. That, and the sprites had never bothered us before. In the gods' name, we'd only been contacted by the sprites a handful of times ever since the Fall. His apparent objection seemed laughable at face value.

But the abbot looked around the table intently. "We will send parties to investigate the village and identify any creatures we do not normally see. Brothers Sedimont and Camdal, you will make this happen?"

"Yes, Abbot," they both replied.

"Excellent. I would also like a patrol."

"I will see it done," Brother Sedimont answered him.

The abbot nodded, then looked down to the healer. "This will reassure the villagers, yes?"

"Yes, Abbot Dreise. Their elder, Cor Tam, specifically asked if something could happen like this."

"Good. Then it is settled. Is there anything else before we continue?" Everyone looked around the table in silence. "Then I believe we were discussing the types and numbers of potions we will offer in trade for your mountain tarn. We will recess to the refectory for lunch in a few candles."

The healer left accompanied by a brother protector, both taking with them further orders made by Brothers Camdal and Sedimont, but I noticed that the people of Lehntarn watched them closely when they took their leave.

Ghaan most of all, despite him trying to hide it. I remember wondering what had interested him so much.

Capitula 18

"What are we looking for, Ghaan?"

"A book of plants to begin with … with illustrations, if one can be found."

I glanced his way, thoroughly surprised. "Illustrations? Only in the most ancient of tomes can illustrations of any accuracy be found, and even those are faded," I hedged. "I would need special dispensation from the entire council of seven to access any of those. There are some illuminated treatises and works on vegetation that are more easily accessible. Can we access those instead?"

Ghaan sighed, but readily acquiesced. Pormult was accompanying us in our descent into the library, with another two of their people following along behind. This did not include the plethora of brothers escorting us, who were almost wringing their hands with outsiders being allowed inside the library.

It had taken the abbot forcefully putting his foot down to let them inside the library in the first place, over top of their many heated objections, but his rationale was simple enough: Only Ghaan and his people knew what the living plant looked like, as all they had left was dried and crushed to be used. And, they could not read our tongue. Carrying the various tomes into and out of the library would take time and effort, both of which would also expose the books to damage while being transported, and this was something none of us wanted.

Ghaan and his countrymen could sit in one of the private studies of the council members and be presented with the books that they need, while their recollections of the elves could be communicated in private and set to record. Since no one was quite sure about even the name of the plant they sought, it would take some time to conduct the search. And since the story they agreed to convey for access to the library was not a short one, the time spent waiting in private for the various books to arrive would not be wasted.

So, down into the library we went.

It surprised me that Pormult was the one accompanying us to search for a plant, but it really shouldn't have. Apparently, the burly warrior had a lot of knowledge on herbal remedies to help with post-battle care. And though he could communicate to us the plant's description they sought, no one was quite sure if it could be positively identified without seeing a picture of it first. But the tomes with illuminated descriptions were of course the most delicate ones, thereby necessitating the plethora of brothers to help and escort the people of Lehntarn, and to further turn the pages for them for those irreplaceable books they sought.

When the Lehntarnese discovered that it was being proposed that Ghaan would descend to a restricted area without any of the others, in only my company, a strong objection was made. A very strong objection, indeed. One that included the dwarves. So, Pormult and the other two accompanying Ghaan were apparently others of their people who had some knowledge of plants, along with various herbs and the descriptions of them, but I suspected they were simply there for muscle.

I kept those thoughts to myself of course, but my suspicions were verified when the unnamed two came along with us with their arms and armor. Their gear was polished and shining as best they could, and the reason for it being worn was relegated to 'respect for the tower' and 'being ceremonial', but I suspected this was untrue. Pormult was brought his gear to adorn as well, and now Ghaan had a conspicuous though apparently ceremonial dagger, but I didn't believe the fiction they presented in the least.

To say Brother Sedimont was unhappy was an understatement. However, he was overruled.

To this day, I do not know why I remained silent regarding my suspicions.

Led to another private study that was not that dissimilar from the one I was in before, I sat with Chaltic beside Ghaan's party while my brothers left to retrieve the first books.

"Will there be any refreshment?" Ghaan asked.

"Not within the library," I told him. "Nothing is allowed in here that can possibly damage the knowledge we hold."

"Knowledge is kept up here." Ghaan tapped his forehead.

I noticed the two armored men from Lehntarn casually move to take up station on either side of the door. "It is also recorded inside the tomes we save to protect." I raised my eyebrows in the two men's direction, but Ghaan made no comment.

"You are correct," Ghaan agreed, then looked around the somewhat bare room. It was quite obvious that things which had once been here had been hurriedly removed. "What is this place?" he asked.

"A private study. I recently learned that all of the members of the council have them for their private investigations and research."

"We are not inside the library?"

"We are, but somewhat removed."

"I see. No one goes in there?"

"No. Generally no one gets behind the door in the scriptorium except a chosen few. Not even most of the monks."

"Yet you have access?" He nodded towards my robe, having seen me use my medallion to open the scriptorium's door.

"Yes. I am one of those few."

"So, this is highly unusual."

I looked at him somewhat oddly. "You heard the discussion before the council."

"Discussion?" Ghaan quirked the side of his mouth. "If that is what you call it. A select few yelling at some of the others would be a bit more descriptive."

Chaltic interrupted whatever I was going to say. "How come you speak so much better than your countrymen?" he asked.

"Blessed, I suppose." Ghaan grinned.

"Seriously," Chaltic protested. "Don't get me wrong. We can understand your countrymen, but they are not well-spoken. You have a heavy accent, but speak our tongue readily enough. What is the difference between you and them?"

"Imperial."

"Excuse me?" Chaltic asked.

"You speak Imperial, not 'our tongue'." Ghaan frowned.

Chaltic looked as confused as I was. There was his naming of our speech 'Imperial' again. I hadn't had a chance to question his naming it that way as of yet, nor had we had the time to discuss it, and it was one of the many things remaining on my list that I'd been asked to figure out. With how cautious Ghaan and his people were about revealing everything, I suspected the subject had to be handled delicately. However, Chaltic just leapt right in.

"Imperial?"

"It surprises me you do not even know the name of your tongue," Ghaan told my friend

"And you do?"

"Every descendant of the towers should know of its naming."

"And you are familiar with it?"

"Yes. I am the only descendant among my people that remains."

"I thought you were all people of Lehntarn," I interjected, confused by the distinction he'd just made.

"We are," Ghaan agreed, saying something in his own language to the rest of his people. Then he looked at Chaltic before turning his gaze on me. "This is your friend?"

"Yes. My best friend, really. We grew up and took our vows together."

"Does your friend have a loose tongue?"

"Hey–" Chaltic protested.

"He is my friend," I insisted, allowing some heat and annoyance to enter into my words.

Ghaan's questioning of Chaltic so openly annoyed me, rapidly. The tone of my voice must have offended the two nameless people from Lehntarn standing there by the door, as they both stepped away from the wall and headed in my direction. But Pormult waved them back, saying something to them while Ghaan paused before continuing.

"You have the learning of our tale, Makun Derring," Ghaan said. "There is still much to learn. Why should we trust him?" He waved to indicate his people.

"Because *I* trust him."

I was now thoroughly annoyed. Ghaan knew as well as I did that everything I recorded was reported to the abbot, and then it was discussed in council. We had discussed this point only yesterday, and I had spent long hours answering his questions around that point. Talking while Chaltic was here would make no difference about my people learning his tale, and inferring it might, made absolutely no sense. So, I decided to tell him so.

"What difference does it make to you, Ghaan? If you had any objection, you should have voiced it before we descended. There will be plenty of my brothers here to hear."

"I must be sure for my people."

There was that distinction again. "I thought you said they weren't yours."

"I am the most fluent," he hedged.

"And the one in charge?" I challenged.

Pormult grunted, but I did not take my eyes off of Ghaan even once.

He knew as well as I did what had been agreed upon upstairs. I didn't understand his challenge, or the apparent distinction he was making … or not making, depending on the time of day you were talking to him. But whatever else could have been learned was interrupted as my brothers entered in through the door, each carrying one of the tomes we'd previously requested. They sat them down upon the vacant desk, then moved to open them and begin turning the pages.

"I can turn the pages myself," Ghaan protested.

"We are not allowed to let you handle the books," a brother told him. "The brother recorder and the abbot were very clear."

Ghaan frowned but allowed the limitation, agreeing to begin perusing one of the most common tomes on healing they'd brought. It didn't make sense he'd brought that point up again. He'd known about the restriction before we descended.

"Turn to the pictures, I cannot read Imperial," Ghaan told the monk. It honestly sounded to me as if he was a bit put out.

"But you speak it?" Chaltic quickly interjected. It was exactly the question I was about to ask.

"It is the language of the towers. All who live there are required to speak it."

"Why?"

Ghaan frowned, glancing at me, and then Chaltic. "If they wanted you to know, your council would have told you."

I frowned, not understanding that in the least. "Why are you being so objectionable? We are here looking for the plant you require. All you have to do is tell stories in return. Why are you being so defensive about answering our questions?"

"Because we do not know you."

"You've come to know me well enough."

"Yes, you."

"But not the people of my order," I clarified after his pause.

"No."

"Why the distinction?"

"… For I now find myself a stranger in a strange land …" Ghaan mumbled. He looked off into space before asking, "Wouldn't you be?"

"How so?"

"Make the distinction between certain individuals and an entire people?" He glanced down at the various illuminations depicted in the tome before him before telling one of my brothers, "Next page please."

"I guess I can see your point."

"You are very endearing, Makun Derring. You are smart and approachable, and very open about what you do, or are trying to accomplish," Ghaan went on. "It is refreshing to meet someone like you since we've sought shelter here. With your people," he clarified. "Not everyone is that way."

"Which doesn't explain how you speak 'Imperial'," Chaltic mumbled.

"Or if you are the leader of your people," I said.

But Ghaan responded to Chaltic, not even glancing at me. "No. The elves didn't speak Imperial well either. They were out of practice."

"Yes?" I prompted.

Ghaan ignored me, becoming silent for a moment, then had the brother helping him turn more of the pages. "No. We almost started a war upon our arrival. We'd taught them better …"

"We taught them?"

Ghaan frowned. "There were more of us originally." Then he asked something of Pormult in the language of Lehntarn. Pormult looked at where Ghaan was pointing and shook his head. "Can one of you flip pages for Pormult?" Ghaan asked one of my brethren.

Silence accompanied his question. "We were instructed that access has only been granted to you," a brother spoke up.

Even I was a bit annoyed by this. "They have dispensation from the abbot and the entire council to be here," I reminded my brethren. "It will make their search go quicker."

"I will have to get permission," the brother insisted.

"They are just looking at pictures," I said, but my brother seemed adamant. "I am a historian. I will take responsibility for this until I know better."

The brother nodded, not entirely comfortable with my solution but apparently happy to allow me to take the blame. He sent someone off to speak with Brother Ansilin or the abbot, then motioned for someone to help Pormult.

"This is why we trust you," Ghaan remarked.

"Why? Because he lets you look at a book?" Chaltic challenged.

"No. Because he can see reason beyond rote teaching," Ghaan answered. He said something further to Pormult, then looked to the brother closest to the burly warrior's side. "He will let you know when to stop or to keep turning the pages."

The brother nodded after looking at me for reassurance, but he didn't look happy. He very cautiously opened another book for the brawny warrior, turning the page to the first picture. Pormult grunted and leaned closer, then motioned for him to turn the page.

"So, you almost started a war?" I prompted, looking back to Ghaan who was studying a page intently.

"Yes. The elves were not expecting our arrival. Vortiid has explained what he told you, but I'm sure there were limitations in what was said."

"He did, and there was."

"And he explained the reasons for our coming?"

"He said your people were running from the dead, somehow brought back to life."

Chaltic whipped his head around at that, obviously having not heard the explanation for their arrival. I thought it had made the rounds of the tower by now, but the abbot and the council must have kept its telling more protected than I had assumed. Then it hit me that neither Chaltic nor Jan had been around for that part of the story, and I wondered how much various people knew.

Ghaan pursed his lips after I said that, and then frowned. "Yes," he agreed. Ghaan ritualistically stroked his cheek with his thumb, the other people of Lehntarn doing the same while he did so. Then he continued. "We had retreated to the final redoubt when they invaded the tower. Then we came here."

"How?"

There was a significant pause before he answered. "Once we arrived here, it very much surprised the elves," he said, ignoring my question entirely.

"You still will not tell us?"

"The elves were taken aback by the arrival of a few hundred humans they did not know," Ghaan answered, still not replying to my question. He went back to the tome's pictures. "We were all armed and armored coming fresh from battle. They didn't like that very much either," he mused.

"Two hundred and twelve of you," I said, remembering what Vortiid had told me.

This captured Ghaan's attention. "He told you, eh?"

"Yes. That and more."

"Two hundred and twelve fighters." Ghaan turned back to the book before him. Then he added, "There were around five hundred of us who originally escaped."

The entire room went silent.

"What happened to them?" I asked.

There was another long pause.

"They died."

The simple explanation he made was somehow stunning. The fact that saying it affected him was readily apparent, but he spoke the words like he was absently telling me the time of day. The incongruity between his words and what I saw on his face threw me.

"Died?" Chaltic asked. "There's barely fifty of you. Died doesn't even come close to explaining it. Were you in heavy fighting?"

"Not since we left. Some of our people we killed ourselves after we arrived. To save the rest. They'd been infected you see," Ghaan explained. "The elves didn't like that at all."

I couldn't believe what I was hearing. *Over four hundred of your people died since then? By the Pantheon ...*

"So, what happened?" Chaltic asked.

I wanted to know that as well.

Ghaan took a moment before answering. "They killed some of us when we arrived. We didn't attack back …" I noticed Pormult was paying close attention to everything Ghaan said, and the rest eyed my brothers around the room with interest. "They eventually noticed and stopped fighting," he said after a pause. "There wasn't much we could do anyway."

"They just stopped?" I asked.

"In essence." Ghaan looked to the brother who was helping him. "I don't think what I'm looking for is in this one. Is there another book? Perhaps an original?"

The brother nodded, setting the bound text aside before reaching for a much older tome. He put on a protective pair of fine woven gloves before opening it, admonishing Ghaan not to touch the book at all while he turned. The artwork I saw in there was much older, more charcoal sketches than anything else, blurred by the passage of time.

"What happened then?" I prompted, remembering what I'd been asked to do by the abbot.

"We spoke." Ghaan frowned towards one sketch in particular, before he kept going on. "It was difficult. They hadn't had an Imperial speaker for over a generation, and they most certainly did not speak Lehntarnese."

It was becoming obvious that Ghaan didn't want to talk about the elves in specifics, and he fell silent perusing the pictures again. I wasn't sure if anyone who didn't know him as well as I did would have picked up on it though. But he was coming across as deliberately evasive to me.

"I bet that *was* difficult," one of my brothers suddenly spoke up.

"Yes," Ghaan agreed, nodding towards the man. "It was similar to what Vortiid described first speaking with your Derring here was like."

"Why do you call him Derring instead of Makun, or Makun Derring?" Chaltic asked.

"Derring is your name, is it not?"

"Makun Derring, yes." I nodded my head. "Derring is my family name; Makun my given."

"Ah. A cultural mistake."

I wasn't quite sure I believed that.

"Makun was the name your family gave you?"

"We think. No one remembers naming me that, but they remember it being my name, along with my family name. I am an orphan," I explained. "I was found after an attack. My parents had been killed beside me."

Ghaan nodded his understanding. "Rahdimus Ghaan, then."

"But your people call you Ghaan and not Rahdimus?" Chaltic asked.

"Yes," Ghaan answered, but did not explain further.

I frowned, but decided not to pursue it, the elves being more important. "So, you stayed with the elves?"

"For roughly a year," Ghaan agreed. "They were adamant about that."

"Why only a year?"

"And why adamant?" Chaltic questioned.

"It was what their leaders insisted upon. We were in no position to complain."

Pormult frowned.

"They provided you food and shelter?" I asked.

"For payment," Ghaan agreed.

"What did you pay?"

Pormult said something to Ghaan in Lehntarnese, which sounded cautioning to me, but Ghaan didn't even look at his man.

"The elves we found are similar to you here," Ghaan continued. "They are led by a council as well."

I noticed that he did not address my question again, leading me somewhere else in our conversation quite subtly, though obviously very deliberately. "Yes?" I asked, and some of my frustration must have entered my voice. He glanced up, and by his look, I think he noticed me realizing what he had done.

"They have a hierarchy of leaders, Makun, based on their family's bloodline. We were assisted by one family, but there are six in total. Always six with them it seems. That number is very important to the elves."

"Why?"

"I don't know." Ghaan answered, finally directly answering a question of mine. He grinned without looking up from the tome he was studying. I wondered if he knew he'd finally answered one, and was now teasing me about that, too. "They were very mysterious and closed mouthed about their rationale and traditions."

"Not so dissimilar from you," Chaltic complained. Apparently, he'd picked up on what was going on as well.

"Somewhat," Ghaan agreed, then he looked up towards me. "I begin to like your friend. He is refreshingly honest as well."

"He is," I allowed, noticing Chaltic shifting his position out of the corner of my eye. I knew a quick way to get underneath his skin was to talk about him like he wasn't there, and spoke up before any argument between them got started. "Why did the elves let you stay?"

"Their views on Life." He stressed that last word like it was somehow important. "They have built up an entire religion around it. Because of their beliefs, they could not turn a non-enemy away."

"That was very lucky on your part."

"Yes. Very lucky," Ghaan readily agreed. "They let us settle in a small village the locals called Sirikii, on the banks of a large river." He looked off in the distance. "It took some of us months to relax."

"Relax?"

"We have been fighting for our entire lives, Makun Derring," Ghaan explained. "There was no danger for us in the Vale."

"The Vale? That is what they call their land?"

"It is. It is surrounded by mountains on almost all sides. I was lucky to see some of it, travelling to our host family's many estates."

"Estates? You make them sound rich. Like the nobility of old." I waved towards one of the oldest tomes for reference.

"Rich? Yes, the elves of the Vale are very rich. Rich in all things, only found inside their domain." Then Ghaan got a faraway look. "It was magical to see."

Pormult gave him a hard look, saying something to him in their tongue. I wish I understood what was said as the two of them spoke back and forth, then even more when the two by the door shortly thereafter joined in. I was only able to glean that some admonishment about being careful was made, but some agreement was decided upon before I could determine anything more, though they had talked about it for quite a bit. Then Pormult turned back to his book, and waved for another page to be turned.

And after that, Ghaan looked up at me, then started rubbing his head.

To this day I have no talent for languages unless they are written, and Lehntarnese is a very liquid tongue. I think back often and wonder about how things would have turned out if I'd been better about it then and understood. Yet, despite my wants or desires, that was not to be.

Capitula 19

"Your headache?" I prompted as the silence stretched, not saying a thing about the Lehntarnese's discussion.

"Yes." My question seemed to surprise him, and he focused his attention on me. Then he gave me a slight nod. "It is why we are here after all. To find the cure for my headaches."

"Why is that so important?" Chaltic asked.

But Pormult cut everyone off. "Find plant. Important."

Ghaan said something to him, but the brawny man almost glowered back. Ghaan rubbed his forehead again before answering, almost like he was thinking about how exactly he would answer before he did so. "I've had them since we arrived. My people arc insistent upon it."

Chaltic and I looked at each other, then Chaltic shrugged. "I won't even pretend to understand that answer."

"Do you not get headaches?" Ghaan asked.

"Me?"

"Your people."

"From time to time," Chaltic explained. "No one has suffered from debilitating headaches for generations."

"You are very lucky then." Ghaan looked over and met eyes with Pormult. "They are a trial."

"Not luck," I explained. "Careful breeding."

"You breed out your headaches?" Ghaan asked.

"They can be a sign of lingering mutation," I explained. "Your headaches are one of the reasons both Brother Barkon and Sedimont have issues with you and your people."

"Mutations?"

"Like the altered beasts of the wood," I explained. "Humans suffer from the results of The War of the Fall as well."

"You may be assured that my headaches are not because of that," Ghaan demurred. "The elves explained I was allergic."

"To what?"

"Pollen," he said after a pause.

I didn't believe that for a moment.

"You didn't have pollen in Lehntarn?" Chaltic asked, also disbelieving.

"There are many different plants between here and there," Ghaan explained.

"Seems strange to go through all this effort to treat an allergy," I insisted.

"It leaves me debilitated. My people are very concerned." Ghaan shrugged. "When they get bad, I cannot move."

"And this plant solves it?"

"Yes."

We fell silent for a time, Ghaan and Pormult studying their various tomes, but something was still bothering me. "You don't practice selective breeding, do you?"

"No. The elves do."

"They do?"

"Yes, for generations … and as a people. You monks do as well?"

"Yes, ever since the Fall. To breed out mages and magic," I further explained.

"Breed?" Pormult questioned. His question once again reminded me that the people of Lehntarn understood much more than they spoke.

"Selective partnering," I explained. "We've practiced it amongst our people since the Fall."

"There aren't that many of you," Ghaan commented.

"No. There are not," I agreed.

"Why?"

"Death, disease, monsters, magic," Chaltic listed the reasons.

"You live inside a tower."

"Trapped inside a mountain," I disagreed. "There are things we require outside our halls. The tales of our forefathers are limited, but they describe much, and their struggle was profound."

"How so?"

"They first fought off a monster invasion during the Fall. You remember The Book of the Fall?"

"I thought that was a religious text," Ghaan questioned.

"Religious only in that it speaks of our people's past with the gods. It is mostly historical."

"You worship a history book?"

Every last one of my brother monks frowned.

"No. We worship the Pantheon. We remember them best through

174

The Book."

"Strange," Ghaan commented.

"Do you not worship the gods?" one of my other brothers questioned.

"Some, yes," he allowed. "Please turn the page." He waited until the page was turned before continuing. "But to make a religion out of it? No. My people do not do that."

"You will show proper respect for the Pantheon!" my brother demanded.

"Respect? I will show respect to the gods, but I will not bow down to you or your religion."

I waved my brother down. "This is off topic. You did not control your people's breeding?"

"No. Family and children are most important to us. Especially after what you describe as the Fall."

"But did you have mages?" another brother asked.

"Yes. But none of the An'pac."

"An'pac?"

"You do not know of them here," Ghaan explained. "Or at least I don't think so. The elves were unclear." He shook his head. "But you selectively pick your mates?"

I allowed his change of subject with the mention of the elves. "Yes. Our forefathers were decimated during the time of the Fall. There was no limitation on breeding then, but within a few generations our forefathers had already begat more mages. They weren't aware of it then, and as it is told in The Book, some generations later the mages grouped together and revolted. It led to another time of death and devastation inside the tower. Beating back that revolt led to the election of the first abbot, who brought into being the practice of tracking our bloodlines, and then selectively breeding."

"To what end?"

"To ensure there could never be any more mages."

Pormult grunted, then spoke to the other two in their tongue.

"How long has it been since you've discovered a mage?" Ghaan asked.

"Beyond the boy?" Chaltic asked.

"Eldso," Pormult forcefully corrected. He didn't look happy having to do that, either.

Chaltic waved the correction away, but I interrupted when I saw Pormult frown. "Over a hundred years ago," I stated.

Ghaan didn't look up from his book. "It seems as if your solution is effective."

"It is," Chaltic agreed.

"The Pantheon shall save," another brother stated.

"Your Pantheon asked you to do this?" Ghaan asked.

"We eliminate the mages in their name," that brother explained, then partially quoted, *"… so that the Pantheon can return to us again."* I noticed he thumped his chest in the manner of one of our more conservative believers.

"The gods will come back when every mage is long dead?" Ghaan asked.

"Yes," my brother answered simply.

"Seems a little too easy," Ghaan replied, motioning for another page to be turned.

"It is our way," I interjected before an argument could be made. "What are the elves' view on mages?" I inquired.

"They have no issues with them."

"What?" came the exclamation, in many forms, from every last one of my brethren who were present in the room. Ghaan's simple answer had touched off an explosion.

It took some time to calm everyone down. "We did not know this," I explained.

"Obviously." Ghaan looked around towards everyone in the room. "However, you are quite removed from the world hiding in your tower here."

"How can they stomach magic and mages?" one of my brethren demanded. "They slaughtered the gods!"

"People, at least. We have no knowledge of what anyone did to the gods directly," I cautioned.

"Semantics!" my brother insisted.

"Nor do we," Ghaan agreed. He eyed me strangely while thinking about something for a moment. "Though we did fight them during the War of the Apocalypse."

"The Fall?"

"The same thing." Ghaan nodded.

I was learning more from him now than I had in days. "Thank you for sharing what your people call it."

Ghaan turned back to the book. "It began our war with the dead."

"One thousand five hundred and eight years ago," I clarified.

Ghaan glanced up at me. "Six. We've been travelling here for two years."

"One of which you spent with the elves."

"Yes."

"Who have no problems with mages."

"You are correct."

"Then you've surely been damned through exposure!" one of my brethren thundered. He was clutching his medallion quite forcefully on his chest, hidden underneath his robes.

"They have since left," I reminded that brother, "and then arrived here with the loss of almost all of their people."

"A sign of their damnation!" he insisted.

Ghaan sighed. "No. That would be because of the orcs."

His mention of orcs threw the entire conversation off stride. "Orcs?" I asked.

"That's a story for children!" the brother insisted.

"No, the orcs are very real."

Pormult grunted once again. One of the men by the door stroked his cheek with his thumb, while the rest followed. Ghaan never looked up from his book, but the motion made me nervous.

Eventually Ghaan continued. "When we left the elves, they pointed us towards other human settlements. We travelled through the mountains, but as a people we didn't listen. Not to the warnings they gave."

"Ghaan listen," Pormult declared.

Ghaan nodded, then said something in Lehntarnese to him before he continued. "I did, but the leaders at the time did not listen. We were traversing one of the passes when the combined tribes attacked. Over a hundred and fifty of our people died there."

"Ghaan save," Pormult insisted.

"Yes." Ghaan patted the warrior's knee. "But at what cost? Regardless, I played an important role in the fighting. The orcs fled, and we survived to reach the keep of Ancilar on the eastern side of the mountains. They thought we were ghosts." Ghaan snorted. "Didn't much like us either."

"Ghosts?"

"The people there consider the mountains to be haunted. That keep there guards the pass against the orcs, but it wasn't equipped to take us in."

"Ghaan save."

"No. I just told them about the orcs who were possibly coming," Ghaan explained to Pormult.

"Ghaan save," Pormult insisted.

Then Ghaan shrugged, not making any further argument against what Pormult had said. "We eventually left, heading further east into the lowlands through a series of villages. And over time we reached the coast, and sought to settle there."

"You obviously did not settle," I prompted.

"No. They did not like our people much."

Pormult grunted. "Hunt, fish, farm, make go." Then he said something in Lehntarnese.

"Yes, they did," Ghaan agreed. "There wasn't enough food for us there anyway." Something about the tone of his voice told me he was hedging, but Ghaan continued his tale. "They did tell us about Tatdavarr, though."

"The lost city," Chaltic said with wonder.

"Not lost, just a long way for us to travel," Ghaan explained. "It took us three months to get to the outer city of Shardal … a haven on the plain."

"Shardal?"

"A little bigger than a town, not quite as big as the city of Tatdavarr. It sits on a river where it enters the ocean. That was where I started to run out of the plant we are seeking to treat my headaches."

"Did they have some?"

"No. But they did have something similar. They held us there for a week before they escorted us to their king in Tatdavarr."

Pormult grunted again.

"Sounds grand," Chaltic mumbled.

I could see he was totally enthralled by their story. He always had liked grand stories when we were kids, no matter that he said they no longer interested to him now.

"Sore feet," Ghaan explained. "It took us a month to get there at the pace we travelled. The old roads were in shambles, so we mostly moved with our escorts cross-country."

"Escort?"

"Basically, an army. The country is wild, probably not at all like the stories you have here. We'd lost almost another hundred people by this time, but our losses were becoming fewer as we neared civilization over the plains. We knew nothing about this land or its dangers, you see. It took us a long time to gain that learning."

"Ghaan warn," Pormult stated.

"Yes. I did my best. But even my best could not prepare us for everything we faced."

Pormult grunted again.

"In any event, we arrived in Tatdavarr amidst pomp and ceremony."

Ghaan motioned for my brother to turn the page. The brother jumped slightly before he did so, riveted as he was by the tale.

"We were greeted by the king, but cloistered by ourselves inside a certain section of the city. It took us a while to realize this, and bluntly, it was because I wasn't paying attention."

"No?" I asked.

"I was out of my herb. I did the next best thing, which was drinking, but I suffered for my lack of sobriety."

"Alcohol?"

"Just so," Ghaan agreed. "It dulls the pain in a pinch."

"We have a limited quantity here," Chaltic offered.

"I'd just as soon as refrain." Then Ghaan had another page turned. "While I was incapacitated, my people found a similar plant in the market used to help women with childbirth. It helped, and the limited amount we have left still helps me, but it was not native to the area. It was also not as effective. We discovered the plant we found was native to an area west of Tatdavarr, near a fortress outpost named Devalket, and we eventually travelled there."

"You left the lost city of Tatdavarr for a plant?" a brother asked.

"Yes," Pormult answered at the same time Ghaan said "No." They looked at each other before Ghaan once again declared "No." Pormult glowered, but turned back to his book. Then Pormult angrily motioned the brother helping him to turn the page.

"The king was not … accommodating," Ghaan continued.

"The king," I prompted.

"They still have a Gate intact in Tatdavarr. They wanted our help in opening it."

The silence radiating from myself and the rest of my brethren was profound. "Ghaan," I said to get his attention. "The Gates were lost during the Fall. The mages destroyed them."

"Not all of them," Ghaan disagreed.

His statement was stunning.

"How did he expect you to open one?" a brother asked.

"I have absolutely no idea," Ghaan quickly answered, glancing towards Pormult. "Perhaps it is because of where we were from."

"He knew you were from Lehntarn?" I asked.

"We made it no secret," Ghaan agreed. "The only thing we kept to ourselves was of us living with the elves."

"For good reason," someone mumbled. "They sided with the mages."

"They did not." Ghaan sounded offended. "They did not take part," he insisted.

"Which is the same thing as taking their side."

"To you," Ghaan allowed while eyeing the man. "The elves had their reasons."

"Which are?" I asked.

"Their own," Ghaan responded, turning away from frowning at the man.

"We refused the king and then travelled back over the plains to Devalket, not receiving any aid when we arrived. The king had sent a runner ahead, ordering them to withhold any aid until we agreed to do what he wanted us to. We refused, then wandered further west towards the mountains in search of the plant. The villagers we passed knew of it, but said it was on the other side of the mountains, which ended up being the same mountains we had originally passed through … and this became an issue. In short, because no one wanted to go through the mountains again."

He looked to the brother helping him. "Not this book either. Do you have anything on the herbs involved with childbirth or the rearing of children? Maybe it's included there." The brother nodded, then left to go get another book.

"They pointed us to another pass and we travelled through it," Ghaan continued. "We were attacked by the orcs once again, but it was less brutal this time. That, and some tribes of goblins in the night. Then on the other side of the pass we came upon a remaining citadel."

"Goblins?" one of my brothers scoffed.

"Citadel?" I asked, glancing over to quiet the man.

"An intact Imperial citadel," Ghaan explained. "From before the War. It's controlled by a warlord who is afraid of Tatdavarr, and at first he thought we were an army from them. It sits at the entrance of a pass we found and utilized, along the banks of an inland sea."

"There is no inland sea in this area," I said with absolute certainty.

There were no remaining maps of the area, but this entire side of the mountains was wooded hills. The constant cover which hid the monsters around us was one of the main reasons we stayed to our mountain.

"With all of your books and knowledge, you, Makun Derring, are wrong," Ghaan emphatically said. "We stood along its banks, and I defy you to tell me that we were imagining things. Decidedly cloudy, almost dirty, the water has a strong and distinctive taste to it. Something like metal is in its flavor, and the people there strain and boil it before its use. Even the fish are odd looking to me, one of them being a mutated thing with eyes almost on the side of its head. But the people there fish for it and eat it, along with the rest of the sea's harvest, and doing so does who knows what to them in the process."

"That sounds unclean."

"It is." Ghaan nodded. "Bathing in it leaves a distinctive odor."

"You are having fun at our expense," Chaltic insisted. He was much more knowledgeable than me about the tales of our surrounding area, considering his interests, but even I knew there was no sea anywhere nearby.

"Truth," Pormult insisted.

"It cannot be true," Chaltic maintained. "The only notable feature east of here is the city of Són. It's fabled to be located against the mountains you supposedly came through. The tales of our forefathers' state there are not even supposed to be any mountains there, between our tower and the plains I mean. The only reason we know that mountains exist there is because apparently the ancient sprites told us so."

"There is no city where you speak, though the mountains definitely exist," Ghaan said. "Though 'son' sounds similar in Imperial to what the people have named those peaks."

"Tatdavarr exists, so the city must, too," Chaltic eventually replied. "And it's pronounced Són, not son."

"All I can say is this fabled city of yours is not there. Though there are multiple villages in the area. They, at least, knew of the plant."

Chaltic frowned.

"So, you stayed there?" I interrupted, not wanting to get off track.

"No. The warlord wanted nothing to do with us. He bluntly told us to take our herb and go. With the king waiting beyond the pass behind us, and the warlord insisting we leave, we basically had nowhere else to go. Then the common people of the area started warning us about what to look out for, filled with stories of creatures and monsters in every tale we heard. This is when we started learning about a fabled tower of learning and knowledge, hidden somewhere beyond the forest, with golden walls and enough food inside to feed the entire world."

He screwed his face up into a sarcastic grin. "You can see why this interested us. That, and the common people telling us the plant we sought grew more commonly in the western woods. We were down to around a hundred and fifty of us by then, left out of basically five hundred who had escaped the fall of our nation, and even if we discovered only the ruins of a tower, we'd hoped our medallions would open it. That, and we could use the knowledge and supplies we found therein to survive."

"Which is what led to your journey here," I concluded.

"Which is what led to our journey here," Ghaan agreed. "It took about a month and a half for us to get here. Unfortunately, this area of the world has become inundated with monsters," Ghaan explained. "The journey was much more difficult than we feared."

"Fight. Poison," Pormult added.

"Yes, many predatory creatures haunt the woods," Ghaan confirmed. "And then, of course, I was poisoned."

"How did you meet the sprites?" Chaltic asked.

Ghaan looked to Pormult, who shrugged, before Ghaan answered. "Apparently, they were looking for us."

"The sprites?" I clarified.

"Yes. There are no sprites or history of sprites in Lehntarn. They are a fantasy tale to us. Most likely much like we are to you. When the sprites first arrived, we thought we had died and gone to our final journey under the Way. But before I had all but succumbed to the poison, I learned they had been tasked to watch out for us."

"By whom?"

"The elves," Ghaan explained. "Apparently, they must not have been as ready to let go of us as we thought." Ghaan got a faraway look in his eye before he shook himself to continue. "In any event, they led us here."

"To when you arrived … That was quite a tale of your journey."

Ghaan shrugged. "I am simply happy to be alive." Then he dug his fingers into his forehead, wincing as he rubbed. "Though another headache is coming on. Is there somewhere to lay down?"

"Not in the library."

"That couch looks most comfortable," Ghaan said, ignoring my comment entirely. He got up and then laid down on it, closing his eyes while he continued to rub.

"We can pick this up tomorrow," I offered.

"No. We will remain here. I just need to rest," Ghaan explained. "Pormult can look while I do."

Chaltic and I looked at each other and then shrugged, the two of us not caring as long as the books were protected. The hours stretched on, Chaltic leaving to go get my things for my writing, and then returned so I could record Ghaan's tale. Then that first monk who had left returned, telling us that after eventually being admitted to speak to the council, that they said it was fine for Pormult to look through the books … as long as he did not touch any of them. By this point, the permission was so redundant it was silly to receive it, but I appreciated it had been asked and that permission was given.

We broke for the evening meal in the refectory before we returned to our search, Ghaan and his men joining us to eat with the rest of our order. Then we returned to the study, continuing to allow Pormult to peruse the books with my brother's assistance. We didn't find what they were looking for that day, but I was able to make a coherent record of Ghaan's journey with his assistance, Ghaan lying on the couch with his eyes closed the entire time I was writing. And he was open about making corrections when I made any errors in recording it, explaining he was simply upholding his part of the bargain that allowed them to search.

When it finally became too late, we left the library and Ghaan was escorted back down to the village. We said our goodbyes before he left, and admittedly I enjoyed my time with him in the library, but I knew he was still holding things back. He was open about what he would and would not say in mine and Chaltic's company, something I found very refreshing, as were the rest of his people. And Chaltic and I seemed to have made an impression on them, the people from Lehntarn being more relaxed in our company than they ever had before.

But it wasn't until later that night that a thought hit me as I reviewed the overall day. How Ghaan and the rest seemed to shut down when the rest of my brothers were present. Something I remembered Vortiid saying when we first spoke.

No say all, he'd told me in his broken common … *No say all*.

And it left me lying in my cell wide awake, wondering what Ghaan and the rest had not said with the rest of my brothers present.

I had no doubt that Ghaan had not told me all.

Capitula 20

"Punch!"

I threw my fist forward, hitting the stuffed target to the best of my ability, which admittedly wasn't great. My attack was accompanied by a plethora of grunts and sharp exhales around the courtyard as my brothers did the same. Practice was normally something I avoided, only doing it when it was absolutely required, knowing combat of any type was most certainly not part of my calling. However, I was the target of much greater scrutiny today, and could not disappear into the crowd to avoid embarrassment this time.

I'd missed many of the brother protector's weekly exercises in my time spent with the Lehntarnese, and Brother Sedimont had apparently made an issue of it. Speaking before the council, I suddenly found myself caught in the middle of some sort of power play between the abbot and the brother protector because of my lack of exercise and expertise. But despite the long, ever-so-polite conversation the two of them had had over it, and their disagreement over my priorities, I found myself here.

"Sloppy, Brother Derring," one of the brother protectors called out. "The brother protector was right to insist on you training today."

I frowned, but that was all the reaction I made.

I'd never been particularly interested in fighting beyond studying the strategies and tactics mentioned in some of the older works I'd seen. However, every brother in the order was required to be minimally proficient in defending ourselves, despite our individual postings or duty. Everyone participated in the defense of the Spire and our community whenever it was required, no matter who you were.

So, here I was.

"Makun," Vortiid called out from the far side of the courtyard.

The older warrior stood and started ambling my way from where he had sat and observed since our practice began. He and a few of his other people had come from down in the village to watch when I was recalled for practice with Chaltic. I think it amused him to see me struggling based on the comments his people shared, but I'd noticed they'd watched the protectors as much as they'd talked about me.

I had a suspicion they were taking the protector's measure. I had another suspicion they were not impressed by whatever they saw. And it made me feel better thinking about that fact while I sweated.

"Makun. Turn fist," Vortiid directed as he came closer.

He told me to punch out again, and then stopped me mid-motion after I did so. Chaltic watched as Vortiid took my fist and rotated it sideways before it was fully extended, then nodded emphatically as if doing so was somehow important. Then moving my arm, he repeated the gesture, extending my arm while rotating my fist through a series of guided punches, before backing away and motioning for me to do it myself.

I did, not really noticing much difference, but Vortiid seemed satisfied with what I was doing. I did notice a change in the sound the target made as I hit it, but that was about it. That, and the brother protector wasn't riding me while Vortiid was offering one-on-one instruction. Chaltic looked down at his own fist then started copying what I'd been shown, trying a few practice punches while the brother protector looked on, but I didn't notice much difference with him either. But nodding in thanks to Vortiid, that brother protector wandered down the line to bother another one of my brethren, thereby leaving us alone.

It could have been Vortiid's flat look that'd helped him turn away, though.

I wiped the sweat out of my eyes and got back to it, worried the brother protector would come back once the older warrior's back was turned. And off I went, punching out again and again while the brother protecter returned to calling out the cadence of our exercise.

"Punch!"

The day had begun oddly strange with a noticeable tension underlying the mood of the village. I didn't understand the source of the increasing uneasiness, but then again it wasn't my job to investigate. I had my own duty. The lay brothers kept a finger to the pulse of the village and its people, and looked into any odd happenings there.

I'd heard they'd found nothing regarding the most recent death, and as far as I knew, everyone's fears had been put to rest. No hint of any altered beast was found inside the village, and likewise the patrols outside had found nothing as well. My brothers even gave credence to Untark's man and his rumor regarding the supposed 'creature' he saw during the mage storm, and searched diligently for anything they could find out about it.

In the end, they didn't find a thing.

No, I imagined the uneasiness had something to do with the dwarves now that they were staying with us, situated not that far away from the Lehntarnese as they were. Between the two groups, these 'strangers' made up a little over an eighth of the total number of villagers, which was a large amount of people for them to take in. And, I was fairly certain that superstitions were now surfacing in private, no matter how much they were publicly denied. I'd have to remember to ask Jan when practice was done, but I was almost certain my thinking about their tally was accurate. Then I remembered I hadn't seen her recently, and wondered what she was up to.

"Punch!"

I threw my fist forward, sloppily turning it like Vortiid had shown. It hit firmer this time, something I finally noticed as a brother protector continued to call out the cadence of our strikes, and the courtyard was filled with the sounds of grunting as me and my brethren continued our practice. The brother eventually called a halt to what we were doing, the lot of us backing away from the targets we'd been abusing with a series of happy deep breaths.

"I think he's out to get us now that you're here," Chaltic complained as he bent over, placing his hands on his knees to rest while he breathed.

"Me?"

"Yes, you," he griped. "This is the first time he's led practice in ages."

"Who? Him?" I asked, nodding my head to one of the older brother protectors who'd been making my life miserable this morning.

"Yes. Or anyone else for that matter."

"They always lead practice when I'm around."

"I know." Chaltic glared. "When you're not, we practice on our own."

Another one of our brothers nodded his head, obviously listening in and just as tired as we were, agreeing with everything Chaltic had just said.

"We will finish with a light run, brothers," a brother protector called out. There were sighs of relief before he continued, "Three laps up and down the switchback to the village is appropriate, I think. Let us be about it, brothers."

Now I was certain he was just trying to hurt me, picturing the switchbacked trail in my head. To be sure, I walked the trail every day, sometimes multiple times a day, but I took my time like everyone else did. To run it three times in a row? That was going to be torture, and by their reactions, most of my fellow brothers felt the same.

We had just left the gate when we noticed a commotion below. It was the dwarves with a bunch of Lehntarnese, surrounded by a group of villagers. They were being yelled at by Untark Mar, the muscled villager accompanied by a bunch of his followers, and armed as well. I wasn't certain what the problem was, but by the posturing whatever was said was heated, and it couldn't be good.

Vortiid and his men caught sight of the commotion as well and then caught up to us before we reached bottom, and I couldn't help but notice that none of them seemed to be worn out in the least by their run.

"… had another man die!" a villager accused.

"No kill!" one of the Lehntarnese insisted.

"Aye, laddie," a dwarf put in. "We not be havin' anythin' ta' do wi' it."

"Nobody died before you people showed up!" Untark Mar exploded.

Frowns were on everyone's faces all around. Both the dwarves and the Lehntarnese faced off with the upset villagers, everyone's countenance tense and grim. But after that last accusation, the dwarves and the Lehntarnese faces became suddenly flat, and cold expressionless eyes became abruptly worn all around.

"Hold!" I cried out, not knowing what else to say. Untark Mar had absolutely no idea what he was doing, and I needed to stop this before it led to bloodshed over him insulting their honor.

Untark spun around on me. "Why should we? For all we know they're harboring more mages. They already turned one of our own!"

Vortiid looked like he was about to lash out and I grabbed ahold of him without thinking. It was like grabbing onto a moving block of stone. "They had nothing to do with it, Untark," I rebuked the man as calmly as I could. Vortiid's arm was vibrating under my own. "Now what's going on?" I demanded.

"Blasted monks!" He glared my way. "The stranger's brought something with them! Carden Nalt was just found dead. Dead! We need to search them for whatever evil they bring!" he said, pointing to the dwarves and the Lehntarnese.

The dwarves were reaching for weapons, then Vortiid sent someone running away.

"Did you let the brother healers know?" I hurriedly asked, looking past them for anyone with more authority than me. This was rapidly going to devolve into blows if I couldn't put a stop to it. I moved to put myself between him and the dwarves, but there was no way I was going to move Vortiid.

"Not yet! And why should I? I know they had something to do with it!"

"To do with what?" the village elder's voice called out, breaking through some of the tension before me. I looked over, seeing Cor Tam being helped to hurry in our direction by a young boy. The elder looked more upset than worried, which was a good sign as far as I was concerned.

"The killing of Carden Nalt!" Untark shouted.

"Who's killed Carden Nalt?" Cor Tam asked.

"One of them! We found him dead in his home!"

"And did you see any of them around? Standing over him?" Cor Tam demanded, waving his hand to indicate the dwarves and the people from Lehntarn.

"Don't need to! I know they had something to do with it!"

"Gods save me, Untark. You can't go accusing people of killing if there's no proof! Even if you don't like them!" Cor Tam shook his stick at the burly man. "Especially the dwarves who are our allies! Do you like milk?" he asked, verbally pointing towards the mountain Tarn we were trading the dwarves for. Then he waved his stick towards Vortiid. "I don't be liking them either, but them people have been here without issue for weeks!"

"Untark! Carden has the marks!" one of his men shouted, trotting up from behind.

"What marks?" I asked.

"The same ones Mastin did." The man glared my way, almost

bristling that I had asked.

"Bite marks?" the village elder questioned.

"Yes, same as before."

"Did they ever find the bug that did it?"

"Them monks never found nothing," the man said disgustedly. Then there were a lot of glares suddenly cast my way.

Chaltic and the other brothers from our run closed in tightly around me. The conversation and mood was definitely devolving, with distinct groups being formed. There was me along with the rest of the monks from the tower, the villagers, and then the dwarves and the Lehntarnese. Each group was standing a bit apart from each other, and all were staring at the others warily and with heat.

I sent one of my brethren off toward the Spire to summon the healers. "Elder Tam? I sent for the healers. If we could go see Carden Nalt's remains?" I prompted. It took everything I had to remain calm.

The elder eyed me for a moment, then spat before nodding his head in agreement. Then amidst objections and grumblings from Untark Mar and his men, the lot of us wandered further into the village to see the poor soul's remains.

Thank the Pantheon what little calm we had remained.

"How die?" Vortiid asked.

"I thought you knew," Untark accused.

"Untark! That will be enough," Cor Tam admonished him. "It is a question that all of us want to know. Answer it."

"Aye, laddie. I'd be doin' tha' afore ya' go throwin' more accusations around," a dwarf said.

I noticed then there were a lot more dwarves around than there had been a moment ago. The villagers that weren't accompanying us were hurrying away, and there were shutters and doors being closed all around. I think Untark noticed that too, him being a little less brave as he caught sight of all the armed dwarves around him.

At least no blades had been drawn yet, but I was worried it was still a close thing.

Untark frowned but complied. "His wife found him, said his boy told her his dad had a funny look on his face. She said he was sat outside, eyes bulged out with the marks all over him."

"And the dwarves and the other people did this how?" I asked.

"He was outside!"

"Oh, aye. We lured him out here on the other side of the village," another dwarf sarcastically replied.

Untark spun around to glare at him, but Vortiid cut him off. "No kill," he quietly said. Somehow, the simple statement stopped whatever Untark Mar was going to say.

"We are being led to the other side of the village from where they camp," I put in. "It doesn't make any sense for them to be a part of it, Untark. The entire village would have seen them come this way to get here."

"Carden has the marks all over him," he insisted.

"And we still don't know what made them."

"We'll get nowhere until we see them," Elder Cor Tam interrupted us both. "Let's go."

As a group we arrived at Carden Nalt's house, a well-kept single story home with a loft above, just like most of the homes in the village. There was a woman weeping on the doorstep, and another woman hugging her who knelt by her side. Cor Tam took one look at them and somberly asked where Carden was, being directed out back to the yard behind. And there we found another group of Untark's men who were keeping everyone else away, all of which backed off as soon as Cor Tam raised a fuss for them to allow us to enter.

And there we found Carden Nalt, an older man about the age of Vortiid if I had to make a guess about it. His face was weathered from being outside, his dead eyes vacant and glassy while his body sat slumped in a rickety chair. He had the strangest expression on his face, something between wonder and terror, and his mouth was hanging wide open.

But what was most noticeable about what I saw there was the random scattering of palm-sized round marks that were here and there all over the bare skin of his corpse. They reminded me of insect bites, with an even red tint to the skin that encompassed the entire area of the mark. They looked raised, well maybe just the tiniest bit, but definitely a little. And I agreed at first glance with what had been said: they looked like insect bites of some kind.

The only problem was their size. They were the size of my palm, every last one of them. My entire palm, mind you, which was much larger than any bite or bites I had ever seen. Cor Tam leaned down to study one, the bite appearing larger the closer he got. And I had to wonder what creature had made them, finding myself agreeing a bit with Untark's wild and angry alarm.

"It ain't natural," one of the villagers said.

I found myself wholeheartedly in agreement.

"It's the same as before," Elder Cor Tam muttered, then looked to catch my eye.

"Exactly the same?"

"There's more of them this time, but that's it." someone said.

Cor looked up from the marks, then turned to gaze about the yard. "Besides that, they're the same," the elder agreed.

"And no one's seen anything new?" I asked.

The village elder shook his head, but one of Untark's men took that moment to open his mouth. "Nothing new except them people," he accused.

The dwarves had obviously had enough of that. "Ya' want ta' be doin' somethin' about it, laddie?" one of them asked. Then another one drew a blade.

"No blades!" Cor Tam thundered. "They had nothing to do with it, you idiot! Do they look like bugs to you?"

Untark's man frowned, but remained silent and didn't answer. He didn't look even the slightest bit apologetic, though.

"Who looks like bugs?" another voice asked.

A brother healer walked into the yard, accompanied by a few of the brother protectors. He took one look at Carden Nalt's remains and made a sign to the Pantheon, then pulled out his medallion to kiss it. Then coming closer, he leaned over to close Carden Nalt's eyes. "When was he found?"

"Moments ago," the elder explained. "We actually just arrived."

"I still say they had something to do with it," Untark mumbled, not quite loud enough to be offensive, but enough to carry.

"No one here had anything to do with this," the healer definitively stated. Then he leaned in even closer to study the remains.

"How do you know?" someone asked.

"I examined Elder Mastin's remains," the healer answered. "This looks exactly like what we saw there. It's some kind of insect."

"You didn't find nothing!" one of Untark's men accused.

"No, we didn't, but we'll look again." The healer looked up from the remains. "Brother Derring, could you go inform the council?"

"The whole council?"

"They're in closed session," the healer explained. "That's why I'm here and not Brother Camdal. As far as I know, you're the only one they've recently let in."

"Absolutely." I nodded my head, wondering why they were in closed session in the first place. There had been a lot of them recently.

"Let the brother healer know I'll secure the house and the surrounding area. We'll need more people to conduct a search again. That and more healers depending on what we find."

"We help," Vortiid offered.

"We can do it ourselves, outsider," another one of Untark's men objected.

"Ya' want ta' say somethin' ta' us again?" a dwarf challenged.

"What are you going to do about it if we do?" someone else replied.

"I said enough!" Elder Cor Tam interrupted. "We better do it ourselves," he said to the people of Lehntarn, somewhat apologetically, but nothing hid the suspicion I saw there.

There was a bunch of grumbling from the villagers, and frowns from everyone else around, but Untark's people looked smug. They eyed the dwarves and the Lehntarnese, hands firming on weapons as the grumblings grew.

"Come on, let's go," the dwarf said to the people from Lehntarn. He eyed Cor Tam and his people before turning back to me. "An' tell your council we not be happy abou' tha' accusations," he added. "No' happy at all."

I nodded, then followed both groups out of the courtyard and back into the village. I escorted them part way to their compound, then turned away towards the Spire, feeling the eyes of the villagers on me as I hurried away. And I remember hoping beyond hope that I made it to them and got the help we required, before anger, suspicion, and the many attitudes below devolved even further to descend into blows.

Capitula 21

"They have almost unfettered access to the library!"

"Completely untrue!"

"True enough to deliberate," someone else shot back.

I stopped outside the door to the abbot's chambers, stunned I could hear people shouting from inside.

"It is an offense against the Pantheon!"

"To give an ailing man a chance to find a plant?" the abbot asked. Even I could hear his sarcasm through the door.

"None except those of our order have descended into the library in generations," the brother recorder rejoined.

"Exactly!" It took me a moment to recognize Brother Barkon's voice as the one speaking. The brother chanter sounded furious to my ears. "The first formed our order to protect the library!"

"Which we have done," the abbot replied. "Ghaan and those that accompany him go nowhere except where we let them."

"You let them into the library!" the brother chanter retorted.

"We are all well aware," Brother Randilon replied. The lay brother was often the peacemaker during disputes in the village, and it seemed he found himself in the same role within the council as well.

"There is no precedent," the voice of Brother Sedimont broke in. "I still say we should have the brother protectors guard them at all times when they enter."

"Why? Do you seriously think they'd harm one of ours? They come from their own tower!" the abbot insisted.

"So they say," Brother Sedimont retorted.

"You honestly are going to sit here and tell me you doubt them?" The abbot sounded incredulous. "You've seen their medallions."

"No one doubts the medallion's veracity," Brother Ansilin answered. "However, there is no record of any person or persons of any tower being so militant. I have looked."

"You've heard what young Makun has reported," the abbot replied. "They've been fighting an implacable enemy since the Fall."

"The dead?" Brother Sedimont asked. "That sounds as made up as any children's story. How can we verify the truth of their claim without putting the lot of them to question?"

"Which we shall never do," Brother Camdal insisted as he broke into the conversation. "What is the root of the problem here? Would we deny a man a plant that would help him? No. The issue, Abbot Dreise, is allowing them access to the library in the first place to find it. You made that decision without consulting the council. I would suggest we find it for them to resolve our dispute."

"That bird has already flown now," Brother Margonest said. "You cannot take back something that has already been offered and given."

"We most certainly can," the brother protector declared.

"And yet we shall not," the abbot answered the man. "None of us have seen this plant, not how they describe it. Would you know what to look for? Would you?"

I glanced behind me down the speckled stone hallway, stunned by what I had heard. Such a heated and uncouth argument between the council members was unimaginable, but my curiosity got the better of me. I wanted to know what they said. No one could catch me here listening though, and my nerves became frayed upon thinking that.

"Of course not," the brother recorder answered. "But we could bring a selection of books to the scriptorium for them to view."

"Which is still unacceptable," the brother chanter replied. "Strangers given access to the library? The scriptorium where we work? It is an offense to the Pantheon, I say."

"How?" the abbot answered. "The dwarves have been given access before. The Pantheon did not strike us down then."

"Abbot Dreise!" Brother Barkon thundered.

"Enough shouting," Brother Randilon cut in. "This is getting us nowhere. Ghaan and a few of his people have been down to the library. Have they learned anything?"

"About the plant? Nothing," Brother Ansilin answered him.

"And about the other thing?"

"They walk by it every day. Ghaan keeps his medallion on him at all times."

"You've seen it?" the abbot questioned.

"He pulled it out of his shirt to place it in the slot where we place ours in the scriptorium," Brother Ansilin replied. "He asked after seeing me use mine. It fits but does nothing. Besides, it is bronze."

What does that matter? I thought to myself, but someone else started talking.

"How does his medallion fit? It's square," Brother Barkon asked.

"The outer design is an eight-pointed star," Brother Margonest said, and then pointed out. "An eight-pointed star is basically two squares."

"Which is beside the point," the abbot interrupted. "Their medallion does nothing. There is no danger or risk."

"No danger?" Brother Sedimont challenged. "They admit to staying with the elves!"

"Over a year ago," the abbot retorted.

I heard a scrape down the hall behind me, and I whipped my head around to see what was there. If anyone saw me listening at the abbot's door there would be questions. Hard questions. Questions I did not want to be answering.

My nerve almost broke, but I saw nothing there.

"It does not matter. It's the elves. Do you want anything that has to do with the elves here?" Brother Sedimont sounded like he was at wit's end.

"There are no elves here, Brother," Abbot Dreise soothed. "Just the survivors of a lost tower. A tower we," the abbot paused, "that we all thought was lost. By the Pantheon, all of you, don't you see what an opportunity this is? What we can gain?"

"At what cost?" Brother Barkon retorted. "Access to the library is bad enough, but if they find some way into the sanctum, everything we have will be lost."

"Lost?" the abbot chuckled. "Nothing will be lost Brother Barkon. There is no way for them to get in. It is as simple as that."

"That we know of."

"Which is why we need to assimilate those people into our order as soon as we can."

"But how can we, when we don't know what they suspect?"

"Which is why I sent that young man Derring down with them."

"Who is doing a remarkable job," the head of the brother recorders reported. "His reports come daily, without skewing anything that he reports with personal opinions or shading," Brother Ansilin continued. "And what he does think, he marks as a personal insight of his own. We are lucky they have accepted him, and even more so that they are willing to share with him what they have."

"See?" the abbot stated. "Precautions are being taken."

"I do not like it," Brother Barkon answered.

"Neither do I," Brother Sedimont immediately said. "Nor do I like–"

I heard another scrape down the hall behind me and could no longer wait. I knocked firmly on the abbot's door, and conversation in the office immediately ceased.

"Yes?" the abbot's voice rang out.

"Abbot Dreise, there is a situation in the village," I called. "I've come to inform the council."

"Can it wait?" came Brother Sedimont's frustrated voice.

"There's been another death, Abbot," I replied. "Tensions are high."

There was a significant pause before the abbot answered. "You may enter."

I opened the door and strode in, and was immediately hit by a wall of tense emotion not normally found among those in the tower. Abbot Dreise sat behind his desk, but the rest of the council was spaced around the room seemingly at random. I nodded to one and all before speaking, and ignored the tension I felt.

"Abbot, Brother Camdal, Councilors, there has been another death in the village. An able-bodied man, Carden Nalt, was found only this morning. The healer who responded has requested the presence of the brother healer."

"I will go then," Brother Camdal said, raising his aged bones off the couch where he sat. "Is there any more information?"

"And why are you not at your assigned practice?" Brother Sedimont sharply questioned.

I bowed my head generally toward the room and everyone in it. "The practice was finishing when there was an altercation at the foot of the trail to the village. Untark Mar was accusing the dwarves and the Lehntarnese of killing a villager. I helped Elder Tam defuse the altercation, but the situation remains tense. A group of us travelled to the house of the deceased villager where the body still lies. It is covered with marks. The healer said they looked like the marks on the other villager who died before."

"I believe we should all go," the abbot said. "Calmer heads and all that."

"We could all do with a change of venue," Brother Margonest agreed, causing eyebrows to raise around the room.

I almost stopped myself from speaking, but I could not. "Excuse me, Councilors, but the situation remains tense. Accusations were made by Untark Mar and his people that led to drawn weapons. The dwarves and the people of Lehntarn have returned to their areas, but their anger at the accusations he and his people made remains high."

"Damn. I will meet you there with more protectors," Brother Sedimont said as he hurriedly left the room.

"Come, Brother Derring. I wish to hear your observations while you escort me to see Carden Nalt," Brother Camdal said.

"The body can be brought to you," the abbot offered.

But Brother Camdal waved his words away. "No, Abbot Dreise. I will take these old bones down to the village. They know me there. I was present for most of their birthings, after all. My sheer presence alone may defuse the situation before it erupts."

And upon hearing that, the abbot acquiesced. Which was how I returned to the village in the presence of the entire council of seven.

✳✳✳

"They are the same marks. You are correct, Brother," Brother Camdal patted the brother healer on the back. "We will have to examine the body further in the Hall of Healing to be sure, but I personally have no doubt."

We were back in Carden Nalt's yard, and his property, the council, and everyone else present surrounded by almost every brother protector in the tower. The village was still quiet, a sense of foreboding exuding from it, but not from Untark Mar's men. Those villagers with him were wandering around aggressively, turning over and rooting through everything they could find in an apparent effort to search for the insect or insects that did this. Untark, however, remained at our side.

"It's more mages," the burly man declared.

"These marks are most certainly not magic or mages," Brother Camdal scoffed.

"It's a hex! The bastard mage put a curse on us all before he died!"

Someone sighed, Abbot Dreise simply turning away from the man to address the rest of the council. "Another search must be made. Your thoughts on the creature?"

"Something small?" Brother Camdal pondered. He turned towards the village elder. "Nothing was seen that could have caused this?"

"No." The village elder shook his head. "His wife said nothing was amiss. The neighbors reported nothing unusual either."

"Then most likely it is something small with a foul humour. I would guess something smaller than the size of a hand. Maybe even smaller. It could easily be the size of a fly or something like that, Abbot Dreise."

"Which will be almost impossible to see, let alone find," Brother Sedimont added. "We will conduct another search."

"Interesting that it found two people who were alone," Brother Barkon said.

"We cannot make that assumption," Brother Ansilin objected, raising his brow. "Both men were found alone, true. But we cannot assume they were targeted because of it."

"But we cannot dismiss it either." Brother Sedimont motioned for one of the brother protectors to begin his search. "We will need greater access than before. We should probably search the houses."

"Search houses?" a liquid voice called out.

Everyone there turned to see Rahdimus Ghaan walking closer to the gathering, being escorted by a few of his men and some dwarves.

"Why are we searching houses?" Ghaan went on.

"To find the culprit that did this." Brother Sedimont waved his hand towards the body of Carden Nalt. "Unless you have something to add? Or that you might know?"

"Beyond my people and the dwarves having nothing to do with it? No." Ghaan looked to the abbot. "It seems certain accusations have been made."

"So it seems," the abbot agreed.

"I can speak for my people the same as you. Is there something the monks wish to say?"

"No."

"Or you?" Ghaan turned towards Cor Tam, steadily meeting the eyes of the village elder. "You think my people have something to do with this?"

It stood out to me that Ghaan was calling everyone 'his people' right now. It was something he had been adamantly denying in both public and private to me before.

"No," the elder eventually answered, and he didn't look happy answering that. "Though people are a right upset."

"An' they have reason ta' be," a dwarf growled before Peltic pushed past the speaker to come forward.

"Aye, ya' have a right ta' be angry an' mourn yer' dead. But the Spire needs ta' have a care with what they say abou' their allies."

"My brother monks have given voice to no accusation," the abbot soothed. "I'm certain whatever was said was in the heat of the moment."

The abbot very deliberately looked at the village elder, who joined him in turning towards Untark Mar. The burly Untark glared at Ghaan and the dwarves but remained silent, almost obstinately so. There was no missing his knuckles turning white on the shaft of his spear though.

"Good," Peltic answered, eyeing the man.

"Have the dwarves ever encountered markings like these?" the abbot asked.

"No. No bastard bug big enough to be leavin' welts like tha' be livin' in tha' mountains tha' don't bite yer' head off in tha' first place."

"Ghaan?" The abbot turned towards him.

"No," he answered shortly, the man back to rubbing his head. "What we fought does not leave welts." He said something to one of his people, that person looking back and forth between Ghaan and the corpse with a frown. His people looked gravely concerned, though I doubt anyone else picked up on it.

"Then we will conduct a search."

"All houses and structures," Brother Sedimont quickly put in.

The abbot raised an eyebrow in his direction but it was Peltic who spoke up. "Ya' meanin' ta' search our dwellings?" the dwarf challenged.

"In an overabundance of caution, I'm sure," the abbot soothed.

"Yer' meanin' ta' invade our privacy?" Peltic demanded.

"Your pavilions only."

"And anything large enough to contain an insect," the brother protector added.

"Ye'll do no such thing!" Peltic protested along with a loud mass of grumblings from his countrymen.

"There will be no search of our things by outsiders," Ghaan

added, now firmly rubbing his head.

"They have something to hide! I knew it!" Untark Mar shouted. "I knew they did it!"

"Be silent!" Elder Tam shouted back, but he didn't look like he entirely disagreed.

"I agree, such accusations have no place here," Brother Randilon added, returning to his role of peacemaker. "I agree a search must be made to eliminate anything that may kill us, but I also understand the need for our visitors to retain their privacy. Is there some compromise that could be made?"

"Yes. Is there?" the abbot said, looking to Ghaan, Peltic, and Elder Tam for an answer.

"Allow them to conduct a search of their own belongings," Brother Margonest suggested. "The dwellings we know and can search, but their things are rightfully their own. I'm certain no one wants to deny that a search must be made if there's something hiding in the village that can kill us."

"Killing us, not you!" someone shouted from the back.

Elder Tam turned to glare, but whoever had said that kept their head down. However, Untark Mar's people were remarkably closed faced in that direction, almost suspiciously so.

The following silence stretched.

"We can agree to that. I offer to allow Makun Derring to observe our search," Ghaan said after a moment, nodding towards me. "He has proved himself honorable …"

The abbot and Brother Barkon both raised their brows before turning in my direction, but I didn't miss Brother Sedimont's disapproving frown.

Ghaan continued before he could speak. "… Peltic, could he perhaps observe your people, too?"

"Aye," Peltic hedged, obviously finding something odd about Ghaan's suggestion by his tone. "If tha' fighters suggest it, I can be agreeing to it."

Ghaan dug his fingers tightly into his head and then looked up. "We do." He smiled my way as the man he'd previously been talking to started to say something and then continued to speak in Lehntarnese. But Ghaan waved the man away after listening for a moment. "I believe that will address your concerns, Abbot?"

"It will." The abbot nodded, looking to the brother protector.

However, Brother Sedimont did not look pleased.

"Then the issue is resolved," Ghaan concluded. "What will happen if we find nothing?"

"Then we need to search outside the village," Brother Sedimont declared.

"My people will volunteer for such an expedition."

"Aye, as will mine," Peltic agreed.

"Then we will arrange for it." The abbot turned to face Brother Sedimont directly. "Actually, arrange it now. A party to patrol outside the stockade, made up of all of our peoples. Outfit them for combat."

"Yes, Abbot." He still didn't look pleased. "We should start with ten men."

"Ten of yours for an insect?" a dwarf challenged, which started a debate into who and how many people should go.

I, however, was pulled aside by Brother Ansilin. He directed me to go and observe the dwarves and the Lehntarnese's search of their belongings. We were joined by Brother Barkon, who also directed me to make a record of what they did and did not have for the council. The brother recorder remained silent as he said this, and I found myself uncomfortable to do what he asked.

But I had no way to refuse.

Which is how I found myself leaving the sad corpse of Carden Nalt as the talk of armed parties went on, to go make a record of everything the dwarves and the people of Lehntarn had.

I felt decidedly dirty as I walked away.

Capitula 22

In short, nothing was found.

This led to a period of heightened anxiety within the village, and between the brother protectors and our two groups from afar. The continuing accusations made by Untark Mar did not help, and the comments by him and his men only added to the villager's unease. Ultimately, after another day of searching, the investigation was called off, but not without a slew of objections. And one of the greatest objections was made by the dwarves, who were told in light of the mysterious killings, they should not leave to return to their homes for their own safety.

The supplies we would normally give them for their return journey would now not be provided, as we didn't know if we would need them for an outbreak of disease or infestation, which is what Brother Camdal was now most concerned of. It seemed a hollow reason to me, as I didn't recall any concerns besides insects stated before now, but it was the will of the council, so it is what it would be.

After this, the trade talks continued unabated, though they noticeably no longer made any headway. The dwarves' anger at being kept confined to the village was readily apparent, and they complained about it during the ongoing talks in the Spire quite loudly. But Peltic said he saw the reason for the restriction even though he didn't agree with it, so their protests were voiced only to us monks who lived in the tower. However, they stopped holding back against the accusations down in the village, a few of Untark's men sporting noticeable bruises as the days went on.

The Lehntarnese were noticeably relaxed with what had happened, making no comment about me observing them searching their things. In complete opposition to the dwarves, they readily opened their bags and packs in my presence, diligently searching through them for anything to be found. As I said before, there was nothing discovered, but the differences between them and the dwarves was distinct. And beyond a few tomes and foreign curiosities that I greatly desired to handle, there was nothing of note that stood out beyond their concern about Ghaan.

Reporting this greatly frustrated Brothers Sedimont and Barkon, who I recall taking me to task over some of the things I had written. But the abbot put an end to my heated questioning, pointing out repeatedly that nothing they feared was there. Strangely, it was his insistence that nothing of the elves was found among the Lehntarnese things that finally put a stop to it, continuing on to say that it had come out quite clearly that the dwarves didn't trust the elves either.

It was a strange time and a strange series of days. One that has stood out in my memory ever since they took place.

"The Pantheon shall save," my brethren and I replied, our voices echoing around the Hall of the Pantheon.

I was not sitting in my usual place, this morning assigned to escorting visitors to observe our worship. The council of seven had closed the library until tempers were less frayed, citing that the manpower needed to assist Ghaan in his search was required in the village instead. I found this an empty reason, but Ghaan and the Lehntarnese accepted it readily enough, though they did seem a bit put out being kept from their search.

However, Ghaan expressed an interest in observing our worship since he had nothing else to do. He petitioned the abbot, and his surprising request was discussed in council. It was reasoned him visiting the Hall was a harmless enough request over minimal debate, though they did wonder why he did not want to hear from the friars or the chanter himself, so I found myself at his side for our worship.

The man seemed greatly interested in the proceedings, grunting periodically and making curious noises as certain things were said and done. I found his reactions annoyingly distracting, considering the solemnity of our worship, but it did make me think and wonder while his reactions continued unabated as the service went on.

Brother Barkon advanced to the dais, standing before the alter behind its gilded podium. From our position down in the hall, he seemed silhouetted on the circular engraving imprinted upon the wall behind him. Its curious markings made an ovular arc that looped around his head, framing him in some strange manner that stood out to us all. And Ghaan had seemed curiously intent upon its engravings, pointing it out as soon as he had entered the Hall of the Pantheon, along with every other engraving he saw.

"Today, I chant to remember from The Book of the Fall," the brother chanter intoned, beginning his almost ritualistic opening. "Chapter three hundred and twenty-two, page eight thousand two hundred and three. I turn to the words of Abbot Crell Tó, 'On the Alteration of Beasts'."

A suitable subject for today, I thought as Brother Barkon slowly turned the page. Ghaan's escorts for the day whispered quietly to each other in Lehntarnese, but fell silent when I glanced their way.

"I begin my chant … beginning verse six." He paused, and it seemed almost for effect. *"The gods are lost to us, and in this time of our damnation the mages have further cursed the worthy. For though they achieved their dastardly aim, their demonic desires were not sated by this alone. No, brothers, in this time of desperation, the authors of our beloved Pantheon's fall have unleashed their hated creatures upon every last one of us. Not satisfied by achieving their goal, they seem to take great delight in tormenting the faithful with their ongoing death and destruction.*

"Taking simple creatures, the hare, the squirrel, the songbird, they alter them, working their despicable desires upon innocent flesh. What was once a pleasant and godly creature in the eyes of our Pantheon is now a hated invader.

"The destruction of Cordatal, Maisus, and Talonthall to the altered hares ... " My brethren and I thumped our chests with our fists, whispering the names of those long-lost cities as they were spoken. *"... Naked in their visage, with teeth like daggers and claws of wrought iron, the altered hares devoured them, eliminating their peoples.*

"The desolation of The Golden Plains by the harmless mole, growing hair like thorns and a stinger of acid, burrowing to attack the desperate farmers as they walked overtop of them. Their spread eliminated our crops in this time of doom.

"Even the gentlest of songbirds has become the crier of oncoming heartache. Speeding with barely observable speed to impale its target upon its lengthened beak, then sucking upon its blood until only a husk is found, they sound our doom. These are the things that the mages have left us, brothers. The terrors they inflict upon us. This is what our world has become."

A few of my brethren continued to thump their chests, their displays of marked piety making soft sounds throughout the hall, but

Brother Barkon continued.

"Be warned, brothers. Be steadfast. Be slow to trust. For the mages are everywhere, hiding their evil in the guise of travelling strangers and gentle things, offering to help us survive when in fact they look to destroy us. They seek to kill, my brethren. To root out every remaining scrap of knowledge that we retain of our gods' greatness, so that they may achieve their ultimate aim one day."

I couldn't help but think about Eldso, but my wandering thoughts were interrupted by the next question.

"Do I know their aim? Can I speak of it? No, in my shame I cannot. But as we bury our most recent dead to the slaughter of the altered beasts that slew them, that our world now has wandering afoul among it, I turn my mind to examining the conundrum of their aims. And I ask myself, what is or was their ultimate gain?

"Our world is now destroyed, brothers. Civilizations have been slaughtered or crumbled. Contact with the far continent is lost. Mountain ranges have been leveled. Seas have dried up. The races are almost completely divided. What in every gods' name was their aim?

"The elves, assistants to the gods, who once worked openly with every race around to help and hold have disappeared from the land ... all contact with them has been lost. We hear rumors from varied survivors that the dwarves have gone to ground, disappearing into their homes and shutting their doors upon the world. The halflings have been trampled, their innocent and joyous selves totally unsuited for what our world has become. The gnomes ripped from their studies, thrust out of their institutions, and forced almost criminally to defend and fend for themselves in place of learning.

"And even the warrior races, once combatting the dangers of our ancient world have been slaughtered with wild abandon. The hated orcs and goblins have spread, breeding uncontrollably in this altered world without the checks or balances that were once upon them, and they conquer the land around us. Word coming from the sprites stating that they are combatting their spread into the forests and hills that surround the mountain we hold, but that it is a lost cause, and hope is lost. Meanwhile, this diminutive people who helps us, appears to be devolving to become one with the trees, like it was rumored from whence they had originally sprung.

"Then there are even taller tales of horrible new creatures,

further alterations and abominations made from animals that we the pious once knew. And dare I say there are now fabled to be thinking altered creatures, reaching the pinnacle of unholy aberration, that the mages have decided to inflict upon one and all. That these new threats continue to wage their war of annihilation upon the peoples of our land, seeming to target any abode of safety that comes into being. To lay waste to any memory of that happier time before the Fall."

Ghaan shifted in his seat, turning this way and that to gaze upon the rapt attention of my brethren and their reactions to Brother Barkon's words. The solemnity of the moment was at odds with how he was looking about, and I was pulled out of my intent attention by his motion. Then he met my eyes, something in them looking back at me, before he quickly turned away to pay attention to the rest that was chanted from The Book of the Fall.

"No, brothers, these last few hundred years have been our downfall. We are a dwindling people, eking out our pitiful existence only by the grace of the gods. Our piety saves us, protecting us against the evils the mages have inflicted upon our world.

"One was found only a week ago now past, and I must say it brought great joy and satisfaction to the people when the witch's life was brought to an end. Her cries for mercy while she burned alive were horrible, but our hearts must become as stone so that the threat all mages pose can be punished and eliminated so that none may return."

I thoughts shot to Eldso again.

"Harden your hearts, my brethren. Become like the stone that the dwarves so greedily harvest. The mages brought about the Fall, to this there is no debate any longer. By inflicting their apostasy and creations upon our world, the resultant apocalypse that followed was either by design or by accident, but it matters not. The perversions they created now do haunt us, and we must be ever vigilant against their demonic incursions unless we would have them come to kill us again.

"For even the simplest of ants may one day be our downfall. The tiniest of creatures someday being mutated through the mages' apostasy into a monster. One that gives warriors and steadfast men horrifying nightmares while their hive advances to kill us all. These thoughts do worry me my brethren, in this time of our survival after

the Fall.

"For I know; I have fought them."

Brother Barkon stopped talking, raising his medallion to kiss it softly before returning it to his chest. Most of the rest of us did also, the quiet sounds of rustling cloth a soft undercurrent to the mood as the brother chanter closed the Book of the Fall. And the dull boom of our blessed tome as it shut authored in a pregnant silence that descended upon the Hall.

I must admit, I was moved.

Brother Barkon took his time to meet all of our eyes before saying, *"The Pantheon shall save."*

His gaze seemed to linger on Ghaan and I most of all.

"The Pantheon shall save," I replied along with my brothers, bowing my head in the brother chanter's direction.

He frowned, a miniscule thing, barely a shifting of his lips, but I saw it anyway. Then Brother Barkon stepped away from the podium to begin his sermon.

"Before any of you ask, yes, I chose that passage on purpose. And its purpose should be obvious to any of you who have a brain. Abbot Crell Tó lived over a thousand years ago, the third abbot of our order if you remember your history lessons." He nodded to Brother Margonest, acknowledging the brother teacher before he continued on. "Abbot Tó lived when incursions were common. When hard lessons had yet to be learned. When the threat of alter beasts, which we later simply grouped under the moniker of 'monster', were much more common."

He waved a hand over his shoulder. "I asked the abbot there to check our records to verify what I thought. Abbot Tó lost close to three hundred survivors during his time as abbot. The brotherhood was newly formed, our strictures yet ill-defined, but he and our brethren strove on to survive.

"They did not relax their watch. They did not wave our restrictions to take any and all in." He glanced towards the abbot. "They formed the area outside our walls as a holding area for any who might approach. To vet and sequester. The village that area became almost forming into a waiting area for penitents before becoming accepted into our order. And the decisions that they and our forefathers made in that horrible time of hardship and struggle still guide us all."

He seemed to look in my direction. "And today, even when new challenges and experiences come to face us, we can turn back to that time to see for ourselves what those who came before thought and tried. To see for ourselves how things worked out for them. To see what succeeded or failed … and how our brothers survived."

I wondered if he was trying to give me some kind of message, but he kept going.

"And Abbot Tó also dealt with a plethora of invaders. Not men, so much, true. But invasions of altered beast seeking to inhabit the tower." He waved his hands around the room. "Monsters that even invaded here. To where you now sit. To defile our great Hall and turn it into a cave of death and depravity haunted by gloom.

"Did he and our brethren of that time allow this? No. No, they did not. And as we have just heard they fought against the mages of that time, burning them as we do today, to ensure there is nothing left of them to return. Nothing left to heal. Nothing left to remember them by, but for the absence of our gods. To the Pantheon, to whom we all pray."

Brother Barkon looked down at his feet, then shook his head. His voice was quiet when he began speaking again.

"Do you know the true role of the chanter?" he asked, raising his head to gaze at us all. "The villagers think it is to shove worship of the Pantheon down their unappreciative throats. But the true role of the brother chanter, and all the brother chanters before me for that matter, is to speak to what we remember. What those who came before went through, and to give voice to the cautions of the past so that we, the Monachi Spirae, can make the most informed decisions to protect our order. To preserve the knowledge we guard for the betterment of all, in hopes of a bright and glorious future."

He turned away from the congregation, then ran his hand along the altar in an almost delicate caress.

"Do we pray for the return of our lost gods? Yes. We most certainly do. And you hear our songs and prayers daily as we lift our voices in high hosannas to our many gods. But our main role is giving voice to the memories the brother recorder records … and the brother teacher instructs us on, during the times of our lives.

"And the memory of that time before has been both recorded and instructed upon. Just as Abbot Tó fought the mages and the altered beasts of his time, we have killed a sorcerer and are being attacked by a monster in ours. We have met one challenge, hardening our hearts to end the life of a mage that sought to infect us all by spreading its very evil. But now we are facing the deaths of those waiting in the village below. Deaths by some unknown creature, authored in by that vile mage, which attacks the pious and those we protect, in its corrupted desire to rid the world of any and all.

"Will we let this diabolical creature ultimately win? No. In the Pantheon's name we shall not. But just as we hardened our hearts to burn that child mage, we must harden our hearts to the cries of anyone who resists us in stamping out this unknown monster that infects us now. And we must listen to the hallowed words that guide us from the past, as they are written, so that we do not make the same mistakes that our forefathers once did."

He paused to look out around the room once again, then nodded firmly before returning to the podium. "For the chanters remember the words of the past. And hear me brothers, we chanters will not allow our brethren to forget them." He looked out upon everyone in the room.

"The Pantheon shall save," he sang out.

"The Pantheon shall save," we all replied.

Then Brother Barkon turned and bowed to the abbot, then to that lone candle the chanters kept ever burning that represented the Pantheon. Then he kissed his medallion once more and slowly returned to his seat.

The mood was solemn and somber, and I thought about the trials my brethren had endured in those times long before.

But Ghaan's eyes seemed to burn from his seat.

Capitula 23

Ghaan had many questions.

"You put much faith in the words of this book?"

"It is basically a record of our civilization."

"In one book?"

"Well, no," I corrected. "The formative years only. It tells of our survival during and after the Fall. They are the recollections of those who came afterwards, and the stories they were told of what happened leading up to and during the War of the Fall."

Ghaan nodded his head, then leaned back into the pew to look up at the altar. "An interesting book."

I glanced back and forth between him and the altar, his comment seeming inane. "It is," I hedged, not quite knowing what he meant by that comment. "Though Brother Barkon would be a bit upset about the Book only being thought of as 'interesting'."

"He would," Ghaan agreed. "From what little I know about the man, he most certainly would."

"Ghaan?" I waited until he met my gaze. "It strikes me again how much better spoken you are than any of your countrymen." I waved a hand towards his ever-present escort.

"I am." Then he nodded further into the room. "You call this the Hall of the Pantheon?"

"Yes."

"This was the entry room to our tower."

"Entry room?"

"Yes. I recognize it. Well, without all the decorations. It is from where one came and went when they visited our tower in Lehntarn."

"You had no edificium?"

Ghaan nodded, glancing over his shoulder that way. "We did. We called it the vestibule." Then he descended into thought.

"Strange."

We fell into silence, myself trying to imagine the room without all of its idols and decorations, though his people continued talking quietly in their tongue.

"Are we allowed to wander the room?" Ghaan asked.

"Yes, though the chanters will return in a bit to begin their songs."

"Songs?"

"Prayers for the return of the gods. They sing in remembrance before meals every day."

"That is a lot of singing."

"It is."

Ghaan rose, waving for his countrymen to return to their seats. They did so, I assumed being content to let their leader wander about since there was only one entryway to the room, which was behind them. I rose to follow.

"These are the depictions of your gods?" he asked, approaching one of the pillars lining the wall. Atop it stood a bust of Zebbad, god of the fields and farmers.

"Of all of our gods," I said, watching him run one finger along the face of that figure. It made me decidedly uncomfortable watching him do that.

"Not mine," Ghaan said. "I give my loyalty to Aspiros."

"Aspiros?"

"God of learning and knowledge."

"Do you mean A'Piron?"

"I have no knowledge of that name, but it sounds close."

"Brother Ansilin would be very interested in hearing your names for the gods."

"I'm sure he would." Ghaan turned away. "Would he have you write it down for him, then store it away in the library?"

"Yes."

He fell silent for a time but then asked, "Would anyone but you know the difference?"

"Yes?" I looked at him in confusion.

"I am not so sure that they would," Ghaan replied, turning away from the bust. He started to rub his head as he walked, stopping to peer at one depiction or another the further along he went.

"We are not a bad people, Ghaan."

"I do not think that you are. Misguided perhaps, but no, not inherently evil."

I stared at him, thinking he looked somehow ... lonely. "Strong words for someone who is taking shelter with us."

"Yet I think they are true. The people of Lehntarn, my people, value truth and honesty before all, Makun. Almost embarrassingly so. Will you tell me now before your idols, that your leaders are being completely open and honest with us? … Or you?" he added shrewdly.

I didn't even think about lying to him. I simply met his gaze as dispassionately as I could, copying how he sometimes looked at me.

"I thought not," he returned, then turned away to continue his walk. "Admittedly, we do not know each other, but your leaders and the people below have not extended us much trust."

"I disagree with that sentiment. You yourself have descended into the library. That has not happened in generations. Many generations, if the rumors are true. That is more than a little trust for us."

Ghaan acknowledged the point with a nod. "So the dwarves have told us. However, your people are exceedingly stingy with the books you protect, I'm told."

"They need protecting."

"They do."

Something told me he was waiting for me to ask a question. I thought of a few, but resisted opening my mouth. I wanted to hear his reasoning without any influence of my own, and I was prepared to wait him out to get it.

"What you protect also needs shared," Ghaan eventually uttered.

"We do share our knowledge."

"For a price. Always a price, the dwarves have said."

"Is that not fair?"

"To a point," Ghaan granted. "It becomes miserly when people die from being unable to afford what you ask."

"I have not heard of anyone who's died from a lack of knowledge about something we did not share."

"No. It doesn't surprise me you've heard nothing."

I was taken completely unawares by that comment. "You make it sound as if you do," I challenged. "Someone who's only been here for a few weeks, I might add."

He glanced to meet my eyes for a moment, then turned away towards the next bust without answering. "Zaxxon?"

"Zax Xona, god of thieves and assassinations."

"An interesting god to display."

I thought to say something in response, but Ghaan abruptly turned away. I studied the aged bust, the scar across its face the only defining feature left to be seen to distinguish it from most others. I'd honestly never looked at it in that much detail before to see it.

"Did you not protect what you had?" I asked.

"You forget, Makun. Our tower fell to protect every last one of our people."

"Yet you did guard it?"

"Yes. Against any and all, we guarded it."

"And did you just let anyone enter your tower to search what you held?"

"No. But we were under siege, Makun. You, most certainly, are not."

"Then you chose who could access your tower the same as we."

Ghaan stopped to study me, seemingly searching for something in what he saw. It looked like he was going to say something further, but then he turned away and began rubbing his head.

"The headaches are getting worse?" I asked into the silence, when long moments had gone on without a word.

"Yes. They were especially bad the night before that man was found."

"A curious coincidence."

"An annoyance is what it is." Ghaan sounded frustrated. "Some of my people think my headaches warn of oncoming danger."

"You are a seer?"

"No." Ghaan's instant reply was emphatic. "Absolutely nothing of the sort." He glanced back towards his people. "Simply headaches, ever since I came here."

"Allergies you treat with a plant."

"Supposedly. The elves had a bitter tea which treated it better."

"Yet this is not the plant you seek?"

"They said they feared their ingredient could not be found outside of their territory."

"The substitute being the leaves from the plant you are looking for?"

"Exactly." We'd reached the end of the line of pedestals and figurines. Ghaan stopped for a moment to look around, then looked up towards the altar. "Can we ascend the dais?"

"You may. Please respect the altar and candle."

Ghaan nodded, then ascended the stairs. It felt strange to ascend the dais like this. Like I didn't belong there, or somehow would be getting into trouble if I did. But Ghaan appeared as if he was completely unmoved, walking up and then onto it as if he had not a care in the world.

He was silent as he looked out from on top, his eyes unfocused, and obviously deep in thought. I didn't want to disturb him, but I remembered my orders and could not refuse. "The elves provided the tea you have?"

"Originally." Ghaan grunted. "Your abbot is still interested in the elves?"

I remembered what Ghaan had said about his people moments before and went with the truth. "Yes. I'm under orders to learn what I can."

Ghaan half-turned to look at me before running a gentle hand over the altar. "Is that the complete truth?"

"Yes. You said you value it. I do listen."

Ghaan grunted, but returned to silence.

"Ghaan?" I prompted after a bit.

"The truth then. Yes. The elves made the tea. Their mages did."

I glanced his way.

"Their civilization is filled with magic," he said as if talking to himself. "Everywhere, and in everything. It is much different than it is here."

"You met mages?"

"Yes. Many mages. Many of them were good people."

"Which means that some of them were not."

"Can you say that every person who is not a mage is good?" Ghaan challenged. "Here? Before your Pantheon?" He waved his hand about.

"No."

"I appreciate your honesty. I don't think I would receive the same answer from your brother chanter."

"No, you would not." Ghaan seemed more open with me right now than he had ever been before, so I took a chance. "Vortiid told me he would not say all when he spoke your tale."

Ghaan nodded.

"Will you?"

Ghaan did not answer, turning away from the altar and walking up to the engraving on the wall. He ran his hand over a part of it, tracing some of the symbols that were chiseled into the wall around the oval with his finger. "Do you know what this is?" he asked, tracing another symbol after he'd asked that.

"No. No one does. It is not in any of the languages we know, even other race's languages we have a copy of we've been unable to translate. Some of the examples we've compared it to are in languages we can't even identify, just like this one. We assume it's in the language of the gods, but we do not write or speak it."

"Close enough," Ghaan muttered before turning away. "No, Vortiid did not tell all."

"Will you?" I asked again.

He seemed surprised I'd heard. "No. No I will not."

"May I ask why?"

"Did you listen to what your chanter said a short while ago?" Ghaan asked.

"Yes?"

"Then you know why."

I cocked my head at him, asking him to explain by the gesture itself.

Ghaan placed both hands upon the altar, planting himself firmly, and then looking out over the room before he responded. But what he said wasn't an answer. "A thousand men."

"Excuse me?"

"A thousand men were below me the last time I looked out from above." I squinted my face up in confusion, but Ghaan continued. "Your chanter would wage a holy war against the civilization that helped me. That helped all of our people, Makun, whether you would believe it or not. Would you turn your back on that if it'd been done for you?"

"No."

"That is why I will not answer your questions."

I tried another tack. "We are taught the elves shut themselves off from the world during the War of the Fall."

"Yes. Your book makes great complaint about it." He waved his hand towards the tome on the podium. "The author blames the elves for everything, including society's fall, from what little we've been able to figure out."

I'd forgotten I'd given him a copy. He must have read more than I'd known. "Then you know my next question."

"Not until you speak it."

"Why you?"

"Excuse me?" My question seemed to surprise him.

"Why were you allowed to stay with the elves? Why were your people granted permission to stay for a year if they hid themselves away? Why did they give you that tea?" I paused but then added, "What makes you so special?"

"Can it not be simply because of the kindness of their hearts?" He was back to rubbing at his head again.

"Not if both you and Vortiid openly tell me you have not told me all." I watched him, waiting for him to respond, but he remained silent. "What makes you so different?" I prompted him again.

"Ghaan?" one of his men called up. Ghaan looked up and they discussed something in their tongue, the liquid syllables of the Lehntarnese language echoing weirdly throughout the chamber while they spoke. Then the man rose and looked to me once Ghaan had sufficiently answered. "Makun, Ghaan go Vortiid."

Ghaan waved the man down, a short conversation going back and forth again before the man settled back down. "They are concerned about my headaches," he explained.

Something told me that wasn't quite right. I'd become more adept by simple exposure at reading their body language and picking up on what was said. Ghaan's escorts seemed somehow tense, and there were a slew of guarded words they'd said that I did not recognize.

"Treated by a tea made by the elves and elf mages."

"Treated by a plant which was provided by elves who happened to be mages that knew better," Ghaan corrected me.

It was a blatant evasion.

"One of the things I always enjoyed was learning about other races," I said, completely changing the subject. "They have always caught my imagination. Elves living wherever they are; the dwarves in their holes; halflings in their hidden homes; the gnomes in their halls of learning; but one race has always stood out to me."

Ghaan turned my way, obviously confused by my sudden change in subject.

"We don't know much about the sprites even though they live in the forests surrounding our mountain. They don't bother us, and we leave them alone, only seeing one every couple of decades or so. We saw more sprites when you arrived here than we have in a generation, and I wished I could have talked to one before they'd gone."

"They are a strange people. Slow to trust or speak."

I nodded my head. "Two things stick out. The first is something that I was told … that the sprites were told by the elves to look out for you. I think it was Vortiid who said that." Ghaan frowned, but didn't interrupt me while I continued. "The other is something I read. How the sprites as a race were allied with the elves before the Fall."

Ghaan frowned even more, but held onto his silence.

"Now I don't know much, Rahdimus Ghaan, but I do know some things. And one thing I know is that a sprite will hold their oath as firmly as a dwarf will, which my people know a dwarf will die over before they break it. It is simply who they are. And even if we no longer believe the sprites evolved from trees like we once did, we do know one thing the sprites comprehend quite well, which are plants and what you can do with them. And the sprites said they did not know of the plant you are searching for, from what your people have said."

I stopped talking, gazing pointedly at Ghaan. For once, the man turned away. It seemed my conclusions had struck home, and what I'd said had made him uncomfortable. But I didn't want to shut him off.

"I have said nothing of my suspicions, Rahdimus Ghaan, but if I can follow that line of reasoning, I'm sure others can, too. And now that I know that elven mages provided you that plant? And that they made your tea with it? Well, that raises all kinds of questions. Questions that provoke other questions … and questions that you and Vortiid are not answering."

But Ghaan said nothing.

"What is the risk you pose to my order?" I asked.

"Will you tell the chanter and your abbot?" Ghaan asked in return.

"My people have reasons not to trust the elves."

"Less of a reason than you know." Ghaan sighed. "Would you blame an entire race for hiding when your people hunt them?"

"No. And we do not hunt them."

"Your abbot and chanter would," he disagreed. "Your protector would, also."

And there was nothing I could say to deny the truth of that. The reason for Ghaan and his people holding back was becoming quite clear.

"The dwarves do not trust the elves, either, Ghaan."

"They have a history that explains this."

"Yes?"

"It is a history that is not my story to tell."

I frowned. "Someday, you will need to speak more than what you have now."

Ghaan nodded. "Agreed. Here is something you can say to your abbot. I was the reason we were allowed to stay with the elves."

"Excuse me?"

"The elves. Their reason was me."

"Again, what makes you so special?"

Ghaan sighed. "I am the last of my tower."

I raised my brow.

"You call yourself monks. The Towers of Knowledge had no such position. We are all keepers; tower's keepers is what we were called before the war. You have forgotten through using your bastardized Imperial. I am the last remaining keeper of my tower."

"I've never heard that term."

"No. It is not even hinted at in your book." He waved his hand towards the gilded tome on the podium again. "There is much you've forgotten."

"And you remember?"

"Yes. Though there is much knowledge you have that I wish we had known."

"You should share what you know."

He paused before speaking, then all he said was "I know."

"Will you?"

"I don't know."

Then Ghaan stood and pulled his amulet out of his shirt. It was square where mine was round, but I recognized some of the symbols on it with only a glance. What surprised me about it though, was that it was not the medallion I'd seen when he'd first arrived. This one was golden, a shimmering, almost glowing, amulet that was the same color as the one the abbot wore.

He traced the symbols on top of the altar, coming to rest upon the circular symbol of my order. I recognized the eight-pointed star that surrounded it as the two squares I'd heard Brother Margonest talking about, and Ghaan seemed to recognize it as well, slowly taking his medallion over his head and slotting it into one of the squares. It fit snugly, almost like it was made for it, but it did nothing else besides emit a soft click once it had settled.

"Ours were turned on their side," Ghaan mentioned, then looked off into the distance. His hand he kept gently placed over the medallion as he stared.

"Ghaan?"

"The symbol was rotated."

His eyes went unfocused again, and it seemed like he was studying something that was not there.

"Ghaan? Are you well?"

"I will help with your inconsistencies to pay for this burden, Makun."

"Burden? What burden?"

"The burden of keeping us. The dwarves were very clear it would only be a matter of time before payment for what has been provided came due. Payment cannot be set by your order, and it is already becoming an important matter. The matter has been discussed, and there are now some things I can share."

"I guess thanks are in order."

"They are." He nodded my way. "I will share them with your Brother Ansilin and the other record keepers, that is all. We have no problems with that part of your order."

"Thank you. The brother recorder will be very appreciative."

Ghaan nodded, descending into silence before speaking once more. But what he said initially made no sense to me.

"Special classes."

"Excuse me?"

"The elves taught special classes, Makun. That is how I speak your Imperial so well. There were a few of us in them. The rest of them died. It took us almost a year."

"They let you stay in their realm until the classes were over?" I guessed.

"Yes."

I didn't quite believe it, and knew he was holding back, but I somehow also knew he wouldn't say anything more. "Thank you for telling me."

Ghaan grunted, but still kept looking far away. Then he stood up from leaning upon the altar and retrieved his medallion, tucking it back into his shirt. He stopped when he got close to me, then looked long into my eyes.

"I would not be, Makun Derring."

"Be what?"

"Thankful. You have been fair with us, and I will be fair with you. I would keep the knowledge of what I have told you this day to myself, Makun Derring, if I was you." Then Ghaan walked away to join his people, before the lot of them left the room.

I stood behind the altar and that gilded podium, deep in thought for some time. When I finally came back to myself, the lone candle to the Pantheon was the only one watching me, and I felt decidedly uncomfortable under its gaze.

The flame flickered while I thought about the many secrets that had come to my order. Some were now open, some were partial secrets, and some were only my concerns and suspicions. But I was keeping them anyway from the people in charge, from those who led our blessed order.

And the candle flickered again when I realized I had already decided to do just that. To keep them. To keep those secrets.

I left the Hall before the chanters returned.

Capitula 24

Ghaan was true to his word after that curious conversation, descending into the village but returning every day to meet with me and the brother recorder. Adding to the annals with what he knew, he spoke of the various gods, their names, their attributes, and what he knew of them to the ecstatic reception of the tower. Even Brother Barkon was thrilled, emerging from his hostile suspicion of anything new and strange to marvel at what Ghaan decided to tell them.

And what he passed on I could tell was the complete truth, even if I hadn't known what I knew about the Lehntarnese before now. He was completely open, correcting what was said and discussed as best he could, while admitting openly the things he did not know. His depth of knowledge was amazing, though limited in scope, only having the barest knowledge about anything considered even the littlest bit esoteric.

What he did know was about hands-on tasks, and his depth of knowledge there was amazing, and it was obvious that some of the daily tasks he described he himself had taken part in. He showed an example of written Lehntarnese, and then translated the first few pages of The Book of the Fall into his tongue in his curiously spiked hand for the council. It was a treasure trove of knowledge the tower was giddy to receive, only interrupted by his worsening headaches and the many breaks that his pain required.

It was obvious whenever his head pained him, and I was present one morning when Brother Ansilin challenged the abbot and the council's decision to close the library to him. In short, Brother Ansilin was completely on the side of turning Ghaan loose in the library to find the plant which would cure his headaches. The knowledge he shared was just that great. Brother Barkon and Sedimont were appalled, and a few of the others remained hesitant, but the Abbot, Recorder, and the Brother Healer were firmly on the side of finding the plant the man needed which was required to heal him.

It was a strange time. Especially since it came to light one day while I was in the room with our leaders that the council had made the decision to lie about why the library had been closed. And I made myself as inconspicuous as I could when that point came to light in their discussion, then tried to make myself even smaller when Brother Sedimont noticed my presence and glared my way.

I think the only reason I was even in the room while the council discussed that point was because of my relationship with Ghaan and the Lehntarnese, and something told me that would come to a quick halt if I made a fuss. Especially after I heard Brother Sedimont report in detail about Eldso's mother's questioning, and then her purification which concluded with her eventual ending, thus leading to that bloodline's ultimate demise.

The entire ordeal sent shivers down my spine.

Like I said, it was a strange time for a new brother recorder, and dare I say, a brother historian. A very strange time, indeed. Especially once the deaths continued.

"Another one?"

"Yes, Abbot Dreise. A woman this time, known to wander outside the stockade in search of the herbs she uses."

"Where was she found?"

"Just inside the gates. She was found by the Lehntarnese on their way out to patrol further down the mountain."

Abbot Dreise scrubbed his face. "And they still insist on doing this, Makun?"

"Yes, Abbot. It is their way. Expecting them to stay idle behind the walls of the stockade is simply not what you should be expecting of them. Passiveness is not their way, and the dwarves have joined them in their search for the plant, along with whatever's causing the bites."

"Do they interfere with the protectors?"

"No," Brother Sedimont admitted. "They make an effort not to interfere. We do not need their help, but it is as Brother Derring said. They refuse to stay in their dwellings no matter what we ask. At least the villagers have the sense the Pantheon gave them and have decided to stay safe."

The abbot sighed.

Why exactly I had been called to this meeting of the council of seven wasn't entirely clear, and therefore I'd been as quiet as possible. There was a curious atmosphere to the room. One of annoyance when discussing the mysterious deaths, then frustration and impatience when it came to the people of Lehntarn, and finishing with a resigned distraction when discussing the dwarves. I had always thought our leaders discussed issues that involved us with solemnity and grave poise, and it was an education for me to see the council's unguarded and unscripted reactions.

"What is Ghaan doing?" the abbot asked me.

The entire council turned towards me. "He has taken to bed in the home we provided. His last episode seems to have taken it out of him, and he almost had to be caried back to the village this time. We haven't spoken since he retired."

"We must find the plant he seeks," Brother Ansilin said. "The depth of his knowledge is amazing. It is a gift of the Pantheon, and we must have it recorded."

"Dangerous knowledge," Brother Barkon challenged. "Some of what he says is in direct contradiction to our teachings."

"Yet what he says is remarkably consistent," Brother Margonest said. "What he reports is very obviously considered common knowledge to them, and where they come from."

"But is it true?" the brother chanter asked the room.

"There is no way to know," the brother teacher admitted. "It is not as if we can go to their tower to check."

"If they even come from a tower," Brother Sedimont mumbled.

The entire council looked at him.

"What?" He glared back. "Since when does the entire population of a tower take up and become so comfortable with arms? They could be escaping invaders, having sacked that tower."

"I'm not even going to address that," the abbot stated. "But I sympathize with Brother Barkon. There is no place in my heart for the elves. They refused to help the gods when asked. Our records tell us that much. And, they refused all contact with our forefathers immediately following the Fall. Ghaan's apparent friendliness towards them is concerning."

"But is that enough of a reason to deny a man knowledge of a plant that might heal him?" Brother Camdal questioned, the elder monk cutting to the heart of the problem at hand. "It is obvious his headaches and condition are worsening ever since their meager supply has run out. I believe they only have a pinch left. They've asked for alcohol to dull the pain, something I am loathe to provide, but I think we should do it."

"Maybe a drunken tongue will reveal the truth?" Brother Barkon suggested.

A few of the others simply looked at him in surprise.

But Brother Sedimont cautioned, looking directly at me, "Which is a matter for private council."

I suddenly found myself under a plethora of eyes.

"Open the stores," Abbot Dreise said into the awkward silence. "Brother Randilon? We have enough?"

"More than enough, Abbot. We barely drink what we brew. There is enough to recklessly trade away to the dwarves if you wish, and still meet our needs for the next year or two."

"Ale?"

"For consumption in case the water is fouled, yes," Brother Randilon confirmed. "Then there is still our experiment with wine, and the clear alcohol Brother Camdal's predecessor requested for use by the chirurgeons."

"That wine is foul," Brother Barkon complained. "It tastes like a decadent syrup with the undertone of the bottom of my shoe."

"If you know of a better fruit or method of production, take charge." The lay brother looked annoyed by the wine's description.

"We are getting off track." The abbot looked around to the rest of the council. "Brother Derring? Go with Brother Randilon and take some ale down to Ghaan. I believe your friend Chaltic has been helping you? Use his assistance to take it down. Then stay down there and see what else you can learn while he drinks it."

"I report everything to you already, Abbot," I protested.

"Yes, yes, but more of a focus needs to be made on the elves. Get him drinking the ale enough to loosen his tongue and see what else you can find out. There has to be more to his tale. Get him talking about their tower as well, if you can. Hold out on there being more ale if you can't, and see what else they have to say about that if you do."

I was taken aback. This was the first time I'd been blatantly ordered to spy on them, and it made me uncomfortable. Uncomfortable enough that it must have shown on my face.

"Is there an issue, young Makun?" the abbot asked.

Brothers Barkon and Sedimont seemed keenly interested in my reply, almost predatorily so.

"No, Abbot."

"Good. See that there remains none," he admonished. "You may go."

And so, I went.

"Brothers, let us have that private council …" I heard the abbot say as I slowly closed the door.

✳✳✳

"Ghaan thanks," one of the Lehntarnese women said as Chaltic and I set down the ale.

I'd known we'd had a stockpile of supplies, but I'd never realized the extent of it. Taken deep into the sublevels of the tower by Brother Randilon, Chaltic and I had passed room after room that was stacked floor to ceiling with goods. By the layers of dust, most had remained there untouched for a very long time, and I was simply amazed by the quantity.

"Is he awake?"

"Yes," the woman said, then led me to him when I asked.

Lying on a simple cot was Ghaan, his fingers dug into his forehead like he was trying to massage his brain through his skull. He was very pale, almost ghostly so, with a sallow color underlying his skin that made him seem both ethereal and unreal. He slowly turned his head towards me as I sat down, squinting his eyes as if the darkened room was inundated with a light that only he could see.

"Come to interrogate me some more?"

"No." I sat by his side. "We brought ale and are hoping it will help. Gritilli said that it might. I am simply concerned about your condition, Ghaan."

"If there is enough of it, it might."

"There is," Chaltic said, a little too loud which caused Ghaan to wince.

The room darkened from what I assumed was a cloud passing over, Ghaan seeming to become even more pale as it did so. Then the woman leaned past me, patting dry some sweat from his head. She said something quietly to him, seeming to be very concerned for the man that lay prostrate before us.

"We will let you be," I said.

"No," Ghaan replied. "Talking will help keep me awake."

"You need sleep from the look of you."

"No." Ghaan shook his head, then winced with the motion. "No,

I do not. Sleep will not help, even if I could. It is best for me to stay awake." He took a large drink of the ale that another woman brought for him, grimacing at its taste. "You call this ale?"

"It is what I was told to bring." Chaltic and I looked at each other.

"Children made this."

I shrugged. "The monks do not drink."

"It shows." Ghaan grimaced at the taste, but took another long drink. "At least it is potent enough. It's bitter enough to curdle milk," he grumped, finishing it off and then motioning for another cup. The woman nodded, saying something else in their tongue before leaving the room.

I watched as a bit of color returned to his skin, though admittedly the color was mostly green. "The ale helps?"

"Helps?" Ghaan rolled on his side, groaning a bit as he did so. "It dulls the pain, enough so that I can concentrate." Then he groaned again. "If I can get enough of it, that is."

"There are barrels of the stuff," Chaltic said. "We had no idea."

I nodded. "More than enough."

The news seemed to help him relax. "That is good. Has Vortiid returned?"

"He's gone?"

Ghaan nodded, waiting to respond until he'd drank a few more swallows of the ale the woman had returned with. It was like watching someone getting something their life depended on for the first time, and I took note that his eyes were dilated while he drank. It was easily seen despite the dimness of the room. Then the cloud passed, the increasing light hitting his eyes just right for them to seem to shine from somewhere inside.

Ghaan winced, then the woman put her hand to his brow. Ghaan closed his eyes while she did so, seeming to relax. She mumbled something to him, and I waited until she was done before I continued.

"He's left? Vortiid?" I prompted.

"With some of the dwarves to go find a particular weed." Ghaan nodded. "There is hope."

"You've found it?"

"No. But Peltic's man said the bitter taste and its effects remind him of a weed that is found all over the area. He's going to collect some and then we will see."

"I hope so," Chaltic said. "You look terrible."

Ghaan huffed and then smirked, leaning his head back into his pillow to watch. He lifted his mug in an ironic salute and then said, "This helps."

"I'm glad," I said, glaring at my friend.

Chaltic lifted both hands, asking "What?" with his eyes, but made no further comment.

Ghaan drained his second cup, the woman placing a third in his hands as soon as he was done with the second one. "This helps," Ghaan said, nodding towards the ale while closing his eyes. "You make a potent brew, even if it does taste terrible."

"As I said, we do not drink." I shrugged. "I wouldn't even know. I've never tasted it."

"Don't drink at all?" Ghaan cracked one of his eyes open towards me.

His pupils were still dilated, and the light shining in from outside of the room continued to reflect in his eyes. He squinted, and then another cloud passed overhead. The light dimmed before that one passed to, and then it rapidly brightened inside the room. Ghaan closed his eyes while it did so, taking another long drink as a soft gust of wind blew.

"No. Wine at the turning of the year during our service to the Pantheon, but that is it," I explained. "The villagers drink much more than we do."

"Your tower is very reserved."

"It's all I know." I shrugged.

Ghaan smirked, reclining back into his pillow and seeming much more relaxed than when we had first entered the room. Color was returning to his skin, and the greyish-green undertone seemed to be going away. Another slew of clouds passed overhead, the light coming and going from the room while they did so.

"You all need to relax. Life is too short," Ghaan commented. "You and I shall share an ale."

"I really would rather not."

"Nonsense. What grand duty do you have that requires your time right now except me?"

"Ummm, nothing. Not at the moment, at least."

"Then your assignment wants you to share a cup of ale with

him," Ghaan said as the sun came out from behind the clouds once more.

Then it hit me.

"Share a drink?" I asked. This was the first time I'd been offered anything from the Lehntarnese. I could see it in his eyes that he knew I'd guessed the reason and what he was offering.

Jan had been eating and drinking with them for days now. Me? Not a thing. Something seriously must have changed for them to offer me something.

"Come. A drink, Makun. Will you refuse to drink with me?"

"No," I hurriedly answered, wondering what I had done for this thawing.

Then he said something to the woman, her leaving and then shortly returning with another cup. She evaluated me before offering it, then nodded towards me once she had done so. Regardless, I took the offered cup in silence, peering suspiciously down at the brown liquid before I eventually heard Ghaan snort.

"You drink it, not stare at it, Makun." He grinned.

So, I cautiously took a sip. The most revoltingly sour and horribly bitter flavor hit my tongue, so bad that I actually spit. It tasted like I licked the bottom of my shoe. He was lucky I did not throw up.

Ghaan chuckled, then Chaltic as well. "Not like your ale?" Ghaan asked.

"How can you drink that?" I exclaimed.

Yet the man took another sip. "You get used to it. Come, drink. I'll tell you no more tales until you do, Makun."

The woman brought his fourth of fifth cup, Ghaan steadily drinking as I lost count while I looked down at mine in revulsion. I looked back to Chaltic for help, disappointed when he backed away while raising both of his hands.

Maybe I can tell the abbot Ghaan's sleeping ...

"Drink, Makun. If I can drink enough of this so I'm coherent enough to speak, you can drink enough to listen. Maybe if you get some for your woman you can finally put a child in her belly. It's taking you long enough."

"She wouldn't touch this if her life depended on it."

"Lucky for her, it doesn't." Ghaan grinned. "Come. Drink! Put some hair on your chest and be a man."

The sun was shining in his eyes now. Ghaan grimaced and sat up, bobbling a little while the woman made unhappy noises as soon as he moved. He said something to her, the woman returning with another cup as Ghaan worked his shoulders and then groaned while he moved.

It was amazing how quickly he recovered because of the drink. The paleness and unhealthy color was mostly gone by now, and it was improving while I watched. But he was noticeably unsteady as well, the amount of ale he'd imbibed bringing on what I'd read and heard about was described as drunkenness. I'd never actually seen the effect, and if his mercurial mood was any indication, what I'd heard about it was true.

He eventually convinced me to finish my cup, quite set in his ways that he would say nothing more to me until I had done so. Then he proceeded to regale me with the most ridiculous tales as he steadily continued to imbibe drink after drink, his people taking turns to ensure his cup was never empty. The amount he took in eventually slowed until he only sipped at it, though he sipped almost continuously, his cup never far out of reach. And it amazed me how much he took in.

His people seemed to relax as they saw him up and about, talking and coherent, albeit being helped around because of his unsteady feet. But they relaxed as a group anyway, the oppressive air of their camp lifting as word seemed to spread he was up and about, as well as being in good spirits.

And it stayed that way. Right up until Vortiid returned with a shout.

Capitula 25

"Ghaan!"

The man in question was a bit unsteady as he looked towards his shouted name. Vortiid stormed in through the door, looking furious and very concerned. Then someone said something quickly in their tongue, Vortiid's entire countenance changing by what he had heard.

"What's going on?" Jan asked me.

She'd come over in the intervening time to join Chaltic and I when she'd heard we were with the Lehntarnese. I appreciated her company, not only because it gave me an excuse not to drink more of the foul brew, but because I hadn't seen her in a while. It had been getting harder and harder not to ask the brother healer about the genealogies, and I think the old man knew, but I still hadn't asked.

Jan actually thought the ale was pretty good, daintily drinking the cup Ghaan had forced on her as soon as she'd entered. How the two of them could drink the stuff I had no idea, but her presence and the conversation that ensued between her and Ghaan ensured that I was mostly ignored, and my cup remained untouched and full.

"I don't know," I replied to Jan, listening to the Lehntarnese speak and trying to get a feel for their conversation. "Vortiid's reporting something that has alarmed him."

"Sprites come," Vortiid turned to me, breathing heavily from what appeared to have been a long run. He'd obviously heard what I'd said. "Warn, Makun."

Ghaan asked something else in his tongue, Vortiid answering before Ghaan turned to me. "Your people are idiots, Makun Derring," Ghaan said, weaving a bit in his chair. "He tried to warn them but your protectors won't listen."

"Listen to what?"

"The sprites say there are creatures coming. They told Vortiid and the dwarves that they were going to try and lead the creatures away."

"What creatures?"

"He doesn't know. The sprites say many people will die if we do nothing. They described something similar to what had poisoned me."

Both Chaltic and I jumped to our feet. "The alarm?" I asked, looking to my friend.

"You have to ask?"

"But what if you're wrong?" Jan put in.

"Then we'll get into trouble," Chaltic declared as we hurried out of the room.

Trouble? If we were wrong, what he had just said was a complete understatement.

The two of us scrambled to the village square, flying past people who looked at us like we had gone completely crazy as we hurried on by. Sprinting as fast as we could, we rushed to the elder's house and the bell that hung from the lashed tower in front of it.

Shouting the alarm as we went, the people we passed stood frozen in place until we reached our goal. Then we began pulling the rope to start the bell and its tolling.

BING-BING! BING-BING! rang the high tone of the bell as Chaltic pulled the rope twice in quick succession. Then he let it return fully, before he pulled on it twice more smartly again.

The BING-BING! BING-BING! of the alarm bell echoing its way around the village made its way up to the outer gates, where dozens of eyes hurriedly looked out and locked onto us. It was a sound that had only one meaning to those of the Spire when sounded that way, a meaning that had been pounded into every one of us since birth …

That enemies were coming.

A great commotion rose up in the village as we continued to sound the alarm. Untark sprinted out of his house, the brutish man pulling up his breeches while his shirt and spear dangled from his opposite hand. Village women raced for their homes, shoving their children hurriedly before them. The friars and lay brothers herded their classes home, while the men of the village sprinted in from the outer fields.

Elder Tam ambled out of his house as quickly as he could, staring at us ringing the bell. "What in the Pantheon's name are you doing!" he demanded.

"Sprites warned the survivors that monsters were coming!" I told him.

"Sprites?" Untark shouted as he ran up. "My people have seen nothing! You'd take the word of demons?"

"Would you have us undefended if monsters do come?" I asked

the brutish man.

"But what if it's some trick?" Untark demanded.

"By the Pantheon, man! You'd seriously leave us vulnerable because of a suspicion?" I couldn't believe what I was hearing.

"They're no more trustworthy than you monks!"

"What is your problem?"

"The protectors have raised no alarm!" He waved his hand up towards the wall. "They'd let us know if something was coming!"

"I thought we weren't trustworthy!" Chaltic spat. "Are we trustworthy or not?"

"Why you little shit …" Untark pushed his way forward, but one of his men held him back.

I had a feeling that the only reason the man held him was because we were monks. I looked at Elder Cor Tam for help, but got nothing.

"Chaltic, keep ringing that bell," I commanded, then turned to the village elder. "Will you muster your men?"

Cor Tam screwed up his face, but didn't answer. He knew the danger same as I, but his hesitation right there and then suddenly irked me. I didn't have time for his superstitions, or his apparent mistrust of the Lehntarnese, or what I'd told him, so I ignored him entirely.

I sent a cluster of nervous aspirants sprinting off towards the monastery to report the reason for the alarm, and to summon the brother protectors. The village men were assembling in the center square without orders, readying themselves for Cor Tam and the brother protector's directions, when the elder grabbed me by the shoulder. He spun me around to meet his eyes.

"If this is a false alarm …" Cor Tam threatened.

"The abbot and the council will see me punished." The last man who did had been banished. He'd done it for attention. I know, I read it.

"I'll see that they do," Cor Tam said as the gate to the village stockade boomed shut. "Untark, get those people in order!" he snarled, then shoved the burly man towards the assembled villagers.

I heard a commotion from the monastery above, seeing the brother protectors hurrying to line the stone walls of the courtyard. One was pointing off into the distance, but there was no hope of me seeing what he was pointing to with his vantage point so far above my own.

Two units of brother protectors in full battle gear were trotting down the switchbacked trail as the outer gates boomed shut, only its sally port being left open. The black armor they wore peeked out from beneath their maroon robes as they came, and long hammers held in both hands, wrapped in the black and silver stole of our order, reflected the sun's light while they advanced.

Then a new sound in the village drew my attention. The dwarves and the Lehntarnese were trotting into the square from a street nearby, armed and armored as if outfitted for war.

The dwarves were wearing chainmail, full suits of it jangling as they smartly came to a halt. Weapons I had no knowledge or name for, what looked like axes combined with spears on long poles, were carried in every hand. It gave the unit the look of some prickled creature you'd be a fool to attack.

The Lehntarnese assembled beside the dwarves in their glazed and painted armor. Outfitted in deep blues and rich reds, with masks now affixed and adorned with fearsome visages, they stood in a loose formation devoid of any strict cohesion. But they radiated a deadly experience, like this was any other day, despite being completely focused and alert on everything around them.

Cor Tam hollered for Chaltic to stop wringing the bell, shouting down various questions from the men until he knew more. The villages men were massed in a cluster, individual people moving chaotically within it as they looked for their friends, but eventually the noise of the assembly died down as they waited for the elder to speak and take charge.

"Untark, get your men to the north gate. You, get your people to the south," he said to another man. "Heller? Your people in from outside?"

"Yes."

"Get your hunters up on the roof. Cry out what you can see."

"You got it, Elder."

Heller was one of the village hunters. We didn't have many bows, but those that shot them trained with them endlessly. Heller was passing out quivers of arrows, a precious commodity as their production was almost a lost art. Their makers had to descend into the trees for wood, you see, and there was no ready supply of feathers.

A shout from the switchbacked trail turned our heads, a friar with a cluster of aspirants there was pointing east over our heads. We turned to look, but only saw the stockade wall before someone shoved something into my hands. It was Vortiid, closing my fingers around a strange long-handled mace that had a head on each end.

"Makun, come," he ordered, grabbing Chaltic and I and returning to his own men. Then shoving the two of us between his armed countrymen and the dwarves, he began barking orders in his language to the lot of them, both units changing formation as he spoke. A second unit of dwarves trotted up with only chain shirts, every one of them outfitted with a short spear and a sling. Then the lot of them fell silent listening to Vortiid speak, before Peltic arrived with Ghaan in tow, speaking quietly to the man.

Vortiid frowned on seeing Ghaan arrive but said nothing to him, directing a few of his men to surround the two leaders with a series of sharp orders. Then another shout came from above and behind us, the brother protectors picking up speed as they charged down the last turn of the switchbacked trail to join us.

My heart thudded hurriedly away as some commotion rose up from the north gate, someone shouting orders overtop of a few cries of alarm. Elder Cor Tam ordered another group of armed villagers to run that way and find out what was going on, or to back up whatever Untark Mar was encountering. No one was quite sure. Then a commotion came from the south, turning even more heads in distraction that way.

My hands began to sweat.

"Elder! Elder Tam!" one of Heller's archers cried from the roof.

"What is it?"

"Alter beasts!" the man screamed. Then he pointed towards that first horror as it scrambled over top of the stockade.

I will never forget my first vision of that horror left over from the ancient war. Like someone had stomped on my chest, the fear that took me as first one, and then another creature came over the wall had a vision and life all of its own. And I sought shelter in a hurried prayer to the Pantheon as I saw that perverted horror, then I recoiled as it advanced.

Furry only in a scraggly sense, the monster chittered away evilly as it leapt for one of the men. Roughly the size of a dog, it flew through the air like a bird, wrapping its legs around a villager's head as it bit and chewed while he screamed. Then the next, and the next, and the swarm after that came over the wall, chittering madly as their three-eyed heads took in the placement of our defenders. Then charging lighting fast down the wall head first, the horde of mutated animals that were still scaling the wall rushed towards us in a wave of uncaring death as their forerunners swept on.

Vortiid shouted orders overtop of the chaotic commotion the alter beasts produced while that one man screamed. The dwarves lowered their strange pole arms, shouting out something guttural in their tongue. The village men backed away the same as I did, their axes and scythes waving warily as the chittering horde advanced. Then as the man with the beast attached to his face fell off of the top of the roof, the dwarves behind Vortiid's formation responded to a shouted command.

Swinging back, the slingers flung shining balls down upon the enemy from over top of the heads of the defenders. The balls dropped, shattering amongst the foul creatures before scattered detonations occurred. Scraggly fur and torn limbs flew from amongst the animals, causing some to flinch and pause while the rest ran on, but it did not stop the horde. And as they got to within a distance that the alter beasts could obviously leap, they did so, throwing themselves bodily against the village men who had massed to defend against them.

The villagers took that first assault, their bravery stunning my eyes. My heart-frozen fear grew as screams rang out here and there amongst their formation. Then the dwarven line advanced, every step the shorter people made sounding alongside a gravelly chant. The Lehntarnese ran to their sides, their masked faces like a flock of horrifying specters that danced around the edge of the battle before they struck.

Yet in that shrieking center, the villagers still fought.

Yelling, screaming, shouting, and hating, the villagers used whatever was on hand to kill the foul creatures that attacked us. I saw one man bury a hatchet in a creature's skull, only to be bowled over as another one flew in from the side to bite him. Two horrible monsters attached themselves to some poor soul's leg, chewing it right off in a flash before my astonished eyes. An arrow took another one in the side as it leapt through the air, deflecting it off course to crash into another creature, but still the monsters came on.

One ran between the legs of every one of the defenders, then fixed its chaotic three eyes on me. Leaping straight for my face, I choked up on my weapon, swinging for all I was worth and hitting it in the side. I heard and felt its ribs break, but before that shock could hit me a blade flew by my face to impale another monster I never even saw. A scream sounded from almost beside my head as another one of those terrible animals latched onto the face of one of the dwarves, the dwarf going down while stabbing repeatedly at the thing on his face.

Someone else killed it, yet still the battle raged on.

A woman's scream rang out over it all. I watched as Chaltic ran for a broken-down door, disappearing inside as I swung and missed at another beast who dodged. One of the Lehntarnese men got that one, but Chaltic was yelling for help as a group of villagers rushed in.

Then more glass balls flew by overhead to land with their accompanying detonations, shocking and distracting me as it was something I'd never heard before or experienced. It was as if the mages had come. Then animal parts flew wildly around us all as the combat continued, drenching me in their gore, but all I could think about was my friend while I slammed my mace down upon another mutated animal's head.

Only a few of those hideous creatures were now coming over the wall. Scaling it like mad spiders, they seemed to rush to join the fray, in some kind of crazed frenzy to feed. One was already impaled by an arrow when it appeared over the wall, but the rest ran towards us, chittering wildly as they came.

Their insanity in the face of our defenders amazed me, and the altered beasts attacked almost without regard for their lives. It was horrible; a hideous thing to see. And it was an insult to the life provided to us by the Pantheon because of their very being to me.

I slammed the back-end of my two-headed mace down upon the body of another one of those foul creatures, pinned into place by one of the dwarves' strange-bladed spears, and I found myself suddenly glad for its screams. Then I watched as the men of Lehntarn broke off into pairs or threes, dancing around each other while keeping their blades ever outward at all times.

Their masked forms drifted around the chaotic battlefield, and anything that came close to them was either an ally or dead. There was no in between. And I recognized Vortiid in his feral blue armor as he skewered one of the animals right out of the air, flicking it off his sword tip before he stabbed out to kill another with ease.

It was chaos, complete and utter chaos. Villagers were down, a few of the dwarves were down as well. A few of the men of Lehntarn were injured, but any that were mobbed were instantly helped back up to their feet by their brethren.

Chaltic dashed out of the house, a sobbing woman draped over his shoulder as smoke started to pour out of the door behind him. Then the men with him charged out also, the last two moving backwards to defend against something they were fighting against inside.

Then I was suddenly shoved off my feet, a Lehntarnese man in his animalistic armor bodily standing over me gripping one of the altered beasts by its throat. I was pulled out from between his legs by one of the dwarves while another man helped to kill it, the thing shooting out a mass of spines from its back as it died.

The spines ricocheted off the Lehntarnese armor like it was so much useless rain flying off shingles, and a few of them landed nearby. And for some odd reason one of the spines stood out to me, a drop of some orange substance gleaming evilly in the light from the tip of the projectile. It was barbed, white on the end, with a tip so long and fine it disappeared from sight before my eyes. Then I lost track of it as I was pulled to my feet, another man shouting at me in the Lehntarnese language as if he expected me to understand.

I noticed the battle was beginning to wind down. Brother protectors were cornering groups of the wild creatures, working as one to destroy them just as they were trained. The dwarves were almost unassailable, only a few of them appearing injured while I counted two of their own down. The Lehntarnese continued to drift wherever they seemed needed, their prowess undeniable as they slew and slaughtered wherever they went, but the villagers had taken horrible losses, quite a few of them slaughtered from what I could see.

Then it suddenly came to an end. Two clusters of altered beasts were backing away as a group. The men chased them, cutting off their retreat, because we knew if we let them go, they'd only come back later with more to haunt us later. Chittering madly, the monsters crouched down, one of them with a strange arrow in it that suddenly stood out to me. Then firing off a hail of spines from their backsides they leapt, throwing themselves bodily at the defenders.

It was their last gasp of defiance, the last vestiges of their hate. And I watched as they did everything they could to kill all who remained, while Chaltic dropped that unconscious woman as softly as he could to the ground by my feet.

The woman moaned, a soft sound amidst the screams of those mutated creatures while the defenders killed them. Chaltic brushed the hair out of her face, the daughter of some matron much younger than I had assumed being revealed. I stood with both hands on my mace as I placed myself overtop of them to defend them, but there was no need. That last assault had come to an end, the creatures slaughtered and broken, Heller and his remaining archers now targeting and killing those that tried to escape.

Vortiid and his men ran off to the south in the direction of sounds of more fighting, but the dwarves stayed with us along with that Lehntarnese man who'd saved me. Peltic and Ghaan stood in their center, directing the defense of the villagers as a few of the dwarves broke off to see to the wounded. The brother protectors ran off to the north, but the sounds of battle there began dimming as the cries of those injured around us rose to the fore. Then the woman Chaltic had saved woke up with a scream, causing me to jump as she seemed to explode right next to my feet.

Another shout went out, with the archers suddenly loosing arrows again towards the wall. I looked up to see a short sprite standing on top of the stockade, its huge curiously-shaped eyes taking in the remains of the slaughter. It casually moved to the side as the arrows flew past, looking somehow annoyed at the archers while it did so. Then it seemed to almost look straight at me, before it hopped down out of sight on the other side of the wall. My last sight of it was it holding a bow and arrow in each of its hands, the arrow looking exactly like the one I'd seen in the flank of the monster before.

I panted while I recovered from my exertions, letting the double-headed mace rest near my feet. Shouts went out from the dwarves and the people of Lehntarn to not shoot at the sprites, and eventually the panicked archers stopped loosing their arrows at it. I propped my hands on the mace as I gasped, sweat dripping from my head and then falling into my eyes while I leaned, but the sting came only distantly. My mind was still on the eyes of that sprite, and the memory was somehow comforting to me.

Then the dwarves surrounded us, their polearms never lowering as they made a circular defense, shuffling me, Chaltic and the weeping woman he'd saved into its center. There we joined Peltic and Ghaan, the two quietly watching and talking while Elder Tam was also found and pushed into the center to join us.

People ran about following orders as I slowly relaxed, looking down to observe one of the dead creatures I found at my feet. Its scraggly brown fur was matted by a reddish orange blood. A bit of that fluid was leaking from its impressively wide maw, slowly pooling underfoot while I watched. And I tried to ignore the sour stench it gave off, while wondering from what it had originally evolved.

Elder Tam determinedly kicked the thing before he prodded the corpse with one of his feet, then he pulled a spine he found imbedded out from his arm. His skin was already swelling around where it had been, a reddish circle developing which expanded and grew while I watched. Another squad of brother protectors trotted by, brother healers dropping to their knees amongst the wounded. Then a chirurgeon set up not that far away from us, Brother Camdal there by his side while the elder monk directed his healers into the village.

It was then that the screams of the wounded and dying hit me, as if the sound around me had suddenly come back to my ears. My thoughts flew to worrying about Jan, hoping she was well and wondering what had become of her during the attack. I could only hope she'd stayed where I'd left her with the people of Lehntarn, knowing that if she was there, she would have definitely survived. I had not a single doubt about that at all, but I forced my concerns out of my mind as I drug Elder Tam over to the healers, interrupting Brother Camdal to show him his arm.

"The mark was made by their spines, Brother," I said to him, picking up a random spine from the ground around me for him and the brother healers to see.

"Poison," the brother healer declared as he took in the orange dollop of evil that dripped from one its sharp end. "Well done, Brother Derring. An antidote will be researched and made with haste."

Then he shouted for a cluster of novices and aspirants to gather up more spines as the sounds of the injured and dying men echoed in from all around me.

I will never forget the horror I saw that day. The blood and the loss ... It haunts me to this day.

Capitula 26

In the end, close to sixty villagers died, two of the dwarves, and a single man who had survived the evacuation of Lehntarn and made it all the way here, hoping for peace. All had either had their faces eaten off, which was horrible enough all by itself, or were skewered by the poison spines to die in what seemed like a paralyzed agony. The woman who Chaltic had saved had her family's house catch fire, which spread to four other homes before the flames were put out, but the rest of the village survived intact and endured.

Dozens more were injured, all of us learning that anyone pierced by one of those spines would become somnolent before turning violently ill. And we learned that the more spines a person was struck by, the faster they became somnolent. Then anyone injured by the monsters' bites or claws were infected by some foul humour, an angry rash being raised almost immediately upon the wound in their flesh, to spread wildly around the insult and bleed. This only added to the horrible sight of those gruesome injuries, which wept some rancid orange foulness, in conjunction with the circular redness, that accompanied the prickling spines.

The healers worked tirelessly for hours, only losing maybe two dozen or so more souls who passed on to their final rest before the Pantheon. I hoped they would be received into their bosom, to rest in enlightenment after what they had endured, but none of us would ever know for sure.

We considered the day a great victory.

The last alter beast incursion like this one had occurred before I was born, over a hundred of our own killed that abominable night before our people could even fight back. And the one that happened before that was when the entire village had been almost wiped out. The histories described something that may have started out as a bee or a wasp, that combined or conjoined with some unknown abomination to form stinging tentacles.

To be attacked by the swarm of deadly creatures we had this day, and only lose a few dozen in the process with moments of time to prepare, it was a gift of the Pantheon, and all of us were eternally grateful.

The abbot opened the tower, taking any of the villagers into it who felt unsafe to stay inside the courtyard. And in an unusual show of sympathy, the entire council of seven came forth, doing what they could for all of the wounded as they wandered about the battlefield. I saw the abbot comforting a weeping woman, Brother Barkon solemnly chanting the last rites over the victorious dead, Brother Sedimont making sure that every soul who had lifted up their arms in defense of the village was formally acknowledged for their efforts by the brother protectors.

All of us came together in our moments of grief.

Even the dwarves and the people of Lehntarn were acknowledged, their contributions to the battle not going the least bit unnoticed. And I witnessed a thawing occur, as even the villagers who had held themselves apart and suspicious, moved to thank those armored warriors who had come from another people. Telling tales of how they had moved like ghosts throughout the village, killing demonic creatures wherever they went, no matter who was attacked.

The people were very grateful.

Ghaan took their acknowledgements in stride, and so did Peltic, both of their peoples seemingly curiously detached by how great of a victory the battle actually was to us. But both leaders made sure to accept the thanks they received graciously, not turning down a single kind word or thankful gesture that was sent their way. Even when those words and gestures were couched in shades of prejudice, that the villagers could not seem to leave behind no matter what they did, their words were well received.

Knowledge spread about the spines and their accompanying red circles, putting to rest the cause of the mysterious deaths that had been haunting us. And the people relaxed, now having an answer to what had been killing them to refer to, which caused an even further thawing amongst the villagers. It seemed that suspicion would be put to rest and aside, though the Lehntarnese seemed curiously unimpressed by what had happened.

Brother Camdal was surprisingly able to produce a remedy to the monster's poison in a single day. Crushing an herb that was known to ease breathing, simply applying that plant over the wound in a paste-like poultice ended the afflicteds' suffering. And that discovery spread hope and joy with the news.

Jan had indeed sought safety with the people of Lehntarn, and I later found out that Ghaan had ordered her protection inside their compound. She told me of the women of Lehntarn fighting alongside their men in a great battle that took place inside their courtyard, their prowess no lesser than their men's own. And there were stars in her eyes as she described them, warrior women who fought like the Pantheon's own, blades spinning gloriously around them in a whirling tribute to death that forced the beasts to atone.

And as the recovery went on, Chaltic seemed to have found his mate through his actions, whether he wanted it or not. I grinned towards my friend as the woman he'd saved followed him around, amused that she was older than he was, but no less interested by what she saw. She studied him whenever he wasn't looking her way, her face holding an intense look of concentration while she did so. I eventually learned her name was Soriese, one of our farmers' daughters, yet someone who'd never come to our attention before. But now, she followed him, and I was pleased by what I now saw.

The same day Brother Camdal discovered his treatment, the abbot declared a celebration, announcing that food and drink would be provided from our stores once everyone had returned to their homes. The village was ecstatic, and curious as well, having heard rumors of the monastery's supposedly bottomless stores. They were all untrue of course – those rumors – no matter what I had seen, but the villagers had never believed us. And anything we used came out of the supplies that I found out were set aside for us in case we had to retreat completely inside the tower once more.

Brother Randilon had explained that after I'd asked, on seeing room after room of supplies when we had gotten Ghaan's ale, but the villagers wouldn't believe us, just glad to be on the receiving end of those mystical stores. And as we carried them out with the villagers' assistance, we prepared for a feast. Even I got caught up in the excitement, as an unplanned festival was something unheard of beyond the annual celebration we hosted at the turn of the year.

But the festive air was muted for some, especially the Lehntarnese and the dwarves.

I witnessed my first dwarven burial. A solemn affair, where the entirety of their people, excepting a small few, descended to the treeline and harvested enough wood for a pyre. After removing their dead's beards, they arranged the body on top. Decorating the platform with sweet smelling herbs, they lit it, then arranged themselves around the burning remains, droning a solemn bass chant. It rumbled through my soul, standing there as I was, yet not a single one of those diminutive warriors cried. And after the burning was done, they gathered what remained of the bones and the bodies' ash, grinding it into a powder, and interring it in the earth in case their Maker may come.

The Lehntarnese did something quite different. In a brutal display, once it was determined that one of their own was dead, they quickly severed the man's head in a swift decapitation. It was Vortiid who did this, just one rapid strike with his razor-sharp sword, his friend's head rolling to the side after the sword's uncaring thunk. He gathered it and then set it gently upon the corpse's lap, while another one pierced the man's heart with a sword. Then solemnly carrying the body to their courtyard they stood vigil over it, watching it without pause for that night and the next day, before the entirety of their people relaxed. Then, and only then, did their people inter the body, wails and crying coming from one and all while they did so.

But it was not all depression and solemnity, as the second day after the battle the celebration took place. Adding something to the ale we provided, the dwarves sweetened its taste to something more palatable, and even I began to enjoy the drink. Then with everyone's guard lowered, and the effects of the alcohol taking place, singing and dancing commenced.

I have never been a good dancer, but Jan refused to allow me to refrain, dragging me out into the village square to dance to the amusement of her friends and many others. There we experienced a dwarven dance, one where everyone lined up in two columns, and took turns stately spinning the one opposite them until one of the lines moved. Or the Lehntarnese dance, which was similar to a jig, but depended on two partners twirling each other wildly and seductively about until everyone was hilariously dizzy.

Our many people danced and sung well into the night, joining each other in a celebration of mutual survival … it was a celebration of life, and of peace… something all of us needed.

"Brother Derring?" the abbot said to me as I watched Jan dance with one of her friends.

"Yes, Abbot?"

"Come. The council wishes to speak with you."

There was nothing odd about his manner, but I found myself suddenly on guard. "Abbot?"

"Come," was all he said, turning his back and leading me away.

Set back a bit from the celebration, the council of seven was arranged around a small table, with Peltic, Vortiid, and Cor Tam by their side. They appeared in good spirits, but I could detect the mood was somehow serious beyond what I could see. It was almost like they were intentionally putting on airs, and I couldn't for the life of me understand why.

"Sit." Brother Barkon indicated the last remaining chair, gesturing for me to take it.

"The council has been informed it was you and Brother Chaltic who sounded the alarm."

I didn't understand the looks I was getting. "Yes. We were talking to Ghaan as the abbot directed. Vortiid came in and said the sprites attempted to warn them." I waved a hand towards Vortiid.

"I see." Brother Sedimont responded, then looked around towards the assembled people. He didn't look pleased. "The brother protectors were telling me about the sprites' warning when the bell sounded."

"Makun warn. Warn good," Vortiid interjected when Brother Sedimont paused to take a breath.

"I know I threatened you boy, but you saved our asses," Cor Tam put in, then nodded my way. "If they'd come over the wall before we were ready … I don't want to think about what would've happened."

"Yes." Brother Sedimont said in agreement, but something told me he was holding back another frown.

"You are to be commended for your actions, Brother Derring," the abbot said. "Your quick and decisive action saved many lives, and we are all in agreement on that." I didn't think Brother Sedimont and Brother Barkon agreed by their looks, but they nodded and smiled as well, everyone there chiming in with their thanks.

"Thank you, Abbot."

"You are welcome. We will shortly call over Brother Chaltic to offer him our congratulations as well, however we wished to speak to you in private before then."

"It has come to our attention that you may be considering a villager for a possible match?" Brother Camdal asked me.

"Y-Yes?"

Brother Camdal looked kindly on me, then to Brother Ansilin before he spoke again. "There is no record of your parentage, young

Derring, beyond tales. There is a reason for this, something which has been purposely withheld from you, and you have been the subject of intense scrutiny since your inclusion with us."

"Inclusion?" I asked, noticing Vortiid was looking oddly at the other members of the Council.

"Yes. What you have been told thus far is true. You did have parents, their names were known, they did reside with us in the village, and they did name you. But what has been withheld is that you and they were not born in the village. You were brought to us."

"Brought?" I responded dumbly.

"Yes, brought. To a patrol of brother protectors, actually." Brother Camdal looked towards the abbot.

I felt my stomach sink.

They eyed each other for a time before the abbot nodded. Then the brother healer continued, "By the sprites," he concluded.

Vortiid looked sharply my way and then back to the council, and Cor Tam eyed me with a renewed interest. Even the other brothers of the council observed me with keen eyes, but my mind was not present. No, I was suddenly not present in the least, as my world came crashing down and fell into a dark depression.

My desolation was complete.

I placed my hands into the opposite sleeves of my robes, then formally bowed. "I understand, Brother Healer. Brother Healer, Lord Abbot," I nodded to each of them as I named them, "I will withdraw my interest. I ask for the Council's consideration and make a formal request to enter into seclusion."

I kept my head bowed, thinking about Jan's kiss just moments before while we danced. There was no way any relationship with her could be made now. My bloodline was completely unknown, not even originating in the village. The strictures were clear. There was no way our match would be approved now. I might as well be mage-born.

"See?" the abbot declared into the silence. I looked up in surprise but he continued on, pointing his hand at me all the while. "See? You challenge his devotion to our strictures, his duty to the words of the Pantheon? You have for years! But see? Did he wail? Did he challenge? Did he rail against it all? Did he do anything else that anyone might take offense to? No. No, his only request was to descend into seclusion."

I still had no idea what was going on.

"I still say it is not in our best interests," Brother Barkon replied.

"He is a model of what a monk should be," the abbot continued. "And you've been saying that since I granted that babe mercy. Despite all your prejudice and warnings, he did everything right. What could a soul possibly do differently?"

Brother Barkon frowned but said nothing.

"I will grant he is a model monk, Abbot Dreise," Brother Ansilin put in. "I have enjoyed my time with him, and so have the other brother recorders, but the strictures are there for a reason."

"They are," Brother Camdal agreed. "Yet, the Abbot's suggestion and his dispensation at the time does have merit. We are a closed society. The risk for inbreeding is great. And we did watch his entire life."

"But what you suggest is dangerous," Brother Sedimont answered. "I know. The brother protectors train against its returning."

"In twenty-three years has he shown any of the signs? Any sign at all?" the abbot asked.

There was a long uncomfortable moment of silence before it was Brother Barkon of all people who answered. "No."

"There has been no signs of Brother Derring being a mage, or showing any indication he has the slightest bit of magic," Brother Margonest agreed.

I was stunned. I suddenly understood why the abbot had followed my life so close and with such great interest. Why I had always been housed in the tower. "Abbot, I …"

He simply held up his hand to cut me off. "And the concerns about how he and his family was brought to us by the sprites?"

Brother Randilon frowned. "There is no teaching in The Book of the Fall that I am aware of against the sprites."

"They did not help," Brother Barkon quickly put in.

"But they also did not hurt," Brother Ansilin responded. "There is no record of them acting against any one of the gods, and they once helped us in times of need."

The entire group fell silent. I did not understand, not understand in the least. I was overwhelmed with what I'd been told. A sharp ringing began in my ears as the sounds of singing and celebration came from behind in the village. There was a loud cheer.

"Then we shall vote," Abbot Dreise eventually broke the silence. "I place before the council that Brother Makun Derring needs to be recognized and rewarded for his actions. It is the agreement of the council, as well as the representatives of the tower of Lehntarn and the dwarves of Nächtaltom, that his quick actions saved many lives and possibly the entire village. I therefore formally request that the strictures be modified where it comes to Brother Derring. I ask that he be allowed to pursue his match with the villager Jan Isterlin, whose interest he holds, which has been verified by the Elder, Cor Tam."

Cor Tam nodded when he was named, but I was further stunned. I had made no request. Sure, Jan and I had an understanding, but I hadn't talked to anyone about it. And here that match was already to be approved before the entire council.

"All in favor?" the abbot said.

I was stunned by how fast everything had moved.

One by one the council of seven agreed, until it came to Brother Barkon and Sedimont. "I disagree," was all Brother Sedimont said, but it was Brother Barkon who surprised me.

"I move for the invocation of sancorpus cloture," Brother Barkon decreed.

"Sancorpus cloture?" asked the abbot.

"Sancorpus cloture."

"Sancorpus cloture has not been invoked in generations, Brother Barkon. Almost from the time of the founding," the brother healer replied. "Would you take away his bloodline?"

"The danger is too much."

"Sancorpus cloture?" I asked, not immediately familiar with the term, but the abbot waved me to silence.

"I agree to the invocation of cloture, to be revisited upon the birth of a child from this match. Will this satisfy the brother chanter?"

"It will." Brother Barkon looked surprised.

"Then do you agree with that limitation?"

There was a moment of intense silence, but Brother Barkon eventually nodded.

"Brother Makun Derring? Hear the will of the council. Brother Makun Derring, for you and your friend's actions, the Monachi Spirae congratulate you. Your names will be entered into the annals, and your actions will be remembered for all time. Your match with Jan Isterlin is approved, to pursue or not as you desire. However, the invocation of *sancorpus cloture* has been invoked, and therefore no other match will be heard or considered as it comes to you. Do you hear the will of the council?"

I was stunned. "I-I do, Lord Abbot."

"Then go. The council anticipates your progeny with great interest. You are directed to beget an heir for the continuation of our bloodlines as soon as possible, Brother Derring. I invoke *iubet graviditatis* on my own authority, as abbot, for consideration by the brother healer at his earliest possible convenience, then *iudicium sanguinis* when your progeny arrives. Is there any objection to this by the council?"

There were marked looks of surprise, but not a single one of the council disagreed. Brother Barkon looked completely mollified by what he had heard, but Brother Sedimont still frowned.

"Good. Then go, young Makun. Know that you have the approval of the entire council of seven. You are a symbol of what monks should strive to achieve. I will continue to follow your life under the Pantheon with great interest, Brother Derring. May you go in peace."

"Thank you, Abbot." And then I bowed my head to them all before I left.

But I felt eyes on me, many eyes, eyes that did not seem very friendly. And my mood was entirely thrown off as the night went on, not an ounce of celebration left in me as my mind whirled and then spun.

I was elated that my relationship with Jan was approved. To receive the blessing of the entire council? It was almost unheard of. It was as if every god of the Pantheon had come down and then blessed our union, giving their approval for our lives together to begin. I couldn't wait to tell her, and finally find my bravery to actually ask her if it was something she wanted, no matter what I'd inferred.

Yet I also remembered my histories, something I had been instructed on when I became a brother recorder. The ancient rites and diktats had always interested me, as well as the struggles from those earlier times. And I knew from my studies some of history the names of the invocations the abbot and Brother Barkon had used, though I had never expected to hear them stated so plainly in the modern day.

The two that had come up had last been used many generations ago, almost seven hundred years to be exact. Once it had been determined that magic was passed on to a mage's descendants, those lines had been culled, and anyone since who showed even the slightest possible inclination for magic was put to death. Their living relations with no signs of magic were watched, and put to work for their sin, but it was ensured that the living could no longer breed.

Most did not survive the procedure.

That time was hard, with brother sacrificing brother, and mothers drowning their own daughters. And where suspicion was spoken or held with no other evidence to deny it, before a line was put to death, in the past a child was forced to be born, and then put to the test, to determine if mage-blood had been passed on.

It was a terrible time, one of fear and suspicion, and I had only one thought as I remembered that past.

That Jan would not be amused.

Capitula 27

"Your people are barbarians."

Ghaan's disgust at what I'd explained to him was readily apparent.

"You seriously agree to force a baby on her and then have it tested, after which you could both be put to death?"

"It is our way."

"It is the way of madness. I thought where we came from was horrible."

I had no reply to that. For him to compare the eradication of mages to fighting the undead was almost heretical, and I didn't want any word of it getting out. I liked and respected this man, but he was still a newcomer here, and only knew the barest bit of our history.

He shook his head, looking over at Vortiid who was the one who had told him. It was the day after the celebration, and I was back in Ghaan's rooms having been summoned there to clear away Ghaan's confusion. He was appalled when what Vortiid had told him came out to be true.

"Have you told her?"

"Some of it, yes. I was interrupted to come here."

"I cannot believe this. This is truly sick."

"You would have me spread mages if my blood is unpure?"

"Makun Derring, you forget I knew mages. I lived beside them. There were a lot of good people I met."

"And also some who were not," I reminded him.

He waved a hand in denial. "None of which deserved death."

"It is not for me to say."

There was a long pause while Ghaan emptied another cup of ale, having the next placed before him. "How can you do this? Are you blind?"

"Ghaan, they do not know my bloodline. If testing it this way proves clear, it will remove any suspicions of me."

"Which grants you what?"

"Me? Nothing. Any children I might have? The ability to live and contribute to our society."

Ghaan looked like he wanted to vomit. "Contribute? You mean breed. Like an animal!"

"Yes, if you look at it simply. I choose to look at it like this: I've been awarded the chance to be with the one I love, and love her. If she'll have me," I added after a moment.

"That woman would no more turn you away than she'd choose to not breathe. Naisa there has confirmed it." He waved to one of the Lehntarnese women nearby. "Your Jan Isterlin is only waiting for you to ask."

Now I knew what her and the women around here talked about so much. It gave me hope. Naisa asked Ghaan something, obviously about what he had said after I watched her blush. "Thank you," I said to her. She only guiltily blushed more.

"This is besides the point. What woman would agree to this?" he demanded.

"We will not allow another mage to come into being." I waved my hand towards his copy of The Book of the Fall. "You know this, Rahdimus Ghaan. All of our people here will agree."

He looked completely nonplussed, shaking his head like he couldn't believe it.

"Makun, sprite?" Vortiid interjected after a moment of silence.

"I don't know." Understanding the question even though he didn't know enough words to ask it. "Apparently my parents were guided here much like you were. The only difference was, they led my parents to a patrol of brother protectors. I was a babe. Almost immediately after was a monster attack. My parents and anyone who knew them were killed during the attack. Honestly, it's lucky that anyone survived that one."

Vortiid grunted, but it was Ghaan who spoke up. "The auguries already knew this. They pointed towards a connection between us."

"A connection?"

"That we were both led here by sprites." The importance of that didn't make much sense to me, but Ghaan kept talking. "You are being forced to beget a child, Makun. A child of your own blood, that will be under suspicion and tested from the time it is born. And if it's determined it's a mage, you, Jan, and your child will be put to death. Don't you see how barbaric that is?"

"It is our way."

"Don't you realize that mages–"

"Ghaan!" Vortiid interrupted.

He held a mighty frown, and I noticed that his hand had

descended onto his knife. He stared at me with those flat, dead eyes, and I was reminded that he and his people were merciless killers. Nothing had made that stand out to me more than the way he looked at me now.

I suddenly knew that somehow my life was now in the balance.

Vortiid spoke to Ghaan, an angry hissing cadence to his speech that expressed massive and complete dissatisfaction. Ghaan quietly replied, then he lay back on his bed with a sigh, emptying another cup. Vortiid said nothing more.

"It seems I have said too much. Go, Makun. Speak to your woman. Practice your barbarity. Do whatever it is you must."

Then recognizing the dismissal for what it was, I got up to leave, never once expecting to be dismissed so hurriedly. The mood was tense and yet strange, like there was something yet to be said that should have been. I felt as if there was some subject that still needed to be discussed as I reached my hand for the door.

"Makun," Vortiid said, which stopped me. I turned to meet his eyes. "Makun, no speak." He waved a hand towards Ghaan. "Lehntarn no say all. Ghaan no speak. Vortiid no speak. Naisa no speak. Makun no speak." Then looking intently into my eyes, he continued. "Speak some-day. Today, no speak." Then he drew his thumb down his cheek in that ritualistic manner, never looking away from my eyes.

I nodded, not understanding in the least.

"Makun speak?"

I noticed all three of them were looking at me very intently, and I remembered my promise from before. These people had never hurt me, and nothing they'd done had hurt the tower. And we already knew they'd had contact with mages, Ghaan's familiarity didn't surprise me. I didn't understand the intensity in the room, but I had to answer.

"No. I will not say anything about whatever Ghaan almost said here… though I do not understand it."

"Good. Makun no speak." Ghaan said something to him in Lehntarnese and Vortiid nodded, turning back to me and drawing his thumb down his cheek. "Vortiid remember."

I nodded, still not understanding. Then I left, quietly shutting the door behind me.

✳✳✳

No matter my unusual conversation with Ghaan and Vortiid that day, Jan was ecstatic. I eventually worked up the courage to formally ask her, and she immediately thereafter smothered me in kisses. To say I was pleased would be idiotic in how much of an understatement that was, but our pairing was momentarily put on hold while I explained the stipulations we would be under.

Jan understood, as I knew she would be. We both knew the risks, and even Jan, who only had a villager's education, was well familiar with the tales of what the mages had done before. And the knowledge that there was some unknown to me and my bloodline actually helped me a little, adding a bit of mystery to the man she knew. Then not waiting for more formal nuptials, Jan and I joined by the light of the twin moons, her and mine cries of complete ecstasy that echoed that wonderful night leading to the amusement of all who heard nearby.

A few days passed, and then the public celebration of our union occurred. Amid joyous dancing we feasted again, the abbot and the council of seven agreeing to use mine and Jan's partnering to raise the spirits of the village. And as I looked on with pride, Jan danced with one and all, even Ghaan, who had come in spite of his headaches to witness the celebration. And he'd seemed better recently, spending a lot of time with the dwarves, drinking and speaking with them.

I was given a gift by Peltic, a bead I wear in my hair to this day, and then a strong knife by the Lehntarnese, as well as being instructed to keep the two-headed mace I had used which they continued to drill me in practice. I admit never being very good with the thing, but I look on it fondly as it has served me very well over the years.

Yet all of that paled in comparison to Jan's happiness, which we remember fondly to this day. How she had glowed and then glided as she wandered around, always returning to take up my arm or grace my lips with a kiss. And the cheers as she did so seemed to add a light to her eyes, and offer bliss because of that kiss. Much to everyone's amusement I danced with her friends, which brought a good laugh, but nothing took away from my happiness that day, or our joyous union under the eyes of the Pantheon.

I felt truly blessed.

✳✳✳

Yet, no matter how happy I was, the ending must come. More days passed and eventually we recovered. We saw no more sign of the sprites, and after searching for them or any more signs of monsters to come, we determined the risk of another attack was over. The abbot rescinded his order that prevented the supplies for the dwarves return journey from being released, and they decided almost immediately to return home.

The trade talks were over, being quickly concluded once the supplies were no longer held up. A set amount of potions and other miscellaneous things were determined to be of equal value for the herd of mountain tarn they provided, and they even traded us some iron ore, something of which we desperately needed.

Ghaan and the Lehntarnese were disappointed to see them go, but seemed to understand. Why some of them could not stay was an issue of great importance and long debate to them, but eventually their talks were over. But the dwarves of Nächtaltom agreed to come by more frequently, a solemn promise that I knew they intended to keep. There was something between the dwarves and the people of Lehntarn, something serious, about which neither of them would speak.

Then almost five weeks after the fateful day of that monster attack, Peltic left. He hugged my Jan, who was ever present at my side, before clasping forearms with me in the manner of the dwarves. It rankled the council of seven that I was present I think, but they made no comment as the dwarves said their goodbyes to me first. Peltic and the dwarves said that I was their friend because the warriors had named me a friend of theirs, and every last one of the monks knew how serious the dwarves' declarations could be.

Then after saying goodbye to the monks, the dwarves said goodbye to the people of Lehntarn. Saluting them by beating their fists on their chests, the Lehntarnese made a great cry in their tongue in response. The dwarves stood unmoving, then the Lehntarnese began a chant in dwarven, their human voices strangling out whatever they said in that gravelly tongue. But chant for a long time they did, me only recognizing the name Cathaganlire said again and again before they were done. Then the dwarves clasped hands with them and left, accompanied by another song by the Lehntarnese.

Four more days had passed and the tower and village were returning to normal. Jan had taken to spending equal amounts of time with me in the tower as she had down in the village, and as a couple she'd been given special dispensation to pass the edificium as she pleased. But today she was down in the village, plotting with Soriese on the best way to get Chaltic to ask her to couple from what I had heard.

He still had cold feet.

"And they are still translating The Book?"

"Yes, Lord Abbot. Ghaan and I are about halfway through. Some of the concepts are difficult to translate because of the unstated side of interpretation included in written Lehntarn, but we are making headway."

"Good. And any luck in learning Lehntarnese yourself?"

"I admit I am hopeless at it, Abbot Dreise," I admitted. "My attempts produce much hilarity when I try it, but that is it. I can get my point across, but it is much easier for me in writing. It is easier for them to converse with us in the common tongue ultimately."

"And still no explanation for why they keep calling the language we use 'Imperial'?"

"No, Abbot Dreise."

"Hmmmm. See if you can get to the bottom of this."

"Yes, Abbot."

"Anything else to report?"

We were sitting in his office, our meetings after the evening meal becoming a norm for the tower. Sometimes one or the other member of the council came in to ask a specific question of me, but it had been a while since I'd seen one of them here. And over time, the abbot and I had become comfortable with one another, and I relaxed as I never would have before in the company of someone so august.

"Only that Ghaan and Vortiid want to continue their patrols. Ghaan's headaches seem to have returned in force since the dwarves have left, and I think Vortiid is using the patrols as an excuse to look for the plant they need. They still haven't found the one the dwarves suggested."

The abbot shrugged. "I don't see the issue?"

"Neither do I. But Untark Mar and Elder Cor Tam don't like

them coming and going, and your word of permission would go a long way to quelling their discomfort."

"What is the issue?"

"That the Lehntarn go armed."

"They're descending the mountain, for Pantheon's sake. What do they expect them to do? Go naked?"

I snorted, no longer surprised when the abbot was so open with me. There were a lot of things I was becoming used to, one of which was no longer being solely a historian. I had been laterally promoted, and was now the main point of contact with the people of Lehntarn. My sole duty was to record whatever I could from them, and put it to paper.

I reported directly to the council on this, still considered a brother recorder, reporting to Brother Ansilin, and keeping my access to the library. But my day-to-day duties were my own, determined by finding the best way to bring our brothers from Lehntarn to live as one alongside us in the tower.

"There are still some concerns. Almost all of their superstitions have been eliminated ever since they defended the village, and it helps that they now openly wander around and help out as needed, but they are still somewhat reserved and secretive. One of the villagers made an issue of them 'hiding their women' the other day."

The abbot raised an eyebrow at me.

"The woman in question was having problems turning the man down. From what Gritilli Van told me, he was lucky he wasn't run through."

The abbot snorted again. "So, they are assimilating."

"Yes. Slowly, but they are joining our community."

This wasn't the first time the abbot had talked about the Lehntarnese 'assimilating', and I wondered why it was so important to him. The pure fact that they were here would cause them to eventually assimilate, but I didn't understand why it seemed like it had to be hurried.

"And any more about the sprites or the elves?" I couldn't help but notice his sudden interest.

"No, Abbot. I've passed on all that I know." I cringed a bit internally at this, knowing I was holding back a bit. "Again, if you could only tell me what you are specifically looking for, I could ask more direct questions."

The abbot eyed me for a moment. "No. No, there is nothing in particular. I had just hoped there was more."

"I understand."

"And their journey here?"

"What I've already said." I looked at him curiously.

"I guess I should say their arrival here."

"Oh. No. They are remarkably closed-mouthed about that."

Even I had been surprised that they hinted at nothing when the subject came up. Ghaan still pretended as if I hadn't spoken when I asked questions about that. Even if I was asking while looking straight at him.

"Damn."

I waited before I brought up the next subject. "They are asking for more ale."

The abbot looked surprised. "All of it goes to Ghaan?"

"Yes. He forces a cup on me when we speak, but I don't like it. He drinks it constantly."

"He goes through a barrel or two a week."

I shrugged. "I've seen him without it. His people are right, it's the only thing that keeps him on his feet."

The abbot looked uncomfortable, but then waved a hand my way. Fine, release another barrel. We'll have to brew more."

I couldn't help it, I shuddered thinking about the drink.

Seeing it, the abbot grinned. "We won't have to worry about you becoming a drunkard, will we, Makun?"

"No." I shuddered again, remembering its foul taste.

The abbot laughed, but then we heard the sound of running feet. He motioned for me to sit up, and then the door was flung open. The abbot was instantly surprised at this invasion of his decorum, but the frantic man's statement froze him in place.

"Abbot! A lay brother has died! And a friar!" the monk said.

"Who?" Abbot Dreise demanded.

"Brother Geltin, and Friar Toen."

"How did they die?" I asked.

"It was the marks!" the brother exclaimed, pulling out his medallion and planting a firm kiss on it.

"The marks?"

"From the beasts we killed!"

It was then the bell in the village began sounding, and we looked out to see a group of sprites in the distance. Seeing them again, I was filled with foreboding. I was not filled with peace.

Discessum

It seems I have run out of paper.

I will send Chaltic for more, or another book, I do not care which. He has been my one true friend these many long years, and will understand. Though it is good that the story stops here as I do not want to recount the events that are to come next, and I find my backside is sore from sitting.

Can you believe I almost miss it? That time there before the end? I have thought long about it, and I have earned an unfair reputation for piety as I kneel before the altar in the Hall of the Pantheon almost every day, asking the gods for their rebuke. I have almost begged for their condemnation some days, spending long hours there upon my knees, much to Jan's and the healer's distress.

Their rebuke has never come.

As I cast the sand upon this parchment for it to dry, I also put an end to my endless yearnings. I will bind these pages myself, as all of the brother recorders before me have done throughout time. Then I will entomb these words to the eternal record of the tower, to set them inside the abbot's private archives, where there are many tomes and scrolls that would surprise my brother chanter to find and read.

Dangerous and heretical books that I have studied. Books about heinous ideas, and yes even books upon magic … even the magic I discovered that ultimately saved us that fateful day there in the end.

He would be very surprised.

No, this book is not for prying eyes. I will place this inside our hidden archives, and there I will also place its sister tome that I have yet to write, so that those who follow after me in the office of abbot can understand what I went through. And, in my hubris, perhaps find some guidance someday in the decisions I made, for some future monk by what they find here.

I accept I will never know.

Be that as it may, I end this tome. On the morrow, I will take up my pen and scribe into the new book that Chaltic will find, and set the final events into record. I hope this testimony of events will be of use to someone someday, but I accept that I will never know. And as I lift these old bones from this humble seat to go off to bed, I pray that my efforts will accomplish something.

Someday.

Again, I will never know.

May the Pantheon have mercy on us all,

Abbot Makun Derring
1547 a.f.

Appendere

In our mission to preserve knowledge for future generations I include these explanations for which those of my time consider to be common knowledge. I know not if things will change so much for future readers that they must refer to these explanations, however I will fulfill the tenants that all brother recorders are taught and strive for, for completion. May you find this information useful if you study this work.

Makun Derring, 1547 a.f.

The Spire
The spire relates both to our tower of knowledge and the mountain upon which we live. It is our refuge, our citadel, and our home. Formed sometime before The War of the Fall, its construction is a mystery. But we do know that our tower of knowledge was only one of many, and all were centers for knowledge and learning during the time of the gods.

Whether or not there were some similarities between all of the towers, our tower was divided into distinct areas over the years. There was the living section of the tower where all monks worked and lived, then the unused sections much lower inside the mountain which were kept protected and closed. In the lower sections we kept our stores and the library, but these sections were not open as there was also our shelter and redoubt.

Entry to the tower was through the edificium and its impregnable gate which kept us safe during the war. From there the halls split, and one could find many places immediately accessible once they left the entry. The refectory was where our order ate and drank as a community, all of us as one under the Pantheon. The cells where we slept, and the various public offices were also found on this level. But beyond this, the only other areas open were work stations or the various halls, all of which were very important to us.

Foremost is the Hall of the Pantheon, our center of worship and where the brother chanters led us in prayer. Next in importance was the Hall of Knowledge where I worked during my early days, split into two sections: the Scriptorium where works were preserved and copied, and then the library in the locked section below. Then there was the Hall of Teaching where we instructed those who showed promise amongst the villagers, the Hall of Healing where we treated the ill and produced our many potions, and the Hall of Arms where our venerable brother protectors worked and trained to ensure the safety of us all.

The Monachi Spirae

It seems somewhat ridiculous to put this explanation to paper, but in the desire for clarity and completion I must. The monks of the spire were formed as an official order sometime during the fourth century a.f., the exact date of our founding long since lost to history. Our tenant is to preserve all knowledge for the use of our future generations to bring about the return of the gods. We have since gathered the gods under the broad naming of 'pantheon', for we have lost the names or aspects of most. But we shall remember them as best we can so that you, our children, may one day see their veneration that we, unfortunately, have not.

A monk starts their life as an aspirant, or someone who shows promise and intelligence through hard work and effort. They advance to novice once they are introduced to the teachings of our order and learn them. And if they can remember and adhere to them, after their vigil, they can advance to become monks.

All monks of the order begin as lay brothers, a humble duty which upholds and performs the day-to-day workings of the tower. From there, they can either be selected to specialize in one of the other subsections of our order. Or they can remain a lay brother for their entire lives, possibly to become a friar to work in the village below and look out for other aspirants.

If a monk is chosen to specialize, they have a multitude of paths. There are the brother recorders, chosen for their intelligence and ability with art to keep and preserve the works we protect. The chanters, who study and memorize The Book of the Fall to lead us in prayer, and to remind us of what has come before. The brother healers who study our fragile form to keep us and those poor villagers alive as best they can. The brother teachers who study individual aspects of knowledge and instruct it to the masses, becoming both generalists and specialists in the knowledge they hold. And lastly the brother protectors, who suffer and train to combat the altered beasts of our time, that seek to invade and end the lives of us all.

Each day begins with our summoning to prayer, led by the chanters, as it is before every meal. Then we go about our individual duties throughout the day, bathing every day before the evening meal, after which we have some time to ourselves. Mostly we keep to our cells, simple rooms that offer a bed, a table, chair, and a small lamp or a candle for light, but we also go down to the village when we are allowed to, to associate with those who live there and are less fortunate than ourselves.

We eat a diet of mostly mushrooms, which were provided to us long ago by our allies the dwarves. I personally detest the things, having long since grown sick of them, but I cannot deny the importance of this simple crop for our survival. And their many uses and species are grown and harvested in the catacombs below by the lay brothers, in the only section of the deeps kept open to all, beyond the living areas of the tower.

The Council of Seven

Our order is led by those chosen or most venerable. Of all those positions the most important is the office of abbot. Elected by the council of seven, this brother is chosen to lead us in our daily works and forms the overall direction and vision of our order. The Lord Abbot holds the most sway on the council, being the first among equals and chosen to lead it, but can be overruled if the entire council votes against him.

The rest of the council is made up of the leaders of the various sections and specialties of our order. Referred to by whatever section they represent, they are held above the everyday monks and much deference is given to them. As such, the monk who represents the brother chanters upon the council is referred to as 'the brother chanter', and all of our other specialties follow that form. Each leads and guides their particular sections, but they have other important duties as well.

The brother chanter is charged with guiding our spiritual journey, ensuring that not only do we know the particulars of what has come before, but also that we adhere to our reverence for the Pantheon and do not descend into unknowing apostacy. The brother recorder is charged with the protection of the library and the preservation of its many works. The brother healer is charged with recording the genealogies as well as maintaining the health of us monks. The brother protector is charged with the protection of the Spire and the surrounding territories, as well as putting suspected mages to question and ensuring their destruction. The brother teacher educates the masses, forming and leading classes in both the village and the Spire, but also is in charge of all trade and discussions with those not of the Spire. Then lastly the lay brother, whose members are everywhere ensuring the maintenance and wellbeing of the tower, also keeps an eye out for mages, as the members of his specialty will be the first to encounter them, being the most numerous of our order.

Nächtaltom

Our dwarven allies have always been friendly to us, having discovered us long ago after the Fall. Though we have never journeyed ourselves to discover their home, they come every few years or so to trade for our knowledge. Bringing and providing to us that which we cannot, we gain things such as animals and ores to help us in our struggles. Then in return we provide education and knowledge through teaching, as well as the limited potions we can produce in fair trade. We have a good relationship with them, and they helped us construct some of our protections, but they have always been guarded, holding themselves aloof for reasons they do not always name.

Apostille

1551 – Abbot Darius Fortriid. May the Pantheon have mercy on your soul, old friend. I knew not.

1583 – Abbot Finn Por. Now I know the reason for my predecessors haunted looks. May their souls be ever saved.

1612 – Abbot Tenn Mar. I have read this work.

1662 – Abbot Salius Gartonend. I have read this, and I feel so ashamed.

1698 – Abbot Cor Laran. This, I have read … Pantheon save me.

1703 – Abbot Warl Margonest. I have finished this work, and I stare out this window in deep thought, considering its ramifications. I now know why my predecessor was told to be fearful of the Abbot's position within our order.

1727 – Abbot Olan Reld. I have read this work.

1761 – Abbot Sintilli Artonel. One of the most venerated abbots who led our order to greatness hid this abominable truth? Now I know why all abbots have looked so haunted.

1763 – Abbot Careline Bordeine. The tower is once again under siege. The village is lost. Hundreds have died before the gate was shut. I discovered this searching for hidden knowledge of some way out of the tower. That one of our greatest leaders himself was a mage? I cannot believe it. As acting abbot, I will hold this text for future generations, but it worries me much.

1767 – I do not have time to research this work. Many still die. The monsters found a way in and we battle on the stairs. Pantheon save us.

1774 – We have been pushed into the library and the catacombs. We have no way out. We must find a way out. Abbot Inolt.

1777 – Where is the second volume? The Derrings and the Belns have conspired to save us through lost knowledge, but they say the second volume is the key. Where is that key? We are only a few hundred left. Abbot Vargas Querr.

1781 – Three years since my predecessor went on to live with the Pantheon, and only now do I discover the reason. This is the reason for the endless assaults on the library. This is the key to why he was so focused on regaining the lost offices of the Council. So many have died, so many have gone to their rest. And for what? A book?

No book can save us. I have ordered the library walled off. Thank the Pantheon for the dwarves long ago traded mushrooms, without which, none of us would have survived. We are getting used to the dark. Maybe someday we will retake the upper levels. In all honesty, we know not.

1792 – Chanter Dal Stilrea. This evil book is sacrilege! That the great leaders of our order would hold this vile treatise on apostacy in hiding only for themselves? It sickens me to my core. It will not burn. This evil codex will not burn! It will be hidden. It will not burn! We have won our freedom from the invading monsters, and lost our beloved abbot, yet this demonic treatise will not burn!

2185 – Historian Pal Tin. I have read this text and discussed it in secret with the council. On pain of death, I have been ordered to undertake a vow of silence which was imposed on me immediately after discussing what I have translated herein. I am now a recluse, confined to the tower to guard these words from any who might think to peruse them, until I ascend with joy unto the Pantheon. As Reverent Derring said, may the Pantheon have mercy on my soul.

3794 – Aspirant Zilak. I have translated this work for my master. He has gone mad. This book is cursed.

7841 – Abbot Tarleton For. I admit not being able to understand many of the things discussed herein. This text was taken to our new home after discovering it in a hidden section of the library. It seems that the tales of secret works are true, and I admit to much difficulty in translating it. No matter what it says, its history regarding our founding and forefathers may be more important than we suspect. The pure fact of its condition is remarkable.

7863 – Recorder Fortaine Melinquest. Abbot For bequeathed me this work upon his death, which many do mourn. Beyond recognizing his written words, the text I have been given is hand written, and in an ancient tongue. It will take me many years of labor to decipher it, and I do not understand his interest in it or the reasons for giving it to me. It appears to be a journal of some kind. I will add it to my other work, and complete it after I finish my other studies into the lost mages and magic.

12410 – Recorder Tin Worlaine. Imagine, an eleven-thousand-year-old work, and it remains in perfect condition. If only anyone knew what it said.

13982 – Moved to the section of ancient treatises and unknown works. Librarian Castor.

15679 – Catalogued and inventoried for the archives. Librarian Sentelius Dawn.

18412 – Catalogued and inventoried after being thought lost. It appears this work has been lost and found many times. I wonder what it says. Referred to the historians and the master of ancient works for further study. Librarian Velin Taln.

23662 – Master Alantin Derringbeln Bengal. This text explains much, and I have thought long upon it. May you rest in peace, great progenitors. The Pantheon shall save.

Afterword

Hello,

I hope you enjoyed what you read.

I have intentionally written this book in the way that it is presented, as if this is some old tome that the reader has found. Of course there are some things that the modern day needs, like the copyright page and disclaimer that I wish in this instance I could do away with, but I have to do what is required. So, though there are some things which take away from the presentation I envisioned, the book as read is how I thought this story should be depicted on the page.

I also listened to a lot of Gregorian chant while I wrote this tale. It leant the proper mood or 'air' to how the story is conveyed, beyond sounding pretty. I threw in a bit of Latin here and there, purely for artistic reasons, and I'll admit upfront that I'm no expert on it. I apologize for any mistakes I made.

An intentional decision on my part was not to use roman numerals, as I thought that might lead to confusion since they really haven't been regularly used for over a thousand years. I also thought about spelling the numbers out in Latin, but after I saw that chapter twenty-six converted to 'caput vigesimum sextum', I decided against it.

I considered using Sanskrit instead of Latin, but with this book being intended for western audiences, I wasn't sure if it would have the same impact as Latin would. Regardless, I tried my best where that ancient tongue was included. If there's an error in conjugation, please be kind. I never took Latin growing up.

This novel was difficult to write for a multitude of reasons, the first being that it is my initial attempt at writing to match an outline I previously made. This hampered my creative process a little until I hit a rhythm, but I'll admit it was a struggle to get there. But once I did, the entire story flowed.

Next, it was a challenge to write this story because it is told from the viewpoints of two people, the young and the old Makun. Though they inhabited the same body, they had vastly different life experiences, and separating the two was challenging. Because think of how you might tell a story about a life experience now, compared to how you would have told it maybe a decade ago. Now think about the difference … See what I mean?

This book is also intended to be a two-part story in the world of The Chronicles of the Troop. There is so much background and setting in The Chronicles that it required a reference to be created, and I studied that text a lot as I wrote this story to depict it. But where this story differs from The Chronicles is that it takes place 20,000 years before my original series, and all the changes to people's thoughts and perceptions coming from that different age requires a lot of consideration on my part.

I think I did pretty well.

I hope you enjoyed this tale while reading it, and as I'm writing this afterword, I'm already imagining part two of the book. The dwarves have left, Makun is ensconced in his new position, the Lehntarnese are getting comfortable, and the prior battles and upheaval are now won after executing a mage and a horde of invading monsters. Yet more people have died, and again the sprites have come … Are they heralds of doom? Are they causing the deaths that always seem to follow their appearance? Why have they come?

And then as Ghaan's tale slowly surfaces from what the Lehntarnese have kept hidden, what effect will it have on Makun Derring and the monks of the Spire as whatever they tell comes to light? Only part two of The Book of Ghaan will answer those questions, and I hope part one has interested you enough to find out. Enjoy it when you read it, that's all I can ask.

May the Pantheon hold and keep you safe,

Colin Darney

Oh, and if you could do me a favor, please leave a review.
https://www.amazon.com/dp/B0DNXWJPFQ?ref_=ast_author_dp

Character List

Entirely for your reference, I've included a list of the named characters in The Book of Ghaan. They are presented mostly in the order that they appear inside the story, and everyone is human except obviously the dwarves.

Monks of the Spire
- Makun Derring
- Chaltic Harn
- Vorise, Healer
- Geltin, Lay Brother
- Toen, Friar

The Council of Seven
- Dreise, The Abbot
- Barkon, The Brother Chanter
- Ansilin, The Brother Recorder
- Sedimont, The Brother Protector
- Camdal, The Brother Healer
- Margonest, The Brother Teacher
- Randilon, The Lay Brother

Historical
- Abbot Tó, 3rd Abbot of the Monks of the Spire

Villagers
- Jan Isterlin
- Untark Mar
- Cor Tam, the village elder
- Eldso
- Elder Mastin
- Carden Nalt
- Heller
- Soriese

Lehntarnese

- Rahdimus Ghaan
- Vortiid Beln
- Pormult Dor
- Xer Jeman
- Gritilli Van
- Hestialee
- Naisa

Dwarves of Nächtaltom
- Peltic
- Maess
- Ferdid

Final Thought

Read ...

There are amazing adventures out there for you to discover ...